MW00780575

LEGACY
—THE BEGINNING

DORRANCE
PUBLISHING CO
EST. 1920
PITTSBURGH, PENNSYLVANIA 15238

The contents of this work, including, but not limited to, the accuracy of events, people, and places depicted; opinions expressed; permission to use previously published materials included; and any advice given or actions advocated are solely the responsibility of the author, who assumes all liability for said work and indemnifies the publisher against any claims stemming from publication of the work.

All Rights Reserved
Copyright © 2020 by Kongmeng Lo

No part of this book may be reproduced or transmitted, downloaded, distributed, reverse engineered, or stored in or introduced into any information storage and retrieval system, in any form or by any means, including photocopying and recording, whether electronic or mechanical, now known or hereinafter invented without permission in writing from the publisher.

Dorrance Publishing Co
585 Alpha Drive
Suite 103
Pittsburgh, PA 15238
Visit our website at *www.dorrancebookstore.com*

ISBN: 978-1-6453-0159-2
eISBN: 978-1-6453-0740-2

PROLOGUE

With a beginning
Comes a path
Made into a story
A legend is born
And becomes a legacy

Chapter 1
—A Painful Memory

Morgana woke from a vision, excited but unable to move. After years of search-ing, she was certain of finding the one her Master desired. She wanted to leap from her bed and rush to tell him the good news, but she couldn't move yet. She would have to wait. She had tried using the Acolyte's Sightstone, even her Master's Great Pyre, but the visions were always clouded and uncertain. Though it carried its consequences, this was her truest form of sight.

Simply slipping her soul into a subject's body undetected would allow her to see, hear, and feel all the emotions of that heart as if she were there, living the moment as the other did. She must wait, wait for her soul to set-tle back into her body, finding the anchor points and locking itself back into place.

Whilst in the vision, her body remained lifeless. Her eyes did not blink, her heart did not beat. In every way it was simply an empty shell waiting for its life force to rejoin it. Now, the feeling in her body began to return. She suffered through the experience happily. First, her eyes blinked; the burning sensation sent tears gushing down her face.

How long have I been away? Morgana asked herself. *I must remember to close my eyes the next time I travel. Perhaps they will not get so dry.*

Likewise, her lips and mouth regained sensation. The dryness was almost unbearable. Every swallow felt as if her throat were full of sand. Had she been able to feel her chest yet, she would have coughed uncontrollably, but for now all she could do was lick her lips with a parched tongue, eagerly waiting for the saliva to return. Her eyes began to search the room. The flame of a single candle glinted off the black stone walls of her chamber. The familiar sight comforted her.

Home. A smile found its way to her lips.

The wash of sensation slowly moved down her body over the neck and shoulders and down to her chest. Her heart exploded back to life with a tremendous *THUMP.* She gasped for air as she began to seize and shake. Again and again, each beat of her heart sent an agonizing wave of needles over her body. Each breath burned in her lungs like fire.

Soon, Morgana told herself. *Soon this will be over.*

The pain and the shaking began to subside. She took a deep breath, this one finally cool and satisfying. The last of the sharp pains pricked her fingers and toes, and as the pangs disappeared, she felt the soft furs of her bed caressing her naked body.

Almost there, she assured herself.

She glided her hand beneath the fur blanket, and then exposed it to the cold, crisp air of the room. Removing the blanket from her body, she set it on the other side of the bed. The chill enveloped her quickly. Prickly goosebumps covered her skin from head to toe, a feeling she was well acquainted with.

Getting up from the bed, Morgana placed her feet on the worn obsidian floor. She glided across the room to the other side. With her hands she caressed her figure, starting below her navel and sliding up her slender body to her torso, where the tanned, light olive skin reflected the light. Slowly but surely, the goosebumps disappeared, banished by the warmth of her touch.

She strode to the candlelit wall, where a long, black velvet cloak hung on a nearby peg. Its fabric was adorned by designs of Aramaic embroidery, with white threading along the hem and cuffs. The back of the cloak bore a large shield stitched in dark blue, and a small emblem matching the shield was embroidered on the hood's hem, which crinkled slightly.

A dark chestnut table that looked like it had been scorched by fire displayed a few items of jewelry, bracelets, trinkets, and a small rotating mirror. The rest of Morgana's possessions remained hidden in darkness.

In keeping with her youth, Morgana's mahogany hair fell in a smooth, silky cascade to her lower posterior. Her gaze wandered around the room before resting upon the mirror. It reflected her fresh, youthful countenance. Rosy pink lips, light-gray eyes framed by full eyebrows and impossibly long eyelashes, high cheekbones, and a small, pointed chin.

Displaying marked flesh from fingertips to the neck, she reached out with her right hand, showing blackened lines that traced the tattoos known as *vaynes*. On her other side, the markings did not extend as high, but stopped near the elbow.

Removing the cloak from its resting place, Morgana slipped into the silky garment, covering her naked skin. The soft fabric slid across her fingers, soft as a baby's skin, and the raised embroidery tickled her palms. She looked like a child in adult attire. Her hands barely peeped through the ends of the sleeves, and the hem of the cloak rested on the floor.

I must hurry.

She snatched the bracelets from the table and strode into the darkness. She waved her hand in the dark, and in response, the door swung open with a loud creak. Before leaving the room, she slid on the bracelets over each hand.

Morgana entered the dark corridor beyond, black as the depths of hell and completely silent as if devoid of life. Her bracelets clinked softly, and the blue light of her pulsating vaynes glowed in the darkness. Her hands moved in synchronization, creating symbols to invoke a small flame of yellow, orange, and red fire that floated in midair just a few feet in front of her. The flame danced in a tight swirl, growing to the size of a small grapefruit. Writhing and flaring, the globe of fire resembled a miniature sun.

The shiny black of the obsidian floor glinted and glimmered in the light. Where unbroken darkness and silence once loomed, the corridor now danced with life. The soft pad of her bare feet on the ground and the rustling of her cloak as it swept the floor sounded in the hallway, and from time to time, the clanking of her bracelets striking one another chimed in.

I should have worn my sandals . . . well, it's too late now, Morgana thought.

The miniature sun kept pace with her, remaining suspended in the air a few feet ahead. Every so often, a flare would occur, extending the light to the outer reaches of the corridor. The hood of the cloak did its job of concealing Morgana's identity, aside from the lower half of her face, which lay exposed from the tip of her nose to her chin. Her slender arms moved with her body, hidden by the voluminous cloak.

She walked on, reflecting on life and the afterlife. Staring into the orb of fire that floated before her, she gave a slight smirk.

What simple magic . . . yet how hard it was for me to first learn how to channel that power.

■   ■   ■   ■

ROMAN ERA—80 A.D.

The sunlight gleamed through the open window by which Illythia stood staring out and wondering what life would be like outside the clay walls of her prison. She hoped there was a better life for her somewhere out there. Her skin glowed in the sunbeam, but her light gray eyes betrayed her desire to leave this horrid place. Although she was young and beautiful, she wore a plain white garment that fell from her shoulders down to her lower thighs like a shapeless sack, bound by a rope that was tied like a noose around her abdomen. Her dark brown hair covered the cloth like a tapestry, adding depth in layers. Shifting her head to the side only tightened the collar around her neck.

The door burst wide open, and two guards rushed in carrying an injured gladiator. Blood dripped down onto the sand from the injured man's mouth and back.

"Make room, make room!" the guard called out.

The Medicos man was a middle-aged man of about forty, bald head ringed with graying dark brown hair. His face was rugged and sun-weathered, and he wore glasses that clung to his nose. He evaluated the injured gladiator, whose mouth had filled with blood, his back laid open by savage lashes.

"Lay him on the table, on his side if you would," the medic ordered, nodding toward the dark mahogany wood table. Healing injuries was his specialty.

"You heard him," the other guard responded.

They lifted the gladiator onto the table, making sure he did not fall over.

"If you could leave us and let us do our work."

"But he is the owner's prized fighter."

"Do you want me to heal him or not? Do as you are told," the Medicos commanded.

"Sir."

The guards took their leave and closed the door behind them.

"Illythia . . . bring me the medicine bowl," the medic asked.

Awakened from her daydream, Illythia turned around.

"Over there in the cabinets," he directed her.

As the gladiator tried to roll to the side, blood streamed down onto the table. He moaned in pain, his breathing shallow.

"Whoa, whoa, whoa! Do not try to move."

The Medicos man held the gladiator upright, leaning to the side.

Illythia walked along the outside wall of the infirmary to where the Medicos man pointed. Ever so quietly she moved, like a ghost, as though she barely existed. The collar caused friction on her neck during even slight movements, causing discomfort as though she had outgrown it.

Dust rose from the ground as she padded on bare feet to the end of the small room. A long counter lay just below a few cabinets that hung upon the white painted clay wall. There she opened a cabinet door on its screeching hinges. She reached in to take a few medicine bowls. Clasping them to her chest, she glanced briefly at the window.

All I know is how to be a slave . . . I want to know what it is like to be free.

Setting the bowls at the edge of the table, she waited for further directions from the Medicos man, attending to all his instructions like a student. He then summoned her to fetch a few healing herbs, powder, and tools from another cabinet in the infirmary.

"We need to take that collar off your neck," the medic stated decisively.

"Hmmph?" Illythia answered.

It took her a moment to recognize the gladiator's familiar face, swollen and bruised from the injury.

"Cethin!" she cried.

"Don't worry," the medic reassured her. "We will take care of him."

The door swung wide open to reveal a guard in bronze plate armor patrolling

the area. Briefly he peered in, his curious stare coming to rest on the injured gladiator, disgusted but simultaneously intrigued to see more. He glanced up at the
Medicos man and the slave. His entire grisly quota for the day filled by looking
in on the gladiator, the guard was ready to leave.

"Wait!" said the medic.

The guard paused for a moment.

"Take the collar off the girl."

"What for?" the guard retorted.

"So the girl can work, and so I will not have to attend to her as my next patient."

"Well . . ." the guard considered.

"Do you want me to tell your Master that you killed his prized fighter and
injured another?"

The guard reached for the small dagger that hung from his belt. Unsheathing it, he scurried to the girl, fear written on his features. He immediately reached for the collar around her neck and tugged once to make some
space. The dagger slipped into the small gap, and with a soft snip, the leather
collar released its tight grip on her neck.

Once he'd obeyed the order, the guard left the room.

"We will tend to your wounds once we take care of him," the Medicos
man stated, examining Illythia's bruise. "If you can, hold him in this position
once you are finished."

She nodded quietly, shocked. Collecting all the necessities the medic
needed and setting them on the table, she watched him from beginning to end.
She paid close attention to all the ingredients he added to the bowl, his mixing
and prepping, as he took a few minutes to prepare.

The gladiator's wounds throbbed in pain. His cries were low, with a muffled moan, as if someone had pulled out his vocal cords. The medic used a
cleaning cloth, wiping the wound clean from any dirt or any possible bacterial
infection. Leaving the cloth at the end of the table and scooping the powder
from the medicine bowl, he rubbed the medicine carefully over the wound.
The gladiator cried in agony once before losing consciousness.

Setting a clean cloth next to the injured man, he directed, "You can lay
him on his back now, and keep his mouth open."

Illythia watched in awe as the blood suddenly stopped flowing from her brother's back. The medicine being applied worked miracles. Growing a new fascination with what she'd learned that day, she was intrigued by how things worked.

"Now we have to brand his tongue," the Medicos man stated.

"Is there another way?" Illythia asked.

"This is the only way to stop the bleeding. I am truly sorry."

■　　■　　■　　■

Reaching the end of the corridor, she made a turn. The light of the orb revealed a gaping hole in the middle of the room, dark shadows still looming beyond. She looked across the space to a large monolith, which towered a hundred feet high. No lights hung on chains from the ceiling or clung to the walls to light the way down. Archways stood perfectly spaced out from the opposite sides of the stone walls. Morgana began to make her way down the stairs.

Each passing archway revealed an empty gap that led to the center of the monolith. Descending the circular staircase, she thought about her Master's acolyte's work, the frustration of her instruction as the Master's new pet, and the secrets of the dark gift. She had become so grounded in the hard sciences of medicine and anatomy that she could not comprehend the supernatural at first. It wasn't until she had made the connection between body and soul that she had become adept with magic.

From her years of study with the Roman Medicos man, she had gained such an understanding of the human body that the supernatural was a remote concept, difficult to understand. She could heal most physical injuries, no matter the severity. She surpassed even the most knowledgeable medics in only a few years of study, motivated by her love for her brother, the most skilled gladiator ever to live.

CHAPTER 2
—MOTHER'S BOY

Why? Why do these memories persist . . . ? I just want to sleep.

71 A.D.

A lovely voice rang out within the small, square living quarters.

"Cethin, you are a caring son. You love your sister Illythia *so*."

She looked at her son, a young teen with olive skin, skinny for his height of four-foot-eleven, platinum blond hair, yet eyes black as the night sky. He carried his little sister like a backpack, wrapped in cloth. She slept like a baby, comforted on his shoulder. Cethin wore a white, buttoned shirt, stained with dirt and sweat from long usage, and brown woven pants.

He looked back over his shoulder at Illythia, where she slept snug upon his back, her dark brown hair falling across her face. He could remember the vivid image of her face any place and any time, her pale olive skin, chubby cheeks that he loved to squeeze, and unusual light gray eyes.

The sun's yellowish-orange light began to disappear over the horizon, and a last ray glimmered through the window. The cold chill from outdoors slowly crept into the house. A fire was kept burning in the fireplace on the side of the house day and night, keeping the area warm. Cethin stood before it, soaking in as much heat as possible. Handmade toys lay in the middle of the room, all crafted with love by their father. Stools and a table stood near the window.

The sound of Mother's voice lit up Cethin's face with a smile. As he turned around, his eyes fell upon her pale white skin, hazel-green eyes, high cheekbones and small pointed chin, shiny black hair down to her knees, and her thin limbs under a black dress. She reached out for Illythia, cupping the child under the arms and lifting her from Cethin's back. The girl squirmed, at the edge of wakefulness, fighting the transition of being taken from her comfortable position sleeping on her brother's back.

"It's time to put this little one to bed."

Mother held Illythia over her shoulder like a giant teddy bear.

"When is Father coming home?" Illythia mumbled in her sleep.

Mother left the living room and walked to the corner of the house, where her son and daughter's bedroom was. Dim lighting overlay of the room, revealing a white sheepskin blanket covering the bed of hay. With her feet, and she shuffled the toys on the floor out of the way. Humming a melody for her children, she laid the soundly sleeping Illythia on one side of the bed. Cethin followed a few steps behind, and then tucked in Illythia for the night, kissing her forehead.

"'I'm going to the market in the morning," Cethin whispered to his mother as they left the bedroom and returned to the living area.

"Don't stay away too long . . . She will start to worry once she gets up," Mother replied.

"I won't be gone for too long," Cethin responded.

"Are you leaving now?" Mother asked, concerned.

"I am leaving early in the morning." He comforted her with a hug.

"Okay. Make sure you don't wake Illythia, or she will want to go with you." Mother sighed with relief.

"Yeah . . . I know."

"Now, get some rest. You're going to need it for tomorrow."

"Okay. Mother, I love you."

"I love you too, son." Mother kissed Cethin's forehead.

"Uh-um." Cethin stretched out in bed.

Before the first light of dawn, he stared into the darkness below the roof. Lying in bed for a moment made him feel at ease. Conjuring the energy to get up was more of a challenge. His head rolled on the pillow, toward his sister. Seeing Illythia lying right next to him gave him the strength to push forward. *I do not want to wake her.*

Sliding to the edge of bed, quiet as a mouse stealing crumbs of food, he tiptoed closer to the exit.

A few steps away from the bedroom, Cethin spotted a dim light in the living room. Cleaning the sand from his eyes, he rubbed them a few more times to soothe them.

Cethin blinked a few more times as his vision adjusted to the light. There sat his mother, on a stool, elbows perched on the table like anchors, welcoming him with a whole-hearted smile.

"Mother? You're up early." Cethin looked surprised.

"Yeah . . ." Mother replied. "I couldn't sleep."

"You should get some rest, Mother."

"I know. I just want to make sure you have everything you need before you leave."

"You shouldn't worry so much," he insisted.

"Hang on a second."

"Hmmph?" Cethin looked puzzled.

Mother's hands slipped beneath the table for a moment. "Here," she pulled out a woolen bag. "I also packed you some food for the day."

Accepting the bag, Cethin hugged his mother tight. "You didn't have to."

"I know, but . . . I *felt* that I had to."

"Well . . . I'd better get going."

"Okay . . ."

"Mother, what's wrong?" Cethin questioned.

Her expression showed it all: a measure of fear, shock, and surprise. She noticed Illythia standing in the doorway, quietly looking on. The child stretched, trying to work the morning jitters out and wiping away the sand from her eyes. Still, she looked exhausted, as though it were still the night before.

"You must be tired, sweetie. Let me put our little sleepyhead back to bed. Son, don't leave yet," said Mother.

She guided her little princess back into the bedroom. For a moment, Cethin could neither see nor hear what went on in the other room.

He anxiously awaited his mother's return, contemplating on leaving. As he paced back and forth along one side of the table, he overheard his mother's soothing voice, like a siren singing a sweet melody. The sound carried into the living room, banishing Cethin's anxiety,

Soon, the melody ended, and Illythia quietly rested once more in bed. Mother gently closed the door and returned. Cethin did what he'd been asked and waited patiently.

"One more thing," Mother added. "I wanted to give you this before you leave. I will bring Illythia to the market later on. You know how fond she is of you," she continued, gathering him into an enormous hug.

Cethin smiled and nodded, the response she'd hoped for. She released him from her embrace. He tossed the bag over his shoulder, holding the open end tightly against his chest. His day was about to begin. He opened the door to a cool blast of chilly morning air that tingled to the bone. Without the guidance of light, Cethin made his way in the dark, having memorized the roads.

Mother snatched up the candle from the table and rushed to the window. By its dim light, she watched her son vanish into the dark.

I wish I could give you back your childhood . . . If only your father had been here, things would have been different.

Mid-day saw Cethin hard at work. The fire roared to life among a few blocks of wood stacked together like a triangle. The smoke caught the wind, blowing all around the small fire pit, and Cethin tossed in a few more blocks to fuel the flame. He turned around, wiping the sweat from the excruciating heat off of his forehead. Avoiding the table just a few steps away, he navigated around to set up a couple more workbenches.

Cethin curiously observed a red-hot piece of iron in the shape of a sword, which was cooling down on top of the anvil, waiting to be molded. The hammer was not far away, calling for its master to do some work.

"Thank you, Cethin. My shop is now ready for business," the blacksmith announced.

The blacksmith was an elderly man with golden, sun-browned skin, a balding head with some gray hair remaining on the sides, deep crow's feet like claw marks at the corners of his eyes, and a narrow, hunched back. He limped to the side, to the part of the stall where they were setting up shop, blocking Cethin's view in the process.

"I do what I can to help out," Cethin said with a smile.

"I have a task for you!" The blacksmith huffed excitedly.

"Oh," Cethin replied.

He gripped a wool bag full of metal, clinking with his movements. To the old man it seemed light enough as he handed it over to his helper. "Take this and give it to the merchant on the other side of town on your way home."

The small woolen bag exchanged hands. Cethin graciously accepted the task, but the wool bag almost dropped to the ground as he took hold of it. From its size, he had thought it would be light, easy to carry. Rebounding and investing more strength into lifting the bag, the youth tried not to show any sign of weakness.

"The butcher?" Cethin questioned.

"Yes."

"The one I pass by every morning?"

"That's the one." The blacksmith nodded.

"Okay."

"Here," the blacksmith reached into his pocket, rifling through the change inside. Looking at the money in his hand, he pulled out two silver coins. *This should be enough.* He handed it over to his helper without hesitation.

"Thank you!" Cethin responded enthusiastically.

"Once you have made the delivery, go home. Bring me his payment in the morning, and after that, you can take tomorrow off. I will see you the following day."

"Sure thing. I'll see you tomorrow!" Cethin took his leave.

The sun began tilting toward the horizon as if tired from hanging high in the sky. With a hand, Cethin shielded his eyes from the glare and looked from side to side. He knew that he'd been appointed a task, and wanted to achieve it as quickly as possible. Following the flow of traffic, he merged into the crowd, which flowed like a school of fish.

Cethin tightly grasped the heavy woolen bag, keeping it slung over his shoulder. Whenever his grip weakened, he readjusted to make sure that the bag never fell. Step after step, he was getting closer to the butcher's shop and then home. The bag seemed to take on a life of its own, making the journey more difficult for him.

Time sailed by during Cethin's long walk. His arms ached and shook, but his destination was close at hand. A few more steps and he released one hand to open the door of the butcher's shop.

The butcher greeted him with, "Ah, just in time."

Cethin had no time to look inside the shop, but a giant of a man stood in the doorway: a well-rounded man, face clean-cut, his robe covered in dark red blood. His belly bounced up and down with his loud chuckles.

"I remember you, Cethin, when you were a wee-ol' baby." The butcher raised his hands to approximate the size of Cethin as a newborn child. "Boy, have you grown! Time passes by so fast."

Cethin smiled out of courtesy, unable to remember the man's face. He wanted to say something, yet feared the outcome, so his questions remained unspoken. Still, there was business to be done. The youth took the heavy burden from his shoulder, placing it into the buyer's hand.

"Thank you, young man," the butcher graciously accepted the woolen bag.

Cethin's body was finally at ease, relieved of the burden. Tired from the hard work and long walk, he knew the end of his journey was near. He took a moment to rest, closing his eyes, oblivious that the butcher had left without a sound.

The boy's eyes opened to the sound of metal clinking on the table. The momentary rest had provided him sufficient energy for the day's remaining work. Ready to leave, heels repeatedly tapping the wooden floor, he forgot about collecting payment and headed for the door.

"Hang on a second," the butcher called him back.

Cethin froze just inches from freedom, staring at the doorknob. He wanted to reach out, turn the door knob, and leave, but couldn't. His concerns and thoughts lingered elsewhere, mind petrified by the unknown. *Shit . . . Should I go or should I stay?*

The bubbles in his guts started to churn. He listened to the wooden planks creak closer with the butcher's every step.

"Here." The butcher handed a few coins to Cethin as payment. "Before Cadeyrn puts your head on a spike."

"Oh. I forgot about that."

"And give this to Antha for me." The butcher handed the boy another bag.

Cethin's face was slack with exhaustion.

"Your mother, Antha," the butcher reinforced.

Cethin nodded and replied, "I thank you."

The butcher took a deep breath. "Well—I'm sorry for, um . . ."

At that moment, Cethin knew who the butcher was referring to. The boy fought back the tears suddenly forming in his eyes. The big man quickly embraced the boy and held him tight, not letting go for a long moment. Cethin accepted the welcoming hug, giving in to the comfort. He forbore to weep or make a sound, making the effort to stay strong for his own sake. His face stayed pressed into the dried blood on the butcher's robe until he calmed down.

No words were needed for the exchange, just a brief meeting of eyes between the two as they shared a thought. *"I miss you."*

Shortly afterwards, the store owner and the boy parted ways after their exchange; their connection now on a deeper level. As Cethin took his leave, his emotions lingered inside that little store, always to be remembered.

Cethin stared up at the sky, knowing the day had finally reached its end. His emotions had been on a wild chariot ride through the hills, experiencing both great highs and extreme lows. He gave a needed sigh of relief. Stepping onto the road, he drifted off into a daze, following the normal route home. The shifting landscape was familiar, the houses, stores, and trees passing by. One thing was consistent, though. Two familiar faces drew closer, but as he was fixed in his daydream, he took no notice.

"Look at my hard worker," Mother beamed.

Finally seeing her, Cethin smiled. "What are you doing here?"

"Illythia wanted to come find you," Mother answered.

"Ah."

"And I have to go to the market anyway, so we came."

"Well . . . I'm going home now. The butcher gave me this," Cethin tugged on the wool bag.

"Ah, Arthur has a huge heart. I need to run my errands before it gets dark. Take Illythia home with you."

"Okay."

"I will be home before you know it."

"Alright. Time to go home, Illythia," Cethin said, turning around to walk home.

As they walked down the middle of the road, a young girl about Cethin's age caught his attention. Her pleasant smile dimpled both her cheeks, and her hazel-green eyes complemented her long caramel-brown ponytail, which brushed the fair, peachy skin below her shoulders. She wore a pretty brown silk dress that fell to her toes. She noticed him and waved.

Not too far behind, his sister tried to mimic his every step, jumping the gap of each footstep. The thought of his bed circled around his mind like a shark as he longed for rest after his strenuous day.

"Hey, Cethin," the girl's voice piped up shyly.

"Hey, Tamara," Cethin replied.

Illythia trotted a little faster to grab her brother's hand.

Tagging along, Tamara said, "Thank you for the other day."

"It was nothing," he replied.

Cethin did not yet want to show his feelings for her, so he tried to keep calm and collected. He slowly worked his jaw back and forth as he watched Tamara intently. Butterflies churned and rumbled painfully in his stomach.

Today has not been a good day for me. What is wrong with me? he thought.

As he watched, a blush rose in her face. "You saved my sheep that was sinking in the mud. You rushed right in without thinking. My father would have killed me if he had known," she continued.

This girl really likes you! Illythia thought, looking at the two thoughtfully.

Cethin's head tipped back. "Yeah . . . I really wasn't thinking about it. It happened so fast, I just reacted and did what I could."

"I'm really thankful for that." Tamara's tone was playfully coquettish.

"Well . . . If you like, we can do something tomorrow."

"What do you have in mind?" she asked, interested.

"We are going to the lake tomorrow after I drop off the money at my work. We can pick you up here if you like."

"That sounds like fun!"

"Yes, it will be."

As they reached the edge of town, Tamara announced, "I'll be waiting for you here."

Coming to a stop, Cethin turned to face Tamara. She leaned in immediately and planted a kiss on his cheek. Cethin blushed apple-red as Tamara graced him with a smile. Cethin's world was lost in a haze, the scenery spun giddily, and he grinned as he released Illythia's hand. Tamara then turned and began her walk back to town. Cethin headed back home, twirling around as he strode with renewed vigor.

CHAPTER 3
—MY PAIN

"Wake up. Wake up!" Cethin's whisper sounded in the bedroom.

"Give me a few more minutes?" Illythia answered.

"No. We need to go now," Cethin answered.

"Ah-hhhhhnnnn." Illythia stretched in bed. "Fine-nnn."

Cethin hurried along, bouncing in excitement for the day to come. He quickly changed clothes, thinking of the possibilities of the day ahead and all it had to offer.

On the other hand, Illythia had been awakened from her slumber and dragged along, still tired. She had to put in double the amount of effort her brother exerted to get ready.

Cethin left the bedroom and strode into the living room with extra pep in his step. There his mother stood in the very same spot as yesterday, watching the candle burn on the tabletop. Illythia soon emerged from the bedroom, hair still a mess.

"Someone is looking forward to today," Antha stated.

Cethin smiled. "Yes, Mother."

"Why is Illythia up so early?" Mother questioned.

"I don't work today, so I thought we would go to the lake."

"Oh."

"You can come too if you like, Mother," Cethin invited.

"Oh, no, I have some things around here that I need to take care of. You two go and enjoy yourselves," Mother answered.

"Okay." Cethin guided Illythia to the door.

"You two be careful, you hear."

"Yes, Mother," they responded together.

Cethin opened the door as the first rays of light emerged over the horizon. Being courteous, he let his sister pass through the door first, and following suit, he closed the door behind them. They squinted and blinked, eyes adjusting to the growing light.

Inside, Antha grabbed the stool and candle, setting them next to the window. Sitting down at her usual spot, she watched Cethin lead his sister along the path he usually took to work. Her view of them faded into the distance as the small road passed through a meadow. Staring out at the sky, she thought back to a distant memory.

TWO YEARS EARLIER—69 A.D.

"Hey, beautiful," called an alluring male voice.

"Hmmm. Why must you tease me so, Gildas?" Antha responded, opening her eyes.

A small white fleece blanket covered a patch of grass. Small ornaments of rocks, shoes, and a food basket held down each corner in case a gust of wind decided to wreak havoc. On one side of the blanket she lounged, turning over onto her back. Her hazel-green eyes flicked to the side where she'd heard the voice.

Gildas moved closer, placing his rough, tanned hand on the blanket. His long-sleeved white shirt was folded back, showcasing his blond hair. He inched forward, wearing a radiant smile she would never forget. He wore his softly waved hair to one side, covering his left eye. Every now and then he would push it back behind his ear.

When Gildas reached his destination, Antha raised her head to rest on his thigh like a pillow. They both took in the same view, past the meadow of grass and the endless trees beyond. A sparkling crystal-blue lake adorned the portrait-perfect landscape. Below the cloudless sky, basking in the sunlight that danced across the warm earth, they gloried in the sensation of eternal bliss.

"Hmmm. I could live like this forever," Antha sighed.

"So could I," Gildas responded.

He brushed the shiny raven hair back from her face to behold the perfection he had always adored. *It cannot get any better than this.*

He smiled once more. Bending down to share a kiss, they both melted into ecstasy. Finally, their lips released again as their eyes remained locked upon each other.

"I love you," Gildas declared.

"I love you more." Antha smiled.

Cethin and Illythia frolicked in the field together. Their laughter echoed in the distance. Their joy and excitement were contagious, and their smiles stretched practically from ear to ear. Illythia ran as fast as her little legs could carry her. Her brown hair whipped around as the breeze tugged at it. From time to time, her gray eyes glanced back to see whether her brother was only footsteps away, or farther.

"AHHHH!" Illythia screamed and giggled.

Running behind his sister, Cethin chased her like a cat stalking a mouse, waiting for an opportunity to take advantage. "I'm going to get you!" he teased.

Getting closer with every stride, he waited until she looked away.

With a burst of energy, Cethin sprung forward, closing the distance. At first, Illythia did not realize the pull of grass slowing her down with every stride. Her eyes closed for relief, dry from the breeze. Cethin snatched Illythia up and lifted her into the air. Opening her eyes again to look down, she screamed with joy once more. Then she gazed back at Cethin, happiness shining in her eyes.

"I got you!" Cethin mock-growled.

Gildas and Antha continued to watch Cethin carrying Illythia as though she were a deity flying through the sky. Every now and then, a gust of wind crossed the meadow, flattening the grass in its path, and Cethin would twirl Illythia into the breeze.

Antha studied her lover's face, mesmerized by the sight of him. Her regard became a trance, her thoughts lost in space and time. Gildas gazed lovingly down upon her, and for a second, the world did not exist. They were floating in the clouds, detached from all earthly contact. Their children's laughter did not disturb their state of bliss.

I wish I could live like this forever, Antha thought.

Her abrupt movement swept the candle from the windowsill, knocking it to the floor. With this, the reminiscence faded away as quickly as it had come. Antha blinked for a moment, startled by her own clumsiness, her response a moment late. Reaching down to clean the little mess of wax she'd made, she picked up the candle and set it on the table.

All her energy suddenly drained away. The restless nights she'd continuously endured finally took their toll. Drained mentally and physically, she trudged from the living room to the bedroom.

I must be getting old.

Antha hesitated at first, taken aback, feeling as though someone had jerked her by a rope around her waist. She closed her eyes for a moment to calm her nerves. Then she looked down at the bed.

Who am I kidding?

She did not care to undress and change into her sleeping garments, knowing that her special someone was no longer present. Still, she continued to sleep on the same side of the bed, still feeling his presence there.

Maybe now I will get a good night's rest . . .

"Uhh . . . Ahh!"

Her ears caught the sound of heavy gasping. The darkness pressed in on her at first, then her eyelids fluttered open in a ray of light. With an effort, she focused her gaze. The blur of white slowly dissolved until she could make out the walls of her living quarters. On a small counter, Gildas laid stiffly like a plank, coughing and gasping for air. Antha rushed over to wipe his forehead with a wet cloth to cool him down. The chill of the damp cloth only helped for a short while. His temperature soared, seemingly without limit.

The aged town doctor arrived, bald on top with the lank remains of his white hair falling over his ears to rest upon his shoulders. His features were homely, his beady eyes set in a square head. He reached out his wrinkled hand to feel the sick man's pulse. He was gifted in the knowledge of healing, but today would prove to be a challenge. Through the many patients he had ministered to over the years, this one was unique.

"I have never seen anything like this before," said the town doctor.

"What can we do?" Antha asked.

"Just wait and see," he replied. "Here are some remedies to reduce the fever. There is nothing else I can do." The doctor reached out his hand to feel Gildas' temperature.

Cethin walked out of the bedroom groggily, rubbing his eyes in an effort to adjust them to the light, and hearing voices from the living room. He looked down at the table to see father suffering, and his eyes widened with fear.

Antha watched Gildas for a good moment, anxiously, helpless to rescue the love of her life. The only glimmer of hope she could cling to was the medicine the doctor would provide.

"Give him the medicine in a few hours and make sure he drinks it all," the doctor instructed.

"I will," Antha replied.

"I shall keep Gildas in my prayers and hope the Lord will hear."

The doctor moved towards the door. "I do hope I find something in my books that may help. I will come back once I find something new, that I promise you, and I will pass by in the morning."

"Thank you," Antha felt relief, watching the doctor leave.

"Mother? What is wrong with Father?" Cethin asked.

"Oh! Nothing, son, he is just a little sick," she lied.

"Is there anything I can do to help?" he asked.

"Go to your room and make sure that Illythia doesn't see Gildas like this, you hear."

Antha broke down into tears.

"Yes, Mother," Cethin replied, turning back to the bedroom.

Gildas' breathing became faint, the earlier fight finally taking its toll. Antha stood by his side, applying the wet towel to his forehead. For a moment, he forced himself to open his eyes. They rolled down slowly to see his lovely wife, and he smiled faintly.

"Hey, beautiful," Gildas whispered.

"Why must you tease me so . . ." Antha's tears rolled down her face.

She reached down to hold Gildas' hands firmly, caressing them anxiously.

He twitched slightly in her light grip. Though she tried to smile back through her tears, she knew in her heart what lay ahead

"I love you," he whispered tremulously.

"I love you too." She choked on her tears.

Gildas gazed upon his wife one last time.

"I will wait for you here, forever . . ."

Antha shook her head defiantly, not wanting to hear those words of utmost torture, which pierced her heart slowly, painfully; like a dagger. She watched her husband gasp his last few breaths, accepting his fate. A final calm overtook his eyes, which then closed for the last time, never to open again.

"No! No!" she sobbed, falling upon his chest.

Why . . . must . . . you . . . tease . . . so . . . Come back to me!

CHAPTER 4
—THE VISION

Lightning crackled and thunder boomed in the clouds, like the footfalls of ten thousand men beating upon the earth below. It echoed through the main hallway and out into the wide spiral path. The obsidian floor shone bleakly and rumbled ominously with the monstrous call. A grapefruit-sized orb of light hovered in the air, illuminating the holes of the archway with the colors of sunlight and casting its radiance upon the monolith in the center of the room.

Morgana's pale gray eyes bore into the orb as she focused on the thought she was prepared to share with her Master. Her black velvet cloak covered her youthful figure, exposing only the lightly tanned skin of her face. She glanced down briefly toward the end of the spiral staircase and the final hallway to the Master's chamber. She moved silently like a specter, her footfalls undetectable.

A deep growl reverberated throughout the hallway, making the ground tremble beneath Morgana's feet. The sound brought back a memory when she closed her eyes.

"The Shadow of Death!" the announcer bellowed.

Thunderous, energetic cheers erupted from all over the stadium. Crowds were screaming at the top of their lungs, chanting her brother's name and stomping the ground with their feet, waiting for him to emerge through the wooden gates.

He was feared by even the bravest gladiators, seen as an immortal by many, unbeatable amongst the sands. She'd tended to every wound or scar he attained through his battles. Shadow had suffered by the end of his four-hundredth fight. Not an inch of his body was free of scars. He'd kept his sister safe by winning every fight, while she'd kept him alive through her knowledge of medicine and anatomy. Together, they were invincible.

Opening her eyes, Morgana banished the distant memory. Gigantic double doors of mahogany stood before her. The doorway arched perfectly below a huge dragon skull with sharp, fearsome teeth.

The dragon skull bellowed another monstrous growl. The sound thundered down the hallway as the ponderous double doors unlocked and parted slowly with an ominous creak.

Continuing through the door, Morgana descended another flight of steps, which differed from the previous smooth black footing. Bones protruded from the cold floor like stepping stones. She made her way through the dragon's ribcage, half of which was exposed to the light, the other half buried amid the obsidian walls. The gaps between each bone revealed the black abyss below, an endless, bottomless pit that separated each step. She thought back to the time when the acolyte had told her, "The power comes from within."

The room had been dark and gloomy. Any sound made within echoed back from the walls. The scratch of a match lighting seemed loud in the stillness. It produced a small sunburst of red, orange, yellow, and various shades of blue. A delicate, pale white hand appeared near the small circle of fire, moved the burning matchstick to the candle that stood at the center of the table, and lit the wick. Then the match was shaken, extinguishing the flame.

The candlelight revealed an acolyte clad in a thick black cloak, plain, with no embellishment. The hood cast his face into shadow, hiding most of his features.

"Morgana. Come here, child," he rasped.

As she moved towards the candlelight, she recalled a younger version of herself. With her slender build, she seemed tiny inside the voluminous cloak she wore. The garment was adult-sized, yet she'd worn it anyway.

The acolyte lifted the candle from the wooden surface of a little round table and proceeded to the other side of the room, where a lean, middle-aged man lay upon a bed, his short black hair starkly contrasting with the white pillow. He blinked, revealing hazel eyes. The man was sweating profusely and looked very ill. His lightly tanned skin had faded to a pale, translucent white.

When he summoned the strength to move, heavy coughing and wheezing overtook him.

"Master commanded me to show you something," the acolyte stated.

"But this man . . . He is about to die," Morgana replied, concerned.

"The better to ease his suffering. Time is not on his side," the acolyte replied.

"Is there any way to help him?"

"No."

She watched the acolyte channel energy from within. A blue light glowed around his dominant hand, lighting up the room with the color.

An intense feeling overtook Morgana. *It's like nothing I have felt before. What could it be? He is standing still, yet the room feels . . . different.*

Morgana was queasy, her former control vanishing and leaving her shaky.

"What are you trying to show me?" Morgana asked, intrigued.

"You will see soon enough," the acolyte responded.

He pricked his fingertip, drawing forth a drop of blood. With it, the acolyte drew a small circle on the ground, near the dying man. Closing the circle, the acolyte mumbled some words that Morgana could not understand.

The blood soaked into the wooden floor, and a bright light began to shine forth. Morgana inclined her head to see the spikes of red light flashing up from the floor. Her eyes widened, her fascination piqued by the mysterious sight.

As Morgana watched, the doomed man's breath came slower and slower. Time itself paused for him. She drew close, inspecting him, feeling for a pulse. The space between each heartbeat stretched longer than the one before. *Thump, thump . . . Thump . . . Thump.*

"Watch carefully," the acolyte instructed. "This is what our Master commanded me to teach you." He channeled his energy from within. "Gather your aura from within and use it as energy," as he continued, white light danced visibly around his body.

I can do this, Morgana thought.

The acolyte shifted his gaze to Morgana. "Do not think with your mind. Let it flow from within. Break free from your habits and this power will open to you."

Puzzled, she considered how to react to the remark. In all her experience of healing, she'd never encountered this unconventional approach. *Spiritual energy? Is this possible?*

"Let us continue," said the acolyte.

She looked on, searching her mind for a scientific explanation. No books or teachings on human anatomy had ever mentioned such arcane methods.

There must be something, she thought frantically, *there has to be.*

The acolyte's hands hovered over the sick man's body as he spoke. "You will learn to extract a person's soul." The words rolled from his tongue in Latin.

> The nectar of life slips away,
> Death is near
> It awaits
> Come to me,
> Or be lost in the endeavors
> Follow my voice to find your way

Morgana's eyes opened wide in amazement.

Is this really happening? Can I really do this?

The dying man's life energy began to appear as white light, little bright patches here and there hovering above his body.

The acolyte broke his concentration for a moment to say, "This is but a taste of what you can learn from our Master."

His hands continued to stir the air around the sick man, merging the bright spots into a shape.

The bright energy continued to grow, mirroring the image of the sick man. The acolyte gathered the energy to himself, luring it in with motions of his hands. As the sick man's aura left his body and followed the acolyte, time slowly returned to normal. The dying man gasped his final breath as the last of his aura danced from his chest to the acolyte's hand.

Morgana analyzed those final moments carefully, replaying the events in her head.

Interesting . . . I may have found something. I will have to try it on someone to make sure that this is, in fact, what I think it is.

That day she may have uncovered what no one else could, a link to the human soul's location in the body.

The last few steps of the dragon's bones disappeared back into the obsidian floor. At the end of the hallway, one last turn led to a large room at the bottom of the monolith. The orb that had traveled with Morgana from the beginning of the journey vanished into thin air as she reached the final destination.

The center of the room fell away into a forty-foot crater, like the crash-landing scar of a comet. A huge fire burned inside with flames of bright yellow, orange, and red. The flames danced furiously as if fighting from within.

Around the massive hole stood four pillars, forming a perfect square. Each pillar had a different story etched into its surface. The pillar to the right seemed relatively new compared to the others, only a few hundred years old. The carvings on that pillar realistically depicted a samurai and the battles he had fought, presenting his story for the eyes to see.

The pillar to the left was different from the other three, showing an intertwining of two souls. Shadow, the first of the two, was known to have been the greatest gladiator of his time, having performed illusion-like feats and endured countless battles. The other was a young girl whose extraordinary attributes were her astounding intellect and extensive knowledge. These two complemented each other perfectly like a sword and shield. The third pillar was blank, with no carvings or adornments whatsoever.

The last pillar in the back showed a man of ancient Egyptian times, a giant who towered over all. The story told that armies could not stand against this single man; his strength could not be measured. Throughout his life, people feared this giant and the destruction he caused. His stories were retold as myths and legends.

The floor vibrated with rumbles and thuds as some creatures came running from the other side of the fire pit toward Morgana. Monstrous barks bellowed forth, echoing across the room as two behemoths, wolf-like demon dogs, rushed toward her.

The two frightful hounds were almost identical, with dark ruby-red eyes, small pointed ears, and fangs that protruded from their mouths. One of them had white fur and the other, black.

Oh no. Here come Skoll and Hati. I had better prepare myself.

The hearts' long tails swayed from side to side as both jumped for joy and attacked Morgana's face with licks, pushing the hood of her cloak down to her shoulders. She returned their ferocious affection, rubbing their heads and giggling along with their happy cries. After their quick little scuffle, the two dogs stopped abruptly and retreated back from whence they had come.

Hidden at the entrance, a samurai silently knelt atop a small red floor cushion. The man wore a dark blue hakama from the waist down. He sat perfectly still, not wavering from his position. His hands were mounted on the sides of his hips, his head was bowed, and his eyes were closed in deep meditation as the light from the fire kissed his yellow-tan skin.

A suit of armor encrusted with layers of reptilian scales made of dull reddish-black diamond reflected the light of the night. The armor was supported on a wooden stand next to the meditating man. With the armor assembled, it looked as though another person were sitting next to the samurai. A katana and wakizashi rested on stilts alongside the suit of armor.

Briefly, the samurai's dark eyes opened as he awakened from his deep meditation. He turned his gaze upward to see who had entered the room. The man noticed Morgana, who was now walking along the pillars to the rear of the room. Quickly returning to his previous state of trance, he closed his eyes and bowed his head, resuming the statue-like pose.

Morgana reached the last pillar. A few steps up the staircase, Skoll and Hati slept beside a throne. *Swoosh, swoosh.* The Master's massive wings flapped, carrying him through the room. Morgana looked up, withholding a smirk that itched to show itself.

I knew Master would do something like this!

His feet touched the floor as his wings flapped a few more times, adjusting the landing. His black wings hid his red silk robe. Automatically, he extended the wings once more. He thought himself a fair-looking man. Others thought differently: the most enchanting man, godlike to lay eyes upon, with his shoulder-length light brown hair, hazel green eyes, strongly jutting jaw, and lightly tanned white skin.

His wings separated into feathers, which circled all around and quickly attached themselves to their owner. In seconds, he was covered from top to toe.

The feathers transformed themselves into a black cloak, shiny and silky, fit for a king. The hood of the cloak shaded the Master's eyes as he looked appraisingly at the girl and took his rightful seat. With a blank stare, still and cold, the Master waited for his pupil. The hounds yelped with joy as Morgana approached the throne.

"Master," she addressed him.

"How is my favorite pupil?" he responded, still expressionless.

Both of the hounds sat upright calmly, tails wagging, waiting for the chance to play again with the girl. Though the task was daunting for an energetic beast, they hoped to see another enjoyable day with her. Skoll and Hati knew that her days were long and occupied with hard work, with very little free time.

Leaning forward in his seat, the Master spoke. "I had a feeling that you would come here," his emotionless expression remained fixed in place.

With a sly smile, Morgana stated, "Master, I have something to show you."

Skoll and Hati tilted their heads as if they answered for their Master. She would hear their whining, whimpering, and cries of curiosity and sometimes wonder if they understood what she said.

Hmm, maybe Skoll and Hati's reactions are the Master's after all.

"Continue," the Master prompted.

"A couple named Bruce and Fayth Smith live amongst the free people in the new world. I think you might take some interest in them."

Morgana briefly looked back to see the two hounds inching their way closer to her.

"Go on," the Master inquired, wanting more information.

Morgana continued: "There is a prophecy that has been passed down from generation to generation. 'Followers of the fallen angel' are what they call themselves. They prophesied a child being born, not an ordinary child, but one who could harness a demon. It was foretold that this child would be the harvester of death, as he will take those he pleases."

"Like the Demon?"

"Something . . . better," she responded.

"Hmm?" The Master was curious.

Walking to the crater of fire, she waved her hands in the air, which pulsated and rippled, showing a mirror through particles of light to the other realm. Her Master rose from the throne and walked down the steps, following her. What appeared through the fire had him transfixed with interest.

"This is a remnant of the past," Morgana explained.

Chapter 5
—The Broken One

The massive fire pit in the center of the room cast long shadows of the Master and Morgana. The two shadow figures ran down the floor, blocking the light from the wall. The samurai took notice. The conversation between the Master and his pupil next to the fire was all but a murmur to him.

Deep into his meditation, kneeling on the red cushion, he could hear the restless souls screaming in agony, yet those cries did not hinder him. In his dark blue hakama, his yellow tanned skin glowed slightly from the distant firelight. The warrior breathed slowly and steadily, his hands resting on his hips. Motionless like a statue, eyes closed, he did not waver from his state of trance.

Handprints slowly pressed outward from the skin of his back. Fingertips slid slowly across the muscled plain, running top to bottom and sometimes from side to side before disappearing. Glimmers of a bluish-white aura flew across the samurai's body, yearning to be free.

Under the skin of his midsection, fingertips protruded, moving from one side, peaking at the center, and receding down the other side. A face gasped for air near the shoulder, opening and closing its mouth repeatedly before disappearing. The bluish-white aura danced over his body like a wavering mist. Piecing the once-lost memories back together again was his only focus during these deep meditations.

KYOTO, JAPAN, 1336

Dry wood crackled in a cooking fire surrounded by a small patch of dirt. The rest of the floor was covered with bamboo. The light scent of wood smoke filled the room with a pleasant natural ambiance. A wooden rod rested over the fire, supporting a small pot of rice that boiled slowly. The steam rose like a miniature white cloud, evaporating to fog over the water. A few sticks with skewered river trout were set on the side, roasting near the boiling pot, along with a dead hare skinned down to the meat.

The fire shed only enough light to touch the wooden walls and bamboo trimmings of the modest room. A few windows were open to prevent smoke accumulation. In this room sat a man with his dark hair bundled into a topknot. His oval face bore an angular jaw, sparse black brows, generous but not over-full lips, and deep brown eyes, which now stared into the flames. He let out a long, deep sigh and rolled his eyes upward to gaze at the straw-covered roof above.

A woman approached from the other end of the house, walking quietly upon geta, the traditional wooden sandals. The white kimono covering her from neck to toe displayed flower decorations upon the bosom, and was held together with a pink sash. The lady removed her geta and set them near a small table facing the fire.

She knelt to set down a wooden tray full of bowls, cups, and tea before taking a seat herself. The light of the fire touched her pale skin and her bun of long black hair. Her amber-brown eyes regarded the man of her life, and a slight smile graced her smooth lips.

Placing the bowls on opposite sides of the table, she took up a bamboo stick and began to stir the rice within the pot. Her small, upturned nose flared slightly to take in the scent of the meal slowly cooking, and she closed her eyes in enjoyment. Her small, thin eyebrows raised and her mouth watered in anticipation of the dinner that would be ready soon.

"Gekido, my love, dinner is ready," she called, filling his bowl with rice.

"Hmm . . ." he answered, staring blankly at the ceiling.

She picked up her chopsticks from the table and packed her bowl with rice. She held the bowl near her chest and used her chopsticks to push the rice together, slowly packing it into a ball. Briefly, she glanced toward her significant other.

"You look troubled," she noted as she tore off a piece of hare meat.

"Nothing troubles me, Narumi," Gekido replied, turning to face the table and accepting his bowl of rice.

"You are such a bad liar," Narumi stated flatly. "Something is on your mind."

Gekido let out a big sigh. "I was just thinking about what Lord Ashikaga told me a few days ago. That is all."

"Oh. Well, the only trouble you should have right now is filling your aching stomach," Narumi smiled.

"Yeah. You're right." Gekido's face brightened as he returned the smile.

Silence was their companion as they ate quietly next to each other. Chopsticks scraped and danced on the surface of the bowls, gathering rice, condensing it into a ball as they quietly consumed their meals. They enjoyed their time together just like any other night, even in silence. From time to time, they would catch each other's glances and smile before taking another bite.

In the darkness outside, the red moon glimmered, providing the only light. Even the stars did not come out to play. The land looked as though painted in red, crying the blood of the fallen ones. Through the heavy tree line and thick grass in the fields all around, a small walking path followed the river. A clanking noise could be heard, drawing closer to the house by the second. A man covered in shadow, outlined by the moonlight, breathed heavily.

Narumi's eyes displayed the discomfort of her fear as she sat in the middle of the room, paralyzed by anxiety. All she wanted was a normal night, just like any other night, but the stir outside changed everything. A deep shiver ran down her spine as the tiny hairs on her arms stood up from goosebumps.

"What is going on here?" she thought.

Gekido quickly moved to the mantle on the side of the room, where his armor and weapon laid at rest, grabbing the hilt and sheath of the katana with both hands. He slowly unsheathed the weapon to show a sliver of steel, waiting quietly for the next move. His eyes twitched from side to side as he paid close attention to his surroundings, listening for any subtle movements or noise that might occur.

Taking a moment to catch his breath, the mysterious man outside knocked on the wooden edging of the door. Trying to look in through the paper door, he waited for an answer from within the house.

"Fujiwara," he gasped.

"Koga, is that you?" Fujiwara asked in a whisper.

"Yes," he replied as he caught his breath.

The familiar voice made Gekido's heart sing with relief. Returning his sword to its sheath, he placed it back on its stand and strode to the door. He slid the paper portal open for the man outside in the dark to enter and reveal himself by the dim light of the fire.

A man in a black hakama and dark red hakamashita, his topknotted hair ruffled messily, entered the house. His weary eyes displayed fear; worry lines crossed his tense forehead like furrows in a field. As Koga slid the door shut behind him, the darkness outside vanished like the sun setting on the horizon.

"Koga, what brings you here in the dead of night?" Fujiwara inquired.

"Grave news, Fujiwara," he replied.

A river of blood slowly trickled down behind Koga's ear and flowed down his neck, mixing with the sweat he had accumulated. Adrenaline rushed through his body, flowing from limb to limb, making him shake uncontrollably. Though he steadied his breathing, his concealed injuries caused blood to spill from his hand to the floor.

"Please sit. Tell me everything," Fujiwara gestured to the table.

Koga trailed behind, following his host to the table. Narumi stepped away without notice, to reappear moments later from the next room with a teapot and cups in hand. She lowered herself down to set the cups before each person.

"A few nights ago, one of our scouts spotted a massive army coming toward our shogun's castle," Koga informed the couple.

"How many?" Fujiwara asked.

"Thousands . . ." Koga replied, watching Narumi pour tea into the cups on the table. "Thank you," he continued.

She nodded silently, not speaking a word or making a sound. After pouring the tea, Narumi set the teapot on the table and bowed to the guest before taking her leave.

"What kind of army?" Fujiwara questioned.

"The Imperial Army."

"What about Lord Ashikaga?" He felt a churning in his stomach.

"Safe, for now . . ." Koga looked down.

"What are we waiting for? We must hurry!" Fujiwara addressed Koga, distress plain in his voice.

"Wait! Fujiwara!"

On one knee, Fujiwara paused to look at Koga in confusion. He watched him pull out a scroll from within the hakamashita and hand over the scroll engraved with a wax embroidery stamp.

Just seconds after giving Fujiwara the scroll, Koga pulled out another scroll, this one already opened. Small pieces of the sealing wax crumbled away, falling to the floor. He was slightly hesitant about handing that one to the samurai, yet he did, with a shaky hand.

"This was what they sent us a few days ago," he continued.

Opening the second scroll, Fujiwara asked, "Who sent you this letter?" He watched the parchment roll down from the scroll.

"Ah . . ." Koga choked on the words.

"Spit it out!" Fujiwara fumed.

"The Emperor . . ." Koga's tone was almost a whisper.

"What?" Fujiwara interrupted.

"Yeah . . . Since that day, I have been looking everywhere, trying to find you."

Fujiwara skimmed the beginning of the scroll. It read,

Lord Ashikaga,

You are summoned to the capital. If you do not comply, it will be considered an act of treason.

Fujiwara's eyes paused at the word *treason*, not moving any farther as the other words seemed to vanish from the parchment. Though he tried to read again and again, his emotions latched onto that word, making everything else irrelevant. His hands were starting to tremble with anger, but he decided to roll the scroll back up. Taking a deep breath to calm his nerves and a long exhale to release the frustration, he decided to open the second scroll and broke the seal.

Fujiwara,

I want you to know, by the time you have read this, my life on this world will have come to an end. I have accepted my fate and now I want you to accept yours. Do not come to avenge my death. Instead, I want you to live your life. Take Narumi far, far away and live to the end of your days. Then one day, we will meet again in another life.

Lord Ashikaga

A momentary silence hung in the air as Fujiwara reflected upon the words of his lord. He took a deep breath before crumpling both scrolls into one ball and tossing them into the small cook fire where the flames engulfed them.

"Were you followed?" Fujiwara questioned.

"N-no . . . I don't think so," Koga answered.

I cannot trust him . . . Fujiwara's blood boiled from within, slowly spreading out, reddening his skin. He went straight for his armor that sat on the mantle. As he lifted the iron chest plate with its leather lacing, the front and back pieces collapsed, making a soft clank.

Narumi stepped out from the darkness and into the light of the room once more. Her eyes filled with dread each and every time she watched him put on the suit of armor. She knew she had no choice but to stay strong.

I know Gekido will come back to me.

His thoughts lingered somewhere else as he tied the loose ends of each piece of armor. He did not smile, but only gave her a distant stare. Narumi grabbed the last piece, a kabuto that still lay on the mantle. Like clockwork, she walked to the door, waiting for her partner, and seconds later he followed.

"Come back to me," Narumi whispered to Fujiwara, handing over his kabuto.

"You know I will," Fujiwara whispered back.

As Fujiwara opened the door he commanded, "Watch over Narumi. I will be back soon." He closed the door behind him, noting that darkness had begun to set in.

If they want a fight, I will give them a war.

He ran, away from the yellowish-orange light that shone in rays around the door of his home, toward the darkness that slowly engulfed the landscape, leaving no trace of light.

■ ■ ■ ■

A bright white light erupted like a solar flare above the fire pit. This disruption caused the meditating samurai to lose his focus on the memory, details slipping away. Fujiwara opened his eyes for a moment, and the condemned souls that tried to escape dissolved back into his flesh. He gave Morgana and his Master a distant stare. Their mumbling to each other did not mean anything to him, so he closed his eyes once more. Taking a deep breath, he returned to his original trance.

Pain is all I remember . . .

"Are you certain?" Morgana questioned.

Fujiwara came to a conclusion. "Yes."

Morgana looked at Fujiwara, who lay on the obsidian table. As her hand flicked up and down, multiple ropes simultaneously encircled Fujiwara's hands, feet, and neck, tying him down as though he were sentenced to death.

In the flickering candlelight, she roamed around the table, casting long shadows as she inspected each rope. Following this appraisal, she motioned the ropes to constrict a little more, taking up every last inch of slack.

The samurai stared up at the ebon ceiling, noting slight discomfort, and pondered for a moment. His eyes roamed, searching the room for illumination, but it was a fruitless effort. As he raised his head to improve his field of vision, his gaze finally caught a dull reflection upon the black stone wall next to the door.

"Well, let's begin," Morgana proclaimed, her excitement evident.

Multiple enchantment circles were inscribed upon the floor, surrounding the table to which Fujiwara was bound. Each one featured a different symbol. Turning his head to the side, Fujiwara fixed his eyes upon Morgana, wondering what would come next. As he pondered this, a bluish-white glow appeared from the tattoo on her right arm, extending down its length to the hand.

"What's that light shining from your skin?" Fujiwara inquired.

"This is the color of my aura."

"And the tattoo on your arm?"

"It's called a *vayne*. The more knowledge you possess, the farther the vayne travels up your body," she explained.

"Hmm," Fujiwara murmured, drifting off into another thought.

Revenge is my only weapon.

A dim light at the top right corner of the table began to pulsate, brightening by the second. Slowly forming a circle from one end, the light connected the bond. Morgana lashed her finger like a whip, and a small wound opened in Fujiwara's skin. She collected the blood from the wound and let it drop into the circle of light. The red face of a beast appeared, and then vanished again.

"There's no turning back after this," Morgana warned him.

"I know." Fujiwara affirmed his resolve.

Her hand glowed blue, the light flowing down from the vayne on her forearm. She spoke in an odd language he could not understand:

There is life after death
Hear my voice,
Follow the melody
Come, give it strength
A new vessel is waiting,
Become who you were meant to be

A thunderous roar echoed through the small room. A sense of uneasiness clouded Fujiwara's thoughts as if to second-guess the decision. The ground shivered as if in fear of the ravages of a catastrophic earthquake.

A pair of ears began to take form in flames of bright orange fire that rose from the ground. The untamed flames that fell from the face and body of the beast danced on the ground like sparks. Molten ashes flaked off the apparition like a thin layer of skin as it levitated into the air, and black smoke circled it as it took form. The being became a large, striped feline that glowed blue from within. The sight of it sent shivers up and down Fujiwara's body.

Aaaah! A tiger! This child is more powerful than I expected.

Fujiwara looked at her once more, closely this time. The vaynes weaved around her arm, reaching the top of her shoulder but ending before her jaw-line. The other hand, which saw less use, had begun to show signs as well, but he could not see it clearly due to the gauntlet that shielded most of her skin.

One day, I will surpass her strength.

"This is only the beginning," Morgana stated.

Nor the end.

Fujiwara swallowed the saliva remaining in his mouth, and then exhaled.

The second circle began to illuminate with a reddish glow as Morgana continued speaking the language he could not understand.

Feel the fire
The anger inside his heart,
Smell the fear

The fiery beast began to pace from side to side while Morgana chanted. Palpable rage swirled through the animal as though it had been provoked. The beast's skin lit with a dark red fire, and then pulsated, shifting quickly to a bright yellow-orange color as the seconds passed.

Feed off his hate,
Let the tensions unite
Go to him,
Become one

At the end when silence reigned supreme once more, the beast jumped at Fujiwara with its massive jaws open. Its roar echoed like a sonic boom and, going in for the kill, the tiger aimed for the lethal blow, going for the neck. Suddenly, as it neared Fujiwara's body, the tiger phased into a stream like pure energy, fighting its way backward with everything it had yet still getting absorbed into the samurai's body. The last speck of the tiger's energy touched Fujiwara's chest.

The room returned to darkness. The two lights that illuminated the circles dimmed down to almost nothing. Everything seemed to be going according to plan.

"Well . . . that was not so difficult," Fujiwara stated with relief.

"It has not started yet. Just wait," Morgana warned him firmly.

What is that noise? I do not remember that.

Rapid footsteps padded around in front of the samurai, disturbing his meditation once more. They weren't the footfalls of people, but something else. Fearful growls broke the silence. Fujiwara's eyes opened once more, viewing everything as though through the bottom of a glass. Two figures, one white and one black, moved back and forth, play fighting with all their energy. Their dark ruby eyes glimmered like red oceans of blood in the light of the fire.

Skoll and Hati will stop soon . . . I hope.

Fujiwara's head thudded with immense pain. Tensions spiked like daggers, piercing from one side to the other. *What is this all of a sudden?*

He looked over to the side where his armor stood by the mantle. A glare of yellow-orange shone through the eye holes of his mask.

Concentrate . . . He took a deep breath, watching the glow disappear.

There was a lingering sensation of sorts. Something he could not put his finger on, tingling down his spine. A low, subtle rush of energy began to creep in, from something else . . . Fujiwara knew that something was coming, and soon. *Focus.* He watched the two hounds continue their play, and then closed his eyes.

My fragmented memories, I need to fix them all.

One of the most excruciating pains . . . more than a few lifetimes to bear.

The stench of death ran wild amidst the air like a plague, fires burning in areas other than campfires across the village. The gray smoke that loomed over the area covered the sun like a blanket. Scattered rays of light began to break through the pall, creating a blood red sky.

What remained of the village was the skeleton of a ghost town. Fujiwara approached and beheld a view he did not recognize. Houses and stores alike, once towering among the small trees, were all burnt to the ground. Countless arrows lay scattered everywhere like a gigantic mural. Some of them affixed corpses to house walls and trees, and broken swords, shields, and armor lay in disarray all around. Pieces of wood, charred from the fire, lay on the road. Fujiwara passed dead bodies piled upon each other like a grisly monument. Men, women, and children alike, all were massacred, not one left alive to see the light of another day.

Those bastards! Tears filled his eyes.

Everyone he had known lay slaughtered like pigs. Fujiwara proceeded down the path to the castle where Lord Ashikaga lived. The road was strewn with carnage. He noticed a few dead soldiers from the imperial army amid blood splattered copiously on the ground like paint on a canvas.

Step by step, up the winding stairs, he made his way through a small opening between the two massive white stone walls that hid the Lord's house. Fujiwara paused for a moment to look back over a winding river that coiled like a serpent heading toward the castle.

He turned around, looking over the courtyard full of dead bodies and pools of blood surrounding them, and at the palace where his Master stayed. The west wing of the fortress where Lord Ashikaga laid to rest every night was burnt to cinders, while the east wing made of timber, wood, and stone still stood unscathed.

He proceeded along a narrow walkway, past a small circular koi pond tinged red from the blood of men, the spot no longer tranquil. He spotted a body on the ground, head severed, lying sideways near the pond. The corpse wore a white hakama that he recognized.

Please be someone else.

"No!" Fujiwara screamed out to the heavens above.

A pool of blood surrounded his master, who lay on the floor. The white hakama Lord Ashikaga wore was soaked in red blood on one side, tainting his attire, while the other side still retained its pristine color. As Fujiwara knelt by his departed Lord's side, the pool of blood and water splattered on his knees as they collided with the stained earth. He held the lifeless body of his Lord and mourned for the last time.

This one is special; Morgana expressed the thought without speaking, linked mentally to her brother.

A ripple in the air pulsed back and forth like a vortex tearing through. Something wanted to come out. The pattering of hoofbeats breached the portal, but only bones appeared. Farther and farther it reached out, muscle and tendons then wrapped around the bones, and black skin held everything together. Finally, the black horse with blood-red eyes neighed a fearsome cry.

Morgana wore a black velvet cloak with white embroidery on the hem and cuffs in an Aramaic design and a shield emblem on the tip of her hood and back. Riding behind her brother, a giant considering her own size, she held tight to him. Though her view was blocked, she knew where to go.

Shadow, holding the reins of the horse, displayed scars all along his hands and forearms. He wore a black velvet cloak from head to toe that matched his younger sister's, the only difference being the emblem on the hood and back, which resembled a sword.

Why is he so special, sweet sister? Shadow inquired.

He is like you, never defeated in countless battles, Morgana replied.

Ha! I will show him a true gladiator.

Sure, you should ask him to fight.

Ha, ha, funny. With what tongue? I will just kill him instead.

Master wants him, so here we are.

Turning the corner and onto the road toward the castle, the black stallion trotted slowly. The samurai ahead knelt at the foot of the courtyard in prayer, ready to take his own life. Hearing a horse, Fujiwara looked up to see who it was, lowering his tanto to the side. Shadow pulled the reins as the horse came to a halt, snapping its head from side to side.

Help me down, brother, Morgana asked.

With his right hand, Shadow reached up to pull off the hooded cloak, revealing his olive tan skin and the scars etched all over his head like scriptures on a wall. The only remnant of his platinum blond hair was in his eyebrows, as his black eyes looked up. An awkward dead silence held sway between the two warriors as they stared intently at each other.

Releasing his other hand from the reins, Morgana took Shadow's hand and lowered herself to the ground. With both hands, she removed her hood from the top of her head. Her dark brown hair rolled down to her pelvis like drapes touching the floor, and her light gray eyes were ever so watchful. She smirked, highlighting her high cheekbones and rose pink lips.

"Why are you in such a hurry to die, Ronin?" Morgana taunted in Japanese, walking forward.

"I have failed my Master. I too shall follow him," Fujiwara replied.

Fujiwara had begun to raise the tanto back up when she stated, "There are many different ways to approach this situation."

"What do you mean?" he inquired.

"There has to be a greater purpose in your survival."

"My purpose is to join my Master in the afterlife."

"Maybe your Lord had a greater cause for you in the end."

"What kind of cause?"

"I am sure you already know the answer," Morgana hinted.

Revenge, Fujiwara thought. "What do you have in mind?" he asked her.

"My Master can give you all the tools you need."

"To . . . ?" Fujiwara remained skeptical.

"To give you the strength needed to defeat all your foes, for the injustice they did to your Lord," Morgana finished.

Fujiwara thought for a moment.

Lord Ashikaga . . . What should I do?

Morgana continued her glacially slow walk. With every step, her jewelry clashed, musical to her ears.

I wonder what he is going to decide . . . Time will tell soon.

"As we speak, your enemies are still amongst you, in your shadow," Morgana proclaimed.

In my shadow! What could she mean by this?

Fujiwara gave Morgana a puzzled look.

She gave a clue. "The messenger."

His eyes lit up with rage as he fumed like a ticking time bomb ready to explode.

KOGA! I FUCKING KNEW HE WAS BEING FOLLOWED!

Fujiwara dropped the tanto onto the ground, his only remaining thought that of disappointment.

Narumi . . . I should not have left you.

"Claim what is yours," Morgana called out to Fujiwara.

Nodding his head, Fujiwara got up and approached Morgana.

I have lost everything. Soon . . . Emperor. Soon. You will lose it all.

The third circle sparked yellow, dancing around until it returned to its origin. Once again Morgana's tongue continued in Latin,

One together,
Choice of will
Of blood,
Pain and sorrow
Coming together as one
An everlasting bond, forever

I was not finished with that memory . . . Why can I not go back . . . I need to go back. I need to see for myself if Narumi is still alive.

"AH! What the fuck is happening to me?" Fujiwara screamed.

"You and the demon I put inside you are bonding together," Morgana replied.

"Something is not right!" Fujiwara shrieked in agony, trying to break free from his bindings. "Ah!"

Sudden movements appeared from his belly. A glow followed from within as though his demon were putting on a light show, and a subtle cry carried over with an almost yearning tone. Something inside his abdomen seemed to reach out as the skin tightened.

"What is this?" Fujiwara cried.

The tiger's claws reached out, slashing his skin, moving toward the ceiling and clawing its way out. The glow of red, orange, and yellow lit up the samurai like a glowing lantern when the claws returned inside his body. Seconds later, a face surfaced where the first attack had appeared as the tiger roared with a renewed purpose.

"Fuck!" Fujiwara bellowed.

The pain on Fujiwara's face was plainly visible. The agony was longer tolerable. He squirmed and used every ounce of strength to free himself from the prison that held him. The damage began to set in as blood seeped through his pores. The rush of dark red, almost black fluid filled his mouth as he coughed for air. He leaned to the side and blood gushed from his nose. Spitting the rest of the liquid onto the floor, he gasped for a few more breaths.

The samurai whimpered, "H-Help . . ." as the tiger continued to ravage him from within.

What was once one,

Now are two

But never far,

Always near

Fate is close,

The dreams will be real

The two will unite,

When their calling is the night

Darkness is all I remember . . .

"How did your experiment go?" The Master asked, looking down at the steps.

"It could have gone better," Morgana replied.

"And what about Fujiwara?"

"Broken . . ."

"Broken?" he sounded almost surprised.

"Broken, but . . . alive. The experiment I tried had a flaw that will be fixed. As for Fujiwara, he is something else. A true demon . . . He has the will to live on despite what he endured. Extracting the demon was easy, and the majority of it now lives in the mempo, where I put him. A portion of the demon will remain in the samurai's body. He will serve Fujiwara in time when he has recovered. The demon will give him the strength he needs. As for Fujiwara, I will have to monitor him. His soul is broken. I will fix him as best I can after I figure out what has happened."

"Okay . . . Hmm . . . the Demon. I like it."

CHAPTER 6
—THE PROPHECY

The Master stared through the pixelated screen, into the fire. "I do not see anything . . ."

"Just wait a while. You will see, in time," Morgana replied.

"You enjoy this."

"A little," Morgana gave her Master a grin. "Ah, it begins."

MASSACHUSETTS, 1665

The room was blanketed in darkness with the windows barred shut. Suddenly, the door opened. As the light seeped in, a group of children quietly entered. One by one, each child blocked the light with their bodies, casting a momentary darkness back over the room. Each child sat on the floor next to one another, just a few feet in front of the entrance, forming a line as the door slowly closed behind the last child to enter.

An old woman sat peacefully in the middle of the room. She opened her eyes once the last child was seated, making a creaking noise on the wooden floor. Suddenly a flame flickered into life upon a candle in front of her, and more candles followed suit, surrounding her. The woman wore a black silk dress that resembled a nightgown. Her frizzy white-and-gray hair fell across her cheeks, down her back, and finally, to the floor.

She examined the children with her dark brown eyes. In the candlelight, her wrinkled, furrowed white skin looked almost transparent, sagging from her face and her exposed arms. Slowly her nostrils flared as she inhaled, and she smiled slyly, revealing decayed yellow teeth. The children wiggled their way in a little farther, closing the gap between them as they waited patiently for the old lady to say something.

"A long, long time ago before we all existed, heaven condemned one of the angels," the old lady began in a shrill voice. "That angel had his wings taken away from him. The God he loved and worshiped took everything from him. In time, he then lost his way and roamed the earth for many centuries, cursing the heavens above for what God had done to him. Then he learned the ways of mankind. There, he wrote many scriptures revealing the art of magic for those who wanted to invoke the gods," the old lady continued, her eyes focused on the audience.

The children's eyes were fixed upon the old lady, intently wishing to know more of the story as they devoured every word she spoke. Slowly glancing at each child in the room, she continued where she'd left off. "Many years later, after gaining a few followers, his gathering began to grow and flourish. People learned the essence of magic, being able to control elements at their own will. Suddenly, one day . . ." The old lady paused for a moment, building up the suspense.

"Hundreds of men came, wearing brown robes and leather necklaces with a cross on their chests. They began to destroy what the fallen angel had built, and called our magic, "devil's work." Most of the scriptures containing the magic were burned and forever lost."

The old lady lifted her hand just above her chest for the children to see. A small fire ignited in her palm and the other hand waved in the air, rolling a small piece of cloth with her fingers.

"A few men captured the fallen angel and burned him alive, to prevent any future harm to their church."

She dropped the piece of cloth into the fire. After a brief moment, the children heard a man crying as if he were burning alive there within the room.

"Most of the fallen angel's followers were captured and hanged. Those who remained fled for their lives as the fallen angel told them, to save the scriptures before his departure. One of the scriptures, the fallen angel treasured most. He insisted on keeping that one safe because it held information foretelling the future. Over a long, long time, that scripture was lost from the face of the earth."

The old woman adjusted her posture to sit comfortably.

"What happened to the people who escaped? What did they do?" one of the children asked.

"The followers who escaped, they continued practicing what magic they had learned. After years and years of searching, one of them found the lost scripture. With it, they grew and established our order of the Fallen One. Handed down from generation to generation, we are the protectors and guardians of that scripture until we find the one that is prophesied."

Slowly, the old woman rose.

"Prophecy for what?" one of the children questioned.

"That will be for another day," she answered.

The children grumbled, wanting to know more of the unfinished story. Standing up, one after another, they stretched their little limbs, knowing the end of their time together was near. The door opened behind them to reveal an old man.

"Alright, children. Run along now. It is time for us to have a word with her," he said.

He wore a thick brown fur coat with claws on each arm and a bear head resting back onto his neck. His cheeks were red from the cold winter winds, and with every breath he took, a cloud of white vapor steamed from his face. The wind howled by with another hollow cry, yet his short brown hair, spiked straight up, did not budge. He watched sternly with his hazel green eyes, crinkling his forehead slightly, as the children in their winter clothing walked by in single file quietly out the door.

"You summoned me, Nan?" the man asked, closing the door after the last child.

She got up from the floor, which took all the strength she had. Moving creakily toward him, she replied sternly, "I need to see your daughter."

Without hesitation, he nodded and responded, "Right away."

He immediately exited via the front door in a few swift steps.

Why does she need to see Fayth? he wondered.

A narrow creek continued to flow, slithering like a snake, throughout the land, thawed again after the harsh winter. Tall trees sprouted everywhere, reaching for the sky above, their branches yet lacking any leaves for protection.

At the edge of the ridge, comfortably nestled between the tree trunks as if they were a chair, a young woman sat, covered with a thick woolen blanket. Her light brown hair obscured small portions of her face, her eyes remained closed, and her lips were reddened, chapped, and cracked from the cold. The sunlight wound its way through the maze of trees, illuminating her lightly tanned skin. She breathed calmly, quietly listening to the flow of water, finding a place of tranquility.

The bitter cold felt like a thousand needles pricking her skin, but she tolerated it, for she relished every moment of solitude. Her yellow-green hazel eyes opened in the sunlight, revealing a startling clarity. She watched the powdery snowflakes refracting the light like tiny prisms as they swirled down from the trees. She huddled against the tree trunk as the wind howled, in an effort to avoid the chilling bite of the frosty air.

As her consciousness ventured deeper and deeper within, the world seemed to distance itself from her. She did not notice when the howling winds slowly subsided.

The far cry of a familiar voice echoed amongst the trees, yelling out her name. "Fayth! Fayth! Where are you, Fayth?"

Her weariness allowed the calls to pass through one ear and out the other. Fayth's concentration had passed the distance beyond which the darkness began to descend upon her heavy eyes. Resting her head against the tree trunk as though it were a pillow, and taking another deep breath, she drifted off to sleep.

The shuffling of dirt kicked up from the earth by heavy boots continued steadily, announcing the man's footsteps. The bear head that had once rested on the back of his neck now sat cozily atop his head, baring its fangs.

I cannot believe she likes this type of weather . . . Of all things, she likes to be alone.

He searched high and low, knowing that he was close. Any detail out of the ordinary would provide a clue.

Ah, there she is. He watched a puff of white vapor wisp up from a tree trunk.

He spoke to her calmly. "Fayth . . . Fayth, dear, time to wake up."

The words seemed to dance into one ear and straight out the other. He gave it a few more tries, calling her name again. Finally, he shook Fayth softly to awaken her from her slumber.

"Did you hear me call?" Fayth's father asked.

"Hmmm . . . I thought it was all a dream, Papa," she replied, stretching and yawning.

She peered at her father with glazed, watery eyes. It reminded him of the same blank stare she'd given him in her childhood. Those light green-yellow hazel eyes told him she was lost in thought or imagining herself in another life. He smiled, recalling the cherished memories.

"I wish it *had* been a dream," Papa responded.

"What is going on?"

"Nan wants you to see her."

"You mean the oracle. Did she say why?" Fayth inquired.

"No, she did not say. And don't talk about your grand-Nan like that," Papa responded.

"Hmm." Fayth looked down.

"We will find out soon enough." Papa let out a big sigh.

"Yes."

The gravel crunched under her hands as she rose. She wiped away the dirt and crumbs of tree bark that stuck to her backside.

"Let's get out of this wretched cold," said Papa.

"Hmm." She nodded.

"I do not know how you deal with this weather!" Papa shivered.

"It's no bother. I like it out here . . ." Fayth trailed off.

"You are just like your mother," Papa smiled once more. "In every way, she liked to be out here, all alone."

As the pair walked together down a narrow path along the river, Fayth's father slowed his pace, letting her lead when the path narrowed enough to accommodate only one. A light tune drifted ahead from behind Fayth, who smiled and looked over her shoulder to see her father whistling a song she remembered. She hummed along with him as a distraction from the situation that lay ahead.

Why am I being summoned? Her only thoughts are of us even though she tried to block everything out.

Shrubs, willowy saplings, and tall trees soaring fifty feet in the air, branches still bare from winter, lined the path back to the village.

At the end of the melody, Faith re-experienced the urge to satisfy her curiosity.

"Do you know why she summoned me?" she asked again, forgetting she'd already inquired.

"I do not have the slightest idea. We are close; we will know soon enough," Papa replied.

"Oh . . . Yes. Right," she replied, looking up at the milky-gray clouds slowly covering the sun.

"We're here," Papa proclaimed.

Their destination was the only house on the hill. The other houses were scattered amongst the trees, not far away. Though the houses all looked alike, the people in the village knew the little details of each. The log cabin had a small wooden porch just in front of the doorway. Bundles of branches, mud, and grass were layered on top for a roof, and the windows were sealed shut to keep the cold out. An uneasy feeling danced through Fayth's mind as she approached the door, knowing she did not belong there.

Her father rushed to open the door, and then waited for Fayth to go ahead. She took a moment to muster her courage she had. The eerie feeling of the house seemed to suffocate her. One step after another, she slowly crossed the threshold. She felt the weight of the world on her shoulders, and saw nothing but blackness ahead.

From the center of the darkened room, a shrill voice, scratchy with age, called, "Come here, my child."

Fayth proceeded slowly to the middle of the room, her eyes trying to adjust to the darkness. Her careful steps made no sound on the wooden planks beneath her feet. A flame sprung to life on a candlestick just a few feet before her, revealing a black figure sitting on the floor. Fayth lowered her gaze to the pale, wrinkled feet.

"Close the door," the old woman commanded.

Fayth's father nodded and closed the door, leaving the flickering candle as the only source of light. He sat down on a nearby chair close to the door, providing a silent audience to whatever might lie ahead.

I wonder why Nan didn't tell me to leave. What kind of news is she going to tell us?

Fayth's eyes finally adjusted to the darkness as the candle's small flame grew brighter to her with each passing second. As she fixated on the candle, which rested in its fixture on the floor, the surroundings seemed to disappear.

A loud squeak, like nails on a chalkboard, sounded from the back of the room. Suddenly a chair arrived in the circle of candlelight, just behind the dark figure that blocked her view. Fayth watched the candle levitate and hang in mid-air, slowly casting light upon the darkened form. Attentively, she watched the flickering flame reveal the pale old woman her father called Nan.

Her eyes fixed upon the wrinkled white hand that twirled in a continuous circle several times, then stopped. Fayth noticed a mark on the old lady's hand in the shape of wings, perhaps a small tattoo. A bright yellow light glimmered from that mark. It was enough to illuminate a radius of several feet, revealing the chair behind the old hag as it slid beneath the old lady's body.

Nan's long, frizzy white hair hung down freely, almost touching the floor. The candle shifted to one side of the room, as though carried by a ghost. Nan glanced at the candle and summoned it back to the center of the room with only the movement of her eyes.

"Sit, my child," she bid the younger woman.

"But there is no seat," Fayth responded, looking around for another chair.

"Trust your grandmother."

With grace and swiftness, Papa quietly placed a chair right behind Fayth without her noticing. With trust, she did what was told and sat down, slowly looking back to see her father returning to his seat. She put on a smirk but wanted to smile outright.

I should have known you would do something like that, Papa.

"We have many things to talk about and very little time," Nan stated.

She looked at the candle and swung her arm to the side, commanding it to fetch something. Within seconds, the candle brought back a small square wooden table of rough quality, as though a ten-year-old child had made it. The candle came to rest in the middle of the table.

"Hmm," Fayth mused.

"Someday . . . Someday, you will take my place," Nan began.

"Take your place in what, Nan?" Fayth questioned.

"To be the protector of the scroll."

"Huh . . . what?" Fayth blurted, shocked.

Nan nodded, "I see so much potential in you."

"B-but why me?"

"You . . . you have a gift," Nan responded.

"A gift?"

A few more candles from underneath the table levitated their way to the tabletop. One by one, each candle turned sideways to light the wick. With all three lit, they scattered, looking for something.

The first candle arrived back to the table with an empty bowl that came to rest right next to the candle in the middle. Seconds later, the next one returned to the table, passing by just above the old lady's head with a small wooden container in tow. The last candle remained on the other side of the room, indecisive about which item to bring. The old lady regarded it with her beady gaze and tipped her head to the side, summoning the candle back. A container returned with the last candle, heavier than the others and shaped like a small treasure chest.

Nan leaned forward and opened the little wooden box. As she placed the lid upon the table, an awful stench wafted through the room. Fayth's nostrils flared, taking in the horrid odor. She cringed, hoping something else would happen. As she watched, Nan took some pieces of bone from the container and tossed them into the bowl.

"I see so much potential in you," Nan repeated, opening the treasure box. "You remind me of myself when I was your age, optimistic."

What does she mean? Maybe I will know soon enough.

Nan balled her hand into a fist, hiding whatever was in the box. She brought her hand over the bowl and released her grasp. Gemstones fell to the bowl, glittering in the light. Rubies, diamonds, emeralds, and other gems clattered into the bone fragments. The old lady then reeled in Fayth's chair with a motion of her finger, bringing her closer to the table.

"While we're here, we should read your fortune." Nan took up the bowl.

The eerie feeling still clung to Fayth, leaving her uneasy. She felt uncomfortable sitting in front of Nan, and she wished she could just leave. Briefly, she looked back at her father, who remained silent in the back of the room like a mute. She wanted to scream out to him, but knew this was neither the time nor place. She wished she could be home or in the woods, anywhere but here.

Fayth's eyes skimmed around the room where the candles had made their search. She could still see remnants of the light although it shone there no longer. She could see shelves upon shelves of books and scrolls on one side, medicine and containers on another.

"Let me see your hand, my dear," the old lady requested.

Fayth almost refused, though she knew better. Her hand quivered as she extended it.

"You will know everything soon enough, child," Nan continued.

Nan took hold of Fayth's hand and examined every inch of it. The old lady's sharp, claw-like nails tickled Fayth's palm, causing little spasms and the urge to take her hand back. Slowly moving Fayth's hand to the middle of the table where the bowl remained, the old woman's fingers reached to her grandchild's fingertip. Suddenly, with her sharp nails, she gouged Fayth's index finger. Blood issued from the wound, forming a small drop.

Nan held her granddaughter's hand tightly, preventing the girl from retracting it any further, and squeezed the finger to draw more blood out. After collecting a few drops of blood in the bowl, Nan released Fayth's hand. That hand bore red prints from the old woman's grasp.

Fayth reclaimed her throbbing hand, wincing in pain. The old lady lifted the bowl from the table and began to shake it around and around, combining the blood, bones, and gems. Finally, Nan poured everything out of the bowl. The bones and gems, stained with blood, clunked onto the table.

The old lady raised her chin a notch and squinted at the spread of bones and gems. Though it looked like nothing special to Fayth, she pondered what the significance might be. Nan's eyes opened wide with intrigue.

How could I have let this one slip by? Is it because she is my own kin, shrouding my judgment?

She quickly rose from her seat, creaky old bones notwithstanding, and walked to the wall full of scriptures and books, looking for a certain item. She browsed through each scroll until she located a particular one. Nan mumbled, "Ah hah. There you are," as she pulled it from the shelf.

Fayth looked confused, lost, trying to figure out what was going on. *What is this old lady talking about?*

She watched Nan walk ever so nimbly back to her seat.

The old lady opened the scroll with shaky hands and placed it on top of the bones and gems. She muttered, "Hmm . . ." *Could this finally be the one?*

"What did you do? I don't understand," Fayth replied.

"This is another test," Nan answered. "Look closely and tell me what it says."

"I cannot understand this language . . ."

Nan began to work her magic, speaking an unknown language that sent a tingle down Fayth's spine. It seemed as though she was possessed by another entity. Her eyes rolled back as though she were blind.

What is old is never old,
Is now renewed
Let the dust settle
With broken wings,
Show the path
Shine the light,
And guide us

The letters on the scroll began to brighten into shades of white, illuminated in contrast to the black ink on the scroll. The words began to shift up and down, left to right and vice versa, restructuring the canvas to its content.

"Now, tell me what you see," said Nan.

"I cannot make anything out," Fayth replied.

"Give it some time."

Fayth's eyes opened wide as she suddenly found herself able to understand the words once they were placed correctly.

What is this? She read quietly.

"To whom it may concern:

Whoever can read this will bring great justice to this world. You are the prophecy we have all been waiting for. Your presence will change the world. With the seeds being sown, a new world will manifest.

She leaned back to rest on the seat, her face making plain her shock.

"Is this true?" Fayth asked Nan.

"What does it say?" Nan queried.

"It said something about justice, changing the world, and something about a new world that will manifest."

"Yes, my child. Is there any more?" asked the old lady.

After all these years of searching, she was right underneath my nose this whole time. I never thought I would see this day come.

"No, but how could I read this?" Fayth said sternly.

Nan took a moment to find the right words. "You are the one."

"Wh-what?" Fayth's face registered surprise and shock.

Nan nodded affirmatively.

"How do you know it is me they are calling for?" she demanded.

Clearing her throat, Nan replied, "Over time, I have tested everyone the same way, those who could bear a child. Most of them failed the first test, but there were some that showed promise . . . None of them could read the scripture's translation. Only the guardian protecting the scroll knew of the translation passed down from guardian to guardian, and only the prophesied one could read the scripture."

This cannot be happening . . . This must be a dream. Why . . . Why me? Fayth thought.

The old lady sighed in relief, knowing that her search was over. A slight smile overtook Nan's features, although she normally kept her composure at all times. Something had changed this day.

"Remember this. One day a young girl around your age will come and visit. When that time comes, you will fulfill the prophecy," Nan warned.

Endless thoughts raced through Fayth's mind. It was overwhelming to be chosen for something great, and she was unsure if she was ready for that burden. Adrenaline coursed through her body, making her tremble.

I could just run away. Then the prophecy will not come true.

She clenched her hands together, trying to still her frightened shaking. She asked Nan, "Please excuse me."

She quickly rose to her feet, making the chair rock as if an earthquake shook the floor. As she rushed to the door, her emotions overwhelmed her and a waterfall of tears flooded over her cheeks. Fayth swiped at the tears once with her hand, and then burst through the door. The distress of this overwhelming new burden seemed impossible to bear. Not knowing whom or what could console her, she ran out into the forest.

Fayth's father jumped up in surprise and took his leave from the room. This new revelation was shocking. He turned to follow his daughter, just a few steps behind, and he'd almost left the porch when Nan called out to him, "Stop."

"But why, Mother?" He looked back, confused.

"From now on, she is a grown woman. Leave her be. One day she will come back," Nan replied.

They both watched her disappear into the forest. Fayth's father felt that his heart was being torn from his chest with each step Fayth took away from the cottage and deeper into the woods. He noticed she'd never once looked back.

■　■　■　■

"This oracle you speak of . . . You think this is true?" the Master asked.

He watched the screen dissolve into wisps of smoke from the burning pit beneath. The two hounds looked, puzzled, at Morgana as they howled, seeming to pose her a question.

"My premonition tells me yes," Morgana answered firmly.

"You have never failed me. I want you and Shadow to personally see this one through."

"Yes, Master," she replied, bowing.

Morgana's mind called out to her brother, *Cethin. It is time for us to go.*

You know that he does not like you calling us by those names anymore, Illythia, Shadow replied, as he strode through the dark hallway, over the steps of bone, to the Master's chamber.

Like his namesake, a shadow of the night, he made no sound as he moved.

But it is so fun! Besides, he cannot hear us. Come on, brother . . . she teased.

He can hear when you speak it. Good thing I have no tongue to speak or I would be in the same position as you.

I can make you one, she offered.

Very funny. Or I can take yours, Shadow replied sarcastically.

You would not dare!

Heh, heh, heh. Or would I?

Are you close?

Yes, I am.

Moments later, Shadow quietly entered the chambers as the flames in the fire pit lit up his scarred pale olive skin. His black cloak covered the majority of his body and the laces of his sandals wrapped around his legs like snakes, stopping at the knee.

He stopped behind Morgana and asked, *You summoned me, sister?*

Yes. Master has a job for us, she replied.

Us? It is unlike him to do something like this.

Yes. It should be especially fun, since it's a small family we are after.

Why not just send you?

He specifically told me that we *had to go.*

Alright, I will come as long as you do everything yourself, said Shadow, thinking back to the time when their family was whole.

Maybe she does not remember much or anything at all of our childhood. Illythia has changed so much.

That is fine. Let us go, she responded without hesitation.

The Master extended his arm, and a pulse of energy disrupted the surrounding air, summoning a portal. The ripples in the air sang like a thunderstorm crashing within the clouds. Like a spinning vortex, it waited for its new companions to be sucked in.

"One thing," the Master said.

"Yes, Master?" Morgana calmly replied.

"No one can see you use the dark arts besides those you are going to use them upon, and no teleporting. Do whatever you have to; make sure you conceal yourself," the Master instructed.

Skoll and Hati both barked sternly in unison, reinforcing his message.

Morgana nodded to the Master and walked into the teleportal, vanishing into thin air.

CHAPTER 7
—FREEDOM

Shadow stood there for a moment, seeming almost reluctant to move. He closed his eyes and listened to the sound of the teleportal. The sound was oddly different than he normally remembered, something possibly playing tricks in his mind.

He heard the constant thudding of clashing thunder from what the Master had made. He remembered something else, the constant thudding of thousands upon thousands of feet stomping the floor of the Flavian Amphitheatre.

They chanted his name, "SHADOW! SHADOW!" as though he were a god.

Soon enough, Shadow's eyes opened to the light, but the darkness of the hood hid them. He looked at the Master, took his leave, and followed Morgana to their next endeavor.

80 A.D.

Screams and shouting erupted from the crowd roaring like thunder inside the Amphitheatre. The sun was ready to rest for the night and setting along the horizon. Clouds came to chase the last bit of light away.

Men working all around began to set torches on fire for the center stage preparations. The audience behind the arena watched the men working, cleaning the bloody carcass from the dirt like worker ants. Their task complete, the men rushed off, setting the stage for the next act, and the anticipation began to build

"WELCOME TO THE FINAL ACT FOR THE EVENING!"

The announcer paused momentarily and looked around to catch his breath. Once he was satisfied that the audience was quiet enough, all full of anticipation, he continued, "TONIGHT! WE HAVE A BATTLE WORTHY OF THE GODS! A BATTLE BETWEEN TWO TITANS, A GLADIATOR WHO LIVES IN THE SUN AND ANOTHER WHO DWELLS IN THE SHADOWS!"

The southern gates of the arena opened with a loud thud that shook the ground like an earthquake. The metal chains slowly loosened and the massive wooden cage-like door, formed of many crossed planks, slowly opened. The sands that rested on the door shifted and blew like mist in the air, slowly dropping back down to the earth once more.

In the darkness behind the gate, a clanking of metal sounded forth when a man suited in armor paced slowly into the light. A darkly tanned gladiator with a medium build, he wore a light brass chest plate and carried a sword and shield on each hand. His helmet was cradled under an arm, shifting back and forth with every step he took. Sand crept in between his sandals and feet, causing an uncomfortable friction like the leather belt he wore around his waist.

"A GLADIATOR CRAFTED FOR ZEUS! HE IS BRINGER OF HOLINESS AND FIGHTER OF JUSTICE. LADIES AND GENTLEMEN, I GIVE TO YOU THE RIGHTEOUS LEON!"

The crowd roared to life, screaming at the top of their lungs, praising one of their favorites in the arena. He was a man who purposely volunteered himself time and time again to banish the wrongdoers, or sometimes just out of pure enjoyment. He killed other gladiators for the spectators' entertainment; he defied the rules sometimes, not even listening to Caesar, just to bring justice. Stopping near the center of the arena, he waited for his next adversary.

The crowd slowly calmed down, and a slight breeze swirled around the stadium, giving them new life from the last heat of the sun. They looked to the north gate, waiting for the next opponent to be called.

He walked alone through a small hallway, dimly lit by torches hanging from the wall. A musty odor hung thickly in the air. A loud thudding began to rumble, shaking the pillars around him. His olive skin, tanned by the sun's rays, shone in the nearby torchlight, and he bore scars everywhere from the countless battles he had fought.

Fine dust sifted down from the stone-covered building above. Stepping into a small puddle of water, he continued around the corner where there were flights of stairs to the arena. With his sword in hand, a laced belt, leather shoulder pads and bare chest, an air of calmness surrounded him.

His black eyes stared into the light, framed by platinum eyebrows on a bald head. He peered out through the open-gated bars of thick wood, shaped in small squares, big enough for an adult head to fit through.

How did I change from the old me? he thought. *I used to be a different person back then.*

Only a few memories were vivid enough for him to remember. He entered a trance as he approached the gate.

It only took a blink and the sound of laughter to negate the thudding above. Cethin envisioned the bright blue sky and the field of green grass that reminded him of an ocean. He remembered watching Illythia run across the vast plain of grass, coming closer with every step. He could feel the midday sun shining down upon him and the light, refreshing breeze that blew across the meadow.

Those were the happiest days of my life. I remember as though it were yesterday the delightful picnic that they prepared for us, laid out upon a blanket placed over the soft grass in the middle of the field. Mother was smiling at Father as he was reclined on the blanket. I cannot remember their faces, but it was so long ago. Though I do remember that chasing Illythia was quite a task, but I loved every moment of it. She was chasing a little butterfly around the field, giggling and wearing the biggest smile.

The raucous thudding and shouting continued to grow, getting louder as he approached. It interrupted his thoughts, bringing his mind back to what needed to be done.

Remember who you are doing this for. This is my last fight.

Taking a long-awaited pause for the crowd to simmer down, the announcer sang out, "ON THE OTHER SIDE, A MAN WHO HAS WON

SO MANY BATTLES, I CANNOT REMEMBER HIS FIRST BOUT!" He paused once more and the crowd erupted with life and increased excitement.

They already knew who was coming into the arena and began chanting his name, "SHADOW! SHADOW! SHADOW!" The audience screamed at the top of their lungs, a booming roar like a lightning bolt striking the stadium; continuously clapping, stamping the ground, and cheering for the next gladiator.

The announcer continued where he'd left off, "THE MAN WHO WAS CREATED BY THE GOD ARES HIMSELF! HE IS THE CREATOR OF A NEW TORTURE GAME WITHIN THESE BATTLEGROUNDS, THE REAPER HIMSELF! THE GAME OF SHADOWS!"

The thunderous sound bellowed forth before the gate opened. Cethin looked up to the sky, avoiding visual contact with the audience below. He performed a routine he did before every fight, slashing the sand, marking an X. Thereafter, he kicked the dirt and erased any trace of it.

Another thunderous roar bellowed inside the Flavian Amphitheatre, more screams and shouting. He made his way to the center of the arena to meet his foe for the first and last time. A brief silence stretched between them as the two gladiators stared each other down.

"ONE SHALL STAND, ONE SHALL FALL. THE BATTLE BE-TWEEN THESE TWO GREAT GLADIATORS IS ABOUT TO BEGIN," proclaimed the announcer.

After that, the gladiators turned their attention to the commentator and the important people sitting in the audience, particularly the Caesar. Bowing to acknowledge his presence, they both turned once more to face each other.

The dance of death began and the roar from the crowd was renewed as they squared off, circling each other, waiting patiently for one to make the first move. An intense wordless communication developed between the two opponents, like shadow fighting, trying to gain an advantage from fear or intimidation.

The gap between the fighters slowly closed. What took only seconds felt like ages for the two gladiators. Cethin felt confident and did not want to play nice anymore. He charged ahead with the first strike and kicked dirt from the ground like a raging bull.

This is not like you . . . I wonder what is going on in your head. You usually wait for the first strike, Illythia thought as she watched from afar.

The audience roared out its first cheer. Leon stood his ground, preparing for a defensive stop with his shield near his chest. In a split second, Cethin lunged forward, gripping the pommel of his sword with both hands and unleashing an overhand strike.

Leon countered with ease, absorbing the blow with his shield. As he slid back from the force of the blow, the sand behind cushioned him from the quick jolt. Though he couldn't recover in time for a counter, he managed to gain a little bit of separation from his opponent.

I cannot take any hits from him like this again, with his strength . . . What a monster! I will get him next time.

The crowd roared and cheered as the first strike concluded. Once Leon recovered, the second blow came just as quickly as the first one. He parried the attack by a sliver of an inch, barely avoiding injury.

Oh, this gladiator's speed! I am going to love killing him!

Thinking of a counterattack, Leon swung his sword wildly. Though it was a gamble, it worked and caught the Shadow of Death off guard. With little time to react, Cethin tried to dodge the unorthodox strike, walking away with a clean-shaved chest and a cut on his loincloth.

A rumble of thunder raged in the sky, and dark clouds appeared, rolling in from the west. The last bit of sunlight disappeared, replaced with the flashing of lightning above. Gusts of wind intensified rapidly. Though it brought relief to some, others began to worry.

The announcer got up, quick to give the audience another statement: "THE GODS THEMSELVES ARE MAKING THEIR PRESENCE KNOWN. LADIES AND GENTLEMEN, I GIVE TO YOU ZEUS AND POSEIDON."

Light rain pattered down as the two gladiators continued their bout. Clashes of steel on steel and steel to shield continued. Puddles began to form on the sand, like a swampland, as the rain and wind gradually strengthened.

Leon caught Cethin off guard with a quick slash at the chest. He kept his opponent on the tip of his toes at all times. Watching his foe slip to the ground from a misstep, he tried to take advantage.

This man is fast!

Landing on the wet ground, Cethin rolled in the wet sand, splashing through the puddles. He watched the edge of the blade swish past his head.

Oh, hell! What luck. If he had swung the other way, I would have been dead.

The crowd gasped, reacting to the close call.

Leon continued his onslaught, knowing that he had gained the advantage. He pressed forward with slash after slash at his opponent's body, but with each attack his foe gained distance.

Is this man getting quicker, or am I slowing down?

Cethin's luck wore thin, and then ended entirely. The other gladiator went for the finishing blow. Using his sword as a shield, Cethin absorbed as much impact as possible with the blade. However, the tip of his opponent's sword slid down, pierced the skin of his chest, and slowly penetrated. He took a deep breath and watched the blood fountain from his chest. And he remembered, *I am not immortal.* Another slash struck his left arm, drawing more blood and leaving a wound.

You cannot keep this up. One day I will not be able to heal you. Look at all your scars . . . Illythia's voice reminded him.

I need to do something, and it has to be quick, Cethin thought. *Death does not await me yet.*

Scraping the ground with his hand, Cethin threw mud mixed with sand and water at his opponent, hoping to use the element of surprise to turn the tide. His opponent blocked with his shield, but it was enough time for Cethin to regain his footing.

The Righteous Leon was still relentless, not giving his opponent any time to recover or to defend. He struck out with a flurry of blows from shield to sword, knowing that he was chasing a wounded animal and that time only played in his favor.

Cethin gained renewed vigor. His timing was impeccable. Fending off the sword with his own and dodging the other's shield when he was shoved, he kept his purpose in mind.

He is slowing down. It is time for me to end this duel.

The Shadow of Death used his own set of combinations, finally turning the tide in his favor. Unleashing attack after attack, Leon defended himself perfectly with his shield.

He is lucky I do not have another weapon, Cethin thought.

A gust of wind with the strength of a hurricane swept through the arena. The torches that lit the arena all went out at once. Once they had sizzled out from the constant beating of rain and wind, no light remained for the gladiators to fight by except the occasional flash of lightning.

You are in my world now! Cethin thought, and grinned.

The spectators sighed with relief as the rain slowly petered out and the clouds broke. The moon slowly appeared, shedding light upon the scene. The men surrounding the arena ran around with new torches, trying to fix the situation, but it was already too late.

Cethin's eyes were well adjusted to the night, watching his prey spinning in circles trying to find him. The gladiator's mask obstructed Leon's vision. The crowd's frenzy did not help him either, and their clamor muffled Cethin's footsteps as he neared his fearful opponent.

The Shadow of Death sprinted the rest of the way, his light steps making him almost impossible to hear. A quick slash, and he was in.

"AHH!" Leon screamed.

Both large gates opened and dozens of soldiers with torches came rushing out, lighting up the arena. They finally restored the light, allowing them to catch a glimpse of the Shadow of Death and The Righteous Leon.

One of the soldiers looked down to see a hand holding onto a sword, separated from the rest of the arm. Blood trailed all the way back to the wounded man.

Cethin knew that Leon still had a lot of fight in him, even though his opponent was missing a limb. He took nothing for granted. The crowd watched in silence, soaked from the rain. Time was all he needed now, measuring the best point of attack, watching his opponent bleed out. Like a shadow of the night, he carefully watched Leon's movements, inching forward.

The adrenaline rush slowly trailed off and Leon's forearm throbbed with pain. He still felt a pulsing as if the ghost of his hand remained, his blood flowing down to the sands below, painting a puddle of red. His reaction time slowed, and his breathing became heavier.

Cethin became all but a shadow to his adversary, his movement concealed by darkness. Leon tried to keep an eye out, but could only see the dark starting to consume him. His head would move in the right direction, but the physical image he would normally see vanished into thin air.

Cethin danced fluidly, moving from side to side, stalking his prey. He was taking his time; no longer in a rush, knowing that time would now inflict greater damage than his sword would. The mistakes he'd made earlier were now past, and he knew, whatever came next, the game was already won.

An invigorating cheer from the spectators washed over him. "Shadow! Shadow! Shadow!"

Testing the waters, Cethin struck a light jab with his sword. He wanted to know if the blow would hit flesh or shield. His reactions delayed, Leon barely stopped the strike with what remained of his adrenaline rush.

Now unable to rise from the ground, Leon looked up at the dark sky through a blanket of red which only he could see, and tossed his shield to the side. He waited for his final judgment, searching for peace in the last moments of his life.

Finally . . . I will savor this . . . or maybe not. Towering over his foe, Cethin could not decide how to dispatch him. *Should I give him a simple, quick death, or should I torture him? I cannot remember the last time someone has done this much damage to me.*

Lowering his sword as he'd done in all the other fights before, he would normally call out to his foe, "Remember the name Cethin. Mine will be the last face you see in this lifetime."

Aw, fuck it. Die! He thrust the sword into his opponent's throat, sinking it through into the sand, making sure that his passing was easy.

For the last time, the audience roared to life, chanting "Shadow! Shadow!" once more.

My freedom has come, but there is unfinished business I must attend to.

Come nightfall, the Slave Master's room was filled with candles everywhere, lighting the area like the morning sun. The victor of the fight, his wounds patched up, stood in front of a small wooden table, and the Slave Master sat on the other side of the table, holding a glass of wine.

"Well, you have earned your freedom. In the morning, you are free to go," the Slave Master stated.

Cethin nodded. *But where is Illythia?*

A sense of uneasiness fluttered in the Slave Master's mind as he met the Shadow of Death's piercing gaze. He tried to gather his thoughts before carefully weaving his way through the conversation, trying not to say the wrong thing.

"I—I know . . . what we agreed upon," the Slave Master began.

Cethin stalked closer to his former owner. He did not blink as he waited for a response to the whereabouts of his younger sister. He cared for nothing else.

The Slave Master stammered out the dreaded words. "S-she's no longer he-here."

Cethin's eyes blazed with fury. *Well then . . . where is she?*

His blood began to boil, spreading red fury across his face, like a volcano ready to erupt.

"Re-remember that senator? He c-came with a group of men and took her during your bout," the Slave Master blurted nervously.

You are useless to me. Cethin stood in front of his former Master.

"I am truly sorry. Please forgive me." The Slave Master knelt, pleading.

You should have done something.

Cethin's hand wrapped around the man's head, twisting it until his neck broke with a snap. The fallen corpse of the Slave Master marked the beginning of his new life.

I will kill everyone who took Illythia away from me.

"Hmm." A mysterious voice sounded from the opposite end of the room.

I do not remember another person ever being inside this room. Cethin squinted upwards questioningly. *Am I hearing things?*

"Let me turn off this light. It is too bright in this room and my eyes are hurting," the raspy voice spoke once more.

The acolyte who had revealed himself licked his fingertips to extinguish one of the candles in the center of the room. The black cloak he wore hid the color of his skin.

"I know you are wondering who I am and why I am here. So I will tell you."

The man moved to the dimmest part of the room.

Cethin turned around, hoping to catch a glimpse of the speaker's face, but every inch of the man's body was covered in the black cloak and the shadows. Having never seen such attire, Cethin raised an eyebrow.

I have never seen anything like this before.

"I am a servant to my master, a mere acolyte. He has asked me to help you. I know what you seek," the robed man stated.

He does not know what I seek. He only speaks of madness in hopes that I will listen. I need to leave. Cethin's intention manifested abruptly.

"I can reunite you with your sister. That is what you want most. Am I right?" the acolyte hinted. "And to seek revenge on those who did you an injustice."

I will do anything for her and for myself. Cethin's eyes rose with a question.

"Come with me and we will begin your new chapter in life . . . or forever search for your dear sister. The choice is yours." The acolyte waited for Cethin's response.

With a simple nod, Cethin made his choice clear. No hesitation, no second guessing. He was ready and willing for the next task.

"Good. Our master and your sister awaits."

Chapter 8
—The Birth

1670

Oh, what a beautiful day, Fayth thought.

Her lightly tanned hand released the door knob as she stepped out of the house, a large log cabin in the woods mostly concealed by the surrounding trees. A few windows on each side let the precious light shine through. A few narrow pathways had been worn over time in the surrounding grass by the passage of humans and animals alike.

Taking a few steps forward to the porch, she stopped and waited patiently where the wood met the grass. She blew a strand of hair away from her eyes. The child in her belly was the size of a watermelon. With a little smile, she caressed it through her black silk dress. Brown boots peeked from below the hem of the dress where it kissed her ankles.

A soft neigh sounded from the corner of the house, but Fayth was distracted to notice. The hoofbeats were a little more commanding, and she looked toward the sound.

A man's voice rang out, "Fayth, are you ready?"

Bruce led the horse around to the front of the house. His rough, blistered hands held the reins, the skin showing below his rolled-up white shirtsleeves a reddish tan from hours of hard labor in the sun.

He smiled at Fayth, beaming proudly with smiling black eyes set in a clean-shaven square face. A gust of wind blew, ruffling his short hair and the mane of the brown horse that trotted behind him.

"Yes, we are ready," Fayth replied.

He guided their mount to the porch, stopping it in front of Fayth. Swiftly moving to the other side, Bruce planted a kiss on his wife's cheek before hoisting her up from the waist and setting her on top of the horse. She sat on the horse side-mounted, content and comfortable as her husband held the reins, leading them on their next journey.

Slowly they moved down the gravel road, away from their home. Fayth took a quick glance back, happy with everything she'd wanted in life.

As they arrived at a three-way intersection, Bruce directed the horse northward, heading to town. Fields of crops sprawled along both sides of the road, with trees sprouting out like weeds in a yard. Looking at his lovely wife, he thought back to the time when they'd first met. Reality started to fade away like a dream as he followed his thoughts down memory lane.

1665

It was a winter day, complete with snow slowly fluttering down from the sky. The flakes moved in an endless dance as they descended, wafting from side to side as the wind decided in which direction it would take them to the ground. The clouds shielded the sun like a gray blanket, allowing little light through. Midday felt like an evening waiting for night to come.

Bruce, encased in a thick fur coat, traversed the crisp, glazed snow, his footsteps crunching loudly. His skin was winter-pale, his hands thick and rough from manual labor. He traveled aimlessly through the forest, meandering from tree to tree as if he were tipsy, and whistling a tune. He turned his carefree gaze to the sky to admire the peacefully falling snow, when his reverie was suddenly broken by a distant cry.

Bruce stopped and listened carefully. It sounded like someone crying, but he wasn't quite sure. He circled around to see if he were being followed, but saw nothing. He shrugged his shoulders and resumed walking, whistling again softly to see if the noise would be repeated.

Maybe I am hearing things.

As Bruce made his way deeper into the forest, paying attention to his surroundings, a different sound echoed through the trees.

"Help me!"

Definitely a woman's voice, he thought. The voice sounded like a whisper in his ears, surreal and improbably close. Bruce whirled around, once again looking for the source.

I must be going crazy! There is no one close to me.

His temper flared with frustration, leaving him unsure of the once-familiar surroundings.

Not knowing what else to do, Bruce walked vigorously on and ignored the cries. As he took a step forward, the snow collapsed below him like a sink-hole. He stumbled, falling to the ground on what he thought were tree roots, but no trees were close enough.

That is odd.

The cold, snowy ground kissed his skin, sending chills all over his body. Immediately picking himself back up, he wobbled from left to right as he re-gained his footing, trying to prevent another fall.

I must be tired.

Looking down at the ground with its white blanket of snow, Bruce looked for the cause of his misfortune.

Everything is covered in snow . . . It is so hard to see.

Then he detected something moving, maybe breathing. *What the . . . ?*

It was an unfamiliar figure, possibly a body, under a thin layer of snow. He moved in closer to brush off the white powder.

What is that?

The wind blew the white cover of snow off the woolen outer clothing, making its last descent to the ground. The curves of a body started to appear, and the slow motion of inhaling and exhaling started to click for Bruce.

What? It's a person!

Quickly moving back a few steps, he became an observer.

"Hmmph!" She moved, with a grunt.

The woman woke from her deep slumber. Tears flowed from her hazel-green eyes. She stretched, still unaware of her environment. As she pushed back her hood, her light brown hair cascaded down her back. She took a deep breath and watched the white cloud of steam from her exhalation.

Bruce was baffled. *She is gorgeous. What should I do? Is she okay? Does she need help? I cannot just leave her here . . . Or should I?*

As he took a step forward, the sound of snow crunching beneath his boots alerted the young lady to his presence.

The noise startled her, and she turned to look.

Is this a dream? She stared at him, hoping he would disappear.

Maybe I should go back to sleep and then, hopefully, all this will go away.

Bruce stood there, clueless. He asked her, "Are you okay?"

The young lady turned to face him, giving him a blank stare.

"Do you need help?" Bruce asked again.

Maybe if I do not answer, he will leave.

"Can you understand me?"

Maybe this is hopeless, but what is she carrying? Is her family looking for her? Why was she all alone? Bruce pondered.

All of his questions and doubts seemed to vanish as he thought about the situation, though.

"Um," she finally spoke.

So she can understand me. "Are you okay?" Bruce asked again.

The young lady nodded in agreement.

"Were you the one who called for help?"

"Help?" She looked surprised.

"Yes, I heard a woman's voice calling for help."

"Um . . . No."

"Hmm . . . Okay. Are you hurt?"

She reached down to her side, where a throbbing pain was coming to life.

"Ha-ha." Bruce chuckled. "I am so sorry. Why are you by yourself?"

"I am always alone," she stated plainly.

"Any family?"

She nodded, moving her hand down the cloth pouch. She stood up, showing some signs of discomfort at the question.

What does this guy want?

"Are you lost?"

"No. Ouch!" She grunted from the pain.

"If you want, I can take you home, wherever that may be," Bruce insisted.

Did Nan or Papa send him to get me? Is this a trick? "No!" she yelled. "I will never go back!"

Bruce was taken aback. "What is wrong with you?"

"You cannot take me back!" she blurted in utter rage.

In confusion, he replied, "I don't even know what you're talking about," his voice trailed off as he took notice of her beauty.

It looks like he does not know anything. Can he be trusted? "Where did you say you were going to take me?" she inquired.

"I was going to take you wherever you needed to go, but . . ." Bruce replied, as shades of red began to suffuse his skin. "It looks like you can take care of yourself."

"Where are you going?" she asked.

"I am going home," Bruce replied, his voice trailing off.

She took a long pause to run through some scenarios in her head. *I can stay here and freeze to death or possibly get captured by my family. Hmm . . . Or I can go with him and start a new life and leave my old one. Well . . . Decisions, decisions . . . He is rather cute.*

The man before her made her temperature rise, and her face accordingly blushed beet red. She tried to think of something else, to bring herself back to normal. Her body took control, one foot after another, first walking toward the mysterious man, and then speeding up to a jog.

What am I doing?

Bruce cast a glance sideways to his companion and listened to the crunch of the snow under their boots. A moment of silence passed between the two walking together.

What does she want now?

She smiled at Bruce and initiated small talk. "My name is Fayth, and what is yours?"

"Bruce. Bruce Smith."

That was the day, oddly enough, that I met my wife.

The afternoon passed and the sun began to hang low in the cloudless sky, slowly inching its way west to the horizon. A light breeze swept through the field, blowing the grass in waves that carried onwards for miles until the field ended where the forest stood. Trees waved along with the grass, dancing with life as the wind passed by.

Suddenly, heavy winds tore over the field, blowing wildly in every direction. A ripple formed in the air just above a small patch of grass that split in half like parted hair. The wind began to spin in a continuous circle, and a small vortex rippled in the air. From that ripple, a young girl appeared, clad in a black velvet cloak with a shield embroidered on the back of the hood, Aramaic script around the edge. She took a step forward, enjoying the crunch of earth beneath her feet. Her exposed hands were marked with vaynes that wound their way up her arms into the cloak.

She stood beside the vortex-like portal, awaiting her companion. A taller person, wearing the same style of cloak decorated with white Aramaic embroidery, entered the realm. This man's cloak had a sword embroidered on the back rather than a shield.

How close are we? Shadow asked his sister through their link.

Very close. They will be coming to us, Morgana replied.

"Ah," she spoke aloud, finding the small piece of earth that had no grass.

Walking to the area, she spotted a broken branch half her size hanging from a tree, and grabbed it along the way.

Come here.

She continued to the open patch of grass, just a few feet away.

Responding to the call, Shadow moved closer to her. He watched his younger sister stand in the center of the open space and twirl around once, using the branch as a tool to draw a circle.

He stopped at the edge of the grass and watched his sister's artwork, standing there silently, waiting for her to finish. She continued by splitting the circle in half and cutting a line in between. Then she pricked her finger, causing a pool of blood to drip down onto the ground. Afterwards, she drew scriptures that were not common knowledge among humankind.

Rise from the ashes,
From within the flames

Your calling is here,
Lend us your strengths
Come to our voice,
You are needed once more,
Hellraiser

The loud cry of a horse broke the surrounding air, but no horse could be seen. Slowly the bones worked their way one by one from the dirt below and levitated into the air, forming the skeleton of a horse. Fire blazed around the bones as the muscles and ligaments began to attach themselves. Its breathing came heavily from time to time as it tried to get acclimated to the air.

The horse neighed as if in pain and kicked its hind legs from time to time as each muscle added weight. Its heart thudded for the first time, short but quick. The muscles tensed and relaxed from each contraction. Dark red blood trickled from the air to what would be the sockets of its eyes. Its skin burnt in a bright yellow, orange, and red flame covering the muscles. The skin cooled down from the heat, turning black, making the creature look more and more like a horse. Slowly the black mane pushed out from the back of the horse's neck, and it neighed one last time. Shadow then mounted the horse, Hellraiser, facing Morgana.

Continuing the other half circle, Morgana drew another set of scriptures, chanting once more in an arcane Latin tongue.

Let it cry,
Darkness looms
Let the fear drive,
Swift with speed
Rage asunder

Loud thunder rumbled through the clear sky like a stampede in the heavens. Dark clouds started to form and grow; covering what was once blue sky, full of light. Slowly, the storm began to consume the sky. Morgana looked up to it and smiled. Shadow leaned down to lift her up onto the horse, mounting her sidesaddle.

They will be heading this way soon, Morgana told her brother.

Alright, he replied.

Head back to the road and go south. We will meet them soon enough. Morgana allowed herself a little smirk.

A loud rumble of thunder rolled from the thickened clouds, dancing its merry way to the young couple. Bruce's state of trance was broken; the past fizzled out of his mind, roaring to a rude awakening. He could have recollected that there were no signs of a storm coming. The more he thought about it, the more confused he became.

"Fayth, do you remember ever seeing a storm brewing earlier today?" Bruce questioned, looking up at the black clouds.

"No, I don't recall that," Fayth replied.

The storm began to lurk closer and closer.

This is not going to be good . . . What to do?

"We need to hurry," Bruce declared, his voice hoarse with fear of what might happen next.

"Yes, we must hurry," Fayth agreed.

The wall of rain slowly swept through the land in the distance. Whatever the rain covered, the land disappeared with it. Flashes of lightning rolled ahead of the wall of water like a warning call. Taking matters into his own hands, Bruce saddled up, jumping behind Fayth.

Kicking the horse, he screamed out, "Yah!"

The race against time began and the storm came barreling after them. Their horse galloped down the small winding road, kicking dirt from the ground. Fields of tall grass and trees began to blur past, but the wall of heavy rain came quickly nonetheless.

Fayth began to feel some cramping pains throughout her body. She tried to keep calm, not wanting to alert her husband, who was focused on the task at hand.

Bruce switched his gaze between Fayth and the road ahead. His heart thumped vigorously with the adrenaline rushing through his veins.

He asked anxiously, "Are you okay?"

Fayth mumbled in a hoarse, tight voice, "Yeah."

A mounting stress began to weigh her down. The pain rushed through her as though something were pulling her insides out, and suddenly she noticed a warm, wet feeling trickling from her dress.

"We have to stop!" Fayth cried out.

"Why? We are almost there," said Bruce, eyeing the nearby bridge.

Fayth's heavy breathing and panting gave it away. He looked down to see a liquid running down the side of the horse's back.

Oh, shit. This is not good.

Thinking quickly, he began to scan his surroundings. There he saw a small tree in front of the bridge, off to the side, with branches hanging like an umbrella for cover.

Thinking it would be the best place for shelter, he pressed on. Nearing the side of the tree, he pulled the reins to stop the horse and jumped down. He lifted Fayth down, carried her to the tree, and set her down at the base of the trunk, which perfectly cradled her on the sides.

"You are delivering this baby," Fayth panted between quick breaths.

"I don't know how!" Bruce responded abruptly.

"Ah!" She screamed in pain.

The rain was practically on top of them, rolling in closer and obscuring whatever was on the other side. Bruce knew that the comfort underneath the tree was not going to suffice. Thunder boomed loudly overhead, like a warning that they shouldn't be there.

Fayth's memories came to haunt her once more. In her head, one scene began to play over and over again: reading the scroll Nan had shown her. *Whoever can read this will bring great justice to this world. You are the prophecy we have all been waiting for. Your presence will change the world. With the seeds being sown, a new world will manifest.* The thought plagued her a while, as she worried and wondered if the prophecy could still be true.

Fayth's cry echoed in Bruce's ears as she began to feel the pain. As he watched helplessly, each of his wife's cries was more intense, expressing more pain and agony than the one before. Noticing something wrong after her first couple of pushes, Bruce watched with consternation as the tiny feet of his child came forth. Blood began to run down, entirely too much of it.

Moments felt like hours as Bruce watched in fear, not knowing what to do. The baby's little leg kicked back and forth, struggling to come out, as though something inside was holding it back from emerging any further. Slowly, the energy of mother and child began to dwindle.

The rush of rain finally poured down over them, the tree filtering as much rain as it could with the leaves deflecting some of the droplets. Fayth, now drenched with water, kept trying to push the baby out with every contraction as her breathing became fainter and fainter. The blood kept flowing, slowly mixing with the rainwater, and Fayth's face began to fade slowly to white.

All Bruce could do was watch helplessly from the side, with no idea what to do. He watched the two most important people in his life struggling on the verge of death.

On his knees, he prayed to whoever was listening. *If there is a God out there, please help me.*

Continuous waves of rain still fell from the sky, but the pace had begun to decrease steadily. Bruce looked up, noticing that the torrent had abated. He turned his head to scan the environment as the sound of rain drumming on the ground faded away to an utter silence.

Soft hoofbeats struck the wooden bridge, which creaked with every step. Bruce turned to see a black horse trotting across. A flash of lightning revealed the black-cloaked rider it carried. Where the raindrops fell upon the horse and rider, they sizzled and evaporated as though their bodies were on fire.

Morgana looked behind her to see a clear path of water droplets like a tunnel made by her brother and their mount.

As they slowly made their way to the couple in dire need of assistance, she asked her brother, *Can you smell his fear?*

Yes, he is desperate, I am sure. Have a look, Shadow answered.

I cannot just yet . . . You always get the best view.

I know. Grow taller.

Ha, ha, brother. Very funny.

Do not worry, sweet sister, eventually you will grow.

I should push you off this horse.

You should. It will be funny.

Bruce stood up from the ground, leaving his wife's side, and approached the stranger. The raindrops moved to the side as he pushed them along, displacing them. Stopping at the edge of the canopy of branches, he waited to meet the mysterious cloaked man.

The man grasped the embroidered sword emblem on the front of his hood and peeled it back, slowly revealing his visage. Scars formed a network on the skin, covering almost every inch of his face illuminated by the flashes of lightning. His platinum eyebrows raised a little as his piercing black eyes took in the man who stood before him.

"Please help me," Bruce pleaded.

Shadow turned his gaze elsewhere as if Bruce were invisible.

This is not my problem.

I know, I know, I just want to hear him beg a little. That is all, Morgana answered.

Uh-huh.

"Please, please, can you help?" Bruce's tone became dire.

"Don't worry, Bruce, we are here to assist you," the young woman's voice chimed in from behind Shadow.

Bruce leaned to the side, trying to see past the massive wall of a man to locate the speaker. Hidden just behind the speechless man, he saw a teenage girl wearing an oversized cloak similar to the garment of the man sitting in front.

How does she know my name? I have never met these people before. Look at the red eyes on that horse . . . I've never seen anything like this.

Her fingers danced around the shield embroidered on the rim of her hood before she pulled it back. Her gray eyes focused on Bruce, piercing through her own brother's body and following until he could finally see her.

She is young, Bruce thought.

Please help me down, Morgana silently asked her brother.

Shadow turned around to lend a hand. She slid off the horse, holding his hand, and by the time Bruce looked again, her feet were on the ground. Turning back around, Shadow became a statue to the other two.

"That's my brother Shadow. He's a mute. I'm Morgana," the young woman introduced them both.

Walking past Bruce with short, quick steps, Morgana continued her way to Fayth. Not too far behind, Bruce followed along. Stopping in front of Fayth, Morgana assessed the situation, noticing the blood flowing like a river all the way to her sandals.

Bruce stopped right next to the cloaked woman, watching, waiting for her to do something. He was panicking and didn't understand why she didn't seem worried at all. Then he realized Fayth was no longer crying in pain as she had a moment ago. He bent over his wife and felt her wrist, detecting a very slow pulse.

"Is this really happening?" Bruce asked.

"Yes," Morgana replied after a brief pause. "Time has been suspended so we can do as we please."

As we please? "What is going to happen to Fayth and my child?" he inquired.

"Look at Fayth. If this persists, she will die a slow and painful death. As for your son, he has already passed over to the other world."

Bruce took a step back and stumbled to the ground, grasping his chest. A sharp, stabbing pain struck him in the heart. He looked at Fayth and soon-to-be-born son with a blank stare as though the very life were being taken away from him.

How could this happen? Can this be happening to me? Why? Why, I ask!

"Is there a way to save them?" Bruce asked, trying to gather himself together.

"There is a way. . ." Morgana paused.

"Whatever it takes." He spoke without hesitation.

That was easier than I thought.

"Are you certain of this?"

"Yes."

"What I am going to need here is more than just a sacrifice. We are talking about a deal," Morgana stated.

"I will do it," Bruce interrupted her.

She slipped her hand into her cloak, searching for something, feeling for an item in the pouch pocket and finding a scroll.

Taking the scroll and unwinding it completely, Bruce looked it over. At the very end was a dotted line, waiting for a signature to be written in.

Morgana explained to Bruce, "In exchange for your son and wife's lives, we will be taking yours at the time when it is needed."

"Deal," he said, after weighing the consequences.

"Let me see your hand," she commanded.

Bruce leaned forward to rest on his knees and raised his hand to Morgana. She poked his index finger with a sharp, pointed nail, and blood began to flow out. A drop of blood fell onto the contract, and the scroll rolled itself up and disappeared into thin air.

"First, we have to get your son," Morgana stated.

"How will you do that?" Bruce asked.

"Your son is in a place where the deceased pass on and exist in another plane. It mirrors the world you inhabit, but instead of life, it resembles death. They only see things in black and gray, and the vegetation is wilted away. We call it "purgatory." The souls of the dead may linger at the place where they died. Others roam the earth until the end of time. They will need to find what they are searching for before they can move on, either sent below or above, and others that have lost their way will remain in purgatory to the end of days," Morgana explained.

Bruce stood there thinking, pondering all the information and how it could add up together. He tried to understand the concept she was trying to explain. Things did not register properly, as he did not understand what life after death really meant.

"Your son, on the other hand, is different from the others," she continued.

"How so?" Bruce asked, confused.

"Your son died before taking his first breath of air. He is different from the rest, forever lost in purgatory, unless. . ." Morgana paused for a moment.

"Unless?" Bruce prompted.

Pacing, Morgana continued, "Unless. . . Your son's body will remain an empty vessel even if we do summon his soul out of purgatory. It has no physical attachments to the living world. In order for it to stay in the vessel, we would have to use a guardian protector to keep his soul in place. That is the only way he will be able to live a normal life," she responded.

Waving her hand, she continued, "I need your help for this, Bruce."

Bruce got up and stood next to Morgana, waiting for her next order. She glanced at him, and then drew a small circle right next to Fayth.

"Your hand," Morgana requested.

Again, Bruce lifted a hand for her to use, and she poked another finger for more blood. With a drop ready to fall, she positioned his finger over the circle, and the blood splashed into it. She then drew a scripture into the circle with awkward markings all along the outer rim and the sign of a goat in the center.

A red light began to illuminate the circle; shining brightly and making the raindrops around reflect the red. Morgana's vaynes were radiant with blue, flowing from her fingertips and dancing near the edge of her neck. A heavy, ominous feeling began to sink in, something dark.

> Within the depths
> Life breathes light,
> Consumed by darkness
> And full of anger,
> Let it eclipse you
> When you are needed
> Listen to this calling
> Be reborn once more

■   ■   ■   ■

PURGATORY

"Damien," Annette cried out. "Damien, help!" The voice he remembered echoed in the back of his mind, forever haunting him.

Damien's black eyes opened to the sight of monochrome black, white, and gray surroundings. His pale forehead wrinkled slightly with concern above his black eyebrows.

I can remember everything . . . Where are you? Come up, come up.

Overseeing the flowing river from his place atop the wooden bridge, Damien watched for any movement. He took a few deep breaths, hoping for the best.

The distant call sounded again:

Within the depths,

Life breathes light,

Consumed by darkness

And full of anger,

Let it eclipse you

When you are needed

Listen to this calling

Be reborn once more

Damien heard the call upon the wind. Outside of the immediate view, he looked upon a barren wasteland. Nothing but sand covered the land for miles on end, except a few dead trees that looked charred by fire, rotting away.

The calling voice changed its tone, now almost alluring.

"Damien, come to me. Listen to my voice, come as I summon you. Follow my voice and bring me the child."

The voice rang inside Damien's head like the loud chime of bells.

Fate

Awaits in desire

Fruits of kings,

Chance of the given

And change for the taking

Come to me

Damien held his hands to his temples as a rush of pain rippled throughout his body. He breathed heavily as he fell to his knees, hands grasping at the sand, balling into fists.

"ARGH!" Damien screamed. *What is going on?*

Patches of hair began to grow all over his body, horns began to grow from his forehead, and his face slowly shifted into that of a goat. Saliva ran from his mouth, dripping to the floor, and Damien moaned in pain. His hands and feet were no longer human, but had transformed into small hooves, and his front feet and hind legs were covered with fur. This was no ordinary goat, but double the size.

Damien cried out once more before his last transformation. His eyes, when they opened next, were blood red.

Again the voice of a young woman echoed in his head: "Follow my voice and bring me the child."

"I can feel the guardian. He is close to your son," Morgana asserted confidently.

A sigh of relief rushed from Bruce's throat, all his anxieties washed away the moment she spoke.

This is a lot easier than I anticipated. I would have thought he'd put up a better fight than this, Morgana thought.

"It is almost done. Let us bring your son home," she said, concentrating once more on the spell.

Damien could hear a baby cry in the distance, across the bridge, where a lonely tree stood. He crossed the bridge and trotted down the narrow path to the tree, where a baby laid on the ground, kicking and screaming, at the base of the tree trunk. His cry seemed to continue for hours on end, calling for someone to comfort him.

Is this the baby that the voice wanted me to get? Damien wondered.

The child screamed an echoing cry. The commanding voice chimed in Damien's head once more, this time even louder.

The voice seemed to enchant Damien, making his eyes widen and flare a brighter red. Examining the baby to see where he could possibly take hold of him without the use of human hands, Damien swung his head back and forth. Finally picking a spot, he gingerly took the baby by the neck, his goat's mouth softly biting down on the flesh.

"This part is tricky," Morgana admitted.

Bruce looked on, puzzled, wondering what she meant by that.

Only she knows what is going on . . . Why would she tell me something I cannot possibly understand? Perhaps she wants me to know.

"After the teleportal is summoned, it will bring the guardian and your son's soul to this world. I only have a few moments to guide them to the vessel and properly seal them into his body. If it is not done correctly, they will forever be lost in purgatory, never to be found again for all of eternity. Timing is crucial for all of this to work," Morgana explained.

Watching her prepare another circle to cast a spell, Bruce watched intently as she split the circle into halves again. Morgana pricked her own finger this time, dripping blood into the circle. She began to draw inside the circle. The top portion resembled a teleportation symbol in the center, surrounded by scriptures. She continued her art, making the bottom portion of the circle a little more sophisticated, consisting of scriptures alone.

On Morgana's other hand, the vaynes were illuminated in blue to the wrist. Sweat dripped from her forehead from the effort. As she continued speaking in the unfamiliar tongue for Bruce to hear, the top portion of the circle began to illuminate with a red aura.

The light, fading away,
Will it ever return?
Darkness is a friend,
Could this be free-falling?
Shortness of breath,
The ice cold touch surrounds
Everything is closing in,
Gasp for help
Freedom is salvation

A teleportal began to form, slowly rippling in the air next to Damien. A large vertical circle began to swirl clockwise, sucking in air, pulling him closer and closer. Resisting with all his might, he refused to go into the teleportal with the baby's body suspended in the air, flailing around like a rag doll. Holding tightly to the baby, he tried not to lose his grip as the force of the suction intensified.

We are not supposed to leave this place, not until I find my Annette.

The young woman's voice called out, "Do not resist, and come to your calling, live with the people. Live as you once did in your past life."

Damien tried his best not to submit to the call. *I—I must resist.*

But then, coming to a realization, Damien became almost possessed by the words and stopped fighting to hold his ground against the teleportal. Her speech became words of seduction, like an enchanting spell. Flying into the open ripple, both Damien and the baby vanished from the land of the dead.

"Here they come," Morgana announced.

Bruce watched, standing between Fayth and Morgana, anticipating what might happen.

Morgana immediately chanted another spell.

A silhouette
Blindness from dust
Darkness brought to light
What lies
In your wake

The second portion of the circle started to glow blue from the first spell. The air near Morgana began to ripple, pulsating back and forth. A white light in the shape of a hand pushed through the ripple in the air. Slowly, a man suited in white and glowing with energy emerged from the teleportal. He stood six feet, two inches tall, and cradled a baby in his arms. His black eyes regarded the empty vessel he would protect to the end of his days.

Bruce looked in awe upon the guardian, taking in his stature, pale skin, short black hair, and strong, jutting jaw.

Morgana repeated the incantation, ignoring for the moment what was happening right beside her. The guardian approached the vessel, slowly closing the distance.

Is this really happening? Bruce thought.

He noted the guardian's smile, acknowledging his presence along the short journey.

The guardian walked right through Bruce. A chill coursed through Bruce's body, and goosebumps formed on his skin as he reacted to the instantaneous movement of energy and presence of another being passing through his own form. The bright white energy of the guardian and baby disappeared for a brief moment as they intersected. Flares of energy bled off from Bruce's body, flowing away and leaving a particle trail as they moved outward. The white light reformed once again, the hands and arms cradling the baby first. Shortly after, the guardian's face and the rest of his body followed suit, all forming together directly behind Bruce. Remnants of energy trailed from the guardian. Turning around to see Bruce for one last time, he bid a final farewell with a nod.

Damien began to dematerialize once again as the energy began to shift. His legs lost their form and became a stream of energy that moved to the baby, diffusing through the infant's skin. Like sand through an hourglass, the guardian's energy left his own form and passed into the child.

After half of the guardian's body was gone, a river of energy flowed to the baby and Fayth. The remaining figure of the guardian then burst into energy particles and scattered like stars in the sky. All the energy flowed into the baby as the light faded with the last remnant.

"What happens next?" Bruce asked, awestruck.

"Deliver the child, of course," Morgana responded, rising to her feet after her last spell.

Her vaynes reverted to their original form as a slight fatigue overtook her body.

"The guardian will supply them the energy they need. You just have to guide the baby out, and with just a few more pushes, everything will be fine," she continued while returning to her brother.

My job is done, Morgana told him.

You don't look so good. Did you overdo it? Shadow asked.

I will be fine.

Alright.

Shadow turned sideways to give his sister a helping hand and lifted her back onto the horse. She sat behind him and pulled her hood back over her head, and her face returned to the shadows.

Kicking Hellraiser's sides, Shadow directed his mount back to the bridge and covered his own exposed head with the hood of his cloak. They headed back north from where they'd started, slowly disappearing from Bruce's view.

Bruce briefly looked down at his wife and saw that nothing has changed. For a moment he glanced back at the bridge to see the two mysterious people on horseback disappear into the distance. Time resumed from where it had stopped, the rain pouring again, drops of water splashing down on the earth, drumming rapidly on the foliage and the land. Bruce heard the screams of labor return as Fayth made the last few attempts to push out the child.

Turning around, Bruce rushed to kneel down in front of her, helping and guiding the infant as he held a small portion of the tiny body. Fayth's heavy breathing and panting did not change. For the first time, Bruce held his son, smiling from ear to ear.

He handed over their son to Fayth and watched her smile, warming up the dreadful gray day. Taking off his drenched shirt, Bruce squeezed out as much of the water as possible and used the shirt to cover the infant, wrapping him tightly to give him warmth.

The pouring rain began to lose intensity, drizzling slower and slower by the minute. The clouds dispersed, breaking into smaller wisps, and the afternoon sky appeared from the gray, clearing up just as fast as the rain had initially come.

The last rays of sunlight beamed over the land, the dusk ready to fall. Fayth sat at the base of the tree trunk, admiring her baby and thinking of a name for him.

This day is one crazy day. She sighed. *I am glad it is all over.*

"What do you want to name our son?" Bruce asked.

"Nathaniel," she replied.

"That is a good name. Now, let's go home."

Fayth nodded.

CHAPTER 9
—A DEADLY MISTAKE

"Mother . . . Father . . . Where are we going?" the child asked.

The boy's mother held one of his hands. She was elegant in a white dress, gloves to match, and a white hat with black feathers that covered her long brown hair. Her fair skin was very soft to the touch, her cheekbones high, her light blue eyes reminiscent of the ocean, and her nose straight. With her other free hand, she held a small purse that matched the texture of the feathers on her hat. She looked down bestowed a perfect, dimpled smile upon her beloved son.

Holding the child's other hand was his father, a man just as fair as his other half, handsome with warm brown eyes and a cleft chin that punctuated his oval face. Today he was looking dapper in a striped black suit and casual leather boots. His free hand reached into one jacket pocket and pulled out a pocket watch to check on the time. Then he returned his gaze to his wife and child to smile affectionately back at them before checking over the crowd.

The boy looked up at his loving parents, and his soft hands held tightly to theirs. He smiled joyfully, knowing he was in good company. Though slender for his size, he dressed nicely to match his father. He'd inherited his mother's blue eyes and high cheekbones, while also sporting his father's distinctive chin. As the breeze tossed his short, dark brown hair, the child turned his gaze upwards to the gray and white clouds that covered most of the sky, with scattered sunbeams occasionally breaking through.

The family traversed the busy street, with its wooden houses and stone towers bordering the road, chimneys puffing smoke, and the busy hustle and clamor of vendors trying to lure potential customers to view their wares. During the midday, everyone walked along the road, moving like a school of fish. Horses pulled carriages along the busy street with a clatter. With careful attention, some of the conversations inside might yet be overheard. The people all dressed with individual style, no two looking the same, from the color of the women's gowns to the suits of the gentlemen walking beside them.

Constant noise surrounded the little family like a light breeze in the air that danced around them. Crowds walked in different directions, trying to reach their destinations, while others gathered together just to chitchat.

"We are going to the market, Rowland," the child's father informed him, looking down with a smile.

"Can I get something?" the boy asked cheerfully.

"Only if you behave, Mr. Chapman," his mother teased.

They heard a loud call in the distance, a young man's voice that could carry for miles.

"Fresh fruits! Come get your fruits right here!" shouted of one of the vendors.

Other vendors tried a different marketing method, letting the merchandise sell itself. Trying to see through the wall of people in front of him, Rowland broke into a radiant, vibrant smile. Moving a little quicker, he tried to push the pace a little faster, pulling his mother and father with him.

"Slow down there, son. We still have the whole day," his father admonished.

At the center of town stood a square fountain with an angel, its little hands held out to the sides, cascading water into the space below. Birds chirped and bathed in the water while merchants of all trades set up shop around it, offering their goods for sale.

Rows upon rows of merchandise lay next to each other, separated only by a few feet of space. Each item was laid out nicely on tables in front of the stalls. Some of the merchants waited patiently, like vultures waiting to steal the kill, while others browsed around to see what was new and interesting. Only few customers shopped only with their eyes and not their wallets.

The crowds began to disperse, and the space seemed to open up, making walking and shopping in the market a pleasure. The aroma of spiced meat cooking on a rotisserie over a small fire floated through the air, dancing with the breeze.

The scent caught everyone's attention as they inhaled the air around them, saliva flooding their mouths. Rowland's stomach could not resist any longer, rumbling for him to hear and loud enough for his parents to pick up the hint.

Rowland chuckled, with a slight smirk, as his parents reacted.

"Boy, am I feeling hungry! Catherine, what about you, dear? Are you hungry too?" Gerard asked, rubbing his stomach.

"Yes, very much so, darling," Catherine cordially responded.

The Chapman family approached the open stall where the cook fire was burning, a piece of meat slowly grilling over the fire. A bearded man wearing a butcher's apron emerged and asked, "How can I help you folks out today?" his smile was friendly and his tone hospitable.

"We would like to try the grilled steak. If you could cut one into a smaller portion for this young man here, that would be much appreciated," said Gerard.

"Coming right up," the butcher replied.

He removed the skewer from the fire and slid the meat off, then placed it on the butcher's block. The roasted meat was still smoking. The butcher then took up a long knife and began to cut through the juicy, browned steak. With each cut, the meat sizzled, the smoke rising into the air. As requested by his customers, he carefully moved the meat to a lilac leaf so he could wrap it up for them.

"It will be two coppers," the butcher requested.

Reaching into his coat pocket, Gerard jingled the coins within, feeling for the correct change.

Standing a few feet away from the family as they made their purchase were a couple of men with skin burnt to a reddish brown and disheveled hair tangled in knots from lack of washing. Compared to the other people in the square, they were shabbily dressed, with holes in their pants, and torn, patched shirts. The crowd around them gave them space, detecting their uneasy tension and their out-of-place air.

"Antoine, listen!" one man whispered to his partner. "This is our jackpot. This guy must be loaded," he continued.

"Okay, Francois. Keep an eye on them. We'll deal with them at the right time," Antoine responded.

"What if we don't get that opportunity?"

"Then we will make one."

Nodding his head, Francois smiled and began to whistle. He walked away ever so slowly, separating himself from his partner.

Gerard finally located the coin purse in his pocket.

"Ah! There we go."

Opening his coin purse by loosening the cord on each end, he picked out the two coppers and handed them to the butcher.

"There you go, sir."

"Thank you kindly and enjoy," the butcher responded, accepting the payment.

Rowland grabbed the food from the table. Hunger had begun to set in, but the boy knew that lunch was around the corner in just a few more moments. He waited to give his father the meat he'd purchased once he'd put away the coin purse.

"Father, here," Rowland said, handing over the food in its wrapping of leaves.

"Thank you, son. Let's go find a place where we can eat," Gerard responded.

He found a spot next to the fountain and led the way. Once seated, they had time to relax and enjoy the scenery. Rowland sat between his parents as Gerard unwrapped each leaf, taking a steak for himself and giving his wife and son each a piece of meat, leaving the lilac leaf with Catherine.

"What a view," Catherine observed.

"Indeed. We don't get to see something like this all the time," Gerard responded as he watched the people walk by.

"Well . . . I miss the countryside," Catherine stated.

"I do too."

"Well, let's eat before our food goes cold."

"Ha, yes. One day we'll move back to the country."

The minutes passed as the family enjoyed their meal together. They listened to the bubble and splash of the serene fountain's cascading water and the voices and bustle of the busy passersby until they'd eaten to satisfaction. Then, they got up and continued with their agenda for the day.

"I want to see what exotics they have today," said Catherine.

"There are a few shops farther down the road that we could check," Gerard responded as they passed a few more food merchants.

Low whistles from behind them sounded like a familiar tune, and Rowland looked back. He remembered the melody from where they'd bought the food, but wondered why it followed them. When he looked back over his shoulder, only empty space was behind them.

A small tent pitched at the end of the market caught the eyes of the Chapman family. Filled with curiosity, as they'd never seen it on previous visits to the market, they went to investigate.

"I have never seen this shop before," Catherine noted.

"Neither have I," Gerard replied.

"Come one, come all, and see the treasures of the world!" the merchant called to the crowd.

His face was hidden under cloth wrappings, with only his eyes exposed, yet his body was half naked. He was tall and slender, with a slightly intimidating air about him. Beads of sweat rolled down his chest. For pants, he wore voluminous white linen leggings that almost gave the impression of a skirt.

"Let the mysteries of the world intrigue you," the merchant continued.

"Mother, this man is huge!" Rowland declared, awestruck. His mother simply smiled in return.

Having overheard the child, the man replied, "I am not huge, I am a giant!" he capped this off with a hearty laugh.

"I have never seen such a shop as this," Gerard remarked.

"'Here today, gone tomorrow' has always been my motto, kind sir. Please come in," the merchant invited them.

After entering the tent, he unveiled the merchandise, carefully removing the cloth that hung over the tables. One by one, he moved from one end of each table to the other. The Chapmans' eyes went wide in amazement at all the items revealed before them. From weapons to ancient artifacts, it seemed as though this merchant had it all.

"Whoa! Look at all this stuff!" Rowland exclaimed.

"Please do not touch. Most of these items are very valuable and fragile," the merchant cautioned them.

Looking at the clothing, which was attractively displayed separately, Catherine thought, *this must be very expensive.*

Her eyes glittered with awe. She wanted to try everything to see if the clothing fit. On the other side of the tent, Gerard examined the ancient books. He looked in wonder at the old relics, translated by others and passed on through time.

Something at the far end of the tent caught Rowland's eye from as he browsed. Slowly, he approached. A small bear, carved of light, glossy wood, stood at the end of the table, away from the rest of the merchandise.

It tempted Rowland to come closer, and it looked so utterly desirable to the young child. It was a one-of-a-kind toy and, oddly enough, had a keyhole at the center of its chest. Trying to resist the temptation, he stood there for a while looking at the bear. The pale wood was perfectly carved.

I wish I could have this.

The merchant moved from the center of the tent and approached Catherine.

"Beautiful clothing, is it not?"

"Quite lovely. I have never seen garments like this. Gorgeous . . . just gorgeous," she responded.

"You will not find anything like this elsewhere. Look at the material. This silk was made for kings and queens of old. You can feel the difference, so soft and delicate," the merchant declared enticingly.

He offered one of the silk dresses for her to touch. Catherine reached out to caress the silk between her fingers, and her face shone with delight.

"Yes, it is. I love the way it feels," Catherine responded.

"This very gown was worn by a servant of the late Egyptian queen. See the subtle lines on the gown?" The merchant lifted the dress, laying it on her shoulder.

"Yes, I do," Catherine replied, looking down at the garment, then closing her eyes and imagining herself wearing it.

"It suits you rather well, Madam."

As she regretfully returned the silk dress to the table, Catherine could only imagine what it would be like to purchase this fabulous clothing. The temptation was certainly there. She looked over to Gerard, recognizing the situation they were in, and her heart sank with disappointment.

Rowland walked over to his mother. "Mama. Look what I found."

He held the wooden bear up for her to see. The merchant's eyes opened wide in alarm, wanting to yell at the boy, but he held his tongue, as he stood next to a potential client.

"Rowland! The merchant told us no touching," Catherine snapped.

"Yes, Mother, but I couldn't resist!" Rowland responded, holding the toy bear tucked tightly in his arm.

Keeping his cool, the merchant knelt down, looked at Rowland, and asked, "Do you know where to find the key for that bear?'

"The key?" Rowland questioned.

"Yes. Look carefully at his chest. There is a small hole for a key," the merchant explained.

"Where do I find this key?" Rowland asked, intrigued.

"Very simple, child. Let me see the bear." He held out his hand.

As Rowland handed the toy bear over to the merchant, Gerard took notice and drew near, closing the distance behind his son. "What's going on here?"

"He is going to show me where the key is so I can unlock the bear's chest," Rowland replied.

Gerard nodded. "That's good."

The merchant pulled the bear's tail. It extended about an inch. He then turned the tail upside down, and a key slipped out from a hidden slot.

"Whoa!" Rowland blurted, enjoying every moment.

Gerard took his wife's arm and, turning, directed her gently to the other side of the tent.

"Do you like any of the merchandise?" he asked her.

"I do, but I know we cannot afford any of this," Catherine whispered, looking longingly back at the dress once more. "Did you find anything you like here as well?" she continued.

"Yes. This shop is amazing. It has everything," Gerard responded.

Listening to the whispers in the distance, the merchant kept Rowland occupied by showing him another hidden trick to the wooden bear. He began to spin a tale about the item.

"This wooden bear was hand carved for a prince in the Far East. I was told that this prince was very smart. Nothing made him happy, as he was also very spoiled. One day, the king himself set off to seek a sculpture to satisfy his son's need on his name day. The king searched near and far, until one day, he found what he was looking for.

The king asked the craftsman, 'Can you design something simple, yet complex; something with an interesting secret?'" The merchant changed his voice, impersonating the king.

"'I have something for you, my king,' said the artisan. Again, the merchant changed his voice to imitate the other man. 'Please give me a couple of days, and then come back to my shop. I will have something for you when you return,'" he continued.

"A few days later, the king returned to this craftsman, anxious to see what he had conjured up. Impatiently, the king demanded, 'Let's see your creation.'

'At once, Your Highness. Please give me a moment to get the gift,' the craftsman replied, turning and proceeding to the back room of his store.

The artisan brought out his masterpiece, a beautifully carved wooden bear. The king regarded the wooden toy with a look of utter disgust.

'I waited for days for something like this? I could have had this toy made by anyone else in this kingdom,' the king huffed.

'But, Your Highness . . . This is more than just a simple toy, exactly as you requested,' the craftsman attempted to explain.

'Well, this is not what I asked for. I'm sorry you wasted your time. Good day,' the king declared as he stormed out of the store.

"As you can see, this toy was made for a prince, but it never reached him because the king did not want it," the merchant concluded.

Rowland stood there, puzzled, trying to figure out the moral of the story.

As the merchant concluded his tale, Gerard rejoined his son and asked, "Rowland, are you ready to leave?"

"Yes . . ." Rowland replied quietly, head bowed dejectedly as he obediently followed his father.

"Did you find everything you wanted?" the merchant asked in a final attempt to make a sale.

"We were very pleased with your merchandise. You have an impressive selection," Catherine replied truthfully.

"We should get going. It will be dark soon," Gerard declared firmly.

"Give me just a moment," the merchant said, giving the wooden bear back to Rowland. He scooped the silken dress from its table as well, and then returned to Gerard, offering him the book he'd been examining earlier.

The merchant turned back to the family and said, "You have been my first and last customers today." He placed the book in Gerard's hands, and then gently handed Catherine the exquisite silk dress. "Please, accept these as gifts."

"Oh, we cannot," Catherine demurred, trying to return the dress.

"These gifts are freely given," the merchant responded warmly. "I have encountered many people in my life and I am an excellent judge of character. The three of you are special. These items will serve a better purpose with you, in any case."

He turned to the boy. "My little prince, please take care of that toy bear for me."

"I will," Rowland promised, hugging the wooden bear tightly.

"Thank you greatly for your kindness," Gerard replied, humbled by the man's generosity.

Nodding his head in response, the merchant turned back to his tent to begin packing up his goods for the day.

The three walked out of the tent and back into the crowd of people, pleased with the merchant's kind gesture. Gerard and Catherine looked at each other for a moment, thinking, *Could this really have happened?*

"That was a nice gentleman," said Catherine.

"Yes, he was very kind," Gerard responded.

"Do you like your new toy, son?" she asked.

"Yes, mother!" Rowland responded with a radiant smile.

Pointing away from the crowd, Gerard suggested, "Well, let's go this way. It will be a quicker way to go home and fewer people to deal with."

"Sure, dear," Catherine agreed.

"Father. Father!" Rowland demanded.

"Yes, Son?"

"Can we go that way?" Rowland pointed back to the crowd. A sense of uneasiness lingered around him.

"There is nothing to worry about. I'll make sure of that," Gerard reassured him.

Gerard led the way, walking farther down the street. As they continued along, the crowd slowly thinned out and disappeared, along with the stores surrounding them, as the sun descended to the horizon. Soaring from their high spirits from their experience at the store, the family enjoyed the silent walk home.

Abruptly, a low-pitched whistle sounded behind them. Gerard and Catherine ignored the sound and continued making their way down the street. Rowland, on the other hand, scanned his surroundings to see who it might be.

The beginning of dusk came fast. Clouds thickened in the overcast sky, the dark gray shapes moving to take over the blue. A light rumble of thunder quaked the sky above, signaling an impending evening shower. In the alley there were no signs of life, aside from the family of three. A familiar whistle became progressively louder with each repetition. The Chapman family, now apprehensive, turned around to see who was whistling. A raggedly dressed man, with offensive body odor, moved in closer to them.

Another rough, ragged man slipped quietly by from the darkness of the side alley, rushing in stealthily from behind. He pulled out a knife from his garments, the end of the blade stained with the dried blood of previous victims, and held it closely behind Gerard's back, leaving just enough space not to be noticed. The other man in front continued to whistle, ambling closer with no obvious care in the world.

"C-can we help you?" Gerard asked nervously.

"As a matter of fact, you can," the ragged man replied, his voice ominous and raspy, tilting his head upwards.

A short burst of coarse laughter sounded from behind the family, startling them.

Gerard slowly turned his head, and from the corner of his eye saw a man standing menacingly behind him, resembling the person who blocked their way in front.

Suddenly, a sharp, cold pain struck his abdomen. Blood flowed from the puncture as the assailant pulled out the knife, now covered in bright red.

The man smiled maliciously, striking again and again, stabbing other parts of his victim's body. The thief was obviously enjoying every second, delighting in the gentleman's suffering. Gerard fell to the ground inertly, like a doll, with only enough energy remaining to look on as the final sands poured through the hourglass of his life.

Everything seemed to happen in slow motion when Catherine looked over to her husband, no longer standing by her side. She screamed in terror when she caught sight of the blood spreading in a crimson pool from Gerard's dying body on the pavement. She fell to the ground beside him, hugging him tightly in his final moments.

The whistling man dashed to her, pulling out his own knife from a pocket. Nothing else mattered to Catherine. The person she'd loved for all these years lay lifeless on the ground, wet red stains seeping through his shirt as tears of sorrow came pouring down her face, mixing with the blood on Gerard's body below. As the first few teardrops splashed on Gerard's lifeless body, a knife came tearing through her back, sending a wave of searing agony through her body. She instantly went into shock, unable to act any longer as she lay on top of her loved one.

"Search them!" the mugger commanded.

They began to pat down each of the bodies in hopes of hitting the jackpot. Rowland, backing slowly away, watched in horror as the two men despoiled his parents, fear paralyzing him to inaction.

Finally, adrenaline overcame the dread of watching these human vultures swarming over his parents' bodies. Rowland turned and ran like the wind, back to the market, without even thinking about his destination. Heavy breathing was the only thing he could remember, as though he'd fled without the use of his eyes. Not once did he look back, afraid of the men might come to finish him off.

"What should we do about the kid?" Antoine questioned, searching the woman's body only to come up empty-handed.

"Forget him. He wouldn't know what to do anyway," Francois replied.

His hands dug into the man's pockets. He felt that he'd hit the jackpot they were looking for when he pulled out a small coin purse. He smiled ecstatically, holding up the money bag, thinking that he'd struck his fortune.

Believing all this effort had come to fruition, Antoine loosened the top of the coin purse and flipped the bag upside down, shaking it back and forth. But the only things to fall to the ground were keys and the pieces of a small, broken metal chain.

Rowland continued to run, tears falling from his eyes and disappearing into the wind. Reality started to catch up with him. He remembered last the sight of his parents dropping to the ground, lifeless. He fled aimlessly into the market, the wooden teddy bear still held in his arms, when a lady realized something was terribly wrong with the young boy and tentatively stopped him.

She asked him solicitously, "What are you running from, little one?"

With her tanned hands, she wiped away the tears from his cheeks. Rowland gazed up at the modest-looking housewife, a little on the heavy side and mother of four. Her children looked on from their place near the side window of their house. Rowland could not comprehend what she asked. He was in a daze, mind clouded by the horror of his dilemma. He tried hard to grasp what she had asked.

She tried again and asked, "What are you running from, little one? Where are your parents?"

The situation started to register slowly in Rowland's brain, as he finally understood what she had asked. He looked up at her, taking in her peach complexion and dark black hair that reminded of his mother, but the words wouldn't come even though he tried hard to speak. The only thing he could do was pull her in the direction he remembered where his parents were last.

"Slow down there, little one," she said. Her long purple dress swished around her ankles as she hurried along, trying to keep pace with Rowland.

"Let's take whatever we can and get out of here before someone sees us," Francois snapped.

Rowland tugged the woman's hand harder, trying to get his benefactor to move faster in hopes that the two muggers were still there and could be apprehended. As they made their way around the bend and back into the alleyway, he immediately pointed to the two bodies lying on the ground, lifeless and surrounded by a pool of blood.

The woman's scream of horror echoed up and down the street. The few townspeople who heard the noise came rushing over to see what the commotion was all about.

As the muggers hastily grabbed what loose belongings they could from their victims' bodies, the two heard a loud scream from behind them. Leaving the clothing behind, they immediately bolted down the alley, leaving no traces to tie them to the murders.

They panted and huffed as they sprinted down the narrow alleyway. Little light remained in the area as the majority of the sun sank below the horizon, plunging the crime scene into darkness. The two thugs darted beneath an overpass and vanished into the shadows.

The small group of townsfolk reached the screaming woman, coming to her aid. She held Rowland's hand and pointed out into the alley, where two lifeless bodies lay unceremoniously piled together. The victims' eyes were still open in death, their horrified gazes frozen upon each other's wounds.

The crowd trepidatiously approached the crime scene. One man asked, "Does anyone know who these two are?"

The woman with Rowland suggested, "I believe they are his parents. He led me to them." A low mutter grew within the crowd as they whispered and speculated amongst each other.

"Did you see which way the killers went?" another person questioned from within the crowd.

"They ran down the alleyway," the woman responded, pointing in the direction they'd taken.

"They could be anywhere by now," another person noted in frustration.

Thunder rumbled in the sky. The crowd looked up to see thick black clouds closing over the deep blue-black of the evening sky. The peals grew louder and flashes of lightning danced through the clouds.

"You should take the child to the church," a woman in the group stated.

"What about the bodies?" another person asked.

A police officer turned into the alley, drawn to the clamor of the crowd.

"He will be able to handle this," a man replied, indicating the approaching officer.

"What happened here?" The officer spoke, making his presence known.

"This young boy, those are his parents. They were murdered here," explained Rowland's temporary guardian.

The officer waved his hands back and forth, gesturing for the people to make room.

"Step away, step away. This is a crime scene," he instructed. "Did you see where the suspects ran off to?"

"Down the alley." The woman pointed.

"Did you see what they look like? Could you identify them?"

"Both men had dirty, tangled hair, a reddish-brown complexion, and ragged clothes. I could not make out their faces because they fled so quickly," she replied.

"Thank you, ma'am." The officer took notes on a sheet of paper. "I will take it from here. In case we need to find you, where are you staying?"

The woman indicated her house in the distance and recited the address.

"I hope these criminals can be caught before they strike again," she commented, the worry plain in her voice.

Turning her attention to Rowland, she addressed the most immediate concern. "Come on, little one. We must hurry little one before the rain soaks us through." She turned the other way, pulling Rowland away from the crime scene.

Thunder clashed again and again throughout the sky, and the first drops began to fall, heralding the oncoming downpour. The officer bent down to inspect the bodies, making sure he did not touch the blood on the ground. Reaching down with his hand, he closed the dead woman's eyes, then those of her husband, who lay beneath her.

"Get me a couple of blankets," the officer addressed the crowd.

One man darted into his nearby home and rushed back out with two white blankets, which he handed over to the officer.

Small drops of rain were now falling regularly from the sky. The officer used the donated blankets to cover up the bodies and preserve the crime scene as best he could for later examination. The crowd slowly dispersed, one by one, as they felt the cold touch of water on their skin. Putting his hat back on, the officer bid the victims a temporary farewell so he could get more detectives to the scene. The rain mixing with the blood tinged the white blankets a pinkish red, hinting at what lay beneath.

Rowland continued to hold the lady's hand, walking with her back to the church, but remained silent to the world. The rain was lighter in the direction they were heading, slowly drizzling and covering them like a canvas of artwork, the little light shining through the clouds causing the raindrops to sparkle like tiny prisms.

The woman looked down at Rowland, wondering what was going through his mind. She pitied him. *This poor child . . .* The boy's blank stare spoke to his state of shock, his expression lifeless and empty, possessed by time.

Reaching the end of the road, she finally mustered up some words to try to break the silence between them. "We are close."

He continued to gaze straight ahead, seldom blinking. She wondered if she was able to give comfort to the child, hoping that it would make a difference.

She sighed, carefully thinking of what to say. "The church will surely take care of you, better than being out here alone, of course. You will have brothers, enjoy their company, and learn the way of the church. I think you will like it."

Rowland looked at her blankly, pointing right at her like he understood.

She responded to his hand gesture. "Oh, no. I cannot, I have children of my own to take care of. The church will set you on the right path, and you will become a fine young man."

They arrived to the church, a small cathedral made of stone. Some glass windows had shapes of angelic human faces, with halos hovering above their heads. The glass above the dark-grained cherry wood, inlaid with crosses, on each side of the double door resembled a full moon cut in half.

They walked up a short pathway and a few steps to the doorstep. She knocked on the door three times, loudly. The noise echoed throughout the church, and one of the priests walked slowly to the entrance. A low rumble in the sky disrupted their train of thought, and they looked simultaneously up to the sky.

About to knock again, she stopped herself dead in her tracks, arm moving forward, when she heard the door unlock from the inside with a loud clunk. The doorknob turned slowly. After a few long seconds, the door cracked open and a faint light shone out from within.

A shadowy figure appeared and asked, "Can I help you?"

As the priest come into view, she spoke: "Father, could you please help us out?"

The priest wore a black outer cassock that fell to his ankles, a vestment over the main attire, a clerical collar, and a necklace with the cross resting upon his chest. From what they could see in the gloom, he was an older man, with some white hair mixed with the black, and wrinkled pale skin that spoke of age.

His eyebrows rose a little, ready to ask a question, when she continued.

"This child's parents were killed moments ago, and he has nowhere else to go."

The priest knelt down to look at Rowland and spoke. "Come here, my child."

Obediently, Rowland walked over to the priest, still wearing his distant stare of shock.

"Everything will be just fine," the priest said, gazing benevolently at Rowland. "We have brothers and sisters around your age who will take care of you. You will learn the ways of the Roman Catholic Church and become a fine young man."

The drizzle of rain lightened up and the dense humidity began to rise. The dark clouds scattered away, letting what was left of the sunlight disappear beyond the horizon as the evening came to an end.

Looking at the lady who brought Rowland to the church, the priest said, "Thank you for bringing this boy to us."

"You're welcome," she replied, walking away from the church and disappearing into the darkness of the evening.

"Have a safe trip back home," the priest called out, watching her traverse the walkway and go back to the street. Getting up from his kneeling position, he held out his hand for Rowland to hold.

"What is your name, child?" the priest asked.

He took a long pause before responding, "Rowland . . . Chapman."

"Well, this will be a new experience for you. It will take some time for you to get used to our ways, but you will like it here," the priest assured him, guiding him into the church.

CHAPTER 10
—ONE HAPPY FAMILY

The aroma of food hung in the air, as a freshly cooked meal of venison sat in the middle of the dining room table surrounded by steamed vegetables. Two plates, with silverware, already sat across from each other. Susanna let out a big sigh of relief, the last candle on the dining table being lit.

She strolled along, heading back into the kitchen, where she cleaned the last of the knives in a bucket of water. A few extra buckets hung on the side of the wall, while the rest of the floor was empty except for a table near one side of the room. The stone chimney rose up the side of the wall, and below it, the fire pit spat its last few embers into the air.

Susanna was lovely and wholesome-looking. She wore a silky blue shirtdress down to her ankles, with a white shirt beneath that fitted closely to her wrists, and brown boots. Her snowy skin had touches of freckles on the cheeks, where beads of sweat formed. She wiped the perspiration away with her sleeve. Her blue eyes were focused on the task at hand, and her long blond hair was tied back in a practical bun so as not to interfere with her work.

As she finished cleaning the utensils, she heard the door unlock from the living room. Briefly glancing at the door to see who'd entered, she dried her wet hands on a nearby towel.

"I'm home, Susanna," a familiar male voice called out.

From the shadow of the outside world, Abraham closed the door. Briefly, he looked up at the staircase, wondering if someone special was there, but did not bother to check due to his exhaustion from the long day. He looked around and saw no one there, but candles were lit on the dining table and food was already served.

Maybe she went to bed . . . It is rather late, after all.

The pictures that hung by the chimney made him smile, with one of his family photo dead center above the mantle.

Joseph must be sleeping, he thought.

The enticing scent of food took over his attention. Saliva rushed inside of his mouth, and his stomach rumbled as though a fight had broken loose in his midsection.

"Sweetheart, sorry I am late. Work was a little busier than usual today," he announced.

"That's fine, Abraham," Susanna replied, bringing another plate of food to the table.

Her heartfelt smile illuminated the room with a welcoming presence. She adored his dimples when he smiled, his square, fair face, framed by short blond hair and adorned with blue eyes that she could get lost in.

"Why did you bring out another plate?" Abraham asked.

Setting the plate down, she walked over to him. For a moment they embraced each other, having missed one another from the time they were separated in the morning. Her hands brushed through his soft, short hair.

"I ran into William earlier this morning and I invited him to dinner. He should be here any minute now," Susanna answered, leaning in closer for a kiss.

Three rapid knocks came from the door. "Right on time," she quipped.

Abraham returned to the entrance and opened the door.

"Look who we have here!" William exclaimed, still standing outside.

A man cloaked in shadow stood at the dim entrance of the house, dressed in a black cassock and clerical collar. His dirty-blond hair rested at the eyebrows and his pale skin first caught the light. They both smiled from ear to ear when they hugged each other, their striking similarities making them look like twins.

"Oh, it has been a while," said Abraham.

"Yes, it has," William replied.

"Please come in," Abraham responded, gesturing into the house and closing the door behind his guest.

Susanna walked out of sight and up the staircase as discreetly as possible, giving the two brothers their own space. Into a dark room she entered confidently, knowing everything in place by heart, carefully guiding herself to her destination. Her hands touched on a wooden cradle that rocked once it moved, and she gathered up the sleeping child. She cradled him in her arms as he let out a deep breath, and she carried him back down the stairs.

The young child was the very image of his father and had a few striking resemblances to his mother as well. Coming to the dining table and passing behind William and Abraham, Susanna paused.

"Let me see the new addition to our family," William said.

"Here he is," Susanna revealed the baby.

"Ah," William whispered.

"He is very good. No crying whatsoever," Susanna replied, moving to the next available chair alongside Abraham.

"What is his name?" William asked.

"Joseph," Abraham responded from the other side of the table.

"How old is Joseph?"

"He is two years and a month."

"Boy... Time does fly," William sighed.

"Yes, it does." Abraham paused for a moment.

"Before we eat, William, can you do the honors of saying grace?" Susanna asked.

William held out his hands, one to Abraham and one to Susanna. They bowed their heads together.

William gave a short prayer of thanks. "Thank you, Lord, for this supper we are about to eat. Thank you for our health and the new addition to our family. Amen."

"Amen," Susanna and Abraham replied.

"Well, let's eat," Abraham continued and smiled at Susanna, who held Joseph cradled in one arm.

Like a gentleman, Abraham served the first plate for their guest. He sliced off a piece of venison meat with a sharp knife, set the meat on the plate, added the condiments and sides, then continued the same process for everyone else. The couple waited for William to take the first bite before starting their own portions of dinner.

"William, thank you for coming on such short notice," Susanna said after swallowing her first bite of dinner.

"Not a problem at all. I would do anything to see my little brother and my sister-in-law. By the way, this is some delicious food," William replied.

Leaning back to sit upright in his seat, he looked around the dining room, pausing before he spoke.

Abraham looked up and saw his brother hesitating. "Yes, William?" he inquired.

"I just thought of this. . . I would like to baptize my nephew this weekend," William blurted.

"I was thinking the same, brother, not a bad idea," Abraham replied.

A little cry came from the baby lying on Susanna's chest. They all looked upon Joseph as he dreamed a sweet dream, happy as could be, and stretched out to find his comfort zone to sleep again.

CHAPTER 11
—THE DEAL

1 6 7 1

"Wah, waaah!" Nathaniel cried.

He continued to wail and flail his hands and feet inside a dark burl wood crib, covered in a thick layer of white blankets. A couple of rocking chairs sat on opposite side of the room; the bear skin rug lay in the middle of the living room, its head facing the stone fireplace and its glass eyes glinting in the fire.

The fireplace crackled musically. The flames lit and warmed the living room where the child lay. Small beams of light shone from the reflection of the window next to the fireplace as the sun began to rise.

With the little time she had left, leaving the dirty carrots in the bucket of water, Fayth got up from her stool when she heard her baby cry. After drying her hands on the towel that sat on top of the table, she used the table to help push herself up.

She took off her apron and placed it on top of the stool that she had been sitting on. She adjusted her white button-up top and black dress back into place, and then briskly strode through the kitchen and into the living room where the crib lay. The first rays of sunlight shone on her lightly tanned skin, and her light brown hair breezed through the air behind as she walked. There she beheld her son, her prize, and her rosy lips curved into a smile.

"There, there, Nathaniel. Mother is here for you."

Fayth tried to calm the child by lifting him out of the crib. She cradled him, rocking slowly back and forth to calm him down, but Nathaniel continued to cry, whining, kicking, and screaming in the arms of his mother.

She hummed a melody that her father used to sing to her when she was young. It did the trick, calming him down and lulling him into a trance. Though he was still barely awake, close to returning to slumber, he smiled at his mother, burbling and flailing his arms with joy.

That's my baby.

Bruce lay in bed, his square face facing the ceiling, his short black hair resting on the pillow and the rest of his body covered by a thin sheet. The cool, dark room had the feel of a cold spring morning. Beads of sweat accumulated on Bruce's skin and his body burned like a furnace. He tossed and turned in bed, the fighting within him like an endless battle he could not win.

This is the happiest day of my life, Bruce thought.

He walked alongside his horse, with Fayth sitting side saddle, smiling down at him. The clear sky seemed endless as Bruce looked up to take a deep breath. With a blink, he exhaled and looked ahead to see the dark clouds rolling in like a stampede. Thunder clashed in the clouds like a ferocious symphony.

Bruce panicked, realizing that Fayth was ready to give birth.

This seems so familiar. . . Could this be deja vu? he pondered.

"This is not looking good," Bruce blurted.

"Yes, we should hurry," she responded, feeling the gentle kicks in her belly from the baby moving around.

Saddling up on the horse right behind Fayth, Bruce kicked the horse with his heels and they sprinted along the road. Green farmlands blazed by and trees flashed past, blurry, too quick to see. A loud thunderclap boomed above Bruce and Fayth, sending a lightning bolt straight down. The bolt of lightning struck his collarbone and electricity crackled throughout his body.

"Ugh!" Bruce woke up, gasping for air. He was sweating profusely, sitting up on his bed. He got up from the bed and was stunned to watch the bed disintegrate the moment he stood. A heavy rain came suddenly and showered everywhere, drenching him. A familiar view came as an instant flash. He saw Fayth lying at the base of the tree trunk, breathing heavily, panting in short spurts.

How in the hell did I get here? Bruce put some thought into it.

"Bruce, help me," she cried from the distance.

In a daze, he tried to figure out what was going on. Looking down, he thought back to when it had been and what had really happened.

She never said those words.

He thought back to a year ago when everything had happened. More thoughts swirled around his brain like insects in a hive as he questioned what had really happened.

Before Bruce could pin down the thought, a girl wearing a black cloak with white embroidered symbols he did not quite understand stood no more than twenty feet away from him. He realized that her face was hidden this time in the shadow of the hood.

I cannot seem to remember her face, but it feels like it just happened yesterday.

Her voice was soft, innocent and subtle when she spoke, "Bruce, I am here to help."

Bruce was confused. He remembered that the rain had stopped and time had stood still, but for some reason, the rain had continued to fall. Nothing seemed as it should have been.

The voice of the girl slowly changed from calm and collected to agitated and raspy with every repetition: "I am here to help you."

Bruce abruptly heard his son cry. He turned around to see Fayth cradling Nathaniel, who slept soundly, in her arms. The cries of the young girl no longer rang in his ears, those hollow words that she'd repeated gone like the wind. She'd mysteriously vanished when he turned back. He remembered where she'd stood, but she was gone without a trace.

This is awkward. Oh well.

Bruce shrugged his shoulders, not much caring where the girl might have gone, but a nagging feeling soon crept over him. He looked over again only to see the same cloaked girl traveling with Fayth and Nathaniel down the road.

He yelled at the top of his lungs, "Fayth! Wait! Wait for me!"

He gave chase at top speed, but the short distance between them seemed to stretch farther and farther.

Fayth, Nathaniel, and the young woman in black reached the end of the bridge, where they stopped and turned around to look back at Bruce. The distance separating them dwindled as he reached the bridge, panting and gasping for air.

"Why did you ignore me? I have been calling out to you for quite some time," Bruce asked in frustration, watching Fayth as she stood in silence.

However, the black-clad girl giggled.

Bruce gave Fayth another once-over, noticing to his dismay that she wasn't her normal self. Instead, she was pale, lifeless, and gaunt, as though the life had been sucked out of her. Nathaniel cried and cried, but Fayth's gaze rested elsewhere and she made no attempt to soothe him.

Bruce moved in closer, and she handed over the child to him in silence. The baby's cries faded away as he lay in his father's arms. Bruce smiled down on the boy, proud of his progeny.

Nathaniel sang out with laughter, and Bruce forgot his wife's eerie presence for a moment. When next he looked up, she no longer stood there. He turned in circles, searching for her. Suddenly, he heard something collapse to the ground with a thud. Bruce stepped forward to where Fayth had been standing. In her place, a pile of bones resembling her shape and a skull still covered in light brown hair lay upon the ground.

He stumbled backward, confused and horrified. Then, to make matters worse, he heard a growling noise coming from somewhere nearby. The disturbing sound grew louder and louder, and a slight laughter underlay it. Bruce looked down at his son and saw that Nathaniel himself was the source. The child looked excited, his face lit up with a bright smile.

"Father," Nathaniel spoke.

What? This cannot be possible.

Nathaniel's laughter changed again into a low, snarling growl. An evil, sadistic laugh came from the child, and the face of a horrid demon flashed before Bruce's eyes. Terrified, he jumped and gasped, causing him to drop Nathaniel to the ground. Everything faded back into darkness.

He woke up once more gasping for air, sweat running down his face profusely. He wiped off the sweat and sat up.

Why are these things in my dreams of late? They are all the same, but only little things change here and there. What have I done?

Tossing the sheets to the side and getting out of bed, he stretched out and walked naked in the dark to the dresser, randomly grabbing some clothing. Thoughts of the dream kept replaying in his mind. He tried to figure out what they meant while feeling the garments to make sure he put on the clothing correctly.

Bruce opened the bedroom door and emerged into the living room. He looked spaced out, face emotionless and distant. He headed for his rocking chair in front of the chimney.

"Good morning, love," said Fayth, in an effort to penetrate his deep study.

Without responding, Bruce walked like a zombie to his seat.

"Are you okay, dear?" her voice was laden with concern.

Bruce's distant look vanished as he focused on Fayth holding Nathaniel.

"No, no, no, no. Everything is fine," he finally replied.

"Are you sure? I heard you screaming in your sleep."

"It was just a bad dream," Bruce replied.

"You have been having those bad dreams for quite some time now. Is there something you want to share with me?" Fayth asked.

Bruce got up from his seat and walked closer to the fireplace, leaning his forearm on the cold wall of the chimney and looking into the blazing fire. Pausing for a moment, he tried to think what to say, but dead silence loomed in the air.

Fayth set Nathaniel back into the crib. His deep breathing let her know he was sleeping like a rock.

Finally composing the right words, Bruce spoke out. "Do you remember the first moment we fell in love?"

"Yes, I remember that day clearly. It was the day you found me sleeping on the ground," Fayth replied.

What is he getting at?

Enigmatically, Bruce continued, "A year later we got married, and we've always had the greatest time together."

"I know, dear, and we still do."

"Do you remember my vow?" Bruce questioned.

Fayth walked up behind Bruce and hugged him.

She responded, "Of course I remember."

He softly caressed her hands, his eyes closed so he could savor the moment. He knew she wouldn't like what she was going to hear very soon.

She began to describe the details of their wedding day as though it had been only yesterday.

MAY 21, 1667

"We were behind the church in the courtyard that day. There was a small archway in the middle of the yard made of roses and flowers. It was a beautiful sight, with a few columns that stood on each side of the archway. There were no clouds in the sky, and from what I remember, the sun shone brightly. You were wearing a stylish black suit, tailored to fit you. Do you remember the dress I was wearing?" she asked.

"Yes, I remember," Bruce responded.

He turned to face her, returned her embrace, and then went back to his rocking chair.

"You wore an elegant dress that looked like it was made of white crystals, and your favorite red rose veil. You looked like a goddess."

Fayth smiled and sat down next to him in the other rocking chair.

She continued, "It was a very small and private wedding, but it was the way I liked it. Only a few people from town attended. They sat on wooden chairs spaced around the middle aisle. Of course, the most important person there was the man in front of me."

Bruce smiled, acknowledging his importance to Fayth. He reached over to hold her hand. Her kind words radiated deep to his soul. Needless to say, she was his world.

"Father William Newman stood before us with his Bible in hand," Fayth continued.

Next to Bruce had stood the priest in his black cassock and clerical collar, with a wooden cross that hung upon his chest. He had kind blue eyes set in a calm oval face, dark blond hair, and pale skin. After years and years of experience officiating weddings, it felt routine for him. The priest's gaze skipped around the courtyard, then returned to Bruce and Fayth.

"Dearly beloved, we are gathered together here in the sight of God, to join together Fayth and Bruce Smith in holy matrimony, which is an honorable estate, instituted of God in the time of man's innocence, signifying to us the mystical union which is between Christ and his church. Which holy estate Christ adorned and beautified with his presence at the first miracle which he wrought in Cana of Galilee; and is commended of the Apostle Paul to be honorable among all men, and is therefore not to be entered into lightly or inadvisably, but reverently, discreetly, and in the fear of God.

"Into which holy estate Bruce and Fayth come now to be joined and to unite two hearts and lives, blending all interest, sympathies, and hopes. I charge and entreat you, therefore, in entering upon and sustaining this hallowed union, to seek the favor and blessing of Him whose favor is life, whose blessing maketh rich and addeth no sorrow. Let us now seek His blessing." Father William stopped and paused for a second.

"Our Heavenly Father, we beseech thee to come by thy grace to this marriage. Give to these who marry a due sense of the obligations they are now to assume, so that with true intent, and with utter unreserve of love, they may plight their troth, and be henceforth help meet for each other while they journey through life. This we ask in Jesus' name. Amen," Father William concluded the prayer.

"It felt like time stood still when William said those words to us. I wanted that moment to last forever," Fayth reminisced. "It felt like a fairy tale that I never wanted to end."

"Bruce, will you have Fayth to be your wedded wife, to live together after God's ordinance in the holy estate of matrimony; will you love her, comfort her, honor, and keep her, in sickness and in health, and forsaking all others, keep yourself only unto her, so long as you both shall live?" asked Father William.

"I do," Bruce affirmed.

Turning to face Fayth, Father William addressed her next. "Fayth, will you have Bruce to be your wedded husband to live together after God's ordinance in the holy estate of matrimony; will you submit to him, serve him, love, honor, and keep him, in sickness and in health, and, forsaking all others, keep yourself only unto him, so long as you both shall live?"

"I do," Fayth responded.

Looking at Bruce again, Father William asked, "Do you have anything you want to say to your bride?"

Bruce switched his gaze from William to Fayth as he took a deep breath and sighed. He tried to clear the jitters from his system before he spoke.

"The moment you stumbled into my life, my world turned upside down. I knew you were the one, my love at first sight. My loneliness was replaced with joy. You mean the world to me, and whatever it takes to make you happy, whatever is in my power, I will do it for you."

"Yes, I remember those words. They still ring in my ears like you just said them to me, like it was yesterday," Fayth reminded Bruce.

"I remember those words as well," Bruce replied.

His distracted look carried a hint of foreboding. The truth on his mind would cut like a dagger, and knowing this, he would still have to tell her the truth.

"What's on your mind?" Fayth questioned again.

He took a few deep breaths and a long sigh, focused his gaze on Fayth, and finally responded, "Do you remember the day of Nathaniel's birth?"

"Yes, I remember," Fayth replied.

"When you were lying at the base of the tree giving birth to Nathaniel . . ." Bruce began, searching for the best way to tell her.

Fayth watched him, waiting and wondering what he was going to say next.

"Rain was pouring heavily and we were soaked through from head to toe. The tree that gave us cover really didn't help us much," Bruce continued.

"Yes?"

He let out another big sigh, trying to collect himself. "You were having contractions and screaming in immense pain. For the first time in my life, I didn't know what to do. I stood there clueless and helpless while you were slipping away from me."

"But you helped me deliver Nathaniel," Fayth commented.

"I did . . . But there is more," Bruce paused. "You were losing a lot of blood and everything seemed to happen so fast. Slowly but surely, you were fading away. I could see that you were becoming pale."

"Uh-huh . . . ?"

"Then, I heard hoofbeats coming across the bridge, and I turned my head around to see who was approaching. There was a horse as black as night with blood-red eyes, carrying a cloaked rider, who made their way to us. The rain stopped in mid-air as though time itself had stopped," Bruce recounted.

Fayth's eyebrows rose in suspicion. She thought, *I do not remember any of this at all.*

"I remember the cloaked rider came to us, and when the raindrops touched their skin, the water would evaporate. They stopped a short distance away from where I was standing, and the man in the cloak took off his hood and revealed himself. Oddly enough he did not say a word when I asked him for help; he stood there like a statue. All he did was stare straight ahead as if I were not there. A young woman's voice from behind this man called out to me, "Don't worry, Bruce, we came to help you," he continued.

Fayth took some time to think about it and slowly, something tingled in her brain. She thought back, and a memory resurfaced.

Something is not right here. I know there is something more, I just cannot remember what. Nan came to mind, the more and more she thought about it.

"A girl around your age will visit when the time comes," Nan's voice echoed inside her head.

What did she mean by this? Why do these words keep haunting me?

"When I walked to the rear of the horse, I could see her. She was hidden behind the cloaked man, a young woman about your age when we first met. When she took off her hood, I remember she had dark brown hair and strange, unforgettable light gray eyes. The man helped her down to the ground and I followed her as she approached you. She assessed the situation by observing how much you bled. She told me that Nathaniel had already left us, and she explained to me that you were soon to die as well if she didn't act quickly," Bruce continued.

This sounds a little odd, but I wouldn't know, Fayth thought.

"Before she continued, the mystery girl and I talked for a little bit as we made the deal."

Keeping her tongue still, Fayth said nothing, even though she wanted to ask the questions she knew he couldn't have the answers to. The thought of what deal was made increased her curiosity, eating away inside her. She wanted to know what damage had been done

"Then she drew a circle on the ground right next to you and placed a line in the middle. She spoke a language I could not understand, and the top circle began to glow bright red. The energy I felt around her was different than it was earlier. The air around her felt stagnant and heavy. Her focus and concentration were solely in her work. With every mark that she drew within the circle, the light seemed to follow, lighting whatever she was drawing."

"What kind of drawings did she make inside the circle?" Fayth asked.

"From what I could see, she had written some weird scriptures that looked like words surrounding what looked like a goat," he answered.

"A goat?" she questioned.

"Yes, a goat."

"Alright."

"Moments after the first half of the circle lit up, the sound of a goat bleating could be heard echoing in the distance. She spoke a few words to me that I cannot remember. A low, soft cry echoed around the girl, and it got louder and louder. Then she began to draw on the other half of the circle. This time there were no drawings of an animal or anything, only in writing in a language that neither of us could understand. This time the light illuminated the bottom half of the circle in blue," said Bruce.

"What happened next?" Fayth asked.

"The young girl said, "Here they come." Then next to the young girl, the air rippled from top to bottom. Suddenly a foot appeared from the ripple in the air, and a man, the guardian walked out. He glowed with a white energy that surrounded him. I remember he looked like an angel, with short black hair and eyes, wearing a suit, and he was a little taller than me, carrying our son in his arms. He briefly glanced at me and then continued to make his way to you. When he reached you, he flew apart into a million different pieces until he was no more. She called it energy and went straight to the baby, and he also vanished into thin air. From there on, the young girl told me to help deliver our child, and there was nothing more to it. From that day on, I have been haunted by these dreams."

Fayth leaned back in her rocking chair, thinking of those lingering words that Bruce had repeated. Silence filled the room except for the crackling of the fire. Seconds turned into minutes as they both sat in their chairs like statues, leaving the awkward silence lingering in the air.

"Did the girl have a name?" Fayth asked.

"She called herself Morgana." Bruce replied.

Suddenly Fayth recalled something that she had forgotten a long time ago, and immediately darted for the bedroom.

Why does that name sound so familiar?

Chapter 12
—A Sacrifice

Sounds of laughter filled the air. Little children chased each other around the surrounding teepees like cats chasing mice. The sun shone brightly from the clear sky. At the center of the village, wood smoldered in a large fire pit. There was calmness within the community. The elders of the tribe worked on their tasks and cared for the younger children while the strong went out for the hunt.

A young woman arrived from the outskirts of the village carrying a bag, in the plains where she felt free. Her long brown hair was tied into a ponytail, her reddish light brown skin had a healthy glow, and her light brown eyes had a clarity that could pierce through mountains. An emblem of a comet beamed across her tunic, with stars and constellations finishing the rest of the design. Normally she wore deerskin leggings but the day had turned out warm, so she wore her favorite skirt and finished off the outfit with moccasins. She always wore her cherished beaded necklace with a single eagle feather, never leaving that item out of sight.

The lady was greeted with warm hugs by the children, who ran around and played their games. They smiled in appreciation, leaving her with their warm welcome, and laughter continued to fill the air. The village elders slowly straggled along to catch up to her.

"Healer, your presence is welcomed. Thank you for coming. I am Crow," one of the elders began.

Crow was an older man with grayish-white hair in streaks at the top of his head, which faded down to a darker black mix. His wrinkled face showed his age, beaten from the sun and time, but still radiant with a reddish-brown skin tone. When he smiled, the gaps of some missing teeth were revealed. His brown eyes showed his concern.

"Warm welcomes are always appreciated. Please call me Shooting Star," she replied with a smile.

"Our children have gracious spirits," he smiled once more.

"The wind guided me with haste. What troubles arise?" Shooting Star asked.

"One of our own has fallen ill," Crow explained. "Since the last few nights, our child's spirit has been diminishing. Calling upon the Great Spirit has come up empty. One of our elders had a vision and sought you out."

"Our ancestors will guide me straight and true," Shooting Star replied. "Please guide me so we can begin."

Crow led the way toward the teepee where the sick child stayed. As they passed the great fire pit, the watchful eyes of members of the tribe followed the elder and the healer. The young children ran up to her and gathered around again, playful as ever and curious to know what was going on.

She smiled at the children playing around, enjoying the company they provided. Examining the teepee ahead, she was astonished by all the designs on the skin. She could hear the soft voice of a child coughing and occasionally moaning in pain from outside.

"How many moons have passed?" Crow asked.

How does he know that I am carrying a child? "Three full moons," she replied.

Stopping in front of the teepee, Crow said, "Please give me a moment."

He opened the animal skin cover hanging over the doorway and entered.

In the middle of the room lay a young boy sweating beads of perspiration all over as though he were being cooked in a furnace, covered with a blanket of buffalo skin, with grass surrounding the blanket, and a small fire next to him. His face plainly showed his pain as he fought for his life with an illness unknown to them. The sunlight shone in from the small opening at the top of the teepee.

Behind the child sat his mother and father, their faces furrowed with anxiety. His father's face showed it all, the fighting spirit that he would exchange places if he could, his sense of urgency, knowing he could not fight his son's battle, and his powerlessness in the fact that he could only watch. There was nothing left but sadness in his eyes. Tears rolled down the chief's wife's cheeks as she sat still like a statue, worry written all over her features, wondering if and how her son would make it.

"Walks with Bear, the healer has traveled great distances and is outside," Crow announced.

Without looking up, he responded, "Please bring her in."

"Yes, my son." With this reply, he turned back to the door.

Popping his head out of the opening, Crow called out, "Shooting Star, your presence is welcomed. Please come in."

He lifted up the cover higher for her to enter. She stepped inside the teepee, and the children of the tribe dispersed in every direction behind her, scattering like leaves in the wind.

Shooting star entered the room and felt the gloomy, sad atmosphere. It loomed in the air like the despair on their faces when she looked at them.

"This is the healer Shooting Star, and this is my son Walks with Bear, our chief and his wife Moon," said Crow.

Shooting Star gazed at the chief, his skin kissed by the fire, his gaze only upon his child. Walks with Bear wore a buffalo war bonnet that flowed with feathers from head to toe, a deerskin breechcloth, and an intricate breastplate, woven around the neck. She saw sorrow in his black eyes and the set of his thick black brows almost heavy enough to obscure them.

The chief's wife was just as marvelous to look upon. She wore a one-piece buckskin dress decorated in light brown and blue dye, layers upon layers of strings running down from the chest to the knee, and moccasins, her top painted white to look like the moon, with a wolf howling underneath. Her light brown skin almost matched the color of her eyes, and dark brown hair, tied neatly behind her, caressed her back.

Breaking out of his daze, the chief looked up at the healer. The long face that he gave her summed everything up. He tried to give her a warm welcome despite his stern appearance.

"You must be tired from your journey. Please have a seat."

He gestured for her to sit in front of them.

Shooting Star accepted the offer and sat right beside the sick child, carefully monitoring him. Reaching out her hand, she slowly caressed the child's pale forehead and noticed his color slowly fading away. She felt that he was burning with fever, much higher than expected.

The child made a soft grunt, recognizing that someone was there, and tried to open his eyes to see who was touching him.

She leaned forward and whispered to him, "Shhh, rest. Everything is going to be alright."

Then the chief's son turned his head back and closed his eyes once more.

Shooting Star looked up and stated, "Crow has shed some insight upon your son's ailment that began a few nights ago."

Walks with Bear looked up and said, "That is correct. My son, Lonely Wolf, was hunting around nearby. He told me he found a small man-made contraption of a house in the foothills and explored inside."

Shooting Star nodded, trying to envision the story.

"That contraption Lonely Wolf spoke of was deserted when he looked, until he came across the last room where he caught sight of a white-skinned boy lying in bed. I asked him, "What did the white-skinned boy do?"

Walks with Bear took a breath before continuing, "Lonely Wolf replied, 'the boy woke from his slumber, and with fretful eyes, he stared at me. Arising from the sheets, he scared me a little. He wore some awkward clothing not the same as our own, and he had a shiny item that looked like a star on his chest. There were interesting things around the room. The boy left the room, grabbed a stick with a horse head on top, and went outside. I followed him, curiously watching.'

"I asked him why. Lonely Wolf knew to keep away from the white-skinned people.

"Then Lonely Wolf told me, 'I know . . . I stood in the middle of the field and watched him run with the wind. The boy made some weird noises at me that sounded like 'bang bang, bang bang' with his first two fingers pointed at me, and when he made the noise, his thumb would snap down. There and then, I would see him cough. There was happiness in his face; when I imitated him, he fell to the ground. Afterwards, we chased each other around his house, laughing and playing. At the end, he looked very tired and breathed heavily. Hearing a voice call out my name, I ran back, leaving that boy. He coughed some more while I was running.'

"That was all Lonely Wolf said to me. Over the next few days, a few of our men searched for the house where Lonely Wolf had been. We went to the location and saw the white devils standing there. The woman and another child were crying in front a small cross made of wood that was at the side of the house. They mourned for a moment. After a while, a man guided the woman and child to the house. They left with haste, taking all their belongings.

We went inside and examined the contraption after they disappeared. They left some of the belongings of this child Lonely Wolf was speaking of. The child himself was nowhere to be found. Inspecting the grounds around the house, we found blood spilled on a rock. Everything came together when we saw blood on the ground and the cross by the side of the house. We rushed back to the village. Now, over the last few days, my son has been fighting the illness that the white devil child had been fighting," the chief finished, plainly fearing the outcome.

"Let us hope that the ancestors hear my prayer," Shooting Star spoke.

"You have our thanks," the chief replied.

She set her medicine bag on the ground and began to dig through it, item by item, only taking what she needed. She laid out a couple of bowls, a small water bag, herbs and a couple of lilac leaves wrapped tightly with a string. She filled the bowls with remedies, placing them right next to the sick boy.

Placing the herbs on top of the bowl, Shooting Star began to unwrap the lilac leaves, unveiling a red powder in one leaf and a green powder in another. She pinched up a portion of the red powder and placed it into the bowl, then repeated the same process for the green powder. She went back into looking through her bag, settling on a small grinding rock.

"This should help," she murmured to herself.

She began to crush the herbs and mix them together. Finally taking the bag of water, she poured a little into the bowl and continued to mix, stopping when she felt the time was right.

"Only time will tell if Lonely Wolf will get better," she cautioned.

The chief and his wife looked on with hope, wishing for this to cure their son's ailment.

Shooting Star picked up the bowl and leaned forward to whisper into Lonely Wolf's ear, "Drink up."

Lonely Wolf heard what he thought was a saint's voice from a distant dream. He tilted his head back a little to the side where he heard the voice. With all of the remaining strength he could muster up, his mouth opened, a bit shaky, but wide enough for the bowl to fit.

Shooting Star began to pour the liquid medicine in the boy's mouth. The bowl slowly drained as she rested the bowl on his lips. He began to swallow, each forceful gulp showing that he was still there. A sigh of relief passed between the adults as the atmosphere changed from the thick feel of gloom to one of hope.

"Give him the night to rest, and let's hope he improves," Shooting Star broke the silence.

The chief gazed at his son, checking to see if there were any immediate changes. Gradually, the pallor of Lonely Wolf's skin slowly disappeared and his natural color blossomed. Smiles filled the room as the mother and father felt their son coming back from the brink of death. The sound of a deep breath from him confirmed it.

"I will check on him tomorrow. There is still a long journey ahead that he will have to conquer." Shooting Star gathered all her belongings and set them back into the bag.

Walks with Bear got up from the ground and spoke, "You have blessed us with your help. My home is your home. Is there any way we can assist you?"

"A place to lay my head for the night," Shooting Star responded.

The chief nodded his head and his father left to help the healer in any way that he could.

Stepping out of the teepee, Crow broke his silence and said, "Thank you again for helping us. You have our gratitude."

Shooting Star smiled back and replied, "The wolf still needs to howl at the moon. Lonely Wolf has a long road to travel."

Small campfires lit up the night all around the teepees, scattered throughout the village. Crow and Shooting Star walked past livestock, people, and other teepees to her residence for the night. She looked up to the sky to admire the vast darkness and the stars that glowed like fireflies.

I wish you were here with me.

Reaching the door to the teepee, Crow said, "You have our thanks. We are grateful you came on such short notice. This will be your sleeping quarters." He lifted the door flap for her to enter.

"Thank you for the hospitality, and have a good night," she replied, entering the teepee.

The next morning, Shooting Star heard noise from outside. The livestock made their animal sounds, and people chattered outdoors in the gray dawn. As she stared up at the top of the teepee, gathering her thoughts, a familiar voice broke her from her trance.

"Shooting Star! Shooting Star! Are you awake?" Crow's voice was frantic.

"Yes; is something wrong?" she asked.

"Lonely Wolf is getting worse. We must make haste," he replied.

Getting up from underneath the covers, she shivered from the morning chill on her bare skin. The fire that had kept her warm through the night smoldered, and smoke rose to the top vent. She looked for her tunic and clothing nearby and began to dress. Lastly, she put on the necklace and moccasins, and, snatching up her medicine bag, she rushed out the door.

"What happened last night?" she inquired while tossing the strap of her bag over her shoulder, wearing it like a purse.

"Lonely Wolf's color returned a little after you gave him the medicine," Crow began as they hastened to the chief's teepee.

"Yes, I remember," she replied.

"The night was quiet with no intrusions, and his breathing returned to normal. But suddenly, before the sun could rise, he coughed up blood and his fever began to rise once more. His color returned to white, and he now looks as though he is ready to join our ancestors," Crow finished as they reached their destination.

Opening the door flap for her, he offered, "Please, after you," gesturing for her to enter first.

The chief looked up to the entrance as Shooting Star and Crow arrived.

"I hope we are not too late," Walks with Bear said.

Shooting Star nodded, agreeing with the chief.

"Is there anything we can do to assist you?" Moon asked.

"I have just one thing," she replied.

Everyone watched her, waiting for a response after the unusual request.

"I would like to be alone with Lonely Wolf. No one is allowed to enter, no matter how long it takes for me to heal your son. That is all I request," she said.

The chief, his wife, and the elder passed a look among them and nodded in agreement.

"Very well," Walks with Bear assented. "If you need anything, please let us know," he continued, rising from the ground.

"There is one more request," Shooting Star added.

The chief looked back, eyebrows raised in silent inquiry.

"Have a celebration. Ease your mind, and come morning, your son will be fine again."

The chief nodded his head, and in a single file, the family left the teepee.

In the evening, the sun neared the end of its daily travel across the sky and darkness began to consume the land. Flickers of light shone from the stars as they appeared against the deep blue that faded swiftly to black.

Shooting Star selected some essentials from her medicine bag, beginning with candles, which she placed around the sick child. Then, she chose a few essences and set them near Lonely Wolf's head. The nighttime darkness gathered in the confines of the teepee, making it harder and harder to see.

The healer got up and gathered a few pieces of wood and dried shrubbery from their spot near the wall of the teepee, and placed them at the center of the room. With a bow, a drill, and the wood, she started a fire by friction. Smoke began to rise from the shrubbery that served as kindling.

Quickly, she blew gently on the spark, and it ignited the twigs and dry leaves into a small fire. She carefully placed more wood on top of the fire, layering increasingly larger pieces to keep the fire burning. She reached for the candle closest to hand, lit the wick in the fire, and then used it to light the other candles one by one.

Shooting Star began a healing chant.

Find
The everlasting oasis
Guidance,
From your fears and doubts
From the shadows
Soar, soar
Into the light

Outside in the center of the village, a large bonfire, practically big enough to be seen from the stars above, kept the darkness at bay, and everyone in the tribe came for the festivities. At the northern edge of the bonfire, Walks with Bear sat amongst the people, who formed a big circle. He had respected the healer's wish and held a celebration. The men passed around the peace pipe. People were talking amongst one another, others were dancing to music, people sang near the fire, and some feasted on the meat of a buffalo that some of the hunters had provided fresh from the morning kill. In the dead of the night, this celebration of life prevailed.

Shooting Star took one last item from the bag, a white powdery substance that she kept always on hand. Pinching up a small portion, she blew it in the air. She then stretched her limbs, took a deep breath, and exhaled. As she felt the comfort of serenity all around, her body began to wind down. Her eyes roamed around the room one last time, and her weariness grew substantially. Finally, she closed her eyes and fell into a deep slumber.

Clouds surrounded every inch of her like a giant pillow as she woke up. Small wisps of vapor followed her like the untamable wind. An eagle screeched its call into the surrounding sky. She looked up at the bright blue firmament as the sun blazed forth beams of light. She knew that she was no longer present in the chief's house. Against the bright sunlight, a small black spot grew like a plaguing shadow.

Shooting Star made out the form of a gold-headed eagle with black feathers, dark as the night, with golden talons. It quickly dove into a nearby cloud and vanished. She waited quietly for the majestic bird to reappear. Seconds later, the scream of an eagle echoed in the clouds as a bright white light beamed through, making the entire view go white for a second.

The eagle transformed from a bird into a lean, golden-bronze man among the particles of light. He wore a golden war bonnet that matched his breech-cloth, which had images of the sun. It was difficult to make out the features of his square face.

"Hello, my child," said the Great Spirit.

She levitated through the clouds to meet him, up in the sky. Shooting Star was about to speak when the Great Spirit interrupted.

"What brings a child of mine here?" he questioned.

Shooting Star looked down into the clouds.

"Ah, the young child lying next to you."

She nodded.

"Why show sympathy to someone who does not belong to your tribe?" he questioned.

The Great Spirit sent them back flying down to earth with haste, right back to where she was sleeping next to the sick child. They hovered over the two bodies as though in a state of astral projection. She thought long and hard to find the answer to his question.

"Every life is as important as any other," she finally answered.

"This child is ready to join us in the stars. Why do you want to stop him from such purity?"

"His loved ones still have hope. I do not want such suffering or heartache."

"But that is part of life," he reminded her.

"I understand, but letting the caterpillar become a full-fledged butterfly is worth the reward," Shooting Star countered.

The Great Spirit knelt beside to the sick child, caressing the boy's forehead.

"I see why you want this child to live, but do you understand what you are asking for?" the Great Spirit asked.

"I am well aware of it," she replied.

"The consequences will outweigh what you receive," he admonished her.

She looked at him in puzzlement, wondering what this meant. *What is his intention?*

"This child is on his last breath. He will not survive the night. Let him join his family in the stars where he belongs," the Great Spirit repeated.

"What can I do?" Shooting Star asked.

"There are two paths that you can choose. One is to let the child join us in the stars and be at peace, an existence without knowing pain or suffering that he will otherwise experience later down the road, or the heartaches from those he will soon lose to natural causes or in battle. The other path is . . . since his time is passing, there is only one way to bring him back. That way is for someone else to take his place."

"I can be that person," she offered.

"I will not allow it. You are a healer, and you serve a greater purpose. One day you will understand the words spoken today." The Great Spirit motioned.

She thought long and hard about the choice she had to make. Her options grew slim and slimmer with each and every person she could think of. Placing her hands on top of her belly, she thought of the perfect person to take the sick child Lonely Wolf's place.

"I will offer my unborn child," Shooting Star decided.

"You do know what you are sacrificing?" the Great Spirit cautioned her.

Thinking back a few months back left a bitter taste in her mouth. The anger rushed through her face, and the memories of her past left her with nothing but bitterness.

In spite of her thoughts she responded, "Yes, I understand the repercussions."

"When it is done, you will not be able to have another child."

"Yes, I understand," she stated again.

"Why this child, Lonely Wolf?"

"I believe he is meant for something greater," Shooting Star explained.

The spirit went to Shooting Star and gently rubbed her belly. She felt a force tearing her apart inside. The excruciating pain was torture to her, and she cried out in agony.

"It is done."

The Great Spirit held an aura in the shape of an orb. It covered his hands in a bright white light, a cluster of energy. Bringing it to the sick child, he merged the two energies together and extracted a black orb in its place. He announced, "Come morning, the boy will be fine."

Returning to Shooting Star, the Great Spirit gave her the energy of the dark orb.

"As for you, go to the nearest river and cleanse yourself from this child's sickness. Say your farewell. Your body will return to the way it was before, but you must make haste. Afterward, you will be fighting the sickness yourself for a few nights after you have entered the river. A dream will come to you when you least expect it, and that, you must follow. Now, wake up."

The morning became a new day, and she took a deep breath, inhaled, and exhaled when her eyes decided to open. She turned her head to see the boy sleeping silently. She gave a sigh of relief, but a burning, throbbing sensation lingered at her pelvic area. She got up from the ground aching and crying in pain, and her body trembled. She moved over to Lonely Wolf for a moment and knelt down. Her hand caressed his face, from his forehead down to his chin. He suddenly moved to readjust his sleeping position, and his shirt loosened on his right shoulder, revealing a birthmark for Shooting Star to see. Moving to the door, she thought of something long ago that lingered back in her memory. It was vague, but she hoped the details would come back to her. *The mark looks like a comet. Hmmmm.*

Shooting Star took a final look at Lonely Wolf, and then left the teepee. The family waited patiently outside the door.

"Everything is fine. You have a special child. You must take care of him until he comes of age," Shooting Star announced.

They did not quite understand what she meant, and gave her quizzical looks.

"He is resting, but you can go inside," she added.

Walks with Bear rushed into the teepee to check on his son, while Crow stood next to the healer. Ever so thankful, he held her hands and said, "Thank you for everything. I felt that the spirits spoke to you last night."

She smiled and replied, "No need to thank me, but I must go now. My work is done here."

"So sudden?" Crow asked, surprised.

"Yes, I am afraid so. The spirits have asked me to continue my journey, and thus I have to leave."

"Can you stay another day? Your body looks like it's still in pain," he requested.

"I am afraid I cannot. I am sorry that I must decline."

"Where will you be heading next?" he inquired.

"I will know when my dream gives me a sign," she responded.

Shooting Star gingerly walked through the village with Crow to the edge where they first met. They parted ways with an embrace, and she took her leave. The sound of footsteps on the ground thudded closer to her, and she turned around to see who it might be. She was surprised to see Lonely Wolf running to her; just to see him up and about was amazing, not to mention that he could already run again.

Carrying all her belongings that she had left in the teepee, Lonely Wolf called out, "Healer, you forgot these."

She gave him a warm smile. "Thank you. I was in a hurry and forgot my belongings."

While handing over her things, he remembered something. "Oh!"

Shooting Star gave him a look of confusion.

He explained, "I had a dream last night about an eagle spirit that I was flying with. I don't remember much of it, or what he said, but that spirit gave me something. I think it would be better with you than with me."

Lonely Wolf pulled from his pocket a small, white wooden doll, with hair that had come from a horse.

Not sure how to reply, she simply said, "Thank you."

And, just like that, Lonely Wolf ran back to his tribe where Crow waited patiently to guide him back to the village.

Shooting Star examined the doll in her hands. It reminded her of the potential of her past and what could have been as she caressed its cheeks. The memory of the Great Spirit's words kept replaying in her mind: "Head to the nearest river and cleanse yourself."

Chapter 13
—We Are Moving

At the crack of dawn, the first rays of sunlight began to encroach on the darkness. The brisk air left goosebumps on those who had left any bare skin exposed to the chill. The first light revealed a large, two-story mahogany house with a walking path, a few uneven stones that guided visitors to the white fence. On the other side stood the front door. There was a large plain cottonwood tree at the corner near the fence, its branches waving back and forth in the light breeze.

Inside, the dark wooden china cabinet had double doors with rectangular panes of glass, one of which swung open.

"Whoa, whoa, whoa! Careful there; this china set is very fragile, and the missus will have my head," cautioned the man of the house.

"Sorry, Mr. Arnold," replied the butler.

"We will be more cautious," said another servant.

Arnold was a fairly tall man, standing at six feet and two inches, with spiky light brown hair, blue eyes, and an oval head. He wore a formal white button-up shirt, with the sleeves rolled up to his elbows, black slacks, and black leather shoes that shone in the light. He opened the door while watching over the others moving his merchandise.

"Let's take out the china set before anything happens," Mr. Arnold said.

"Yes, sir, Mr. Arnold." the butler affirmed.

"Please, that is too formal. Just call me George. Okay, let's continue," he responded

Two more butlers, each wearing a buttoned white cotton shirt, overalls, and a black cap, came out through the door, carrying the cabinet with more silverware inside. The man who led the way stumbled, having taken a too-quick step on one of the uneven stones. The other halted and peeked over to see if his partner was alright. With the tremors, a white glass plate moved out of place and slid out, falling to the ground. A loud crash echoed as it shattered to pieces.

"Are you okay?" George rushed outside.

"Yes," a butler responded.

"I stumbled on the pathway and the plate fell off," the other servant replied, ashamed for causing a mess.

"As long as you are okay, that's all that matters. Those items can always be replaced," George reassured the man.

"Darling, can you come here, please?" came a sweet, seductive voice from inside the house.

George re-entered the house to see his butlers and maids working like ants, removing the rest of their belongings from the house. The inside temperature of the house was much warmer than the briskly cold outdoors.

In the main lobby, a giant glass chandelier loomed above, still lit with candles from the late hours of work. The metal frame shone brightly. George admired every piece of handcrafted glass on that chandelier, precisely measured to be identical with the others. Fine glass strings arched down to the candle placements, and hanging beneath the frame were glass gems designed to look like emeralds, diamonds, rubies, and sapphires. *What a shame that I cannot take this with us.*

The main room of the house looked like a ballroom. Near the end of the room was a curved staircase covered by a bright red carpet. Each window in the room framed a breathtaking view of the spectacular countryside.

All pictures had been removed from the walls. The butlers and maids had made sure of that, packing them carefully for the move. Just a few steps away from the staircase stood the master bedroom, its white doors wide open. The rest of the hallway was lined with a row of doors that led to the guest rooms.

"Where are you, Constance darling?" George called.

"I am right here, George Arthur Arnold," she responded, her voice echoing from the master bedroom into the hallway.

Oh boy, something must be wrong, George thought.

He noticed her voice had changed slightly. He climbed the curved staircase and entered the master bedroom.

His eyes were graced by a lovely angel, with blond hair that hung just below her shoulder blades, with bright blue eyes and rose-pink lips set like gems in her heart-shaped face. She was pouting, but that did nothing to change his love. Beneath her lovely red corset-front dress and white petticoat, her plump belly already looked ready to explode where she carried their child. George hoped for a couple more months before she would deliver.

She stood in the middle of the room watching everyone work, trying to hide the overwhelming stress she felt over the move.

"Yes, darling?" George asked.

Her face displaying irritation, she pointed to a large, dark cherry-wood chifferobe. It was an imposing piece, with small white designs on the corner edges, a cabinet the length of a small child at the bottom, a large door on the left side sized to fit full clothing, and three cabinets split into lengths matching that of the door.

"They did not move my chifferobe down to our carriage," Constance stated, her voice stern. Her dainty heel tapped the ground repeatedly.

The whole master bedroom was stripped to almost nothing. George scanned the room to see the large bed frame, the chifferobe, and a small table where Constance kept her cosmetics, with a chair in front and a looking glass mounted behind.

"It will be taken down as soon as they get to it, dear," he attempted to reassure her.

"I want it done, and I want it done now!" she insisted petulantly. "This chifferobe has been passed down from my mother, and her mother before her."

"Yes, dear."

"It should have been one of the first few items to be packed!" she shrieked.

Constance began to weep, her emotions out of control. George came from behind to give her a hug and kiss on the cheek.

He whispered in her ear, "I'll get on it right away."

"I'm sorry." Constance continued to weep.

"It's okay. I know the last few days have been very hard for you. You know that I love you," George comforted her.

He released her from the embrace and walked to the door. A loud whistle rang out in the lobby, and everyone stopped what they were doing. George pointed to the four closest able bodies and summoned them over.

"You two." George pointed at the butlers. "I want you to get the legs of the chifferobe. And you two," he motioned to two other men, "I want you to get the top portion, please."

He paused for a second. "Be careful with it, or Mrs. Arnold will not let me live to see another day," he said with an anxious frown.

"Right away, sir," the butlers responded in unison.

What a stressful day.

Nearly all the belongings had been moved to the carriages outside, and George let out a big sigh of relief. He returned to the master bedroom and announced, "Constance, we should get ready to leave. Everything is almost done."

"Alright, dear, I will see you in the carriage," she replied on her way to the door.

She kissed George's cheek before descending the stairs and going outside.

He watched Constance take her necessities and disappear from view. Then, he performed one last check of each room to make certain nothing was left behind, and closed each door for the last time.

As he descended the stairs and entered the main lobby, the memories came rushing back. He smiled, recalling all the good and bad times they'd shared in that house.

I am going to miss this place.

As George closed the very last door, he thought he heard the echoing voice of the house itself calling out to him. He took a deep breath, knowing that some of the memories would fade over time, and took a step toward his next destination.

The sun rose higher in the sky, its bright rays now producing an unforgiving heat that added difficulty to their tireless work. George began to break a sweat, drops rolling down his forehead as he made his way down to the stone pathway.

The neighbor came to the fence to greet him.

"Good day, George," the man was dressed in a formal black suit and tie, sporting gray hair and a monocle.

"Good day, Francis," George replied.

"Finally leaving?" Francis questioned.

"Yes, we're finally leaving."

"You've been talking about it for quite some time now."

"Yes, we have. We're finally committing to it," George affirmed, pulling a handkerchief from his pocket to wipe away the sweat rolling down his face.

"Where are you headed?" Francis inquired.

"We are going to Massachusetts," George stated.

"Why Massachusetts?"

"They have one of the best doctors there for when my wife gives birth to our child. Not only that, but we will also be able to start fresh out there. We already have the majority of our belongings en route; we are just getting the last of our valuables," George explained.

"Well, have a safe trip. I wish you and Constance the best," Francis replied, extending his hand.

"Thank you," George shook the proffered hand.

Francis continued his way down the street to attend to the day's errands. One of the butlers approached.

"Please follow me," the man requested deferentially, leading George to his carriage in the front.

The butler opened the door for George to enter. He stepped in and looked up to see Constance cooling herself with a lacy fan.

"Let's start our journey," said George, taking a seat by his wife.

The butler closed the door behind him, and seconds later, a loud whip crack echoed and the carriages moved forward like a locomotive, one following the other.

A gentle breeze swept through the interior when George opened the window. Constance sat on a comfortable black cushioned leather seat, welcoming the fresh air. Both windows of the carriage were wide open, allowing them a spectacular view of the countryside.

Constance leaned over to rest on George's chest. She felt his heartbeat thump, giving her comfort.

A few hours later, Constance broke the comfortable silence: "I heard your conversation with Francis."

"Hmm?" George replied, waking up from his nap.

Doubt began to swim through her mind, pondering what the outcome might have been if they'd stayed put.

We should have stayed in Diego. "Are you sure this is the right decision for *us*?" Constance emphasized.

"Yes, darling. We agreed upon this a long time ago. Don't worry, everything will be fine," George reassured her.

"You really think it will be better for us?" she replied, rubbing her belly and feeling the baby kick.

"We are starting a new life with a new beginning, and you will have one of the best, most highly recommended doctors to deliver our child. I want our child to live more of a modest life, as we discussed, and we'll be able to enjoy the things we didn't get to do when we were in the city. I just want the best for all of us."

"Yes, I know," Constance smiled, comforted by her husband's words.

"Let's get some rest. We have another big day ahead of us tomorrow."

George noticed the sun beginning to set. He knocked on the wood of the carriage to summon attention. The butler serving as coachman turned around to see what his employer wanted.

"Make camp and have everyone rest. It will get dark soon," George instructed.

"Right away, sir," the man replied, guiding the horse off the road.

They pulled over to some open land where very little grass grew, not too far from the roadway. George closed the windows of the carriage. Outside was a view of miles of vast plain lit by the last rays of the setting sun.

The butler opened the door for George to exit the carriage. He stepped down, stretching as his feet touched the ground. He watched the other carriages slowly make their way behind the lead carriage, parking side by side, one after another. Constance, on the other hand, remained seated until all the preparations were complete with their tent.

Without needing direction from George, every butler and maid began to gather wood to make a fire, took food from storage to cook dinner, pitched tents for the night, and brought personal items out make Constance comfortable. The last bit of sunlight began to disappear in the west, remnants of yellow and orange gleaming from the horizon.

A few servants unloaded tents from the storage carriage and began to assemble them. One by one, the structures rose up around camp. Afterward, they placed a few pieces furniture in the tents for better comfort.

Constance accepted help exiting the carriage, walked out, and stood next to George. She watched everyone work like bees, though she felt a little restless and fatigued herself from the journey.

"See, darling, this is not so bad," George reassured her.

"I hope you're right," she replied, slipping an arm around his waist.

"In a few more weeks, we will be in our new home, enjoying everything we did before, plus a new bundle of joy. Life will be easy," he responded, as they watched the maid preparing food over the fire.

A butler approached and addressed them, "Mr. and Mrs. Arnold, your room is ready."

"Thank you," George replied.

Bowing, the butler took his leave.

"Maybe you should get some rest, Constance. I will bring your supper when it is ready. Our travel has been long," George said solicitously, embracing his wife and caressing her pregnant belly.

"Alright, I will wait. Just please don't take too long. I know how you are," she responded, then followed the butler to their tent.

Darkness consumed the land as the stars danced in the sky, and the crescent moon dimly lit the earth below. The smell of wood burning brought back memories. George thought back to his days of camping with his father and brothers. They'd hunted early in the morning, and cooked their kill in the evening as their father told stories.

The delicious aroma of meat sizzling over the fire interrupted George's reverie. His stomach growled like that of a ravening beast. Then the cook cut the first slab of meat, placed it on a plate, added condiments, and finally handed it over to George.

Handing the plate of food to a nearby maid, he said, "Take this to Constance, and tell her that I will be there shortly."

"Yes, Sir," she replied, taking the plate from George and disappearing into the night away from the fire.

After everyone had received a plate of food, they all gathered around the campfire, which burned brightly and cheerfully in the darkness.

"George, tell us a story," a servant asked as they sat around of the campfire. The others nodded in agreement.

"I cannot. Constance is waiting for me. She will be angry if I keep her waiting for too long," George demurred.

"Aw," they grumbled. "Just for a few minutes?"

"Hmm . . . What kind of story would you like?" he asked.

"Anything," answered a maid.

Chuckling, George searched his mind for something to tell them. "Hmm." George pondered. *What kind of story should I tell them?* "I will tell you a story. But I will have to break it down into episodes so I don't get into trouble with the Missus. Fair deal?"

"Alright," some replied while others nodded.

"This is a story my father used to tell me when I was younger and we used to go camping all the time."

"Ahem," George cleared his throat, preparing to tell the story.

"When you see lightning in the sky, either cloudy or clear, it is not just the lightning that you think it is. It is rather the clash of gods that makes the dancing sparks in the sky. Thunder is the sound of them fighting amongst each other.

A long, long time ago, there was peace throughout the sky. All lived together in harmony. There was no Heaven, and there was no Hell. They walked amongst each other in a time of calm. Everyone was happy. Some refer these inhabitants of the heavens as gods or angels," George began, looking around the campfire.

"Everyone knows how Earth was created, right?" George asked as he looked around to see everyone's answer.

The crowd surrounding him slowly nodded their heads in affirmation. A few shook their heads in disagreement.

"Well, to sum it all up in a short, simple way for those who do not know, the world was created in six days, and on the seventh day, the Creator took a break.

Mankind was tainted with sin early on by a serpent. It convinced the humans to do something that they were not supposed to do; to eat the apple from the forbidden garden. From then on, the humans were banished from paradise. The Creator condemned his cherished angel by clipping his wings, sending him to spend the rest of his days in Hell. Devastated by grief, the Creator disappeared without saying a word.

The other gods heard about his disappearance and the creation he had left. With each passing day, temptation overtook them all. The gods decided to take action.

There was a room where the Creator had left his work. In the middle of that room, the gods converged upon the creation called "Earth." Arguments burst out like wildfire. Not one agreed with what the other had to say, and no one would back down. Anger filled the air like a poison as they all claimed the right to rule over this creation."

"Was there a war?" one of the butlers asked.

"In time, my friend, in time," George responded.

He continued from where he'd left off: "The argument continued, as it seemed, for a lifetime. One of the gods in the back, not really into the argument, decided to take charge another way. He summoned his legion of angels. In a swift and cunning fashion, he dashed through the crowd surrounding Earth and plunged in with his followers behind him.

They were all struck with shock, each and every god, and they all took action. Instead of arguing, the rest of the gods called upon their followers. They rushed and scrambled to chase the first god, and just like that, they were free-falling in the sky. Falling faster and faster down to Earth, the gods and angels took flight. Through the clouds they flew, chasing one another.

As he landed on top of the clouds, the first god to touch down on the cloud warned his followers, "Prepare for battle. They will be here soon." They watched the sky above, and saw the others flying, descending from the cloud cover, speeding down toward them.

The angels who chased the first god passed the front line. Suddenly, in the blink of an eye, the angels in the front row grabbed the flying angels' ankles and drew their blades. In a flash, it was all over. As they slid their blades behind their foes' backs, cutting off their wings, the sound of thunder rumbled in the air for the first time. The rest of the attacking angels retreated back to their gods.

As the angels who lost their wings fell from the sky, spiraling down to Earth, a flash of light followed them all the way to the ground. That was how the first war on earth began," said George.

"Is there more to the story?" asked the maid sitting across from George.

"There is," he responded, getting up from the campfire. "But I will have to tell it another time, unfortunately. It is getting dark, and I am sure Mrs. Arnold is wondering why it is taking me so long to finish supper. Maybe she thinks I got lost."

Laughter filled the air after George's comment.

"I will leave you with this for the night. My father told me that, when lightning touches the ground, a fallen angel will live amongst us for the rest of his days, becoming a mortal, waiting for the day he can return to heaven and join God," George finished, taking his leave from the campfire and walking back to the tent he shared with his wife.

As George entered the tent, she announced, "Well, that was a long dinner."

Constance gave George a glare that would have frightened death itself. The dim flame of the candle gave enough light to reveal it. He walked across a red vintage carpet with black designs of animals in a forest, and to the bed where she lay.

"I am sorry, my love. They asked me to tell them a story and I got a little carried away with it. Maybe you can join us the next time, when I tell them the rest of the story," George suggested.

"Which one?" she asked.

"The war of the gods," he answered.

"You know I love that *story*."

"I know; I should have told you, I am sorry."

The dry air inside the tent did not help. Constance's temper flashed from anger to sadness in the blink of an eye. An eerie feeling of unease pervaded the atmosphere, and she started to cry.

Turning over in the bed, she cried, "You are supposed to be here with me." She wept aloud.

After taking off his clothes and putting on some pajamas, he laid right behind her, giving her the needed comfort, holding her tightly.

"I am sorry, Constance. You're right," George responded, caressing her arm softly. He leaned over to wipe away her tears and kissed her on the cheek. "Everything is going to be okay. Tomorrow is another big day."

CHAPTER 14
—A New Life

In the thick, gloomy darkness, the sound of a familiar whistle pierced the air, contagious, like a viral sickness.

"NO, NO, NOOOOOOO!" Rowland screamed, opening his eyes. Light came bursting through, like the refraction through a prism. He blinked a few times to clear his vision, looking around hesitantly, waiting for the scene to reveal itself.

He could remember the smiles on the family's faces when they left the merchant's shop, and the footfalls of his mother's heels and his father's shoes. The night loomed as they traversed the empty alley and the houses looked gray in the dark, such that he could not remember the structures properly.

Though he tried to banish this memory, it continued to haunt him. He remembered looking down at the ground, at the sight of his parents' lifeless bodies lying together, surrounded by a pool of blood.

"Come here, little boy," one of the muggers cried, his voice ragged and low. The other mugger cackled like a hyena as he stood over the corpses.

The weight of the world crashed down on Rowland. Fear, panic, and uncertainty swirled through his mind, and his knees buckled under him. The blood splashed on his knees as they hit the ground; the warm liquid sickened him. The horrible hyena laugh continued in the background. Rowland watched the mugger in front creep closer and closer. Fear and anxiety began to build like stone walls within his body.

"You are next, little boy," the mugger grinned nastily, his voice much louder than before

Darkness swallowed Rowland up, and everything around him disappeared. The moment he stood, the scene around him vanished. Beginning his free fall to nothingness, he screamed at the top of his lungs, not knowing when he would crash to the ground. The shakiness in mid-air made him feel queasy.

A distant voice rang out: "Wake up. Wake up!"

Rowland took a big breath, inhaling as deeply as he could, and opened his eyes to the sight of the ceiling above and the priest who had opened the door to him that day in the rain.

"Had a bad dream, I presume," said the priest, a cheerful older man with salt-and-pepper hair atop an oval face, pale and wrinkled with age. His dark brown eyes shone with compassion.

Rowland nodded, clearing his vision.

"Sorry for my horrible manners the other day. I forgot to introduce myself. I am Father Jean," he continued, sitting beside Rowland on the bed.

The boy stayed still in bed, staring at the ceiling, trying to forget the dream. His short hair was tousled from rough sleep, and he had an absent look, as though his mind was far away.

"Everything will be alright," Father Jean said reassuringly, patting Rowland's head. "Soon those memories will fade away, and new ones will grow. You will be a stronger person because of this. You will understand, one day."

Tears filled Rowland's eyes and spilled down the sides of his face. He wiped away the moisture, and Father Jean gently lifted him to sit upright. He rubbed the child's back comfortingly, just as a father would.

"Everything is going to be alright," Father Jean repeated.

Rowland could not recall the chain of events, but felt paralyzed. All he knew now were restless days, sleepless nights, and the fear of those nightmares.

"Let me show you around, for starters," Father Jean suggested, getting up from the bed.

The living hall was empty, with no other children in sight. Rowland turned over on his side, to see rows and rows of beds lined up one after another. Rays of light came through the window, and smoke from the candle wicks swirled in the air. The condensation on the glass spread prism-like colors throughout the room.

Rowland placed his feet on the cold, hard wooden floor before putting on his shoes. A different sensation permeated his body, but he could not put the words together to describe it. Father Jean held out his hand for Rowland to hold. As the boy reached for the priest's hand, a familiar voice sounded in his thoughts.

"Hey there, Row." Gerard's voice spoke in his mind. It was so vivid and real that Rowland turned around to face the sound, so sure that his father had come to get him. A quick flash of a vision that resembled his father passed by Rowland and continued on to the door.

"Let's go to the market," he said.

Rowland rubbed his eyes, blinking to make sure it was not a figment of his imagination. He smiled and started toward the door, ignoring Father Jean's hand.

"Father!" Rowland shouted, running to the door.

The priest followed the child slowly. Rowland's vision of his father disappeared at the door. Sadness again filled the air, like a plague, suffocating the life around him.

"In time," Father Jean said, standing behind Rowland once more. "Life sometimes takes you on an unexpected journey. There are things that you are destined to do and others, well . . . you choose them. Everyone is destined for great things, no matter how big or small."

Father Jean turned the doorknob and slowly opened the door, which creaked loudly. The brisk air sent shivers down Rowland's spine and raised goosebumps on his skin as the wind seeped in.

Father Jean took his first step out onto the shaded pathway, where the air felt wintry and the sun could not bring enough warmth.

"Today feels a little chilly," said the priest, taking a deep breath of the cold air. They walked through the shade into the sunlight, which finally began to warm their skin.

Rowland stared at the green grass on both sides of the walkway ahead. He followed Father Jean closely, just a few feet behind him.

The path split into two directions, and Father Jean spoke. "Over there. That is where we first met, remember?"

He pointed to the right, indicating a cathedral three stories tall with crenelated walls, windows on each story, and crosses at the edges of the structure.

It was a lovely spectacle from a distance, and even more so up close, with or-
nate designs engraved into the walls

"That's our church," Father Jean announced, stopping in the middle of
the road to show Rowland the area. "Wait 'til you see the inside. It's like something made by angels."

The young boy's eyes followed where the priest's hand pointed, his eyes
widening to admire the building. Rowland smiled.

Father Jean turned back around to face another building that looked similar, but with less embellishment, though it stood just as tall as the cathedral.
He continued, "This is your sleeping quarters. You will be living with others
who are like you in a way. They will be your brothers, as you will be to them."

For the last time, the priest turned around once more to the path. He held
out his hand, leaving the invitation for Rowland to decide for himself. Without
hesitation, the boy reached out and took the proffered hand.

"Let's continue our little tour," said Father Jean, smiling down at the boy.
As they continued on the path, Rowland saw a circle of tall, majestic trees surrounding the center of the area.

"This is the courtyard," Father Jean explained.

A small grass field lay hidden within the trees, with a fountain in the middle. There were a few stone seats here and there, but the main seats were
around the fountain. Rowland looked back and forth, searching for anything
interesting in the courtyard.

"This is where you will spend time between your studies during
school, and have lunch and recreation with your brothers. You will also
see some of us praying or taking a leisurely walk just to pass the time,"
the priest continued.

At the fountain, Father Jean looked to the left and pointed. "Behind those
trees to the left are the rectory and convent, the sleeping quarters for all the
priests and nuns. One day, when you are older, you will be sleeping there in
your own room, doing the same things I do, or something even better."

"Lastly . . ." Father Jean took a breath and tugged gently at Rowland's
hand, prompting him to walk again.

At the far side of the courtyard, past the wall of trees, stood a small stone-
walled school. The windows were the same shape as those of the church.

"This is where you will be going to school during the day. Your new brothers will help you to be in class on time," he continued.

Glancing at the building, Rowland stood right behind the priest, trying to stay hidden from any watchful eyes from the class windows.

Father Jean turned the corner and continued to the right, following the tall trees.

"There might be some things that I have forgotten to tell you about your duties and your household chores. Your brothers will be able to tell you and help you out when they are all home with you."

As they walked back around the loop that encircled the courtyard, the church reappeared in sight. With every step they took, the building seemed to grow bigger and taller.

"On weekends, you will be here in church for Mass and Sunday Bible classes. In a few years, you will learn to be an altar boy and help the priest during Mass. In a few days, we will baptize you, but as always, one thing at a time," Father Jean opened the door, waiting for Rowland to enter first.

CHAPTER 15
—How We Got Here

"Mr. and Mrs. Arnold," a maid called from outside the tent, "it's time for us to leave. We have a long day's worth of travel ahead of us."

"Alright, we're coming out," George replied.

"Mhmmmmmmmm," Constance sighed aloud, stretching her limbs in bed alongside George.

They opened their eyes and stared up at the top of the tent. Husband and wife breathed quietly next to each other, not wanting to get up, but knowing what needed to be done.

Constance broke the silence. "I cannot believe how quickly and suddenly our lives have changed."

"I can hardly believe it either," George replied, sitting upright in bed. "We should get going. We don't want to hold up the others." He stood up from the bed, gathered his clothing from the floor, and handed Constance a fresh dress that had been left on the night table for her.

George exited the tent once he was properly clothed and felt the arid heat already taking hold of the morning. The sunrise brought a heatwave, normal for a desert day. There was no breeze or any breath of cool air throughout the vast land. Sweat began to break out on his forehead and back. He looked around at the servants removing the tents and putting them away, back into the carriages.

Moments later, Constance stepped out of the tent, wearing a white dress and carrying her hand fan. In response to the heat, she opened the fan with a flick of her wrist. The maids and butlers soon dismantled the last tent once she'd taken a few steps away, and stowed everything into the last carriage.

"Everyone is ready to leave, Mr. Arnold," the head butler announced.

"Let's go before this heat gives me a shower I do not want," George smiled with that remark. Constance led the way to the carriage in the front.

"Mrs. Arnold," a butler was waiting at the carriage door to help her in.

He opened the door the moment she was near, holding his hand out to assist. Constance took a step up into the carriage.

"Thank you kindly," she entered the carriage.

Shortly after, George followed and the door was closed behind them.

They listened to the sound of footsteps climbing above after they were seated. A couple of quick thuds sounded, the carriage rocked, and then there was silence when the butler took the driver's seat and grasped the reins. With a quick, thunderous crack of the whip, the horses trotted forward.

A slight jerk rattled the carriage, rocking George and Constance back and forth inside, like birds in a cage shaken by the wind. One by one, the other carriages followed the leading carriage, adopting the same pace.

George positioned himself at an angle so Constance could lay her head on his chest. She gazed up into her husband's face, admiring his features from the close angle.

"I remember it all," said George.

"Remember what?" she responded.

"Oh, it's nothing," he replied, trying to brush off her curiosity.

Constance gave him a glare never to be reckoned with. "Do not hide anything from me," she demanded irritably.

George responded, "I was just thinking . . . If not for those guys at the pub that day, we would not be here doing this now."

"Yes, you know, who would have thought all this could have happened?" Constance answered. "Well, you can tell me everything; it will kill some time."

"Yes, you're right," he replied. "Where do I begin? Ah!"

The sky was blanketed with gray clouds. Fog hovered above the ground inland and over the bay as rain slowly drizzled down. The wind moaned softly, pushing and pulling the rain from side to side. Buildings made of stone stood along the side of the road, each one a different color from the others. Candles or lanterns shone from each building to show that businesses were still open.

"Visibility was a problem that day, if I remember correctly, a severe problem, at that. We were walking together, doing some last-minute errands, and our stomachs were growling, as we have not eaten yet. With the last few coins we had left, we decided to walk into the corner tavern called the Oyster," George reminisced.

"Oh, I remember that tavern. They had an imitation pearl hanging from the window curtains, and an oyster painted on the glass," Constance chimed in.

"Yes, that's the one." He kissed her forehead.

George opened the door, and the din of bar chatter hit him like a wave crashing upon sand. The owner welcomed George and Constance at the door with a cheerful, "Welcome to the Oyster!"

The tavern was dimly lit. Along the left side, the bar was packed with people sitting on stools, enjoying themselves, drinking the night away. Behind the bartender, the wall was lined with beer and liquors. A server stood ready to dispense more alcohol. Round tables of light wood and comfortable chairs filled the center of the room, where people gathered to talk amongst each other. Booths were set on the right side, running along the entire wall.

"I remember it was hard just to talk to you. It was so noisy. You could hear other people trying to talk louder than the others, unable to hear their own conversation. The whole place was crowded, but we managed to find an open booth at the very end, where we decided to sit," George continued.

"Yes. I remember glancing over to the bartender, seeing him signal the waitress to us. He nodded to our location while talking with the people he was busy serving," Constance added.

The waitress, a fair young lady with brown eyes set in a freckled face and sandy hair, rushed over to the couple's booth. Her plain brown dress and apron swished with her rapid steps.

"I got the feeling that the waitress didn't want to be there," George noted. "She looked like she'd had a long, hard shift. I am pretty sure she just wanted the day to be over."

"I could understand why," Constance sympathized. "Not only was it very busy, but also, the people were very loud and rude. Most of them were surely drunk."

George chuckled. "I don't even remember what we ordered that day."

Pushing herself up from her husband's chest, Constance got up and moved to the end of the seat.

"Well, I remember that day like it was yesterday. Or were you paying so much attention to the waitress that you forgot what you were eating?" Constance teased.

"You have always had an amazing memory, darling, and I wouldn't dare. You know I'm absent-minded to begin with," George placated her.

"Mhmmmmm." Constance's expression was rather smug.

"Well, let us continue, shall we?" George asked.

His wife nodded in agreement.

The candle in the center of the table flickered, casting pools of light and shadow.

The waitress stood before their booth, doing her best to put on a warm, welcoming smile. "How can I help you folks today?"

"What dish is popular here?" Constance asked, seeking a suggestion.

"Well . . . everyone likes our steak, or the lobster."

While his wife made up her mind, George went ahead and ordered, "I would like steak, bread, and some whiskey."

"And for you, madam?" the waitress prompted Constance.

"I would like the same, but with wine rather than whiskey."

"Coming right up!"

The waitress was efficient, even if tired. She committed their order to memory on her way to the kitchen. A moment later she returned to the booth with a cup of whiskey and a glass of wine, and set them in the center of the table.

"Enjoy. Your food will be here shortly."

A conversation near their booth caught George's attention. At the closest round table sat a group of men who obviously weren't locals, chattering amongst each other. They were wearing strange attire, and their faces were grimy, so that their eyes shone startlingly against the dirt.

"I hear there is money to be made out in the west, where the New World is," said the foreigner with a pipe in his mouth. With every word, it seemed the pipe might fall from his lips.

"The New World?" a top-hatted man inquired.

"Yes!" the mustached foreigner replied enthusiastically.

The man with the pipe elaborated. "I hear of people heading out west to the New World, acquiring riches that people have never seen before. There is a nickname for those who strike it rich out there: 'the golden blood.'"

The waitress returned to George and Constance's booth with a plate heaped with food in each hand. She set the meals before them. "Enjoy your food, and if you need me, please let the bartender know, and I will be here shortly."

"Thank you," George responded as they watched her walk away.

Turning to look at the table of travelers next to them, George asked, "And how do you get lucky?"

The foreigners turned to see who'd asked the question. George and Constance sat at their booth, cutting into juicy steaks.

"Sorry for interrupting. I could not help but overhear your conversation. But how *do* you get that lucky?" George asked again.

"I heard that a ship is leaving to the New World in the next three days, taking as many people as it can carry. I also hear that the price of passage will include provisions the whole way as well, room and board," the mustached traveler replied.

"I heard the same thing," the pipe smoker added.

"I am sure that there will be a big group of people saying their farewells to family and friends," the first speaker predicted.

"Is the ship coming back?" George leaned in to catch every word.

"No, lad, this ship goes one way. So, if you do decide to make this trip, think long and hard," answered the smoker.

"I think they have no hope for those traveling to the New World," the man with the hat surmised.

"I think so too," the man with the pipe answered.

"Where do we find this ship?" George asked.

"The port just outside here," the mustached man responded

"Are ya thinking about going on this trip, young lad?" the traveler with the hat asked.

"Thinking about it," George responded.

"I would not go if I were you. A lot of false hope, if I say so myself. They are probably shipping you to your death," the man replied.

"You never know . . . You might get lucky, though," the man with the mustache interjected.

"We'll consider it. Thank you," said George, wrapping up the exchange.

Turning back around in their chairs, the foreigners began to mutter amongst each other once more. Their conversation blended into the general hubbub of the tavern.

On the spur of the moment, George asked his wife, "What do you think? Should we try this out? Move to the New World and hope to strike it rich?"

She looked up, swallowing her mouthful of food, and thought intently about what he'd said.

"We have friends and family here, and we are doing just fine as we are now," she reminded him.

"We could always do better. Remember, we are not doing so fine at all; we are living from job to job just to survive. I would like the change, and I hope that we can find a better opportunity in the New World . . . but we will only do it if you agree."

"Well, let me think about it."

"Hmm? I think we have nothing to lose, if that is what you are worried about," George insisted. "Or . . . do you have a third?" he smirked mischievously.

"You are so dumb," Constance smiled.

"We should get going. I'm full; you too?"

"Yep, that's how it all started," said George.

He reached across the carriage seat to hold Constance's hand.

"Those were the days. It was a tough decision. I don't know how you managed to convinced me," Constance replied, stroking the back of George's hand with her thumb.

"Well, it turned out to be a good decision. We don't have to worry like we did back then. If we had stayed in England, we would still have been doing the same old things to fend for ourselves," he responded.

"You could be right, but I know that you would still have found a better paying job if we stayed," she suggested.

"There were no good jobs available in the first place, at the time. You remember, we argued a lot over it for the next three days."

"That's not the point, eventually you would have gotten one . . . sooner or later."

"True."

"Stop veering off topic and continue the story," Constance demanded.

"Okay . . . alright, darling," George answered.

The call of seagulls echoed throughout the port while the sun shone down through breaks in the gray cloud cover. Some of the birds were wheeling around, like a hawk homing in on its prey. Others scavenged the wooden docks, hoping that passersby would drop morsels of food on the ground.

Groups of people swarmed the wooden walkway like schools of fish. Bells sang out from the sides of the ships as men yelled at the top of their lungs, "All aboard!" as they made ready to set sail.

"We're late!" Constance shouted at the top of her lungs, speed-walking to the port.

Behind her, George shouldered all their luggage. He glanced up at the sun to guess the time, and replied, "It's not noon yet. We still have some time."

"We need to move faster," she insisted, picking up speed.

"Well . . . If you could just help me out with the luggage, then I can move a little faster," George pointed out.

"Ha, ha. Very funny, sweetheart," Constance turned and glared at her husband. "Which dock are we going to?"

"It is the dock with the most people surrounding it," he sarcastically replied in kind.

"No . . . Really?" she answered, slightly annoyed.

"From what everyone has been saying, it is Dock Three. Just up ahead a little."

The closer they came to the ship, the bigger the crowd grew.

"See, it's the ship with the most people around it," George jibed.

"Well, if you didn't notice, the other docks had quite a crowd as well," Constance stated, looking over her shoulder at the docks they'd passed.

People walked to and fro, slipping past each other like grains of sand drifting through an endless desert. They moved with care, trying not to bump each other.

From the middle of the crowd, a woman's voice yelled, "Constance! George!" The shout was barely audible over the din of the crowd.

Husband and wife looked toward the center of the crowded walkway, filtering out the passersby, searching for the familiar voice that called out their names. Again, the voice shouted out, "Constance! George!" as they inched their way closer to the middle and closer to the ship.

"Ah! There you are! I am glad that we caught you in time before you went in," the woman said.

"Mother!" Constance cried, surprised.

Constance's mother was a middle-aged woman, clothed in a brown dress with white threading, a hat covering most of her blond hair.

Pausing for a second, Constance slowly looked up into her mother's blue eyes and asked, "Where is Fa . . ."

Before she could finish her sentence, her father appeared, smiling at her, from the crowd; a blond, bearded man clad in a black suit and a top hat.

"Father!" Constance said.

"Guess who we found on our way here?" said Constance's mother. Her tone unnerved Constance slightly.

"I don't know," Constance replied.

"Mother! Father!" George blurted out from over Constance's shoulder.

"Ah, we could not miss this important day," George's mother said, trying her best to hold back tears.

"It's not an important day," George replied.

"Well, to us it is… We won't get the chance to see the both of you ever again," Constance's mother responded forlornly.

"Don't say that, mother," Constance replied. Her eyes began filling with tears as she came to the realization that it could possibly be the last time they saw each other.

"Don't worry, we will come back to visit. That's a promise," George reassured them.

"Don't go doing anything reckless, you hear?" admonished George's father.

"Yes, I know, father," he answered.

"The road ahead of you is going to be long and tough. Just make sure to take care of each other. You won't have anyone to fall back on besides each other," Constance's father cautioned them.

The ship's bell rang once, and the captain bellowed out to the crowd, "ALL ABOARD!"

The people said their final goodbyes to their loved ones, kissing and hugging one another.

"Well, it's time, Constance," said George. He hoisted their luggage off the ground. Winding their way through the crowd, people began to line up on the gangway in single file.

"We will try to keep in touch with you as much as we can," Constance assured their anxious parents.

After giving their last-second hugs to their parents, the pair walked up the gangway and onto the ship, and then made an immediate turn to the port side to catch a last glimpse of the town and family they were leaving behind. Bells rang again on the ship as the crew dropped its sail and pulled the anchor from the sea.

That was the last time *The Fair Lady* docked in port. Constance and George searched the crowd for their parents' faces and waved goodbye to them.

"That was the last time we saw our parents," George reminisced.

"Yes. . . Are you going to keep the promise you made that day?" Constance asked, suddenly feeling a pang of nostalgia.

"Yes, I plan to, after our first child is born," George replied.

A loud cracking echoed across the plain, like a huge tree snapping. Constance was startled. "What was that noise?"

"I'm pretty sure it's nothing. Maybe we ran over something," George responded calmly.

Seconds later, another loud cracking noise echoed, amplified inside the confines of the carriage. Screams sounded outside, and they heard a shout: "Whoa!"

As the couple looked at each other, startled, the carriage fell from underneath them. It dropped straight to the ground, leaving them suspended in the air for a moment. They came crashing down into their seats a second later.

"Ouch!" Constance yelped as her body struck the seat.

"Are you alright, darling?" George checked in with his wife. "Well, that was something!"

"Yes, I'm fine," she replied, nervously rubbing her plump belly.

George smiled, reassured, and opened the carriage door for their exit.

The butlers ran to the carriage to make sure the Arnolds weren't injured. "Mr. and Mrs. Arnold! Is everything fine? Are you hurt?"

"No, no, no. Everything is fine. Just a big bump in the road, I guess," George laughed it off, still unaware of the actual problem.

"What happened?" Constance asked.

"Well, the first loud noise was when the carriage ran over something. It was either a big rock in the ground or a tree trunk that cracked the wheel on the back-right side. Then, the back wheels gave out, and pieces of wood flew everywhere. What should we do now, Mr. Arnold?" asked the butler.

George surveyed the damage, noting with dismay the broken pieces of wood spread across the road. "Do we have any spare wheels to replace the ones we have lost?" George asked.

"No, Sir, we don't have a spare," The butler called back after checking the other carriages.

Hmmmmm. Okay . . . George thought. Assessing the situation, he selected the first two butlers in front of him. "Jonathan and Frederick."

"Yes, Mr. Arnold?" they replied together.

"Take one of the carriages back to town and stock up on provisions and supplies so we can continue our journey."

"Mr. Arnold, we might need some wheels from the other carriages in case we break down as well," Jonathan suggested.

"Just take what you need and we will replace it when you bring back more supplies," George responded.

"Yes, sir," the two butlers responded, and made their way to the last carriage in the line.

"Tell the others that we will set up camp here for the next couple of days, so they can bring back the supplies to us."

"Right away," said Frederick.

The scorching heat of the sun baked the land below. It began to descend from its apex and was moving west when the tents began to rise from the ground. Shadows fell across some of the area as the Arnolds' servants worked tirelessly setting up the area around them, collecting wood from the ground and harvesting limbs from nearby trees until the sunset.

The sky soon filled with shining stars, sparkling cheerfully as the crescent moon smiled down with the brightest of light. A reddish orange with a hint of yellow glow filled the air as a fire being fueled by the gathered tree branches.

They all surrounded the campfire once again. The servants sat side by side, holding their plates of food on their laps. This time, Constance sat beside George, near the campfire.

One of the butlers spoke out: "Will you continue the story you were telling us earlier, Mr. Arnold?" The others nodded their heads in agreement.

"Where were we last time?" George asked.

"You stopped at the beginning of the battle when some of the angels lost their wings and fell from the sky," a maid responded.

"Oh, that's right," said George. "Well. Let's continue."

"For the first time, a flash of lightning danced in the sky. The lightning guided the fallen angel's descent safely down to earth. The flash of light having come and gone, the fallen angel laid there unconscious. More were soon to follow. Loud clashes continued to roar in the sky. The clouds began to thicken and darken from white to dark charcoal gray, rolling like an ocean of dust in the wind. Perspiration from the angels seeped down into the clouds below, and thunder rumbled uneasily beneath their feet.

Friction from the angels' movements stirred the clouds, causing light to glow and scatter far and wide within the deep gray darkness. Adrenaline surged and spread among the group like wildfire, and a sense of unease pervaded them as they waited for the next move to be played like a chess match.

The sound of thunder rumbled louder and louder within the dark abyss of clouds. Lightning danced inside, and finally another bolt lanced down towards the earth as the first rain began falling to the ground.

Unspoken words began to fuel the fire within the assembled angels. Everyone for themselves, they thought amongst one another. One of the angels, enraged by the fall of his comrade, dashed to the angel who had sliced off his comrade's wings, and the battle began for the second time.

This time, anger was their friend, dancing along with them, helping them swing the sword at their foes who had once been their friends. It gave them strength for combat as they forgot the civility of everyone once living together, walking side by side.

The sound of steel clashed across the battlefield like an open symphony, with the screams of angels roaring in anger. Slowly, one by one, angels lost their wings in battle, and the lightning storm sent them down to earth, scattering them across."

"Who wins this war?" one of the maids questioned.

George smiled before answering. "There is no end to this war."

"Look up at the sky. It is always storming somewhere. My father used to say, 'If you see lightning touch the ground, you might be lucky enough to see the fallen angel.' And as for those angels, they will always roam the earth, looking up to the sky and waiting to join their friends in combat, always waiting for their time to return," he continued.

George stood and stretched, feeling stiff after having sat for so long. "Well, that will conclude the night," he said as he extended a helping hand for Constance to rise as well.

During the walk back to their tent, Constance began to stagger, her legs buckling underneath her. George caught Constance, lifting her up, and asked, "Is everything alright?"

"Yes . . . Everything is fine, but the baby is kicking much more than usual," Constance responded calmly, trying not to show her anxiety for her unborn child.

Getting down on his knees, George rubbed her belly, and spoke softly to the bulge. "Don't go beating up on your mother."

After a moment, he stood up and opened tent flap for his wife to enter.

As Constance passed by George, she admitted, "I hope those two hurry back . . . I cannot wait a couple more days."

Looking up into the dark sky filled with stars that sparkled and gleamed like scattered glitter across a vast canvas, George thought, *Oh, Lord help us...*

CHAPTER 16
—THE FIRST

A loud sound thundered inside the room as the fire danced in a pit large enough to be an asteroid crater. The room filled with gloom and fear as though millions of people suffered throughout the ages inside. Other than the sound of the raging fire cracking from time to time, the room was silent, still as though it were empty. The Master, a man of angelic aspect, rose from his throne and walked a few flights of steps, silently passing the sleeping hounds.

The Master examined the columns, admiring the history that each one had created through the ages for him, and stopped at the pillar in front, wondering when the next chosen one would come.

The first column caught his attention as he slowly strolled by. "Ah," he said.

As he looked over the carvings in the column, he frowned slightly. *Chike, the Goliath, my very first reaper*. The memory was still fresh, as though it had been only yesterday.

EGYPT, 2605 B.C.

It's so bright.

Chike was no ordinary man; those who stood beside him would be dwarfed by his stature and powerful build. Some called him a monster; others called him a god. His head was bald, but his eyebrows were dark brown, contrasting with the light brown eyes set in his square face. His golden-brown skin, covered only by a black silk loincloth, looked like perfect camouflage for the sand.

Chike looked over the city from the west balcony of the room where he slept at night. The sky had no friends out that day, no clouds for the sun to hide behind; just the clear, light-blue ocean above. An arid heat lingered, scorching the land with no end in sight and no breeze to cool down. However, a sure sight of relief finally came when the sun began to set on the horizon.

He watched the sunset until it was engulfed by the sands, then returned inside. As he trod the light granite hallway, his sandals kissed the floor, clapping with every touch. Nearing the skylight, he slightly ducked his head as he passed beneath the archway, something that no normal man would have found necessary. Seconds later, he untied the rope holding the noren on each side of the doorway so that the dark linen covered the room for privacy.

Finally . . . end of day. He yawned like a tired lion, loud and fierce. Stiff and achy from his guard duty all day, he knelt down to unlace his sandals. The room was bare, with a large round bed that barely fit his size. A few steps away from the large bed was the small entrance to the balcony, its door a small rectangle meant for smaller people, but he made do.

A dim light shone underneath the open door with its curtains that hung, shining, like speckled stardust in the dark. This night there was no wind. The day had been stale and arid.

"Sleep." He spoke softly.

Indeed, sleep took him the moment he collapsed onto the bed, regardless of the lack of a breeze which usually sent him to sleep.

Moments later, though, the air did move, creeping in from the balcony, dancing and swirling around the room with no discernible source. A small shadow figure that followed the wind from the outside entered the giant's room.

An uncomfortable, dark, eerie feeling suddenly filled the room. The atmosphere was now gloomy and cold. The giant tossed and turned as though in the throes of a nightmare, drenched with sweat from head to toe.

Distraught, Chike woke from his short-lived slumber. He tried to scan the room, but it was utterly dark. Still, he felt the presence of someone lurking.

"Who . . . are . . . you?" he called haltingly into the darkness.

In response, a voice rang from the corner of the room. "My Master is interested in you. I am his acolyte and servant. Chike, son of Khaldun, I am here to help you," the man's raspy voice continued. His eyes gleamed with a dim light.

Adjusting to the darkness, the giant sat up from his bed and replied, "No . . . Need . . . Help."

"Is that what you want? Or is that what someone wanted from you?" the acolyte questioned.

Those words struck a chord from memories past. "Hmph," Chike grunted.

WHERE IT ALL BEGAN—EGYPT, 2603 B.C.

The last of the light faded on the horizon and the stars slowly revealed themselves, one by one, as the bright blue sky changed to a sea of dark pearl. A crescent moon smiled a bitter bright red color, different from other nights.

A large camp stood in the middle of a sea of sand, where tents dotted the land as far as the eye could see, the horses and other animals locked in their stables for the night. Torches had been stuck in the ground at intervals to illuminate the outside perimeter of the camp, and a few sentries stood like statues at their posts, looking out into the abyss of darkness.

Loud hooves trampled the sand, making their way to the camp. The two sentries lucky enough to be posted there heard the sound and held their spears a little tighter, preparing for the worst. Adrenaline coursed through their veins in the face of uncertainty.

Louder and louder the hoofbeats came, accompanied by heavy breath. On arrival, the shadowy rider pulled the reins for the horse to stop. The two guards quickly dropped their weapons and hastened to their comrade. The scout bobbled back and forth on top of his mount as though drunk.

"Help him off!" one of the guards yelled.

They rushed to unsaddle the wounded man. Blood trickled down his side like a river, flowing from shoulder to leg.

"What happened out there?" the other guard asked.

"I—I—I—I cannot b-be-believe it!" The scout replied in shock. His eyes rolled around wildly.

The guard grabbed the scout's face and shook him back to reality.

"What happened out there?"

The scout's eyes looked up to the stars, which appeared to wheel above him. Concentration was difficult after such heavy loss of blood. Finally, he noticed the others standing with watchful eyes, waiting for news, like hounds sniffing for a scent.

The guard watching over the injured scout barked orders for the other: "Go to the infirmary and get a healer, then go to general Anthony's tent and have him come and see this."

"Right away," the other guard rushed off.

In an instant, he was gone, lost in the field of tents and other soldiers, who had heard the commotion and were starting to gather like bees buzzing around their hive. Little by little, an audience grew. Soon, the healers arrived with a stretcher, and the general tailed them right behind.

"It happened so fast . . ." the scout managed, finally gathering himself.

A pain shot through the scout's missing arm. His face was white from blood loss. His heavy breathing brought another rush of adrenaline, and he tried to gather himself with his little remaining energy.

"We were dispatched south," he continued.

The guard stopped him. "We?"

"Yes, there were two of us. Another scout was with me. We were several leagues south, near a wide river. Our horses needed water and nourishment for the journey back. At the riverbank, we saw a fair-looking woman. We thought our eyes were playing tricks on us."

The guard listened to the scout's tale, thinking, *What is wrong with this guy? Is he truly in his right mind, or is he hallucinating?*

Another sharp pain struck the scout like a bolt of lightning. He clenched his jaw against the pain and continued his tale.

"We happened to come across this woman. She was washing clothing in the water. We both were quite taken back by her beauty, but the woman did not see us. We tried to get her attention. I don't know . . ." He paused for a second. "We kept trying to attract her attention. And then . . ."

EARLIER

The golden yellow desert stretched out for miles like an endless ocean of sand. A light breeze could be felt only at the edge of the water. A woman was at the riverbank, her sandals covered by the water as she worked. She had a basket of dirty clothes nearby, and was washing them in the river. An exotic beauty, she had golden brown skin, flowing dark brown locks, and large, clear hazel eyes above regally high cheekbones.

She hummed a melody softly to herself. Knowing that her children waited for her at home, she tried to work as quickly as possible. In her reverie, she did not hear the men coming from the north.

The two guards were desperate for relief, ecstatic at the sight of real water and not just a mirage. They felt the cool breeze and imagined themselves enjoying the water with every movement forward. At last, the two horses plunged into the water, splashing loudly. The cool water thrown up into the men's faces was a wonderful blast of refreshment.

They dismounted from their horses and crashed blissfully into the water. Relief washed through their bodies with a cool rush. Playing in the water like children, splashing around, they enjoyed the moment.

Water trickled down the soldiers' faces as they circled around, scanning the surroundings. One man walked closer to nudge his comrade's arm, and pointed to the woman, who was gathering the rest of her clothing.

"Well, well. What do we have here?" he pointed excitedly at the beauty before them.

Both men grinned from ear to ear, lusting after the stunning woman. They rushed over to her, hoping that she, too, was not a mirage. Sloshing through the water, they hastened to the edge of the riverbed where the water was knee deep.

"Well, hello there," one scout began in as seductive a voice as he could manage.

"What kind of shit is that?" the other mocked.

She looked over briefly, saw the men, and chose to ignore them and finish her work. She gathered the rest of the clean clothing and started to wade back out of the river, showing no interest in them.

"Watch this," said the other scout. He thumped his partner on the chest and bolted off to intercept the lady.

"Maybe I can help you," the scout winked.

The woman looked up, confused, not understanding the language. She gave the man a brief glance of distaste and walked around him.

Scattered clouds rolled across the sun, forming a cool cover against the heat. Chike, dressed in loose silk clothing and sandals, was focused on his journey to the river. As he departed the large clay hut, it faded away behind him with every step forward.

"I will be by the north part of the river if you need me," Chike's mother, Safiya, had reminded him.

I have to talk to mother.

Safiya leaned her head down and tried to avoid any eye contact, walking around the curiously dressed foreigners. The soldier in front persisted, getting increasingly aggressive over time. The flirtatious voice and polite facade were discarded as he became more forceful.

"Look at this bitch!" he yelled. "This whore does not understand what the fuck I want!" His patience had thoroughly dissolved.

"Yeah! Maybe she does not like your type!" the other scout yelled back, following up with laughter.

"Shut up!"

With this, the atmosphere changed a bit. Sensing danger, the woman picked up her pace, passing the soldier on the side. Water sloshed around her legs.

"If she is not in a giving mood, I will do what I do best. I will take what is now going to be mine!" The scout retorted.

As she passed by the soldier, a sigh of relief passed through her. She felt that the danger was past when she set her feet back on land. However, she was caught off guard when the man's hand shot out and grabbed her. Her basket fell back into the water and she wound up trapped in his arm. Her face registered disgust as she glared at the man and pushed against him, trying to get free.

The scout did not like that one bit. A loud slap echoed when he backhanded the woman, hard enough that her body splashed back into the water. He grabbed her once more, lifted her up, and dragged her along.

Safiya was dazed, but still tried to fight him off. Trying to wiggle free, she slapped and punched at her assailant.

"This one is feisty," the scout grinned.

Moving back and forth almost like a dance in the water, she finally wiggled free from the man's grasp, falling back into the river. He continued the struggle, reached for her clothing and, with a sudden jerk, ripped the silk from her skin, exposing her breast. The tension inside the man's trousers increased; his lustful thoughts were his main priority.

Safiya shrieked in desperation. Then, from the side, she saw a hand come at her fast, too fast for her to dodge. Another slap in the face and she went crashing into the water once more. Stunned, she caressed the stinging skin with her hand.

The grin on the soldier's face was almost psychotic as he stared at the woman's buttocks. He grabbed a thick hank of her hair with one hand to make sure she wasn't drowning. Getting ready to mount her, he grabbed the rest of the silk dress and ripped it from her body. By way of showing off, he made a provocative gesture, thrusting his hips into her repeatedly like he was fucking her. Raunchy laughter filled the air as both soldiers enjoyed the moment.

"Why not fuck her and get it done already?" the other scout commented crassly.

"Oh, I want to enjoy every single moment with this fucking whore," he replied, his features twisted in a cruel leer.

The aggressor began to loosen the rope that served as his belt, and raised his left hand. He was ready to smack the woman and claim her as his prize.

The scout watching from afar widened his eyes in surprise as he spied another man on the scene.

How did this man appear out of nowhere?

With a loud splash the giant entered the water, looming over the man who was ready to mount his mother. The other scout tried to alert his partner, but could only point, as the words died in his throat.

Feeling a sudden jerk on his left arm, the would-be assailant looked over his shoulder to see a huge man towering over him, face full of rage and anger. All of his enjoyment disappeared instantly, replaced by fear of what might happen next.

"Chike! No!" Safiya screamed.

Another jerk to that arm, and the soldier felt a sharp spike of intense pain as Chike yanked it from its socket. The giant held the severed arm aloft like a trophy. Blood rushed out like a red waterfall. The mutilated soldier screeched and howled in pain as tremors of agony shook his body.

Chike dropped the useless limb into the water and grabbed the man by the shoulders, ripping through his armor like disposable scrap metal, and tossed him a few yards inland.

The soldier choked for air as he thudded on the hard ground and began to go into shock.

Safiya inched closer to the basket of clothing and continued to plead, "Chike, stop!"

Fury and rage boiled through Chike's mind. *How dare that fool take advantage of his mother?* He had never felt so intense a sensation. The wrath was addictive, indescribable. His adrenaline rose to a new high, even more than when he hunted dangerous beasts.

Unsheathing his sword from its scabbard, the remaining soldier ran to his comrade's attacker, splashing water with every step, winding up the sword with both hands. In a blink, he was within striking distance. He shouted a battle cry and slashed at his foe.

With one hand Chike blocked the attack, grabbing the hilt of the sword. The man quickly released the hilt with one hand as the giant's enormous mitt ensnared the sword. Chike tightened his grasp on the hilt, crushing the scout's remaining hand.

"AAAAAH!" He shrieked in pain.

The scout felt the bones of his hands snapping, and experienced the desperation of life and death. Emboldened by terror, with his free hand he launched an assault on the giant with rapid blows to the head.

This cannot be happening . . . Kill or be killed. I need to destroy this monster.

Barely budging under the hail of blows, Chike finally noticed what may as well have been someone tickling his head. He grabbed the man's other arm and hoisted the soldier up like a rag doll over his head.

The terrified scout knew that his life was about to end, and kicked repeatedly at the giant in an effort to escape. The last thing the man saw was the giant's grinning face. He screamed, "N-Noooooooooo!"

The cry went quickly to a wordless shriek as the giant separated the man's arms from the shoulders, tearing them off one after the other. Blood spilled into the water once more, painting the river red. The mangled man splashed down into the river in complete and utter shock, no longer registering the pain, no feeling whatsoever.

The scout lying in the sand came back to reality, grunting. "Ugh."

At first, he didn't notice the pain, too traumatized to recall immediately what had happened just a moment ago. As he lay still upon the sand, the sun continued to beat down on his face. The burning sensation of his skin drying and cracking in the heat finally got his attention. As he stood up, he felt the sharp pain throbbing in his shoulder once more as the adrenaline high of the fight wore off. His missing arm was like a phantom, agony pulsing from the torn shoulder as if it were still there. His sight blurred, and the landscape rushed all around him as though spinning in a tornado.

The image became clearer and clearer as he remembered that he had been tossed from the river. He saw the giant looming over someone, and the woman standing naked, and pleading and watching in fear.

Where is my partner? The scout hoped for the best, yet knew the worst was inevitable.

Chike continued the assault, making sure his enemy could not escape. His countenance was radiant with pleasure. Using every bit of strength, punching away, the soldier's skull cracked and shattered into pieces inside the man's skin, finally flattening like a pancake. Sweet, sweet joy lit up Chike's face with a devious grin, which his horrified mother had never seen before.

The scout heard the crack of his companion's bones, and terror overtook him, as he realized that he could've been the one taking that fatal beating.

Fuck . . . I know he is dead. I have to go before this monster comes after me.

Running and stumbling over his own feet on the desert sand, he cowered away from the giant and fled to his horse, splashing water everywhere as he mounted awkwardly. Blood spilled down his side. It was increasingly difficult to maintain focus. He kicked the horse's sides and turned north, rushing back to camp.

Safiya watched the soldier escaping in the distance, quickly vanishing farther and farther from sight until only sand and hoof-prints remained. She walked the few short steps to her son, her legs slow and heavy and wanting to buckle beneath her. She felt pity for the poor soul Chike had butchered, who now looked like gelatin covered in skin. Still, the giant continued pounding the corpse.

She reached out and grabbed Chike's shoulder.

"Son. Please stop."

He raised his hands for the last time and finally stopped. His mother's voice finally penetrated his thick skull, like a tidal wave splashing back down onto water and earth. The former innocence of his face returned.

Looking upon his mother, Chike asked, "Are you hurt?"

"Not as much as you did to the two who hurt me," she replied.

He grabbed a garment from the basket, squeezed it dry, and handed it to Safiya. She wore the wet garment without any complaints, extended a hand for the giant to hold, and together, they walked out of the river.

"No one hurts mother," said Chike.

It took a while for her to respond. "I know son, I know." She could feel something brewing in the near future.

"Careful! Careful!" said the healer. They laid the injured soldier on the stretcher.

"This giant had the strength of a god . . . A god, I tell you! A god," the scout insisted before fainting from his injury.

"Make way! Make way!" the healer called, trying to force his way through the crowd to the infirmary.

"General!" came a voice from behind them.

"Captain?" replied General Anthony.

"Do you think what he said is true?" the captain speculated on the account he'd been given.

"Tomorrow! Get some rest. We will march south and find this man with the strength of a god," the general ordered.

A swift gust swept across the sand like a large serpent upon the sand dunes. The unrelenting sun hung above at its peak, baking the earth like a kiln.

There, a small village of indigenous people lived near the river, secluded from the rest of the world. The only noise came from a group of young children splashing water in the river, chasing each other around and around while the village elders tended their crops and kept a watchful eye on the children at the edge of the water. One hut in the village stood out from the rest, double the size of the others, closer to the river than the rest.

Inside the large clay hut that towered above the others, darkness ruled. The only light shone in from a crack in the wall and through the window. Inside, the house was cooler than the scalding outdoors. Footprints were scattered upon the sand.

At the edge of the room, a gazelle fur lay on the ground, where Safiya sat, patiently weaving another wooden basket in which to carry fish. She tested the top to make sure the flap opened and closed. The curtain hung over the door fluttered open as Chike entered.

"Chike," she called.

"Yes, mother," he answered, as he carried in a freshly killed gazelle slung over his shoulder.

Safiya inspected the dead animal cautiously, inch by inch. She gazed upon the dead animal as though it were a crime scene.

"I see no wounds. How did you kill this animal?" she inquired.

He looked down at his bare hands, raising them so she could see, as he smiled like a little child with a new toy. Safiya cast him a disappointed gaze as she stood up. Slightly abashed, he bent down her height, and she carefully caressed his face with both hands.

"You know you are not supposed to use your gift like that," she admonished him.

He lowered his head a little further, knowing that he had not pleased his mother with his actions.

"You should have used a spear like everyone else. The villagers showed you how to use it," she continued.

"That is not fun," Chike replied.

"Yes, I know it is not fun, but with your gift in the wrong hands, the gods only know what might happen," she retorted.

"Yes, mother."

Kissing his forehead, she explained, "One day you will understand . . . You are meant to do greater things in life. Now, hurry along and get your brother and sister. They should be playing by the river with the other children. It will be dark soon."

"Alright," he replied, laying the animal carcass on the floor and turning to leave.

The sound of a thousand men marching together shook the desert sands, all treading as one, like a beating heart. The light reflected from the sand blinded them as if they were staring into the sun itself. Waves of heat radiated around the mobile army. The general's horse neighed nearby and trotted past the foot soldiers.

This had better not be a waste of my time, looking for this so-called god. We are going to be delayed a few days by this nonsense, he thought.

"General." The captain trailed behind.

"Captain."

Taking a deep breath, the captain stated, "We are close." This brought a subtle change in the atmosphere.

"Send the scouts ahead to find this god-like man or the village he lives in. We march through the night. Come morning, we will have this so-called god."

"General," the captain bowed his head and disappeared among the other soldiers.

Lying on top of the soft animal skin, Safiya slept uneasily, tossing and turning throughout the night. Sweat ran down her exposed skin with every turn. She panted heavily in the throes of a terrible nightmare.

Suddenly, she awoke. *Was this all a dream?*

"Is everything okay? I heard you talking in your sleep," Chike inquired softly, careful not to wake his siblings.

"Yes, dear, it was only a bad dream," she replied.

The thought of what had happened a few days ago kept replaying in her mind. She wished it had all been just a horrid dream that she could snap out of. She wondered if there was anything that she could have done differently. But . . . *What is done is done.*

The hair on the back of Safiya's neck rose as a blast of cool air swept through the window, sending a chill through her body.

"Chike," she shivered and caressed her arms, trying to give herself some warmth against the goose bumps that covered her skin. Her stomach churned as though someone was pulling it from the inside, toying with it. Sharp pains throbbed throughout her body, and the throbbing in her head made her feel nauseated. *Something is not right.*

"Yes, mother?" Chike replied.

Words tumbled around in her mind. It was hard for her to articulate this.

"I need you to do something for me."

"Mother?" he questioned.

"You must trust your mother and do as I say," she responded, waiting for his reply.

Chike nodded in agreement.

This is sudden, so unlike Mother . . .

"The village could use some food for the night. While you were away, they wanted me to ask you. Can you do some hunting for them?"

"Yes, I will do it."

Standing up brought a rush of blood to Safiya's head, and she felt faint and dizzy. She stumbled and lost her footing, staggering to the door as though drunk. At the entrance, she picked up a spear that lay on the ground and handed it to her son with a smile.

"Remember what I told you; be home before dark."

Chike leaned down to open the wooden door. His footsteps were the only sound at the brink of dawn. The desert sand shifted under the young man's weight as he slowly padded away from his home. Safiya silently listened to her son's retreating footfalls, still feeling perturbed.

The sun hung directly overhead, surrounded by clouds. At times they provided shade; at other times they parted, allowing the heat to bake the earth below. The men at arms watched the shimmer of heat rising from the ground. Thousands of men marching together made the sands quiver like a distant earthquake.

A scout came rushing back at top speed, returning from reconnaissance. He moved to the front where the general led the army.

"Did you find anything?" General Anthony asked.

"A small village lies ahead, General," the scout replied.

"How many?"

"No more than a hundred, sir."

"Any fighters?" the general inquired.

"From what I have seen, there were just elders, women, and children. No giant, sir. My guess is that the men of the village went on a hunting party. I saw very few men, no warriors in sight," the scout replied.

"Captain!" General Anthony summoned.

Following close behind his ranking officer, the captain whipped his reins, speeding the horse to catch up to his superior.

"General," the captain responded sternly.

This is our chance to seize this opportunity, General Anthony thought.

"I want our best riders to come with me and raid the village. Capture those who do not resist and take them for trade. For those who try to escape, kill them on sight," the general ordered.

Nodding his head in acknowledgment, the captain answered, "Yes, sir," and backed away.

The day dragged on and the sun began its descent in the west. It was just another day in the small village as the children continued to chase each other around the huts. Some of the elders talked amongst themselves, as usual, while keeping an eye on the children.

The cold feeling still lingered in the hut although it was a bright day outdoors.

"Just another day," Safiya quietly whispered in an effort to reassure herself.

Not once had she left the confines of her home. She lay atop the animal skin, staring up at the ceiling.

Why do I still have this strange feeling that something is going to happen? That disturbing feeling lingered as though someone were watching her. Anxiety was her companion, huddling around her, trying to suffocate the space. A distinct sound became loud and clear as she laid her ear upon the ground.

"Why is the earth rumbling?" she asked herself, trying to figure out what was going on.

Quickly, Safiya went to the door and looked in the direction the sound had come from. A yellowish-gray dust cloud rose from the earth to the sky, like smoke from a wildfire. The rumbling roared louder and louder as a cloud in the distance took form.

Some of the children continued to play, while others stopped to see what was coming. It seemed as though time had stopped. A small horde of men mounted on horses came charging in, disrupting the peace of the little village.

The men and women harvesting crops near the river came rushing back into town as a horseman appeared from their rear. One of the soldiers threw a spear, which stuck in a villager's back. The old man grunted weakly and fell lifeless into the river, staining the water red.

Terror spread swiftly; the village stirred like an angry beehive. One by one the people scattered, running from left to right and right to left, not one following another. The children of the village were paralyzed with terror. Their bodies knew nothing but to assume the fetal position in reaction to the nightmare scene. The Greek soldiers' bloodlust grew as, one by one, they struck down the panicking villagers.

The cries of women and children drowned out all other sounds. The villagers were gathered in the center of the village. Like cattle, they were inferior in strength to their predators.

One soldier bore a torch. Its flames danced from side to side, seemingly eager to touch and catch upon something. Suddenly, the soldier reached out the torch and lit the outer houses, which were made of wood. Within seconds, the homes were engulfed in a towering inferno that reached towards the sky. The people inside screamed and shrieked as they burst, running, out of the doors.

One by one, each house went up in flames, and more and more of the villagers were herded together at the center. Some of the last of few were stragglers; some came willingly and some resisted. The soldiers inspected the clay huts to make none was left untouched.

Some of the villagers who resisted paid with their lives. Those who were unwilling to move were beaten and tossed into the crowd. The wailing and crying of the children was subsumed in the roaring and crackling of the flames.

My lucky day! Chike thought. He crept behind a gazelle that was drinking water from the river a couple of leagues south of the village. A few hundred meters away, the giant inched closer and closer to the animal. He spun the shaft of the spear in his hand, twirling the point of the blade.

The gazelle trotted a bit to the north, scanning the area alertly. Chike stopped when he felt the distance was right. In one fluid motion, he stopped spinning the spear, unwound, and flung the weapon ahead. The spear flew through the air in a shallow arc. It quickly covered the distance and punched through its target, piercing through the skin, shattering bones, and tearing muscle.

The weapon passed straight through the gazelle and splashed down in the river. The gazelle immediately dropped to the ground, twitching in its death throes.

Chike's excess energy dissipated upon seeing the dead gazelle on the ground. He let out a big sigh of relief and walked past the carcass in search of the spear. When he did not see it on land, he checked the clear waters of the river, and found it there.

When he'd retrieved his weapon, Chike returned to the carcass and grabbed up the animal by the legs. The last of the dark blood oozed out from the open wounds, dripping onto the golden sand. He then carried the dead gazelle upon his shoulders, looking straight ahead into the ocean of shimmering sand and blue sky where they met together at the horizon.

A plume of smoke wavered up, like a black serpent reaching for the sun. *Home*, he thought, watching the smoke ahead. Without thinking, Chike broke into a run, heading toward the black smoke.

"I must hurry home. Mother . . . brother . . . sister . . ." Chike uttered.

The weeping and crying of the villagers intensified. The fire consuming the village diminished, with nothing more to burn. General Anthony trotted on his horse to the crowd, and then dismounted, making his presence known.

The people tried to calm one another, and the cries of grief slowly quieted down, aside from the occasional weeping of children. The soldiers began to surround the villagers, like vultures circling a dead body.

The general scanned through the villagers, searching for the person who had injured one of his men and killed another. It was to no avail, as that man was not present. He saw only elderly men, women, and children.

He is not here. How do I provoke someone who is not here? Maybe he is hiding somewhere nearby.

"There is a man. . ." He paused. *Maybe . . . Possibly, one of them speaks our tongue.*

One after the other, the captured villagers looked up to see the man speaking before them, but they could not comprehend a single word.

"There is a man amongst you who killed one of my soldiers and severely injured another," continued the general as he looked around, searching every face for the potential superhuman. "Speak now and save the people around you."

A moment of silence lingered, for the villagers did not understand a word this foreigner was saying. The crying came to an end, and the villagers looked to the ground for solace. Afraid of what might happen, they all stayed quiet and tried to keep calm for fear of watching others die in front of them.

"Very well then . . . Have it your way," the general announced to the captives.

Walking away from the villagers, General Anthony's captain came from the rear and asked, "You think one of them knows who we are looking for?"

"I am certain that one of them knows. They are not willing to talk. We have our ways for that," the general replied with a sadistic grin.

"They might not know our tongue," the captain reminded his superior.

"If that is the case, then I want you to interrogate a few of them and see if they get the picture. If they don't speak our tongue, make an example of a few of them and take the rest as slaves," General Anthony commanded.

"General!" the captain responded obediently. He nodded his head in affirmation and parted ways, walking back to the captives.

"I know that he is out there somewhere." *I must be missing something . . . What did the soldier say again? Think, think, damn it.*

The captain commanded, "Grab one of the captives."

"Captain!" the nearest soldier answered, and roughly jerked an elderly man away from the group. Cries sounded within the crowd, as they feared for the elder.

The captain looked at another soldier and directed, "Hold him down."

A second soldier stood on the other side of the captive, ready for the next order.

I hope the general is right, the captain thought, almost doubting him.

"Bring me my weapons," he ordered. A soldier brought a variety of weapons to showcase for the captain. From knives to whips and other torture items, his selections were vast. *I need to set an example.*

"Ah. This is the one that I wanted." He smiled deviously.

The captain selected a whip. He grasped its leather handle, from which multiple straps hung down. Nodding his head, he signaled the two soldiers, who positioned the captive with his back to the captain. One of them tore the shirt from the man's body to expose his back.

"We are looking for a man who killed one of our scouts and injured another. Do you know of such a man around here?" the captain questioned his captive.

Silence swept the air like a killing plague. The clouds above cast a shield across the sky, blotting out the bright sunshine. No answer came from the captive's mouth. He stood there in silence, not once flinching or moving.

Stubborn old fool.

"Where are you hiding this giant?" the captain tried again.

Again, tense silence hung in the air as no one spoke a word. The captain wound his arm back and used all his strength to bring down the cruel lash upon the man's back. The leather straps descended like a flash of lightning and cracked like the sound of thunder, tearing the villager's flesh open in a raw stripe.

A stream of blood came rushing from the open wound. Keeping his dignity, the old man refrained from screaming, but the pain and shock on his face were obvious. His mouth gaped and his eyes protruded from their sockets.

The captain demanded, "Where are you hiding him?"

Another moment of silence passed as the interrogated villager again did not answer.

Maybe this person does not understand me. Why, general? Why do all of this? The captain brought the whip down a second time. The weapon hit the open wound and blazed new trails of pain as well. This time, the elder screamed in pain and agony. The women whimpered and the children cried in fear.

Reaching the edge of the village, Chike looked upon what used to be his home. All of the houses on the outer rim were burnt to the ground; dark ashes floated aimlessly through the air.

Am I dreaming? Is this really happening? Would all of this have happened if I had stayed?

The smells of death and fire permeated the gutted village. Nothing was left but a catastrophe.

Suddenly he heard the sound of a foreign tongue in the distance: "Where are you hiding him?"

For a brief moment, silence lingered in the air. Then, the clash of a whip thundered once more and the victim cried out in pain. The intervals became shorter and shorter, leaving the brutalized man little time to answer. The captain remorselessly continued whipping until the elderly man wet himself and fainted under the savage onslaught.

Strolling back from his ride, General Anthony welcomed himself back to the middle of the remains of the village, seeking an update. "Anything yet?"

"Nothing, General," the captain replied as the soldiers tossed the elderly man back into the crowd of captives.

"Well, then, continue until someone talks."

"Sir!"

The two soldiers grabbed Safiya next.

The captain remembered something from a few days ago. *The scout did mention a good-looking woman. This must be her.*

Chike sneaked in quietly, saw them seize his mother, and his heart rose into his throat. He contemplated what to do as he stepped forth out from the rising smoke and approached the crowd.

Disappointment and fear warred within Safiya as she caught sight of her son returning to the village. *You should not have come,* she wanted to scream, but instead she held her tongue.

"Ah! So, this is the man my soldier was telling us about," the general announced as he strode toward the captive the two soldiers were holding.

He certainly does look like the giant they described, but does he really have the strength?

"You should not have come back," Safiya addressed him in their native tongue.

"I rushed back because I saw smoke," Chike responded.

"Promise me this . . . whatever happens to me or any people in this village, only use your gift for a greater good."

"Sorry to break up this reunion, but I need some information," said the general.

He tore off Safiya's clothing, exposing her back, and grabbed the whip from the captain's hand. He cruelly lashed her back as she began to cry and shriek.

Chike closed his eyes, pretending not to hear his mother's suffering. *Never use the gifts that were given to you.* He remembered the last time he'd defied her words, and the repercussions that had come later. He could only think about it, trying with every ounce of will not to do anything that she would regret him doing.

"Are you the man we have been looking for?" the general roared before bringing down the whip again on the woman's body. Safiya yelped again in pain as Chike gritted his teeth, restraining himself, pretending that it wasn't his mother crying.

"Well, a little stubborn, are we?" The general declared antagonistically. Trying every way possible to provoke Chike, he finally unsheathed his dagger and held it to her throat. "Is this what you want? Do you want her to die?" he hissed, sliding the dagger through the frail skin near her throat. Blood spilled on the ground, and the answering anger in Chike's heart awoke with a vengeance.

Chike unslung the animal carcass from his shoulder and catapulted it into the group of soldiers, knocking them over like bowling pins. He charged at the killer and the group of men that stood in his path.

The men at arms held their spears, believing that their weapons would stop the angry giant in his tracks. As each spear pierced the surface of Chike's skin, their wooden shafts cracked from the force, but the formidable giant was not slowed. The soldiers were baffled. The spear points were left clinging in the thick rawhide skin of the giant, achieving no actual punctures.

Chike shoved the men aside, sending them flying, and trampled the ones in his path like a war horse. Men were flung left and right, one after another.

The general bellowed, "Attack! Keep this man alive. Do whatever it takes to subdue him. Kill off the rest of the village. They are of no use to me."

In a matter of minutes, the men, women, and children were slaughtered. Their main objective was to trap the man of godly strength. They strung arrows on their bows, shooting wildly in an attempt to slow down the monster.

Chike would grab one, sometimes two men at a time and crush their skulls together. The arrows he felt only as a pinch, but with every shot, he began to slow down. Small rivulets of blood flowed from his legs, arms, and chest.

A man came from his side and swung his morningstar, which collided with the giant's temple. He staggered under the blow, which would have been fatal to any normal human. Chike wavered back and forth before slowly regaining his bearings.

Before the attacker could act again, Chike grabbed the soldier's leg and swung him around like a rag doll, knocking down the crowd around him. When he was finished, the giant tossed him away like a broken tool and continued his way to the man who had killed his mother.

For the first time, the giant noticed his own blood. The amount of damage done to him had finally started to take a toll, but that did not matter. There was one thing and one thing only that kept him moving.

Another soldier came from Chike's blindside with a morningstar and struck his other temple, staggering the giant yet again. This time it was harder to recover. Everything seemed to become a blur. A third soldier used the blunt side of an ax and swung it hard as he could at Chike's head. The last strike finished the giant, knocking him out cold. At last, the mountain of a man collapsed to the ground.

"Bind him and put him in the cage. Take extra precautions for this man. He is our gift," ordered the general.

In two days' time, the giant returned to consciousness.

"Ugh," Chike muttered, feeling groggy.

The world was all a blur. Throbbing pain pulsed like a heartbeat all through his head. The glare of bright sunlight shone between rusted metal bars, hurting his eyes, triggering a migraine. The thump of soldiers' feet on the ground only amplified the splitting headache that crashed violently in waves through Chike's skull.

The moving prison bounced and shook on the uneven terrain. The unbearable pain continued while Chike strove to recall his mother's words. They only came as fragments, at first, like shards of a broken mirror.

Once Chike's memory of the event was fully recalled, his last vision of his mother kept replaying in his mind: Safiya sitting there helpless, being held against her will. He closed his eyes, trying to forget that moment, but it continued to repeat like a recording. *Promise me this   whatever happens to me or any people in this village, never use the gifts that were given to you.* Her words now replayed interminably in his memory.

Every time Chike blinked, the sight of his mother flashed in front of him. *I am sorry, Mother. I have failed you again.*

Kneeling in the confines of his prison, Chike was jostled as the movement shifted the cage up and down and side to side with every small bump on the desert land. Tears rolled down his face like a stream of regret. *I did not do what you told me to, and in return, your life has ended. I caused pain and suffering to others who did not deserve it. Little brother . . . Little sister . . . You wanted what was best for me and I did not heed your warnings.* His hands trembled on his thighs, shaking from the mixed emotions that surged inside.

Chike wept in silence, body shaking in small tremors. He opened his eyes to let another pool of tears escape and stream down his face. Trying to calm all his feelings, he listened to the one soothing voice he knew whispering in the back of his mind. *Everything is going to be fine.*

Chike took a deep breath, and the trembling came to a resolution. The tears disappeared quickly as they ran down his cheeks one last time. *Mother . . . I promise to never use my strength again.* Chike finally understood Safiya's warnings.

The acolyte took a step closer, revealing only a shadowy form against the darkness. "I came here for you."

Chike turned to the side of the bed, placing his feet on the ground, and faced the mysterious man.

"I . . . am happy here," he replied.

"Are you truly happy?" the acolyte questioned. His words hung in the silence.

Words did not come to Chike in the way that he thought. For once in his life, he was stumped. He was unable to reply, as the question brought doubt to his thoughts, which fought with the words he wanted to say.

Hmm. I've got him right where I want him, the acolyte thought.

After a long silence, Chike abruptly answered: "Yes."

"Do you think the people here will miss you? Hiding your strength, not being able to use it as you once did, and serving a master who does not care for you? Everyone around you cowers in fear of the person you are. My master, though, will embrace you," the acolyte stated persuasively.

"I am . . . different?" Chike asked.

"That you are. My master likes you just as you are. If you choose to come with us, you will be forever free from this place."

"No such thing as . . . freedom." *All I know is to follow orders. Freedom is a myth.*

"What about vengeance? The choice to have revenge on those who took away the life you knew. To avenge those you loved dearly, to use your strength as you see fit. You have a choice ahead of you. Tomorrow, I will return around the same time."

The dawn of a new day danced with the night, making the shadows retreat. The mysterious man vanished with the darkness, without saying another word. Chike sat at the edge of his bed, ruminating over the conversation. *Was this all a dream?* He took his sandals from the side of the bed and laced them on, just as he did every morning.

The ache in his foot still lingered, never having had the time to heal. As Chike stood up, a sharp pain spiked through his back. Limping and hobbling along, he tried not to put much pressure on his heels. He untied and opened the curtain that served as a door, and exited the room. *Another day.*

As he walked along between the palace walls, the acolyte's words kept nagging at the giant's mind. "Are you truly happy?" On most days, he would look at the hieroglyphs on the wall and admire them all the same, but not today. His thoughts were focused on the decision soon to come, as questions that had never come to mind finally surfaced.

Chike entered a large room, so grand that it made even the giant look small in comparison. Tapestries hung from the ceiling to the ground, almost kissing the floor. Several servants walked amongst the pillars that stood throughout the room, cleaning as they came and went. At the center of the ceiling was a dome, through which the sky above was visible.

Following the wall, he strode swiftly through the room, not once looking up. He approached a half-circle set of stairs where the throne sat, two servants standing silently beside it. A long, plush red carpet divided the room from the throne all the way to the entrance hall. Large rectangular windows were set in the wall, letting light in from the east. The floor shone in places, catching the light such that it looked like gold reflecting sparkles to the ceiling

Automatically, Chike bowed down at the throne, his eyes remaining downcast. The two servants giggled. He was oblivious to their laughter echoing through the hall, for he was in deep thought. Chike then stood up and made his way to the other side of the room.

I have no friends, I have no family. They were all taken away from me. I have nothing to keep me here. What should I do? His thoughts perplexed him just as the mysterious acolyte had done the previous night. In the back of his mind, the man's voice kept replaying, taunting him. "Are you truly happy?"

Chike left the main room and moved into another hallway, where he noticed the statues did not line up perfectly with each other and the wall as he remembered it. *Maybe this is the distraction that I need to keep my mind off of things.* He lifted each statue and moved them closer to the wall, one by one.

At the end of the hallway, Chike heard someone mumbling in the room ahead and decided to check on it. He poked his head into the room to see a man sitting on a ledge, peacefully watering some plants.

"Come in," the man called from inside the room.

Downstairs, green plants were all around. The walls of the room were barely visible through the forest of plants and trees. In the middle of the oasis, a large rectangular pool of clear water sparkled, the rays of sunlight transforming it into a sea of diamonds.

The man moved closer to the pool and sat, trailing his fingertips back and forth in the water.

Edging through the field of green trees, plants, and bushes, Chike finally spotted the man sitting near the pool. The man turned around to see who he'd welcomed into his sanctuary, and there Chike was, the giant, as they called him.

Chike gazed upon his master and immediately bowed down.

The Master was blessed with good looks, a man of medium build with peachy golden skin. Brown eyes gazed out from a square face, which was fully decorated with paintings that surrounded his eyes, lips, and cheeks. He wore the finest silk, a white loincloth and gold-threaded garment; gold jewelry on his fingers and wrists and ankles, and a golden necklace with the biggest emerald imaginable.

"My King," said Chike reverently.

"Come. Sit, and call me Khaba; we are not in the presence of others," said the king kindly, gesturing for Chike to take a seat and pausing for a moment to let the giant settle down. Chike sat beside the king.

"They call me the shadow king. People fear me. *My* people love me. My enemies are always a step behind me," Khaba boasted. "Do you know why they call me the shadow king?"

"I don't know, my King, I mean . . . Khaba."

"Like a shadow, I can be either your friend or your enemy. They feared what I was capable of; no one could match my strength, and my knowledge that none can measure." He shifted his position to look at the giant. "It has been a long time since you came to be in my service."

"Yes, quite . . . some time," the giant agreed.

"I remember as though it were yesterday. You were a little smaller. The Greeks came to me with you as a gift, or so they said. A gift from the gods, they boasted to me."

"I remember . . ." Chike solemnly looked down into the clear water, which returned his reflection like a mirror. His eyes shifted to the king sitting beside him.

"I never meant to take you in as I did," Khaba said. His thoughts were in disarray, words difficult to form when the servant looked up at his king, uncertain what he was trying to say.

"It is not my way to take my own people as a gift from others," the king finished those distasteful words, which left a sour taste in his mouth.

A deep breath issued from the giant as he took in the king's words.

"I am King Khaba," he thundered. "My job is to protect my people, not to take them in as servants."

"Kha . . ." Chike cut off abruptly.

"The strength of a hundred men, they had told me. It is true that you have that ungodly strength that cannot be measured by men. You are of great value to me."

Why does it seem like he is going to tell me something else very soon? Is it going to be good or bad news? Chike wondered.

"I was thinking as of late, you are one person. If I had ten strong men protecting me night and day, that would be more feasible than having only one set of eyes. I know that you can protect me from an army by yourself. As goes for food, on the other hand, you have built an appetite that could feast a party. No one in my lifetime will have strength like yours to face me." Khaba's hand splashed in the pool, making ripples in the water.

The giant cringed at the thought of the words he would hear next. The ripples glimmered and danced when he touched the water; it shone in different directions like a spinning prism. Chike waited and watched the king in puzzlement, not knowing what to expect.

"You have served me loyally for the past two years. I myself have seen you grow in that time, from a child to a grown man," King Khaba continued.

Chike's face lit up with a smile, hearing his king speak of him in such a way. *Maybe I jumped to conclusions early.*

"You came to me a slave from the Greeks. Today, you have a choice."

"Choice?"

"Yes, a choice. You can either stay and serve me, as you do now, or you may choose to leave the palace and find your happiness elsewhere. You have time to consider what you wish to do."

Those last few words triggered the same thought that had tormented the giant's mind throughout the day. It lingered, taunting him. *Are you truly happy?*

"Thank you, my King," Chike replied. He stood up from the edge of the pool. "I will . . . make my decision . . . in the near future." The giant bowed once more before taking his leave of the king and the lush garden.

Time blazed by. The sun reigned over the day at high noon, and then quickly descended to the horizon in the west. Chike wandered around for the remaining time, rambling aimlessly around the palace, thinking of the conversation with King Khaba and of the mysterious man who had visited him during the night. *I have no friends, no family.*

Chike returned to his chamber at night and continued his routine as he had done for the years he'd stayed in that very room. He untied the knot that held the curtains; they fell to brush the floor and covered the doorway. Sitting at the edge of the bed, he unlaced his sandals and got ready for sleep. As he lay down, his eyes felt heavy, as though being pulled shut. *That man will not show up*, he thought. *It was all a dream.* In a matter of minutes, the giant was sound asleep, his thoughts and worries having vanished.

The sound of laughter echoed all around. Chike opened his eyes to see a familiar place. *Home.* His smile spread from ear to ear as he beheld the children of the village surrounding him. A large fire burned in the open, where the villagers cooked the gazelle he'd killed. He circled around to view all the huts. His own hut stood closest to the river. He inhaled a lungful of air, the mixed scents of the desert and river sending tingles down his spine.

"I am so proud of you!" Safiya praised him.

"I am home," he smiled.

"You have been gone for too long, and now you have found your way back to us."

Chike lowered himself down to give his mother a hug. She patted his head like she used to, giving him the comfort he so longed for. He opened his eyes, and in the distance, he saw a man in a black, hooded cloak standing, waiting, holding an hourglass. The man pointed at the passing sands of time, indicating the need for a decision. He would have to choose.

Everything surrounding Chike began to die. The huts caught flame and fell to dust. The women, children, and elders of the village shriveled to bones, bones that piled at the center of town next to the fire. Safiya's whisper burned in his ears: "You could have saved us."

Icy shock flowed through Chike's body. He wanted no more of this dream. He looked down to his mother, and she was nothing of who he remembered. He held only a pile of bones that once resembled his mother. Then his head snapped up to the man with the hourglass, and Chike charged at him. The mysterious man only continued to point at the time, as the sand continued its countdown.

"Wait! I need more time!" the giant screamed at the top of his lungs, and the mysterious man vanished before his very eyes.

Chike woke up in the middle of the night gasping for air. Sweat drenched his face, and he wiped it away with his hand. He could feel the coolness of the moisture soaking into his bed, and the awkward feeling of someone else in the room lingered once more. *Not again . . .* This time the room felt a lot cooler than the last time, raising goosebumps on his skin.

"We meet again," the voice sang from the darkness.

As Chike's eyes began to adjust, he saw the shadow in the same corner of the room as the previous night. The giant asked, "How long . . . have you . . . been here?"

"Not too long," the acolyte responded.

"You were . . . in my dream," Chike's tone rose a little.

"A dream is only a dream. What you dream is what you want to dream about. You already know why I am here, so here I am."

"Could I . . . have a few more . . . days?" Chike asked.

"I have been waiting patiently for quite some time now."

What the hell does he mean by that? "It has only been a day."

"If you mean while you were awake, then yes, it has been a day. You have been asleep for the last three," the acolyte stated tartly. "My master still awaits your response."

It doesn't feel like I was asleep for so long. If that really happened, then why did the people not come looking for me? The giant turned these thoughts into questions, which turned to more unanswered questions. It started to sink in that he was unwanted by his current master, which was deeply depressing. *I thought I was more valuable to my king.* The pressure to make a decision was immense, like the weight of the world on his shoulders. *They will not remember me when I am gone.*

"Yes, I will come."

The Goliath . . . a man who stands alone, thought Chike's new master.

Chike descended the dragon-bone steps to meet his new master. The acolyte, all but hidden inside his black cloak, walked a few meters ahead of the giant. The bright fire in the center of the room exposed the pallor of the acolyte's face.

"Master," said the acolyte, making his way around the gaping maw of the fire pit.

Nodding his head in acknowledgment, the Master responded, "You may leave."

Walking full circle around the fire pit and back to the corridor, the acolyte disappeared from their sight. The Master rose from his throne, guarded by two now-sleeping hounds, and descended the stairs. Chike stood next to the fire pit, surveying the area. The space was empty, with no windows to provide light from outside. The only light came from the raging fire in the pit.

Looking upwards, the giant saw nothing but a black abyss. Stairs ascended through archways on the sides of the room. His eyes wandered to the two hounds, which slept soundly next to the throne.

"I have been waiting for this day to come. It is an honor," said the Master.

Chike's mind was worlds away from where his body stood. He was no longer a slave, but a freeman with decisions to make. Snapping out of his trance, he felt as though he were back in the palace where he once lived. With the feeling of unease all around, the eerie mood was almost suffocating. He looked to his side, where his new master stood next to him. Chike towered over the man, as an adult would over a child.

"I know what you want," the Master said cunningly.

The giant watched the Master intently, curiosity plain on his face.

"Look into the fire and tell me what you see."

Chike stared into the blazing fire, watching the shifting shapes of flame.

"Nothing."

"Look a little harder. Focus."

Chike squinted again into the shimmering heat and dancing flames, where the image of a familiar face now appeared. The giant's countenance turned sour with anger and loathing. His hands balled into fists, fueled by rage.

"Yes, he is still alive. While you lived like a slave, he roamed his town like a god. A hero, from what they say; considered to have conquered lands with help from your former master, King Khaba."

Pent-up fury roiled within the giant; it was the image of General Anthony he saw in the flames. He turned away from the fire, disgusted by the sight. That was the man who had changed his life forever. Chike turned to leave.

"Wait a second," the Master stopped him.

The Master snapped his fingers, summoning the cloaked acolyte back down the stair sand through the corridor. The acolyte arrived carrying a large blood-red pillow, upon which a shiny piece of metal gleamed in the dancing firelight.

Lifting the weapon from the pillow by its handle, the Master presented it to Chike. "Consider this ax an extension of yourself."

Chike carefully examined the masterpiece that would soon be his. As he studied the end of the double-edged ax, he noticed a small gap at the top.

The Master continued, "This is no normal ax. Turn the bottom of the handle and it will separate, making two. The chain that connects the parts is simply an extension to make it whole."

Chike spun the bottom of the handle, as his master instructed, releasing the other ax. For a while, the giant slashed the air with both axes, getting used to the subtle movements and weight.

Finally returning the weapon to its original form, the giant wondered where he would keep his new toy. Then he noticed that the ax had one more trick at his disposal. Chike turned the handle in another spot, and turned the double-edged weapon into a one-sided ax.

Carefully measuring its size, he noticed the weapon would fit perfectly on his forearm. That question was now answered. He tried it out, placing the ax on his forearm and wrapping the chain snug.

"You are ready," the Master announced, stepping back.

The Master lifted his hand, palm facing Chike. The air surrounding the giant's body began to pulsate. The gradual ripple soon became a vicious spin, like a black hole sucking matter into its vortex.

"Walk into the portal," the Master instructed. "From there, you will find what you are seeking, and you will make the choice when the time is right."

"Yes, Sir."

Chike gazed into the portal. *This is my new life.* The giant took a step into the portal, and his body disappeared, one part after the next. The portal then vanished, leaving the Master alone in the throne room.

So this is how it is done. I cannot meddle in things not involving me directly, but . . . I can get someone to do it for me. Interesting . . .

CHAPTER 17
—A PAST WORTH FORGETTING

Silence filled the room, with not a peep, not a breeze, only darkness. The arid, dry air was like the desert in its slumber. Morgana sighed deeply, breaking the silence just for a moment.

A light sparked in the center of the room, flashing bit by bit, like a miniature thunderstorm. The sparks circled in the air like stars in the night sky as they gathered together, forming a small orb. Light shone dimly from this orb, enough to form shapes of shades in the dark. At the corner of the room lay a bed, its frame made of stone, topped with a thin layer of sticks and straw. The walls shone with ice that glittered like diamonds along the corners.

Morgana took no notice of the orb that hovered over the bed. She slept peacefully, a small portion of her vayne exposed to the air as she snuggled tightly between the straw and thin blanket. She gave another deep sigh, breaking the silence again and sending a tiny current of warmth through the icy room.

A thought made the girl twitch in her sleep; the light flashed a little brighter white for a few seconds and then reverted to its original form.

"Come . . . Follow me," the acolyte ordered, pausing for only a second to look back at Morgana in her bed chamber, and then continuing on down the hallway.

Morgana quickly slid out of her bed and followed the man into the hall. She felt a change in the air, and a chill tingled down her spine. A furnace pumped scorching heat and humidity into the hallway. *That is something I will have to get used to.*

In the darkness, a small, dim light followed the acolyte as he continued down the gloomy hallway. Just a few steps behind, Morgana followed silently, listening to her own soft footfalls. A door opened with a wave of the acolyte's hand. Without a word, he walked fluidly, his movements like a dance, through the open doorway.

The door closed on its own once the girl entered. She turned and looked behind her to see if anyone was there, but no, she was alone with the acolyte.

"What are we doing today?" Morgana asked.

"You shall see soon enough, young one," the acolyte responded.

As the man lifted his hands, fire sprang to life in various parts of the room. The candles lit up, reflections glistening from the obsidian walls. In the center of the room, a little round table stood to waist height. A black cloth covered an object. The acolyte pulled the cloth aside, revealing a white moonstone as big as a grapefruit.

The acolyte took his position beside this object. "I am going to teach you how to look into the past and present," he announced.

"Why not just the future?" Morgana asked.

"The past has already happened. Actual facts and proof, things you cannot change. The present is what is happening at this point in time, and the future is always changing from one thing to another. Only fragments can only show you what you will see, but you can alter it to change its course of direction. It's never guaranteed. That, my child, is something I cannot teach."

There has to be something. There is always another way, Morgana thought.

The acolyte's hands hovered over the moonstone orb. His fingers began to massage the little sphere, and the top of his hand started to glow light blue. Morgana's eyes widened with interest.

"What is that glowing on the top of your hand?" she inquired.

"It is the gift," he replied.

A gift? she wondered. The acolyte's hand illuminated in a bright blue that filled the room and then quickly disappeared as the darkness rushed back around. She took a step forward, inspecting his hand in the candlelight.

"Are those markings?" Morgana questioned.

"They are not."

"Then what are they?"

"They are known as the vaynes of life."

Hmm . . . The vaynes of life? Morgana thought. She continued examining his hand; the tattooed marks started at his fingertips and ran all the way down his wrist.

"Life itself is an essence. Within life, you have energy, and we use that energy, to do things that you see," the acolyte continued.

"What about you?"

"We are neither living nor dead. Some people call us immortals."

"How does this all work?"

"In time, you will understand."

"Alright . . ." this was a little perplexing for her.

"The vaynes that you see on my hand show the endless years of training I have been through, studying magic as well as gaining experiences. In time, you will develop your own vayne once you acknowledge the fact that medicinal healing no longer applies. The world that you once knew will only hinder what you are going to learn. Once you let the old ways go, that will help you excel in this realm."

Morgana's blank stare told the acolyte she was trying to understand the concept, but she was still young. He knew that time and patience would be the keys.

"Think of it like this . . . In your body you have veins, and within those veins flows blood, carrying oxygen to help you function and do normal activities. Well, the veins also serve another role in your body. They also spread the energy that is needed, which we call *vayne*. Once the energy is spent, as I am doing now, it will reveal your past."

"What about the living that use this power?" Morgana asked.

"Vayne is your life force. The more you use, the quicker you age. There are some who have figured a way around it, keeping their place, as it were, but others become old and eventually die."

"Can you use spells for other things?"

"Yes, but you are not going to learn that today. You will have to wait for another day, child."

"Why does it look like an ordinary vein?"

"Essentially, they are one and the same, but they have different purposes. Do you understand?"

"I am starting to."

"Good. Well, then, let's continue."

The acolyte began to massage the moonstone orb with his fingertips again, and once more, the vaynes on his hand illuminated bright blue. Sparks and flashes within the orb swirled like particles, connecting with each other, and started to take the form of her past.

The sun overhead shone brightly that day, the sky clear with a few clouds rolling in, not once covering the sun as they slowly drifted by. Sounds of laughter filled the air as Cethin chased Illythia across the field, through the knee-high grass.

The youth's spiked platinum-blond hair danced like the coat of a wild animal as he chased his sister. She ran as though for her life, though it was all in fun. His black eyes focused on the chase like a beast hunting its prey. He enjoyed every single moment with his family.

"I'm going to get you," he prodded with a smile.

Illythia screamed, then laughed, and tried to catch her breath before screaming once more. As she turned, her dark brown locks flew in the air untamed. Without a glance back, she continued to pound through the grass and more open field. A quick blink to the sky above, and she turned once more, running back to her parents.

In the distance, Illythia spotted her mother. The orb showed a raven beauty with ebon hair, snowy skin, and jewel-like, hazel-green eyes that were made larger-looking by her small, pointed chin. Antha's slender figure, clad in white silk, was relaxed on a blanket beneath a tree. As she caught sight of her daughter, a wide, welcoming smile spread upon her face.

"I do not remember any of this in my past," Morgana stated. The vision in the orb stopped momentarily.

"This is truly your past. If you do not remember it, you probably suppressed it from memory or you were too young then to recall it now. You could always ask your brother, if you really need verification," the acolyte replied.

"Hmmph," she pouted.

"Shall we continue?" he asked.

Morgana nodded, and the acolyte continued from where they'd stopped.

"Ahahahahaha," Illythia laughed, then took a quick breath to laugh again.

Beside Antha on the blanket lay the handsome Gildas. His side-parted blond hair complimented his strong jaw, the pale hair contrasting with his tanned skin and black eyes. His white shirt matched his wife's silk garment. Gildas took notice of the child's footfalls rushing toward him. The grass parted, revealing his little angel running full tilt.

"Uh-oh," his daughter's delight changed to fear as she tripped and fell. Gildas quickly reached out and caught her, cushioning her fall like a human pillow. It would be alright. He let his daughter lie on his chest for a second to catch her breath. Antha and Gildas shared a smile.

"Tickling time!" Gildas announced.

As her parents affectionately tickled the sides of her body, the young girl began to squeal with laughter and tried to escape. Seconds later, Cethin appeared, gasping, out of breath from running. He still found the energy to join his parents in the tickle attack, and more laughter filled the air.

The particles in the moonstone orb shattered and disappeared; the picture was no more. Only fragments of Morgana's past remained for another second as the orb reverted to its normal state of clarity.

"Do you want to explore another past?" the acolyte asked.

A shiver went down Morgana's spine as she assimilated the forgotten memories.

"No. I want to know about the future," she responded.

"That is something I cannot teach you, child. Find your inner energy first, and then we will continue."

Someone has to know! she thought angrily. *If not, I will have to teach myself!*

In the darkness, Morgana saw a bright white light fall from the glittering, starry sky. She moved closer to the light as it fell, on its way to crash land on Earth. She hurried, trying to cover the distance before she lost sight of the light. Morgana came upon a campfire, where men and women huddled together by the warming flames. They laughed and talked amongst each other.

She watched the bright white light from the sky descend to touch a blonde woman, who was pregnant and ready to deliver at any minute. The pregnant woman sat in the middle of the crowd, next to a man with light brown hair and blue eyes. As Morgana watched closely, the light seemed to smile at her as it made contact with the woman. *Why did I not see this?*

Her dream faded away as quickly as it had come. The orb that had hovered over her quickly winked out into nothing. Upon waking up from her short slumber, Morgana summoned a fire, turning it into a sphere with the wave of her hand, as she sat on the side of her bed. *I must hurry.*

She summoned her cloak and jewelry with a flick of her hand. Quickly, she strode from of her room and down the corridor that led to her master's chamber. A loud creak issued from the giant mahogany double doors as they opened from the other side of the room. The doors arched perfectly below a huge dragon skull with sharp teeth. Morgana's light footsteps descended the dragon-bone steps like soft, hollow claps until she passed through and heard the massive doors behind her close.

A slight smile crossed the Master's face as he walked beside the crater of the fire pit to the open corridor. Kneeling so quietly on top of the pillow, the Demon continued his meditation, wearing only half of his dark blue hakama below the waist. His golden tanned skin crawled with souls wanting to escape, screaming in agony. He did not feel the pain, but the shadows hid his face.

The Master passed by without saying a word as the small, dark figure of an adolescent girl appeared from the corridor and proceeded to the main room. The orb that had lit her way disappeared. Her jewelry jingled as she moved, and the hem of her cloak dragged along the floor.

"What news do you bring me today?" the Master asked with a straight face, the former smile wiped away as if it had never existed.

"A child," said Morgana, pushing her hood back as she responded.

"A child?"

"Yes, another child."

"Is this another prophecy?"

"No. This one is special in itself."

She walked to the huge fire pit and waved her hands in a circular motion.

Her right hand wore a gauntlet, and the vaynes, like tree roots, followed the line of her arm to her neck, near her face. The vayne on her hand glowed a dark purple, creating a ripple above the fire. An image was displayed, as though upon a mirror, for them to see. *Who says the future could not be foretold?*

"Here is the child." Morgana pointed. The child had clear blue eyes, deep brown hair, and a cleft chin, and was slender for his size.

"What makes this child so special?" the Master asked, almost disgusted, not wanting to know anything further.

"He is still pure, although he witnessed a devastating event. Not only that, he possesses an amazing motivational drive, which might be turned in our favor," she carefully studied Rowland through the reflection.

"Keep a close watch on this child, then, and maybe he will be useful to us later."

I do not need a glass orb to foretell the future. I have devised a way to use any type of reflection to see what I need to know. Morgana waved her hands again, and the image of Rowland disappeared like dust in the wind. The ripple in the air continued to hold, and another image took form as fragments that scattered like shattered glass. The ripple started to piece the picture together, bit by bit, until it was whole.

"I have seen another vision in my slumber," Morgana added, showing the image of George and Constance.

"What of it?"

"An angel."

The Master stared at the couple in the ripple of light for a while. His eyes were afire with fury, like a laser burning through a photo. "So it has begun," he said, a touch of anger in his voice.

"Master . . . What has begun?"

A ripple of air began to dance next to Morgana, and the Master commanded, "Kill them."

CHAPTER 18
—A NEW PATH

Shooting Star could not remember the last time she felt like this, tired with muscle pain. Even her moccasins did not feel comfortable. She still wore the same clothing she'd worn while performing the ritual a couple days ago. Her eyes were weary; she'd had little sleep during her journey.

She heard the sound of flowing water nearby, covered by heavy bushes. Clouds rolled through the sky, covering the sun and slightly dimming the light. A couple of deer were grazing at the edge of the riverbank. They stopped and stared when they heard footsteps heading their way. The birds chirped loudly in the bushes, singing a melody to the beat of the healer's steps. The clear river water reflected a mirror image of the surrounding landscape, and a couple of trout raced upstream.

Shooting Star looked around, and then stepped onto the gravelly sand, where a small path led to the river. She stopped at the river's edge where the water flowed by, took off her moccasins, and placed them carefully on the ground nearby. She undressed, tossing all her clothing on top of her shoes and laying the bag nearby, then stepped into the river. The cool water raised goosebumps all over her body. Shivering a little, her body slowly adjusted to the temperature of the water.

Farther and farther she walked into the deep area, where the river was fairly still compared to the rapidly flowing water by the bank. She sunk in chest deep, splashing water on her face and washing her hair, taking her time as if it would be her last chance to bathe for a while.

A slight pain throbbed in her belly, making her grit her teeth. She felt short of breath. Sinking deeper into the water, she fought hard to keep her head afloat as the pain intensified. *Cleanse yourself.* She remembered those words and knew what the spirit had meant by them. The water quickly reddened around her body.

Shooting Star wiped the water from her eyes and looked down to pinpoint where the blood was coming from. *Oh, no.* She ached and felt something forcing its way out of her. *Is this what I think it is?* She waved her hands back and forth in an effort to clear the water, with no success. Before long, she blacked out from the pain.

Shooting Star opened her eyes and gasped for air, then scanned her surroundings. She didn't recall getting out of the water, but she was no longer in the river. Instead, she lay on the sand underneath thick brush, near the running water. *Was this a dream? Is this another test?*

She lifted her head to see if she was still naked. A sigh of relief came forth when she saw that she was fully clothed. Everything rushed back to her in that instant, and the world seemed to spin around her. It felt surreal. Exhaustion took over, and fever and chills alternated from time to time, making everything all the more difficult. Laying her head back down on the cool sand, she fell asleep the moment she closed her eyes once more.

"Hey! Get up! Rest can come later," the familiar voice heckled.

At that, a smile spread across her face before her eyes even opened. Shooting Star never thought she would hear that voice again. Upon getting up from beneath the concealing brush, she saw a man standing before her.

The man, clad in deerskin pants embroidered with a flying eagle she'd stitched for him long ago, gathered wood and set the stack right next to her. His glossy black hair brushed the golden-reddish skin of his shoulders. Black almond eyes shone above high cheekbones in his oval face, and a necklace embellished with feathers completed the picture.

"I have missed you so," Shooting Star muttered, tears filling her eyes.

"I have missed you more, my shining moon," he replied, turning around to face her.

"Soaring Eagle," she cried with delight, getting up and running toward her husband with her arms wide open. They embraced each other for quite some time, twirling around repeatedly while time seemed to stand still.

"What are you doing here?" he asked, finally allowing her feet to rest on the ground again.

"I could ask you the same question."

She hugged him again, this time a little tighter. *I wish this would never end.*

"Do not look at the river," he said.

"Why?"

"Please . . . for me."

"Alright . . ."

"You have not crossed over. Why are you here?" he inquired again.

"The Great Spirit sent me on a journey. I am fulfilling my part. Why are you here?"

"I cannot tell you. The one who sits still will understand their surroundings."

Shooting Star released him and leaned back to gaze into Soaring Eagle's face; she opened her eyes and smiled. Taking only the barest glimpse at the river, heeding his warning, she looked back to him, only to see a bare frame of bones clinging to her. They fell to the gravelly sand, and at that, she knew she was dreaming.

I must be sick with the illness, as the Great Spirit had told me. I wonder what he is trying to communicate.

Looking up from the ground, she saw Soaring Eagle again, now on the other side of the river. She ran after him, splashing into the water. The slow current did not impede her, and she was not being cautious. Stumbling on the slippery rocks below, she fell into the river. Though it looked shallow, the water was deep enough to swallow a person alive. As Shooting Star tried to come up for air, she felt something drag her down.

The surface of the water seemed like an arm's reach away, but felt more distant with each passing second. She was running out of air, and the situation was becoming dire. Her struggles were futile. Finally, closing her eyes, she had no choice but to gasp in water.

"Wake up!" Soaring Eagle shouted.

Two voices gave whimpering cries. Shooting Star remembered them. She opened her eyes to a familiar sight she knew all too well. *That day will forever haunt me.* At the center of the teepee was a small fire that kept the room warm. Yellow, red, and orange flames danced around the burning wood with pops and crackles, giving light. Helpless, she sat there next to her partner. *I paid no attention to anyone else but you.*

"Soaring Eagle was as healthy as a wild mustang just the other day," Shooting Star's mother stated.

"A possible confrontation with a neighboring tribe?" Soaring Eagle's father suggested.

"It cannot be. He has no wounds we can see," her father responded.

"Could it be poison?" his mother asked.

"That is blasphemy. Who would do such a thing?" retorted his father.

"It could be the illness that the white devils have brought along with them," Soaring Eagle's mother said.

"It could be," they all agreed.

Surrounding the fire was my family, whom I did not care about that day even though they were closest to me. The only person I really cared about was the man I loved. The words they spoke that day seemed so distant, like I was not even there to begin with, Shooting Star thought, recalling that day.

Tears filled her eyes as she thought back to that day when sadness filled her life. Hours later that night, death struck swiftly and silently. Without a sound, Soaring Eagle struggled for survival. His life ended at last while Shooting Star laid her head on top of his chest, sleeping quietly.

She screamed out loud, "Why torment me?"

"Never forget what happened," answered Soaring Eagle. "It is a memory nonetheless. It will never be forgotten."

She turned around, and that distant memory faded into darkness. He now stood in front of a carriage broken down on the side of the road with many others surrounding it. Soaring Eagle smiled at Shooting Star.

"What is this?" she asked.

"Head east, where the sun rises, and look for this. Maybe you will find happiness here. From that point, you will understand your purpose."

Soaring Eagle spoke his last words to her, and then vanished with the wind. *A gift, a gift. A gift you shall receive. From all the sorrow, you shall be born anew. Come with me, my child, for a gift you shall receive,* he whispered.

Shooting Star woke up, breathing heavily after her dream. *Head east.* Rising from the riverbank, she listened to the stream flowing. Beads of sweat ran down her face. Morning peered from the horizon lighting the land yellow, orange, and shades of red.

The cool dawn breeze dried the sweat on her brow. Plant life seemed to respond to the touch of the sunlight. The smoldering remnants of the campfire remained from the night before.

Shooting Star asked herself, *did someone really watch over me when I was sick?* As she shouldered her bag, she noticed that it was perfectly placed not too far from the fire. *Soaring Eagle?*

She rubbed her belly, and the bump of pregnancy was no longer there. *I must go . . .* she thought only of willing herself to take that first step forward.

Looking to the east, where the blazing sun blinded her and obscured her view, she spied a figure that appeared through the gaps of her fingers as she shielded her gaze from the bright light.

The shadowy figure took the shape of a person standing on the other side of the river. She wanted to scream out at the top of her lungs, "Soaring Eagle! Do not leave me, please do not leave!" only to see the figure point eastward.

Shooting Star scanned the moving river, looking for a small path where she could cross. After a few moments, she spotted a few small flat rocks just above the surface. They guided her to the other side of the river like a serpentine road. Every now and then, the glimmer of the morning sun would reflect from the water's surface, making her squint as she moved closer to land.

She looked up once more to see if the image of her husband was still there to guide her, but he had vanished once she arrived. Her mood sunk into a deeper state of depression. *I am alone.* Stopping where she thought she had seen Soaring Eagle, she took one last glimpse back at the river.

What a view. The lush green shrubs along the edge of the cliff hung over the riverbank, and tree branches hung down to weave and bob over the flowing water. Acknowledging that this view would be the last, she closed her eyes and committed it to memory.

The black blanket of darkness covered the sky with no clouds in sight, and a full moon hung all alone, giving what little light it could to the earth below. Stars slowly spread all along the dark canvas of the night sky like silver glitter. One by one they sparkled and shone, taking turns burning brighter than the others.

A campfire in the darkness flared yellow, orange, and red, flames dancing from side to side. Shooting star slept near the fire for warmth, in solitude. No longer sick, she was simply tired from her long journey. As she lay wrapped in a small blanket, the sound of insects kept her company.

Upon the cold, dry dirt, across the fire from his wife, Soaring Eagle sat. His hands reached out to the fire for warmth. He watched Shooting Star lying there, silently sleeping.

Soon, she stirred and opened her eyes to see what she had longed and yearned for since the days of her devastating loss.

"I do not want this to be the last time I see you," said Shooting Star.

"This is not the last time, my love."

The yellow and orange light of the fire danced along Soaring Eagle's tanned skin. That was all she could ask, for the moment was perfect. She took a deep breath, smelling the scents of the burning wood and the wilderness air.

She wanted to speak, but the words stopped at the tip of her tongue, so she simply lay on the ground, gazing at him across the flames. He did the same, looking at her half intently, bringing back all the cozy feelings and fond memories of what they had shared. For a moment, she was in heaven.

He pointed at her and brought his hand back to his chest, making it into a fist, then moved to the other side of the campfire and sat next to her.

Softly, he whispered into her ear, "You are never alone."

"But I am," Shooting Star replied, looking at the stars that shone coldly above.

As he grasped her hands, she felt the warmth of his body. He carefully guided her hands to her chest and spoke softly, "I am always in here. In spirit, I will always be around."

The warmth of his touch slowly vanished, and Soaring Eagle's human form disappeared from her sight. Feathers fell from the sky as she beheld him changing into an eagle, crying out and taking flight.

Her half-smile widened and tears of joy filled her eyes, blurring her vision. The world seemed to be engulfed in a haze, which slowly cleared away with every blink. Tears slowly rolled down from her eyes and behind her ears. *I am blessed . . . Thank you.*

A swift gust of wind picked up from the west and carried along to the east. As it met Shooting Star's body, the slight chill of morning rushed over her skin, sending tingles up and down her slender form. Her hair danced along with the breeze, frolicking back and forth.

Walking with the wind, she wiped away the tears from her eyes. A landscape of golden-yellow soil and sand stretched as far as the eye could see, with patches of grass and trees scattered here and there. The sun crept slowly higher and higher in the sky. Scattered white clouds appeared to stand still. *I don't know where I am going except to head east . . . I'm going to get lost.*

Perched on the lowest tree branch, a majestic bird followed her with its watchful eyes. Its feathers were white as snow on its face, then deep black down to its massive claws. It stood atop a branch, statue-like, two and a half feet tall.

Caught in between the bark of the tree branch and the massive claws of the bird was a rainbow trout, flailing from side to side as it gasped, out of its watery element. The eagle gave a roaring scream.

Shooting Star gazed thoughtfully at the bird, confused. *Is this the eagle from my dream?* She took a few steps closer, and then stopped a few meters away. The wind died down for a moment and a familiar feeling washed over her.

"Soaring Eagle?!"

Turning its head to the side and back, the eagle screamed its reply, never breaking its focus on her.

I might not be so sure now . . . The feeling is definitely there. The captured trout took its last gasp, and its flailing finally came to an end. The fish then went limp, its death throes past. The eagle grasped the trout in its talons and took flight, screeching, descending to the woman who stood watching.

Shooting Star was definitely hungry, as her rumbling stomach reminded her. The eagle swooped closer, and she lifted her hands and blinked reflexively, unsure what to expect. The mighty bird released the trout and let it fall into her raised hands. She felt the slick skin of the fish in her hands and opened her eyes to see the bird, wings outstretched, lowering itself to perch on her shoulder. The eagle gave another cry.

Maybe this is my gift.

Fire is what I need. Shooting Star's stomach grumbled again, louder this time. The sun hung high above the land, the near lack of shadows indicating noon. She paced the area, gathering fallen branches for a cooking fire. The eagle took flight from her shoulder, soaring back high in the sky but staying close enough to remain visible.

She found shade beneath a tree. A small circle lacked grass, as though someone had already been there. A man-made fire pit stood ready, rimmed by large, gray-blue rocks. Charred firewood from previous use lay within the circle, a brittle pile of black, white and silver.

Hmm. Someone has been here. Oh, well, it will be easier for me.

Shooting Star piled the wood she'd gathered on top of the old charcoal. Sliding the straps of her bag from her shoulders, she eased it to the ground, near the fire. After placing the dead trout on a convenient stone, she looked into her bag and chose an arrowhead, a small line of rope, and a thin stick with a pointed end, and laid these next to the fish. Still . . . *I am missing something.* She sifted through her bag again and located a small rock with an indentation in the center. *Yes!*

A cry sounded from above. She looked to the sky again to see the eagle wheeling above in a wide circle. After a while, the majestic bird broke its pattern and flew west. *I wonder where it's going.*

Arranging the wood in the pit, Shooting Star selected an arched branch in the shape of a small bow. After checking the strength of the branch, she secured the rope to it and tied a knot on one side. She then tied the other side snugly and strung the cord a few times. After laying the dry tinder on top of the branches, she picked up the small rock and the thin pointed stick to start a fire.

Friction from the stick spinning quickly on the tinder created a gray cloud of smoke. A thin line of smoke began to dance up and over her shoulder. Sparks began to dance within the tinder, ready to ignite at any minute.

Shooting Star suddenly stopped and lifted her equipment up, near her face, to kindle the spark. As she lightly blew a couple of breaths onto the spark, it burned brighter and brighter. Suddenly, the spark flared into fire and started to burn the tinder and wood. The scent of wood smoke now hung in the air.

Next, Shooting Star took up the arrowhead that lay on top of the rock next to the fish. Holding the trout's tail, she made an incision down the belly and gutted it. Blood splashed to the ground below, followed by the innards. She then began to filet the meat.

The eagle glided effortlessly in the ocean of blue sky above. Looking down below, it found what it sought. In the middle of the river was a calm spot that split the path of the clear rushing water. Near the surface, a large fish hovered lazily in the middle, flapping one fin, then the other.

Looping in a large circle, the eagle began its descent, slowly making its way to the river. Following the flow of water downstream, the eagle weaved a little to the left and a little to the right, trying to center itself. The eagle's powerful claws opened the moment it neared its prey splashing in the water. The bird snatched the fish from its element, then flapped its wings ferociously, trying to gain altitude as its talons clawed through the skin and bone of the fish.

Flailing furiously, the fish tried to escape, tossing all of its weight back and forth. The shifting weight pulled the eagle from side to side as it gained speed and air space. The earth beneath seemed to fade.

The crackling fire roared, flames burning with orange and red, its translucency revealing the black, white and shades of gray of the burning wood. Shooting Star sat on a flat rock, turning a long stick upon which the fish was skewered, slowly roasting it to a golden crisp over the fire. The aroma of cooking food spread upon the air, awakening her stomach to rumble loudly.

A loud scream echoed from the west. Shooting Star looked up and spotted the eagle flapping its wings to land next to the closest flat stone. She watched the animal for a second as it tore away at the skin and meat of the raw fish, eating and pausing to look up for a second, and then repeating the process. Pulling the skewer away from the fire for a moment, she turned her fish to the other side, inspecting the meat to make sure it was a nice, crisp, golden-brown color. Waiting for a moment before partaking, she began to blow on the meat softly, cooling it down. A small smile crept across Shooting Star's face as she attentively watched the eagle.

He eats the same exact way as you, my love . . . Picking off a piece of the fish from the skewer, she began to eat, staring intently at the eagle. The illusion of appeared before her eyes. *Is this real?*

The bright glows of yellow, orange, and red fused into one as a crackle in the wood sent a small spark of flame into the air away from the fire. The thick darkness surrounded the small illuminating fire, the air trying to suck its life away and smother the light in complete darkness. Feeding fuel to the fire, Soaring Eagle tossed a few more pieces of wood in. Stars in the sky glowed brighter with every pulse and seemed to pull closer as if a man cast a net and reeled in his catch.

"You are not supposed to be here again," said Soaring Eagle.

"Let me keep this for one more day," she replied.

Shooting Star laid her head on his shoulder, looking over the fire where a couple of skinned hares hung spitted over the campfire. The grease of the meat trickled down, falling into the flames and causing the fire to spit, sizzling and smoking. Staring off into the stars above, they both sat in a trance. A gust of wind blew across the couple as the scent of the roasting meat strung their stomachs like a guitar.

"Almost done," Soaring Eagle looked at the food.

"Let me enjoy this just a little bit longer," she replied, squeezing him a little tighter.

Her smile spread practically from ear to ear. Soaring Eagle moved his arm to wrap it around her body, giving her the same squeeze in return. Together for a moment, they gazed up at the stars.

"You are getting accustomed to this."

"Yes . . . So what?"

Slightly shifting from her beloved's side, Shooting Star repositioned her body to lie on his lap, making herself more comfortable while giving him space to maneuver. He lifted the long stick with the well-cooked meat and snapped the wood in two, leaving a hare on each.

"Careful . . ." said Soaring Eagle. Handing her the spitted hare, he continued, "It's still hot."

Sitting up, she stretched out her legs. Lightly blowing on her food, she looked at him, and for a moment their eyes held the gaze, locking their souls together as one.

"I want this to last forever," she said.

"I do too," Soaring Eagle responded, embracing her.

"We should just go and start anew."

He watched her for a moment before answering. "What do you mean?"

"Can we just leave? Just the two of us. We can do whatever we choose."

"We have family and friends waiting for us."

"I know . . . I just do not feel like going back. All I need is you," she bundled herself into a ball and gazed into the fire, then finally took another bite of food. White steam floated up from the open flesh of the animal.

"Well . . . Let's go back, and in a couple of days we will decide."

"Alright," she pouted.

Just as Soaring Eagle leaned down to take a bite of food, a howl in the distance echoed in the darkness. His head shot upwards, eyes wide with caution. Scanning inch by inch from left to right, trying to pinpoint the sound in the darkness, he continued to chew his food.

Shooting Star smiled at Soaring Eagle, relishing every

moment she spent eating beside him. As she took another bite, the howl rang out again, and the brave's head popped up again, like a meerkat looking for a predator.

Laughing aloud, she took a second to catch her breath. "There is nothing to worry about, my love."

"What are you laughing at?"

"Your reaction. It is priceless."

He looked around. "Well, the beasts have fangs and claws to tear our flesh. Hidden in the darkness, they have the advantage."

"You have a bow and a knife that could tear their flesh as well," Shooting Star responded. She took his hand. "They are just as afraid of us as we are to them. Just stay by the fire with me and we will be fine."

"Hmm," Soaring Eagle nodded.

Those were the last few happy days I spent with you . . . The fish in front of her was nothing but bones now, as she'd plucked it clean while thinking about her past. She looked at her new companion. *This eagle really does remind me of Soaring Eagle so much.*

"We have to give you a name," she said, rising from her seat and stretching.

The eagle gave a loud scream in response, stretching its massive wings.

"Your name will be . . ." a moment passed as the name continued to swirl through her mind. "Soaring Eagle." She gave a little chuckle.

A few flaps of his wings, and Soaring Eagle took flight, landing on Shooting Star's shoulder. Responding to the new name he'd been given, he nodded and gave a cry in acknowledgment.

Head east. The thought of her dreams kept echoing in her mind. "Soaring Eagle, lead the way," she spoke.

Soaring Eagle took flight, jumping off her shoulder, flying higher and higher, swimming in the ocean of blue sky.

Something does not feel right . . . I must hurry.

CHAPTER 19
—WHERE TWO PATHS CROSS

Inside the tent, the light was blanketed with a darker shade. Every inch of the ground underneath was covered by the man-made shadow. Rays of light seeped through small holes at the seams and small tears in the canopy top. The door of the tent was left open as wide as possible, yet the air inside felt stagnant. Light inched its way from the door to the center of the room. In the middle, Constance sat on a chaise lounge.

"It has been about a week . . . They have not come back yet." The sound of Constance's voice echoed with a bit of agitation as she rested in discomfort.

"They should be coming back any time now," George tried to re-assure her.

"It's hot, and the last few days were just miserable."

"Yes . . . I know," George responded, rubbing his forehead.

"We could have been in Salem by now," Constance complained, pulling out a handkerchief to wipe the sweat from her forehead.

George gazed absently at his wife's blond hair and lovely blue eyes. His mind was elsewhere.

Yes, we should be in Salem by now, but I have to stay positive for the both of us.

"At least we get to spend more time with each other," he said, as cheerfully as he could manage.

"Ha, ha. I have a bad feeling about this," Constance retorted.

A maid took the liberty of entering through the open tent flap.

"Excuse me, Mr. and Mrs. Arnold. It is getting dark outside and we have already prepared meals for everyone. It's your favorite, steak, potatoes, and broccoli. Would you like dessert as well?"

"No, it's fine," Constance replied.

"Leave it on the table for us, please," George responded without looking at her.

"Right away," the maid nodded and immediately took her leave after placing both plates of food on the table. The couple listened to the sound of her footsteps padding away across the ground.

"Boy, I'm hungry," said George.

"Say that to the both of us," Constance glared at George.

"Right. Are you hungry in there, little one?" George smiled.

He got up to get the food from the table. "Let's eat, darling."

For the first time in quite a while, they ate in silence, not knowing what to say to each other. The clink of silverware was the only sound. The fear of the baby's arrival in the wilderness loomed over their heads, but each other's company was enough.

"I am sure they will be here tomorrow," George declared after swallowing his last bite.

"Let's hope you're right."

"It's getting dark out."

"Yes . . . I think we should have waited to move until after the baby came."

"Hmm?"

"Look at what is happening right now."

"It's just a minor setback, that's all. We should still be there before our child is born."

"Hmph . . ."

"We should be getting ready for bed."

"Fine."

George got up and closed the tent flap for the night.

"Good night, my love."

He lay down beside his wife. *She is not making this any easier for me,* he thought.

"Good night," Constance responded, leaning in for a kiss.

I hope I'm right as well, or we are going to be in a world of hurt. No one knows how to deliver this baby, George fretted silently.

The cool morning breeze swept in silently, colder than the previous days. Goosebumps formed as the air swept across their skin.

Suddenly, George woke from his slumber, alerted by an unusual sound. *She is breathing heavily . . . Uh-oh!* His eyes flew open. Constance appeared to be in pain.

"What's wrong, darling?" George asked fearfully.

"The baby . . . It's coming soon."

Oh, no . . . George was terrified.

A crow perched on top of the nearest tree branch and gave a scream. The pale gray clouds covered the sky like a blanket. No sunbeams shone through, leaving only the drab pall overhead.

"It's a lot cooler today," noted John, one of the butlers, tossing a coat over his shoulders.

"Yes, much cooler than the last few days," a nearby maid, Cathy, responded.

From his place in the back of the carriage, John looked up to the sky, in hopes of the sun breaking through the cloud cover. He wanted to feel the warmth of the sun on such a miserable day. Crows and vultures soared high in the sky, circling the camp like a bad omen. Another crow shrieked, and then landed right next to the other crow already watching the camp.

Cathy pointed up. "Look."

John glanced at her for a moment. His gaze followed her pointing hand. Shock was evident on his face, as though he feared something unfortunate might happen. "This is strange," he replied at last.

"How so?"

He pointed to the sky. "Do you notice something different from the last four days?"

"It's cloudy and cooler."

"That, and for the last few days, there were no birds in the sky. I don't remember any storm or clouds during the night, either. Now there's nothing

but crows and vultures flying around. On top of that, I don't see any dead animals around that would have attracted them."

"Yes, you're right," she looked troubled.

"I cannot take all this squawking from these crows." John massaged his temples.

Swift and silent, an eagle flew above, along the tree line. A faint cry echoed
from the west. Seconds later, the high-pitched scream of the eagle sounded
again, louder and louder.

John and Cathy looked along the tree line to the west. Suddenly their
hearts pumped a little faster. What was going on? Silence filled the air; the
crows stopped their cawing. Approaching from the rear, the large eagle landed
in between the two crows, scaring them away.

"I have never seen anything like this," said Cathy.

"Neither have I," replied John as he watched the birds.

"I wonder what is going on."

"I am sure it's nothing," said John, leaning back on his elbows.

"I guess you're right . . ." she replied, watching at the two small black
specks of the crows disappearing in the distance.

"Well, now, that's definitely something you don't see on a regular basis."
He pointed to the eagle perched on the tree.

"That is a sight to behold."

"AAH!" from a distance, a scream tore the air.

Turning around to see who'd cried out in distress, Cathy looked back at
the carriage and tents. *Could I be hearing things?*

"Did you hear that?" she questioned.

"Hear what?" John seemed confused. He hadn't noticed.

A gust of wind slowly whispered along like the distant howl of a wolf singing to the moon. The sun finally broke through the gray-covered sky, and
beams of light shone down, scattering light through the patchy clouds.

"I thought I heard Mrs. Arnold scream in pain," Cathy answered.

Looking down the same path, John paused to see if he could hear what
Cathy had heard. But only silence hung upon the air, as a light breeze swept
over the two listeners.

"You could be hearing things," he responded as he turned back around.

"I swear I heard her voice a moment ago."

"Sure, I believe you," John retorted sarcastically.

He looked back at the tree and asked, "Did you see where the eagle went?"

"No, I did not," Cathy answered, peeved.

Shooting Star approached a large, unfamiliar object in the distance. Soaring Eagle let out an echoing cry, gliding down to land on her shoulder.

I wonder if this is the place . . . I have never seen anything like this before, except in my dreams.

She looked upon the large carriages sitting on the side of the road, with tents set up between them. Grass no longer grew on the dirt road that travelers had packed down over the years of travel.

Well . . . I guess I should continue.

"Hey. Hey, look," said John, indicating Shooting Star, who was nearing the camp.

"Yes, it's just a woman," Cathy replied. She, like John, was in uniform, despite the rustic setting.

"Not just any woman. Look at her clothes. They are nothing like ours. She's an Indian," John replied as Shooting Star came closer.

"So; what about them?"

"I heard that these Indians are savages . . ."

"Savages?" Cathy cut in, her eyebrows raised.

"Yes, savages. People say that they look for caravans like ours and kill off everyone, and take the women for slaves. Some of them even paint their faces in different colors."

"Well . . . What about the women? You think she is a savage, too?" Cathy asked incredulously.

"I'm not sure . . . Usually, it's just the men, according to the stories I've heard," said John.

"Well, now, we don't have anything to worry about then, right?" *What a moron he is*, Cathy thought. *She is just like us.*

"Come to think of it . . . I guess not."

Hahahahaha! He thinks I'm a savage. Shooting Star chuckled to herself. Her keen hearing had picked up the conversation. Keeping a straight face as

best she could, she watched the two servants react to the cry of her companion eagle.

For a moment, she marveled at the novelty of the Arnolds' camp. *Things
are so different between their people and mine.*

Shooting Star passed the first carriage, from which the two servants
quickly scurried off to the farthest tent. It seemed like a different world. The
only sound she heard now was the padding of her feet treading the ground,
and silence, again, was her best friend.

As she checked the nearest tent, the flap opened wide with a gust of wind.
She looked inside but saw no one. Her heart began to race.

"No one is here," she commented to Soaring Eagle.

*What if I am late? What if I'm imagining things again? No, there has to be
someone here.* Doubt swam through her mind.

The second carriage came into sight, and she passed by another tent. A
white sheet covered some items within, which she couldn't identify, even
though they stood tall. *People's belongings. This is a good sign.* She let out a sigh
of relief, took a deep breath, and exhaled again.

Then, Shooting Star heard a shriek of agony from one of the tents farther
away. She made haste. *That one must be it.* She was relieved to know she was
almost there.

A small group of people stood at the tent's entrance, all of them dressed
alike, muttering nervously amongst themselves.

One maid was just arriving to the little gathering, "What is happening?"

"Mrs. Arnold! She's about to give birth!" an older, experienced maid explained.

"Right now?"

"Yes," another butler responded, blocking the door to maintain the Arnolds' privacy.

"Jonathan and Frederick should be back anytime, though," someone in
the crowd speculated.

"Well, Mrs. Arnold and her baby are not waiting," replied another.

"Lord, have mercy. Please hear our prayers and help Mrs. Arnold," one
of the servants prayed.

The crowd began to become restless and apprehensive, wanting to know everything happening inside the tent. Small groups of servants moved to the side of the tent and others continued to stay congregated in front. They all wondered how it would go, easy or difficult. On the other hand, others, less worried, lounged on chairs, relaxing as if nothing special were happening, just like any other day.

Another bellowing cry sounded from within the tent, and they all paused to look, alarmed for a moment before they continued what they were doing earlier. A group of maids began to speculate amongst each other. Words were muttered back and forth, though they became clear when Shooting Star approached, close enough to hear.

"What do you think is going to happen?" said one of the elderly maids.

"What do you mean?" replied the younger maid next to her.

"What if something unexpected happens?" the elderly maid rephrased her words.

"But what you mean by that?" the other maid answered, frustrated.

"We might not have a job after this journey."

"Or this journey should not have happened."

"That could be."

"If you think about it, we are days away from town, and if Mrs. Arnold does not survive the birth, Mr. Arnold will no longer need any of us."

"I am sure Mr. Arnold would not do that," the younger woman replied. "Or do you think he really would?"

Shooting Star passed by the group of maids. They gave her a cold stare, stopping their chatter until she had passed by. Cautiously, she observed every detail of her surroundings. Seconds later, Soaring Eagle took flight when she neared the tent. The butler did not know what to do or say, but simply gave way to the mysterious woman who'd appeared before him. After all, maybe she could help.

For a moment, Shooting Star paused to watch Soaring Eagle fly back into the sky. The bright sunlight pierced through the cloud cover. She looked to the west, where thick, dark charcoal-gray clouds clustered. No lightning sparked from within, though. *Hmm. This is strange*, she pondered.

An agonized scream from within the tent caught her attention once more, and she opened the flap and entered the tent.

George looked up at the sound of the door flap opening. Fear and uncertainty were plainly written across his face. He did not notice that the person who entered the room was not one of his maids or butlers. When he saw her unfamiliar clothing, he was confused by the unannounced appearance of a stranger, yet desperation toyed with him. He did not know whether to trust this mysterious person or not.

"Are you lost?" George asked.

Undeterred, Shooting Star continued to move forward.

"Ah . . . Can I help you, young lady?"

Through the pain and agony, Constance looked up and noticed George speaking to the stranger in front of her. She grabbed him by the wrist with a death grip and stopped George in his tracks so he could not move. As her grip tightened on his arm, signs of pain fluttered over his face. In low yet harsh tones she ordered, "Don't you dare leave my side."

"Don't worry. I am here to help," Shooting Star addressed her.

"You understand. Thank goodness," said George. "I'm absolutely at sea here."

Shooting Star looked over Constance. "How long has she been in labor?"

"Some fluids came out not too long ago," George replied. He was too anxious to have much sense of time.

"Alright, she seems to be in good shape. This will be easy enough. Just follow what I tell you both and things will go smoothly," Shooting Star reassured them.

"Very good," George answered, and Constance nodded.

Shooting Star stared into the pail of water and at her own reflection. She let out a deep sigh. *I made it in time.* Her hands were covered in drying dark reddish blood from helping the couple deliver a healthy baby girl into the world. She began to clean her hands, scrubbing the blood from skin, as she quietly hummed a melody. The water began to turn a rich, dark red.

Moving from the side of the bed to the meet with the unknown healer, George asked, "May I have a word with you?"

Shooting Star paused for a second to dry her hands with a towel and responded with a nod.

He gestured to indicate they should move outside the tent, as he reassured himself that his wife and daughter slept quietly in bed and could spare him a moment away. They quietly stepped out, and George paused for a moment just a few steps away from the doorway.

Words poured from his lips like a waterfall, coming faster and faster.

"Thank you! Thank you so much!" He let out a big sigh of relief.

Shooting Star nodded and smiled in acknowledgment.

"What is your name?" George questioned.

"Shooting Star," the healer replied.

"Well . . . how did you find us?"

Shooting Star led the way, walking a little farther away from the tent, and George trailed closely behind. She gazed out at the horizon, where the sun was setting upon the land, cascades of orange and yellow yet shining away the darkness that crept behind the vanishing light.

"I saw you in a dream," she ventured.

What? A dream? George gave her a blank stare.

A loud cry sounded from above, and he looked up, startled. He turned to follow the magnificent bird that swooped from the sky and perched on her shoulder. George stepped back a pace, not knowing whether to be afraid or amazed.

"This eagle, his name is Soaring Eagle. He guided me on the journey," Shooting Star continued. "In my dream, a spirit eagle came to me. It took the form of my husband. Then, I saw one of your carriages. The spirit's voice told me to head east. When I woke from my dream, this eagle guided me to you."

"I see," George responded. *I don't think she is telling me everything. Maybe she will tell me the whole story one day.*

"It is getting dark, so I should be going," Shooting Star said, casting her gaze over the open field.

"You can stay here for the night. We have an extra tent."

"Thank you for your hospitality, but I have to decline. I must go back. As for you, go to your family; they need you."

"Where will you go?" George inquired.

"Home," Shooting Star replied. *What did you mean that I might find my happiness, Soaring Eagle?*

George's heart twisted in his chest as he watched the one person who had helped them so much leave without accepting any token of his gratitude. As he walked back to the tent, his legs felt like sandbags, his feet dragging the ground. Turning the corner into the entrance of the tent, he glimpsed his last sight of Shooting Star. Listening to the sweet melody of light breathing coming from his wife, he went to his family, and everything else became irrelevant.

With a sigh of relief, Shooting Star felt the weight of the world lifted from her shoulders. Still, she felt empty inside. Despite the satisfaction of helping these complete strangers, there was something still lingering, unfulfilled. The farther she traveled from the newborn child and her family, the less she wanted to think about it. She looked ahead and remembered the dark, heavy layer of clouds covering the once perfect sunset.

She paused for a moment and glanced back at George's tent, wondering if she should return. *No, I must be going.* Soaring Eagle took flight from her shoulder and into the dark abyss of the sky, soon disappearing from sight. Suddenly a sharp blast of chilly air hit her like an icy wall, raising goosebumps all over her body.

What was that? She looked around, but there was nothing in sight, no wind blowing, and no movement in the branches of a nearby tree. Turning back around, she continued to walk past the last tent, and suddenly noticed that the creatures of the night were not singing their usual melodies. Another freezing blast sent a tingle down her spine.

Something is not right. There! She spied a black-cloaked figure making its way to the last tent. *NO! Why did I leave! I am so stupid!* She quickly and quietly scurried back to the Arnolds' tent, trying not to draw any attention from the unknown cloaked person in front of her.

Something has changed. The atmosphere seemed off, unnatural. As she peeked into the open tent, the light from the candlestick did not flicker or waver, and the people inside were still, like statues.

Is this a dream or another test? Shooting Star finally caught a glimpse of the interloper. Keeping a safe distance, she waited patiently for the mystery person to make a move, like a predator stalking its prey.

As Shooting Star watched, two delicate, feminine hands emerged from their hiding place inside the folds of the mystery person's cloak. Further motion revealed a young woman, still in her teens.

She is just a child, the healer thought with surprise. A throbbing pain suddenly tingled around her heart, and her chest started to strum like someone stringing a harp. One thing led to another as it intensified, developing into a choking sensation, thickening the air around her and suffocating her. Shooting Star felt herself in the presence of immense evil. *It cannot be! It's coming from this girl!*

She watched, transfixed, as the young woman knelt down to draw a circle on the ground with her finger, her hand illuminating a bright blue from the vaynes on it. With this act, the cloaked woman gathered an immense amount of energy around herself. The radiant colors began to draw life, flashing red and blue as she began to speak in a tongue Shooting Star did not understand.

> Let me be your guide
> Come
> Take what is yours
> Enjoy
> The nourishment of the living
> Give them what they need
> An endless slumber

Oh, no . . . I hope I'm not too late, Shooting Star fretted. She began whispering a chant of her own.

> Let the darkness fade
> It does not belong here
> For a time
> Hide within the light
> Show your true strength.

Morgana noticed that someone was trailing her, and flung out her arm towards the other woman, as though throwing a spear. A beam of light left her fingertips and lanced out toward Shooting Star.

Give me strength
With waves crashing walls
Shine
Bringer of light
Let me guide you home

"Hmm," Morgana let out.

Reacting quickly, Shooting Star embraced the magic, stopping the bolt with a small shield of air.

"Pathetic." Morgana remarked.

Shooting Star's face now wore an expression of defeat. *This is the end for me . . .* Exhaustion set in, as her defense had consumed too much energy. Her knees began to buckle. A bare moment later, she was kneeling on the ground, accepting the fate chosen for her. As she watched, the other woman's right arm glowed with what seemed to be a tattooed vein, which spread up the side of her neck, harnessing energy. The shield Shooting Star had summoned slowly consumed her strength, and as her power waned, it faded to a small ball the size of a penny in front of Morgana's chest.

I am going to savor this moment. It has been a while since anyone has crept up on me like that. As Morgana was about to unleash the wrath of her powers, a sudden burst of energy exploded in front of her and sent shockwaves that blasted her back. A portal appeared from the light and engulfed her in a flash.

Back in the dark abyss where it had all started, Morgana thought with a wry smirk, *What a sneaky little wench. She used two spells in one and completely caught me off guard. That will never happen again.*

Time continued unbroken as though no disruption had taken place; the sounds of the night awakened with the buzzing and singing of insects. Chatter from the camp was lively, while peace and quiet reigned in the Arnolds' tent. With the last of her energy, Shooting Star regained her feet.

"May I come in?" she asked.

"Who is that?" Constance whispered.

"Sounds like Shooting Star," George whispered back.

"Who?" Constance's expression twisted a little as her voice grew sharper.

"Yes, the Indian healer who delivered our child," George whispered back.

"Oh," she whispered back, comprehension dawning through her fatigue.

"Come in," George called out.

Shooting Star timidly entered the tent. Everything was still in place as before, except that the pail of bloody water had been emptied out. She noted relief on George and Constance's features, now that the stress of the day was over. A cool calm surrounded the couple, as though they were free spirits.

"You look tired," George remarked sympathetically.

"Oh, yes, I am," the healer replied with a sigh.

"Let me get someone to help you out," George offered. "For now, please make yourself comfortable here."

"Thank you."

"Great! I'll be right back." George got up and exited the tent. In just minutes, servants hurried back at his side.

"We are having them set up a tent for you beside ours," George announced.

"I appreciate your hospitality," Shooting Star answered with a smile. She tried to stand, but found herself completely drained. "Oh! I'm sorry; I'm exhausted. I cannot seem to move," she added.

"It's fine. Help her up, please," George addressed the butler.

"Certainly, Mr. Arnold," the butler scooped up the healer as though she were a child.

"What made you decide to come back?" George asked.

"It was nothing," Shooting Star demurred.

"Your tent should be up soon, but . . . really?" George raised an eyebrow. *She is hiding something from me again.*

Shooting Star paused for a second, "Our acquaintance was not merely one of luck."

George and Constance shared a puzzled glance, their curiosity piqued.

"In time I will tell you everything," Shooting Star offered. "Now, though, I am very tired."

"Fair enough," replied Constance.

"Have a good night, then," said George.

"You too, rest well," Shooting Star replied, disappearing with the butler into the darkness, toward her tent.

George turned to his wife. "I have a feeling that she came to us for a reason."

"What makes you think so?" Constance replied.

"I'm not entirely sure . . . it's just a feeling. Also, I think we should ask her to come with us."

"You think that's a good idea?"

"Yes. For our daughter, I think it is. What name shall we give our little angel?"

Constance was still exhausted, and she trusted her husband's good taste. "It's alright if you decide."

"Grace."

"I love it." Constance smiled.

A commotion stirred the camp bright and early. Cheers and shouts rang out as Jonathan and Frederick's carriage returned in the morning. Waking up well rested for once, Shooting Star stretched her limbs and got out of bed. She looked across the camp and saw George and Constance standing together, cradling their newborn child ever so tightly.

George shouted thunderously, "Let's get moving!"

Constance approached Shooting Star, "We would like you to come with us."

"I have a family to get back to," Shooting Star demurred.

"Well, my husband feels that you are part of our family as well."

She thought long and hard before answering, "I accept. I will come with you." *This is my new family, now. I wonder if this is what you meant, Soaring Eagle.*

CHAPTER 20
—A Tragic Beginning

1674

"Darling, I'm home!" Abraham called out excitedly as he flung the door open. His square face was radiant with a bright smile.

"I'll be right there!" Susanna yelled back from the kitchen.

She quickly finished hanging up the last few pots in the kitchen. Her freckled cheeks plumped with a delighted smile. The light of her life was home! She hurried out to the living room to meet him.

Abraham swooped in behind his wife to give her a massive bear hug, twirling her around in circles. Laughter filled the living room as they chuckled together, enjoying every moment.

"I love you." Abraham gazed deeply into her sparkling blue eyes. He couldn't take his eyes off her lovely heart-shaped face as he brushed her long blond hair back behind her ears with a tender caress.

"I love you too. What are you so happy about?" she inquired.

"I got a job!"

"You did? Which one?" Susanna questioned.

Letting her go, he responded, "The lumberjack job."

"Oh, but that job is . . ."

"Needed," Abraham cut in. "The pay is good, higher than the other jobs around here," he continued.

"Yes, but it's dangerous," she replied, concerned.

Abraham gave Susanna another hug, explaining, "I need this. *We* need this. I've had no work for the last three months, and we've been relying on William to make ends meet." He let out a big sigh. "I am thankful for his help, but it's time to carry our own weight. I know I can do this."

"I know, but I can't help worrying, darling. Who is that stuffed animal for?" she questioned as she rested her head on his chest.

"For the little guy. Where is he?"

"Joseph is taking his afternoon nap. He should be up soon."

"Don't worry, I didn't forget about you! You're my world."

"Hm?"

"Close your eyes," Abraham prompted her.

"Okay . . ."

He hurried to the stairs and back, grabbing up a bouquet of roses he'd purchased at the market. "You can open your eyes now."

"Oh, my goodness! They're beautiful!" Susanna shrieked in delight.

"Now, now, you're going to wake up the little one," he teased.

"You didn't have to."

"You deserve them, though. Thank you for everything you do for us."

She fanned herself with her hands. "Roses are my favorite! Oh, my, I love you so much!"

Tears of joy filled her eyes as she embraced him and kissed him with vigor. She fell speechless, forgetting what she was going to say before. That was a frequent state for her in his presence. Everything stood still for her, perfect; all she could ask for.

"Would you wake Joseph before dinner so he doesn't have too much energy later tonight?" Susanna requested.

"Sure, I'll give him the good news myself," Abraham answered.

"Yes, of course."

Abraham ascended the wooden stairs, which creaked under his weight, each one making a distinct sound. The late afternoon light shone through the window glass, gently illuminating Joseph in warm light. The child lay in bed, wrapped in the sheet. Squirming uncomfortably, he tried to unwind the confining sheet and find the perfect position to fall back asleep.

"Hey there, big guy," Abraham called to his son as he approached the bed, his hands behind his back to hide the gift from Joseph's sight.

The boy woke slowly from his cat nap. His eyes were still bleary from sleep, and his father's voice sounded distant as the child emerged from his dream. Joseph blinked, rubbed his eyes, and stretched each limb to its limit, bringing himself back to the waking world.

"Papa!" said Joseph happily. He swung his legs over the side of the bed, bounced himself upright, and embraced his father.

"I have something to show you," said Abraham, revealing the stuffed teddy bear. "His name is Teddy. He will help you sleep at night. If you are scared, just give him a squeeze and your fears will go away."

Delighted, Joseph squeezed the teddy bear to his chest tightly. He smiled from ear to ear, excited about his new toy.

"Dinner is almost ready. Let's not keep your mother waiting too long. You know how that will go." Abraham smiled.

"Yes, papa," the boy replied.

"Leave Teddy here to keep your room safe."

Nodding his head, Joseph left his new toy on top of the bed. As father and son descended the stairs, the wooden planks sang their creaky song once more.

The scent of food alone was enough to enchant the two standing near the staircase. Joseph and Abraham approached the dining room table, the tantalizing aroma leading them closer. Brand new candles sat on each side of the table, a small flame dancing on each wick, making the delicious food below even more enticing. Two of the dishes each had a large T-bone steak cooked medium well, covered with seasoning and spices. Side dishes filled the rest of the plates with steamed broccoli, green beans, and potatoes. On a smaller plate between the larger two were steak strips cooked well done and cut into small pieces, with smaller portions of the same sides.

At the side of the table, a chair was adjusted a little differently from the rest, with a couple of wooden blocks to help lift up the seat for the child. Pulling the seat out, Abraham lifted Joseph to sit down and pushed the chair back close to the table so he could reach the silverware. Afterward, he pulled the next chair out for his wife to sit.

"Why, thank you," she said.

He smiled and gently pushed her chair toward the table as he quickly moved over to his own seat. His stomach growled. The food before him looked all the more enticing.

"Let us say grace," Abraham sat down.

Reaching for each other's hands, they bowed their heads. Joseph watched carefully as his mother and father held hands. Abraham's thumb caressed the back of his wife's hand tenderly.

Abraham cleared his throat, "Ahem . . ." and took a short pause before he continued, "Thank you Lord, for this food that we are about to receive, and for your blessing of good health. Thank You for everything that you have given us. Amen."

"Amen," Susanna lifted her head.

Taking his fork and knife from the table, Abraham said, "Let us eat!"

"Guess what, Joseph? Your father got a job!" Susanna announced cheerfully.

"That's right, son. You are going to be the big man of the house when I'm not home," Abraham added.

"Yes, we're going to have some fun times in the near future."

"Yay, Papa! I will take care of Mama," Joseph smiled.

"That's my boy."

Three weeks later, rapid knocking on the door disrupted the morning. *This is odd*, Susanna thought. *Usually, no one visits around this time.* She quickly paced out of the kitchen to the living room and approached the front door. The knocking started again when she neared the door.

"Who is it?" she questioned.

"Mrs. Newman?" the stranger inquired.

Susanna opened the door to see a young man with light brown hair above an oval face, blue eyes, and a curved nose. His white shirt was stained sweat under brown overalls, and he wore heavy black work boots.

"How can I help you?"

"I am Jimmy. Jimmy Ainsley. I work with Abraham Newman at the lumber yard," he replied, timid at first.

Now she was concerned. "Please come in."

Closing the door behind her, she led him to the dining table, where he sat down on the nearest chair. Quickly, Susanna vanished into the kitchen to fetch a cup of water for her guest.

"Thank you," said Jimmy, his expression distraught.

Susanna nodded cordially, asking, "You are young . . . um, how old are you? And what brings you here?"

He gave a vague smile. "I am fifteen years old, and like I said, I work with your husband in the lumber yard."

Susanna gave him an apprehensive frown, waiting impatiently for the reason behind his visit, though she knew that it would come soon enough. She began to twiddle her thumbs nervously as her hands balled together. The doubt was difficult to endure. Looking up at the ceiling and back to the youth, she was obviously uneasy. *I hope Joseph doesn't wake up anytime soon.*

"It was just like any other day. I've worked with your Abraham since he started, and we have been working together as a group to make our days go by faster. He acts as my older brother, and we would help each other out. Well . . . in the morning, we would meet at the house just outside of the lumber yard and put on our equipment. We would talk about just about anything . . ." Jimmy continued.

At the crack of dawn, when the sun had just begun to crest the horizon, Abraham arrived at his workplace, dressed heavily to keep the frigid morning air at bay. He took a few deep breaths of the crisp air, producing the white vapor with each exhalation. *I wish the sun was up already.* A few steps ahead lay a small shack that looked more like a storage unit with a door, with one window no bigger than a melon on the side.

"Jimmy! How are your folks doing?" Abraham called out as he opened the door. The dim interior of the shanty was lit only by a candle on a little table.

"They're doing well," Jimmy replied. "Ma is running around the house more than usual since Pa hurt his back. The other day he must have done something on the farm that strained his back, but he is feeling a lot better now."

"Well, when you see them later tonight, please send them my regards, and I hope your pa gets better," Abraham said kindly as he donned his tool belt and slung an ax along the side.

"Thanks, Abraham. I'll pass that on."

"What are we doing today?"

"Nothing out of the ordinary. I'll show you," said Jimmy as he strapped on his own tool belt. He opened the door and led the way out the shack that served the lumber yard as an office.

Upon stepping out, the chilly air gave them goosebumps and made them shiver slightly. The dawning day sent a glimmer of light into the darkness they'd grown accustomed to. Another cool blast of air greeted them along with the first rays of light. They followed the river bank together, listening to the flow of the river singing its sweet, gurgling melody, and they inhaled the clean scent of fresh water.

As they climbed the side of a hill on their path, Jimmy explained, "This is where the logs are going to travel." He pointed ahead. "We will be heading up there, just a little bit farther down."

It was actually a few miles' journey to their destination, but their conversation made it feel shorter. The forest around them came alive as the sun continued to rise from the east, illuminating branches and plants. Near the end of their destination, Abraham spotted some logs lying horizontally by the river bank. *They are not rolling in?* he wondered.

A loud creak sounded from the second floor, and Jimmy stopped speaking. He looked up toward the ceiling then ran his eyes along to the staircase. Joseph had quietly crept his way to the staircase, trying not to make any noise. He sat at the very top of the stairs, closely listening to the conversation that had awakened him from his slumber.

"What was that?" Jimmy asked.

"It's probably Joseph turning over in his bed or moving around," Susanna replied. "Please continue."

Jimmy resumed, "We reached our work site, and . . ."

"So what are we doing now?" Abraham asked.

He examined the trees on the shoreline. It looked as though half of each tree was buried by the sand to keep the logs in place. Along the side of the logs, a few pathways had stacks and stacks of trees piled up together; and others lay on the ground by themselves.

"We'll move all these trees into the river," said Jimmy.

"Um . . . How the hell are we going to manage that?"

"Easy."

"Okay, let me see you do this," Abraham replied skeptically.

"Well . . . alright, then. Usually, it takes two or three people, but I can do it by myself," Jimmy boasted, his head held high.

He walked to the tree standing closest to the path along the sand. A rope was revealed when he untied it from a branch. Abraham looked up to see a contraption of ropes hanging above.

"Usually it takes about two to three people, and you're new, so don't attempt this alone," Jimmy cautioned.

Oh, I see now. Jimmy almost had me there. For a second, I thought he was really that strong. Ha! Funny kid, Abraham thought.

Peering at the contraption hanging above them, Abraham wondered how it functioned. It looked as though miles and miles of rope surrounded the four trees near the river.

"If we did it all ourselves, we would need more manpower. For the smaller ones, we can do it with just the two of us no problem, but for the bigger ones, we would need some help," said Jimmy.

"And how does this work?" Abraham asked.

"Let me show you."

Abraham approached the pile of stacked logs. He noticed that one side of the rope was slightly higher than the other side. Near the lowest point was a small sheet metal carrier formed into a U shape. Jimmy indicated the corner of the carrier to show Abraham the holes in it.

"See each hole? I had the blacksmith make fittings to go inside the holes. The rope fits through the holes. It honestly looks like he cut a horseshoe in half and attached a rope. Make sure you unhook one side and do your best to wiggle the metal sheet up. Sometimes you have to move the log the best you can and then attach the hook. With the rope that I untied, tie a knot on the tree and pull it toward the log path. Once you hit the very end, the fitting should come loose on its own and the log will fall to the ground. Any other questions, Abraham?"

"When is our help coming?"

"Soon, but they will be cutting down trees more than helping us out."

"Once the tree is on the log path, what do we do then?"

"Easy. You can do it, either from the back or the front. If you are in the front, you can tie the knot like this—" Jimmy demonstrated"—and pull the tree into the river. Make sure you are very careful doing this. I don't want you to get soaked, or worse, die. Another way is that you can push the log from the back. Eventually, you will find the best way for you. Make sure nothing is loose. You don't want to get pulled into the river with the tree."

"Alright."

"I showed him the process to use that equipment that day . . ." Jimmy drifted off.

"What happened next?" Susanna questioned, impatient for more answers.

"It felt as though everything happened so fast. I told Abraham that I was going on a break, and I insisted on him joining me."

"You should come and get some food with me, Abraham," Jimmy suggested.

"No, it's okay, Jimmy. I'm going to stay a little longer to get as much done as possible and figure this thing out," Abraham gestured to the logs and the rope contraption.

"The work will be here after we come back."

"Yes, I know."

"Okay, well, if you need me, I will be in the woods just over there," Jimmy pointed to the area where he would take his break.

"I was gone for maybe fifteen minutes . . . when I got back, Abraham . . . well, he was not there anymore. I thought that he might have left and gone home. I was hoping to see him the next day, like we did every morning, but he never showed up. I noticed that his toolkit was gone, and I hoped he was playing a cruel joke on me. Mrs. Newman, I'm sorry. I have to get going," Jimmy finished inconclusively and took his leave.

A knock rang out at the front door. Susanna rushed to get it, with little Joseph trailing behind. She longed to see her husband and hear the words, "Darling, I'm home!" She flung the door open, only to find William standing there.

"William?" Susanna exclaimed.

His face was full of anguish. "They found Abraham."

"And?"

"I'm so sorry." William choked on the words.

Susanna began to shake uncontrollably with the devastating news. William reacted quickly, and caught her before she could fall to the ground. He embraced her by way of comfort. Her sobs of grief were muffled in his shoulder.

Papa . . . Joseph was scared now.

CHAPTER 21
—MY DECISION

1674

"From that day on, I have been having those dreams of mine, which have been haunting me." –Bruce

Lying in bed in the thick of night, Fayth stared at the ceiling. *Another sleepless night . . . Three years ago.* She let out a big sigh, as numerous thoughts plagued her mind. *Nathaniel . . . Prophecy . . . I wonder what dreams Bruce have been having these past few years. Did I not change my future? Why do you keep haunting me?*

Darkness filled the whole room, making the white linen bed sheets hard to see even with the dim gleam of moonlight through the window. *How can he rest so easily?* She listened to Bruce snoring, thinking, *He is not having a bad dream now . . .* His heavy breathing became music to her ears. Wrapping herself around him, she began to doze off into slumber.

Fayth's eyes fluttered open; she sensed a disturbance in the atmosphere. She gasped, scanning the dark room as best she could.

"Oh, my dear child, you have grown," said a creaky old voice, familiar, but just barely.

She thought, *This cannot be.* Light began to creep through the window, chasing the darkness from the room.

"No! This cannot be!" she cried aloud.

"But it is," Nan replied.

"Why are you here?"

"To remind you of what you have forgotten," replied the old witch. She sat in the middle of the room, her pale white skin and her frizzy white-and-gray hair glowing in the moonlight. Her brown eyes looked black, and when she smiled, her yellow teeth seemed to darken.

"I have forgotten nothing," said Fayth.

"Oh, but you have, my child. Come and sit."

In the blink of an eye, a dark wooden chair appeared right in front of the old hag. Fayth thought back to that day in Nan's cottage, and she began to remember. She didn't realize yet that she was already sitting in front of the old witch. Then she saw the scroll that the old hag revealed from underneath her draperies. As she read the parchment, it all seemed to slowly come back. Forgotten memories started to resurface as everything tied together. The old hag slowly indicated the scroll again. Fayth shook her head.

"No, no, NO!" she screamed.

"Prophecy . . . Little girl . . ." Nan croaked. Her voice seemed to move eerily from side to side, behind where Fayth sat.

With fear descending upon her like a hungry vulture, Fayth panicked, knocking the chair to the ground as she leapt up. As the chair thudded to the floor, Fayth sprinted for the door, not looking back. She ran as fast as she could, but when she reached for the doorknob, the distance seemed to stretch for miles, and the only exit disappeared from her sight. The glimpse of a body flashed past the edge of her vision. *Father, help me!*

The doorknob turned and the door swung open. Fayth passed through the doorway and into darkness. She shook her head, her eyes opening wide to find herself back in the dark bedroom, where Bruce slept peacefully by her side. He continued to snore, as before, and she drew closer to him. *Just a bad dream*, she thought.

She held him tight in her arms once more and began to drift away into slumber once again. Suddenly, she felt something pulling her gown. She found herself sinking into the bed, like fighting quicksand, and looking up into the pitch black sky. Without warning, the pull on her nightgown disappeared, leaving her free falling through the black space.

As she fell from the sky, flashes of light appeared all around her. Thunderous roars clashed in the air while she plunged through the dark, cottony clouds where the lightning danced. A familiar sight appeared in the distance.

A wave of raindrops fell from the sky as Bruce looked up. Soon, the rain stopped its motion and hung in midair as silence descended. Soft hoofbeats sounded on the wooden bridge. Hovering behind Bruce like a shadow, Fayth stared at her own image. *There I am, next to the tree. This must be the dream he'd spoken of.* A sizzling noise made her turn. From the north, a black-cloaked man astride an ebon horse was drawing near.

Bruce rose from the ground and approached the stranger. As he moved, the raindrops parted. The cloaked man pushed his hood back, revealing a face covered in scars.

"Please help me," Bruce implored. The man's gaze, however, was fixed straight ahead. "Please, please, can you help me?" Bruce repeated, more desperately this time.

"Do not worry, Bruce, we came to help you," responded the second rider, a young woman concealed behind the cloaked man's back.

As she moved closer to that voice, Fayth recalled the memory of her grandmother saying, "Little girl. Prophecy."

Leaning to the side, Bruce looked over to see who might have spoken those words. The person in question was a teenage girl clad in an oversized cloak, similar to that of the man riding in front. She pulled back the hood of her own cloak, revealing a lovely face with a pointed chin. Her light gray eyes focused on Bruce.

I wonder if this is the girl Nan was going on about, Fayth thought.

The young woman dismounted with the man's aid, preparing to lend a helping hand. The man on horseback simply sat, facing forward, like a statue.

The cloaked girl quickly strode past Bruce to Fayth, where she lay under the tree. Bruce turned and followed in her wake. The young woman began to examine Fayth, who was bleeding heavily. The crimson flow mixed with the rain, running down to her feet. Bruce stopped helplessly beside the girl, watching, waiting for her to do something to aid them. The girl crouched down and held Fayth's wrist, feeling the slow, weak pulse that beat there.

"Your son died before he took a breath of air, so he is a little different from the rest. He will forever be lost in purgatory, unless . . ." the girl, Morgana, paused for second.

Nathaniel died at birth? Fayth, still watching in her dream, was shocked.

"Unless?" Bruce prompted.

Pacing back and forth in a short line, she continued, "Unless . . . Your son's body will remain an empty vessel even if we do summon his soul here. It has no physical attachments to this world. In order for it to stay in the vessel, we would have to use a guardian protector to keep the soul in place. That is the only way he will be able to live a normal life."

A guardian? Fayth wondered.

Beckoning Bruce with a gesture, Morgana said, "I need your help on this, Bruce." He stood next to her, waiting for the next order she would bark at him. She started to draw a small circle right beside Fayth.

"Your hand," she requested.

He lifted a hand for her to use, and she pricked the finger once more for blood. With a drop ready to fall, she pulled his finger over the circle, letting the blood drip into it. She then drew a scripture into the circle with odd markings all along the outer rim and the sign of a goat in the center.

A red light began to brightly illuminate half of the circle from one end to the other, making the nearby raindrops reflect the color. The young girl's vaynes were radiant with blue, flowing upwards from her fingertips and dancing near the edge of her neck. A heavy feeling like no other began to sink in, something dark.

Within the depths,
Life breathes light,
Consumed by darkness
And full of anger,
Let it eclipse you
When you are needed
Listen to this calling
To be reborn once more

"She is chanting a summoning spell!" Fayth screamed at Bruce, making all efforts to stop what was happening.

"Here they come," Morgana announced.

A silhouette
Blindness from dust
Darkness brought to light
What lies
In your wake

What kind of spell is this? Fayth hovered over Morgana.

The other half of the circle was now illuminated in blue light. The air near the young girl began to ripple and pulsate back and forth. A white light in the shape of a hand pushed through the ripple in the air. Then, from the teleportal, a man slowly exited, glowing with a bright white energy tinged with blue, and suited in luminous white that even the energy could not outshine. His skin was pale with a light tan, his hair was short and black, and his striking face bore black eyes and a strong jaw. He stood six feet, two inches tall, and held a baby in one arm. His dark eyes gazed upon the empty vessel he would protect to the end of his days.

Morgana continued the incantation, ignoring all else for the time being. The guardian slowly approached his new vessel, inching closer and closer. A wrenching feeling twisted in Fayth's chest at the sight of the guardian carrying her son's soul. *Something is not right.* She inspected the spirit a little more closely. Something was off. *What is wrong with this guardian's legs?* The toothpick-thin legs did not fit the man's body, and his feet had no toes. *They look like goat feet*, she thought.

The glowing light disappeared as it passed through Bruce, transforming into a massive goat's head as it appeared through Bruce's body, its eyes blood red as though it had no pupils. In its mouth it held the crying baby. It stopped to look at Fayth, turning its head, and uttered the muffled words, "H . . . elp . . . me . . . fi . . . nd . . . An . . . ne . . . tte . . ."

The child held in its mouth turned his head and smiled at Fayth. The baby cried out, "Mama!"

With each cry, the sound of the baby's voice deepened more. Behind the goat, her husband rose from the ground, a spear impaling him from the back. His cries of pain were mute, only his face screamed in agony. Laughter sounded all around. Suddenly, the guardian turned his gaze to Fayth's body, lying by the tree trunk, and began to dart toward her.

Fayth screamed, "NO!"

The white light flashed in front of her, and her cry carried over from the dream. Fayth's eyes opened in the darkness of night. She gasped a few deep breaths for air, and sweat rolled down her skin and onto the bed. Her grip on Bruce loosened, and he began to move, unsettled, soon to wake.

Fayth leaned over and whispered,

Dreams,
Follow them
To your heart's content
But remember them
For one day
They will fade

The little things, she reminded herself as she lit a candle by her side of the bed. The small, warm flame only lit a small portion of the room, while the rest lay in darkness. Fayth lifted the candle for a view of the bed. Bruce still slept.

She made her way to the end of the room, where a large chest was stowed away in the very back, hidden by a wooden wall. Fayth selected just a few items of clothing and a book from the chest. She then returned to the bed to catch a glimpse of her love one last time, and kissed him on the cheek before leaving with a faint smile.

She moved into the other room, swiftly and silently crossing the wooden floor, and then passed through the doorway of Nathaniel's room. Nearing the cradle, she began to weep softly. The light sobs were only a comforting motherly sound to Nathaniel's ears, and he wiggled a little to find comfort.

Fayth lifted her son and left a book at the end of the cradle. She held him in her arms, humming a melody and dancing gently in a circle as she softly rocked him back and forth to enjoy the moment. "One day," she said, "this will all add up for you. Let this book guide you to what you need."

Fayth gave the baby a simple kiss on his cheek and forehead as another tear fell to the floor. She set Nathaniel back into bed, caressing from the crown of his head to his chin as her fingertips reached the end, not wanting to leave.

"Mother loves you," she whispered.

Nathaniel smiled for his mother. She could hardly bear to walk away. Mustering her resolve, she turned around and began to walk out the door and into the living room, not allowing herself to look back. *This is for the best.* Behind her, the hallway disappeared in the dark as she quickly crossed through the living room and to the front door. Only pausing for a second to take a deep breath, Fayth whispered, "Goodbye, my loves." As she opened the door, the chill of the midnight breeze washed over her skin. Then, she took her first step out of the house, quietly closing the door behind her.

One day, we will meet again.

Chapter 22
—A Star in the Darkness

1674

"Rowland," said Catherine.

"Mama?" he responded.

"Let's have some fun, son," Gerard suggested.

"Papa!"

"Can we take off the blindfolds yet?" Catherine asked.

"Not yet. Boy, do I have a surprise for you two today!"

The shuffling of their feet on the ground was the only thing they could hear. Catherine and Rowland were blindfolded and only guided by Gerard's hand and voice. The scent of water tickled their nostrils as the sound of the slowly rushing water serenaded them like Mother Nature's own harmonic symphony.

"Just a few more steps," Gerard said— "and here we are," he proclaimed at the destination.

Rowland and Catherine's eyes opened to a white blur when he untied their blindfolds, as they adjusted to the light. A long stretch of time passed as Rowland looked down to the ground, "Hmmmmm." Then, he lifted his gaze to his mother and father.

Catherine wore an ankle-length blue dress that nicely complemented her pale skin, blue eyes and sweet smile. Gerard stood close to his wife. He had dressed sharply for the occasion in a black suit, as he did every day, only minus the vest. His eyes never wandered far from Catherine and Rowland's faces.

Knowing that he'd chosen a great location for his family to relax made the occasion all the sweeter.

From afar, a drizzle of water consistently trickled down like a light shower. The sun reflected rays of light through the water, casting a constant rainbow. The ice-cold touch of the occasional water droplet gave them goosebumps. Underneath a small maple tree was a welcoming patch of grass, just far enough away from the small waterfall. Groups of decorative trees lined the path to the waterfall.

"I remember this place," said Catherine.

"Yes, it's been a while since we have been here," Gerard replied.

"Where are we?" Rowland asked.

"This is where we used to come all the time when we were younger," Gerard responded. He turned to his son and knelt down, pointing over his shoulder off into the distance. "See over there, that little town. That's where we live."

Catherine turned around, walked to the shore, and stared into the waterfall for a moment. Gerard followed not too far behind to lay a blanket on the small patch of grass and set the picnic basket on top.

Rowland lay within the confines of the blanket, stretching his arms and legs. Gerard caught up to Catherine, the sound of his footsteps drowned out by the splashing and rushing of the water. His hands bestowed a soft, subtle touch along her hips as he caressed her curves for a hug.

"Why did we stop coming here?" she wondered aloud.

"We have someone who is really important in our lives now. We've spent a lot of time and effort looking after our son, whereas we used to have more free time for recreation. This place will always be here for us, our secret oasis," he responded.

"You're right. We should come here more often."

"Yes, we can now, since Rowland is older."

"Oh, those memories."

"They were great."

"Yes, they were. We should go back to our sleepyhead, though," she turned her head, checking on Rowland.

"Yes, let's go sit with him."

Opening the basket full of bread, meat, and fruits, Gerard softly nudged Rowland's shoulder and said, "Wake up, sleepyhead. It's time to eat."

Rubbing his eyes after his nap, Rowland gazed up at the rolling clouds in the sky and the trees, which waved soothingly in the breeze. Though he was drowsy, there was comfort in that place that he could not explain.

Leaning over to block his sight, his father spoke, "One day, you will bring your future partner here to share the same memories your mother and I have of this place."

"*Rowland . . . Wake up, Rowland...*" a distant voice echoed.

"Five more minutes," Rowland mumbled.

The comforting dream swirled away into darkness and the faces of his parents turned blank. He could not seem to remember their faces now. Standing alone in the dreamscape, he remembered the faces of those who had taken his parents away, and anger flared within. *If only I was stronger.*

Flashes of light strobed before his eyes, taking Rowland into another memory he would soon want to forget. His parents lay in a pool of blood in the middle of the alleyway. His mother and father's eyes were lifeless as they stared blankly toward each other, drowning in their blood, and his former self stood in the middle, able to do nothing. He felt so powerless. The only thing he could do was watch the two killers run away into the shadows.

Why does this always happen to me? I don't want to remember this ever again. Rowland closed his eyes in hopes that the view would change. Standing behind him now, Catherine and Gerard slowly reached out and touched his shoulders.

"We love you, son," they said together.

"Then why did you leave me?" Rowland asked.

"We are . . ." Rowland's mother's words were cut off by a splash of water on his face, and he gasped for air.

"Wake up, teacher's pet, or you will be late for school," the water-throwing boy mocked. Laughter filled the air of the orphanage dormitory as the rest of the children joined in.

Reality hit him as the cold water ran down his face. The blanket, pillow, and mattress soaked up the rest of the water, which sent a slight chill down his spine.

Collectedly and calmly, he pushed back the blanket, revealing his pajamas. Rowland had grown lanky: tall for his age, yet skinny, as though he was malnourished, and his brown hair grew so that it fell over his eyes unless he combed it to the side. Gritting his teeth and wiping the water from his face, he tried to show no emotion in response to their antics.

"How's the hot bath, teacher's pet?" one of his orphan taunted with a smirk.

"Yeah, how was the hot bath?" the other boys mimicked the taunt.

"Refreshing, Lucas," Rowland replied, getting up from his soggy bed. *Show no weakness.*

Inside the dormitory room filled with row upon row of beds, all the other boys had already made their beds and were ready for school. He was the exception, the last one to make his bed, just like every other day.

Standing in front of Rowland and blocking his way, Lucas said, "Where do you think you are going?"

"Heading to school," he responded.

"Noooot today!" Lucas shoved Rowland back onto his bed.

All the children stopped what they were doing and watched the confrontation. They all quickly gathered around in a tight circle. Lucas landed a couple of quick jabs to Rowland's stomach, taking his breath away.

Rowland caught sight of the fist coming toward his face and absorbed the full blow with his cheek. The noisy crowd exploded with mixed emotions, watching in either amusement or disgust. The scuffle ended as quickly as it had begun. The front door opened, and like roaches scuttling away from the light, the boys dispersed to the corners of the room.

"What is going on here? Come now . . ." Father Jean looked around the room. "Every one of you should be heading to school by now."

Not a peep came from any of the children in the room. They quickly grabbed whatever items they needed and rushed out the front door. The hall emptied, and the last two still in the room were Father Jean and Rowland.

"What happened here, Rowland?" the priest asked.

Rowland watched the last few of his peers exit through the door.

"Nothing," he responded, watching Lucas stare at him from afar with a glare that sent shivers down his spine. The tension eased as the bully finally left.

"What happened to your face?" Father Jean then questioned.

"I don't want to talk about it." Rowland looked away.

"Okay, that's fine."

With his hand, the priest lifted the boy's chin up and carefully inspected the child. *There is something not right here. In time . . . In time, he will talk. I hope.* "Go on now, child. We don't want you to be late as well."

Rowland rushed out the door, forgetting to close it behind him, and out into the brisk morning. He had neglected to wash up, but that was secondary to the thoughts in his mind. The grass and trees were coated with a layer of white frost that was slowly beginning to melt away in the sunlight.

Clouds of vapor floated above Rowland's head like a locomotive train with every breath he exhaled. Running along the path next to the trees and through the courtyard, he heard the school bell ring. *Oh no! I must hurry.* A wall of trees quickly appeared alongside the boy as he ran, and the path continued in between two trees. The school was in sight once he passed the tree line, and beyond the trees was a field of grass that looked like a sea of green.

Rowland could see the small stone-walled school off in the distance. Standing in front of a small bell next to the building, a young nun reached for the hanging rope. The bell rang one last time for the stragglers finally reaching the door. Meanwhile, he continued to run across the field.

The nun waited for the last student to arrive and gave Rowland a warm smile as he finally reached his destination. He felt welcomed, as always, on the school's premises. The students already inside watched through the window as Rowland and the nun entered together.

"Class!" the instructor called out.

One by one, the students took their places at their chairs and desks. At the front of the room was a small table and chair, just a little off center to the right, and the open space for the teacher to walk around.

"Ahem," she cleared her throat. "Class, we have a new student joining us for a little while. Please listen so she can introduce herself, and give her your undivided attention. Also, do not be afraid to introduce yourselves as well."

As the young girl walked to the front of the room, her long brown hair trailed behind her back. She gave a brief smile from her pink lips. She was quite pretty, with high cheekbones, a pointed chin, and warm light gray eyes.

"This is . . ." the teacher began.

"Illythia, daughter of Antha," the girl finished.

"Would you tell us a little bit about yourself?" the teacher asked.

"Sure," she answered, looking around the room. "My parents are merchants, and we travel a lot. I was raised in Rome, and I love seeing new places."

"Alright . . . Would any of you like to introduce yourselves to our new student?" the instructor asked.

The students cast glances to each other to see who be first to take the leap of faith and introduce themselves to the stranger standing at the front of the class. Seconds felt like ages; each and every one was terrified of the simple task. Mustering up some courage, Rowland stood up from his seat. He did not look around for the fear that coursed through him, as though the classroom were a pool of circling sharks, with him about to walk the plank.

He fumbled the first words: "Ah . . . Ah . . . Hi . . . M—My name is Rowland Chapman."

He finished those crucial words and a wave of relief rushed over him. As he sat down, the redness in his cheeks and ears slowly subsided. One after another, the other students rose from their seats and repeated the same process, mimicking the person before, introducing themselves one by one. At the very end, when the last student took a seat, the teacher walked up to the new student.

"You can take a seat." the instructor prompted.

Making her way to the nearest seat, the new student sat right next to Rowland. *This is the person I was looking for,* she thought.

Rowland glanced at her, and his brow creased for a moment, attentive for the instructor to begin the lecture.

"Very good," said the teacher.

A few murmurs sounded from the class. "Settle down. Settle down. Today we are going to learn about history," the instructor paused for a second to open her book and locate a certain page.

She began to read aloud. "There was a man, taller than the average man. Some say this man was a giant, and in history, some called him a Goliath.

This man started off as a slave and was traded to serve under a king of old in ancient Egypt. There are no records of his early upbringing, as they are still a mystery . . ."

Chapter 23
—My Revenge

"THEY ARE HERE! THEY ARE HERE!" A man screamed out, running to the crowd.

Cheers and clapping roared in the streets and, through open windows. The crowd filled every available space to view the marching army. Houses and buildings made of stone towered amongst one another, with potter's clay covering the roofing. Some other buildings, distinguished by location, were made of marble and limestone. Red and pink rose petals scattered and lay on the ground like a carpet upon the golden yellow and brown ground. A little past noon, the army continued to march in unison, following their general.

Oh, it is good to be home. General Anthony thought, scanning the different faces along the streets. The last of the thousands of soldiers entered the city and the crowd closed off the rear, slowly following them to the capitol. Chants from within the crowds grew stronger and stronger with every passing second, roaring with excitement. *Word has spread like wildfire of what we have accomplished.*

Near the edge of town, the road zigzagged up a hill. The crowd's cheering faded into the distance as they marched farther. The citizens slowly dispersed and returned to their livelihoods as the last line of soldiers started their march up the hill.

A new crowd awaited them at the top. Horns blared, prompting the crowd to cheer along. Pillars made of limestone lined the side of the castle near the coast. Intricate designs ahead of their time were inscribed throughout the structure of the building. Waiting on the steps of their castle, the reigning king and queen welcomed them. The last of the army stopped and another horn blew, different from all the previous calls.

At the steps to the front of the castle, a calm took over and the clamor ceased when the king took a step forward.

"My brothers! Sisters! Our gods have been good to us," King Periphas announced. A roar of cheers echoed like thunder from the soldiers.

"Tonight we celebrate! Our brothers, our fathers, our heroes have returned to us from their journey. We have made new allies and conquered our enemies. We will remember our fallen brothers," the king proclaimed.

The sun began to set over the hills, and along the horizon an orange glimmer cascaded along the cityscape. Day was laid to rest and the night awoke to life. A buzzing stirred within the town, like that of a tourist attraction, everywhere filled with people loafing around. Campfires lit up the night, scattered all across the land like fireflies in the sky.

Inside the grand hall, spacious enough to fit thousands of men, the men-at-arms dined for the night. Lit by torches scarcely separated and candles on the table, the night was forever young. Young servants, male and female, carried silver plates of food, and others bore vessels of wine. They walked back and forth tirelessly for those in need of refilling.

Harmonic music played from the middle of the room, where a woman plucked the strings of a harp. The drunken atmosphere took hold of the men and women alike. Some of the women danced naked while others flirted, whispering in the ears of others, seducing men while they devoured their meal.

The general stood up and spoke before his small group: "Tonight... Tonight, we live like kings."

The music and alcohol began to overtake him; the scene around him seemed to whirl at an alarming speed. Laughter and chatter filled the air for the rest of the night, yet something seemed to linger in the back of his mind. People came and went, which did not bother him, but a sense of unease remained, leaving him unsettled.

The celebration continued through the wee hours of the night as though tomorrow were of no consequence. *I hope that this hunch I feel is false. This is one night that all shall remember forever.*

On the outskirts of town, a stir in the air began to pulsate back and forth, rumbling like a minor earthquake. The tremors moved small rocks on the ground back and forth as though they had feet of their own. Then, a foot appeared from the ripple in the air and touched the surface of the gravel-covered ground.

The man's golden brown skin gleamed in the touch of light from the nearby campfire. Now larger than his younger self, he towered a little over eight feet tall, his square face and jutting jaw full of rage. Chike remained a bald, heavy-set man, but retained a masculine bearing in golden sandals that laced up to the knee and a breechcloth to match. A chain wrapped around his forearm, concealing the ax he carried.

He left large footprints behind as he followed the campfires. Dawn broke over the sea, lighting a new day, and a few of the campfires began to smolder, losing their former strength.

Revenge is mine! Chike thought.

From a dimly lit house, a soldier emerged, taking a deep breath and happy to be back home. He rubbed his eyes thoroughly to get rid of the sand, his focus still blurry as he gazed out to the outskirts of town. *Is this a dream?* he thought. *I cannot remember the last time I was home!*

A massive shadow picked up steam and began to move faster into the city. *Is this really happening? Has our past come back to haunt us?* The soldier quickly pulled out his horn and blew it loudly as if it were a matter of life and death. The alarm stirred the nest of all the weary, the sleepy, and those still drunk.

On a routine patrol, a few sentries toured the outer rim of the city. They conversed with one another, not necessarily paying attention to the fine details, yet still doing their jobs as appointed by the general. As they passed the shadowed figure, they did not realize anything was amiss. Oblivious, they continued their rounds.

One of the soldiers glanced back to the darkness, but the shadow figure was gone. However, the soldier did notice an unusual sound. The moment he paused to think was one moment too many. A large ax descended and split his skull of the soldier with a single blow, knocking his legs from beneath him.

"Oh, *fuck*!" his companion cried as the first soldier's body fell, lifeless, to the ground.

The town buzzed to life like an active beehive, quickly stirring to movement. Screams tore from the throat of a woman looking upon at the dead lying mangled on the ground. Chike reeled in the long chain attached to the butt of the ax, detaching it from the flesh so that it flew back, propping the soldier like a dead fish. Blood oozed out from the man's skull as his dead eyes gazed blankly at the horizon of a new dawn.

"Revenge!" Chike roared.

Soldiers poured out like bees from a stirred nest, rallying around from every house possible. The numbers of soldiers grew from a few to tens, to hundreds. Swords and shields at hand, they clashed together in rhythm, uniting as one. One of the soldiers walked to the back of the group, where General Anthony had arrived.

"The giant is back," the soldier announced.

"This cannot be!" General Anthony responded.

"It is true, general."

"The giant disappeared from King Khaba's service years ago, from what we were told. We thought he had died long ago."

"Go look for yourself," the soldier exclaimed.

The beating of swords and shield came to a halt. "Make way! Make way!" the General called. He moved through rows upon rows of soldiers for the first time in four long years.

For the first time, the giant and his former captor made eye contact. The memory came back, haunting the giant as though it had happened only yesterday.

"Well, a little stubborn, are we!" the general said to Chike. "Is this what you want? Fine; let it be that way."

Constant shaking rattled Chike at his core and resonated out to the giant's skin. *Rage . . . rage! REVENGE! It is all I have left.* Chike took a step forward, continuing to shake in anger. *My home . . . my people . . . mother . . . brother . . . sister . . .* White-hot fury soon consumed him, leaving his sanity behind, only vengeance remaining.

Not showing any signs of panic, General Anthony unsheathed his sword from his belt and gripped the leather strap of his shield. "Just like the last time!" he called, rallying his soldiers. They remembered the last confrontation.

"Today! Today, brothers! We will make history! People will talk about today, remembering us as legends, and we will be written in books as conquerors. But most of all, god slayers! Let us send this being back to the depths of Hades where he belongs!" General Anthony proclaimed.

Soldiers surrounding the general bellowed out a loud roar, taking in their leader's words to boost their morale. "Now march! March for glory!" the general commanded. *The sun may work in our favor*, he thought. *This is our opportunity to strike.*

The sun rose over the sea. "Charge!" he yelled. With swords, spears, and shields in hand, they sprinted to their nemesis. A sudden a roar erupted from the army. As they followed their leader, the rumble of hundreds of footsteps felt like a small earthquake shaking the ground.

"We fight! We fight for glory!" General Anthony proclaimed.

Straight ahead, that man dies last. Chike firmly gripped the handle of his ax. His vision blurred in the blazing whiteness of the early sunlight; he could only hear the yelling of men and feel the earth quaking with their footsteps. He threw his ax into the crowd with blazing speed. A soldier next to the general flew back as the weapon struck him deep in the chest, killing him instantly. The now-deceased soldier flew back several feet, pushing a crowd of soldiers along with him as they were knocked off their feet.

Chike yanked the chain to free the ax, which was stuck in the corpse. Blood splattered on the ground like free art, and the slain man landed on his back. The glare of the sun continued to irritate the giant, although he shaded his eyes with his hand for a better view.

Changing angles for the fight, the giant shifted his position to avoid the blinding light. The soldiers chased the giant with relentless valor.

The gap between the soldiers and the one-man army came to a close. General Anthony was the first to strike. Thrusting his sword with both hands, he used all the strength he could muster in the strike. He lunged forward and Chike parried to the side; nimbly, like a cat, he then grabbed hold of the man who had murdered his mother and tossed him twenty feet back into the assembled soldiers.

In response, the rest of the soldiers came crashing to the behemoth of a man like a tidal wave.

A mounted soldier with a spear was ahead of the group. He came charging alone, faster than the rest. He flung the spear, like a javelin, into the giant's chest, and watched in awe as the wooden pole shattered into a million small pieces. The tip of the spear remained stuck in Chike's thick skin, delivering only a light sting to his chest.

Chike watched the mounted soldier flee. The man retreated, disappearing into the back lines of his assembled companions.

The colossus pulled the spear tip from his skin with a quick tug. Blood seeped from the shallow cut, not perturbing him in the slightest. Instead, the tingle of pain he endured gave him more incentive to achieve his prize. *No matter the cost, they will all die tonight.*

Twisting the lower portion of the butt of the ax, Chike brought forth the double edge. The giant loosened the chain on his forearm, dropping his ax to the ground. With the chain in hand, he whipped the chain in a circle over his head, making the ax spin wildly in the air. Releasing the chain inch by inch, he increased its reach.

Still, the soldiers ran to their peril, following their commander valiantly. Within seconds, the blade devoured multiple targets. Blood, flesh, and bone splattered amongst the other men. The spinning ax was like a human grinder, sending mixed body parts to the gore-covered ground. Other soldiers pushed themselves back, not wanting to die in vain. They watched their comrades being shredded into pieces, losing limb after limb. Nonetheless, they lost their own lives in time, in the same fashion. Within those seconds, many strong men fell to the ground in quick and relatively painless death.

The remaining soldiers began to retreat, cowering back more and more as the giant moved forward. Slowing the motion of the chain, Chike gradually brought his weapon to the ground and then reeled in the chain. When he had retracted the second blade, he grasped the butt of the ax and then wrapped the chain around the handle and his fist.

"What are you doing?" General Anthony screamed.

The men-at-arms were terrified of the giant, remembering that last time, he had fought them with his bare hands. Now, he came to battle with a weapon, as an equal. It looked as though they beheld more than just a giant this time, more like a reaper, as they continued to retreat.

The giant marched inexorably forward, wanting more. He wore an angry scowl as he continued to seek satisfaction in vengeance.

"REVENGE!" Chike screamed in their tongue. "DEATH!"

The giant's roar made the soldiers quiver in their boots. As he continued their pursuit, the soldiers' terror increased.

Then, the general broke his silence: "There are hundreds of us and one of him! Do not let him deceive us; he is still human. He is no god! Surround him just as we did the last time, but this time, it will mean his death."

General Anthony pointed to his troops and captains, instructing them to flank the giant to the left. Following orders, the soldiers moved. Then the general shifted the rest of his soldiers and moved them to the right. Soon enough they closed the gap into a circle, trapping the giant so he could not escape their assault.

Step by step, the gap between the giant and his foes shrank. Circling around as though he were a wild animal surrounded by predators, he cracked his neck and stared them all down with a cold, dead glare. *They will all die the same way!*

Chike screamed, a monstrous roar. The soldiers began to sprint towards him, bent on destruction. Crashing into the front line of the army, the giant swung his arm like a sledgehammer straight into one soldier's face. The blow cracked the man's skull of the instantly killing him, and his body dropped to the earth like a puppet.

The giant stopped abruptly, swung the ax and let inertia do the rest of the work, cutting multiple heads off. Blood gushed out, spraying the giant like water from a fountain.

Terrified screams echoed around the battleground, as men charged at the giant who pummeled their front line. The first few strikes came from behind as the soldiers behind Chike pressed in on him.

If I do not show them that I feel pain, they will fear me all the more, Chike thought. The stinging sensations on his back and sides made him want to laugh, though apart of him also wanted to scream in pain.

"Get this savage down on all fours where he belongs!" a soldier shouted.

As the men stabbed his femur and tibia, the giant faltered to the ground, and the rest of the soldiers capitalized on this advantage. Soldiers jumped all over Chike, piercing his back with blades. Then, more men landed on the giant's back, trying to keep him down. One man used his bow in an attempt to strangle him.

Chike rolled over onto his back, crushing the few hanging on to dear life, leaving them gasping for air. He grunted, regaining his feet, but one man still held on, clinging to his bow. Removing the bow from his neck, the giant gazed implacably at the man clinging onto his weapon and immediately impaled him. Blood gushed from the corpse's mouth, and the two nearest soldiers began to panic, in fear for their lives.

In a moment of clarity, the soldier looked up at the giant. He closed his eyes and prayed to the gods for wife and child's safety. Regretting some of the choices he had made in life, he accepted his fate. The fist of the giant, twice the size of his face, came speeding down. The mighty blow crushed the soldier's face, leaving a crater.

By continuously stabbing him from a safe distance, the soldiers kept the giant close to the ground. Finally, Chike stood up, his back red and slick with blood from the constant onslaught of swords and spears.

The giant chased the men away, swinging punch after punch. Every soldier was on his heels, weaving and dodging to escape the blows by a hair's breadth. Their efforts came to an end when their luck ran out and Chike struck one in the ribs, cracking bone on contact. As a last resort, the soldier pulled out his dagger and stabbed the giant's hand.

Chike smiled deviously, flicking the small dagger away like a toy. With the ax in his right hand, he butchered the man, cleaving his stomach open. The flow of red erupted like a volcano as the soldier screamed and died.

The swarming army continued their wrathful assault. Making split-second decisions, the giant dodged the spears that flew by, snapping his head to the side. He grabbed a spear from a soldier's hand, driving the man to his knees. Chike then head-butted him to the ground.

Pain . . . It is starting to hurt. I must end this. Flipping the spear around, he tossed the spear into his oncoming foe such that the weapon punctured the man's belly and exited through his back. The spear continued its trajectory to find its home in the chest of another soldier.

The army's numbers continued to dwindle, to Chike's advantage. Lifeless bodies lay upon the earth, while the fight continued for the living. Some men began to flee while the giant's attention was focused on others. Haymaker after haymaker and strike after strike continued to fly, without any flagging of speed. *Where is their leader?* Chike wondered. *He is not dead yet.*

Though their attacks were seemingly becoming futile, the army kept up their attack. The giant simply continued to destroy whatever surrounded him. From right punch to left punch, ducking and dodging a few attacks every so often, to kicking a soldier's chest in, Chike enjoyed every moment of the combat with a villainous smile, reveling in the freedom of his choices.

In an orchestrated surprise attack, the remaining men quickly gathered and surrounded the giant. The soldiers moved quickly, like scuttling rodents. The giant looked from side to side and whirled around to see what might brew in the moments ahead. The soldiers engaged their foe simultaneously, moving as one. All swords and spears reached their marks in the abdomen, back and sides of the giant.

Blood flowed from the giant, yet he still showed no signs of pain. Well within his striking distance, Chike spun like a tornado. Creating a bond between steel and flesh, he swung his right arm freely. His blade sung a deadly symphony with the screaming of men. Chike slashed their necks and any other exposed body parts, causing blood to spray and gush forth like a fountainhead.

His eyes were fixed on the man leading the charge. Most of the other men had been massacred. Chike strode to the last few who were still standing, either afraid to fight or paralyzed by fear. They had prayed to be the few who would escape. None of it mattered; in the very end, they all met their fate. No miracles or blessing in disguise, only suffering. Chike's years-old desire for revenge was finally fulfilled as he found himself, at last, toe to toe with the monster who had killed his mother.

Unwrapping the rest of the chain from his forearm, Chike held the double-edged ax in his left hand. One of the few remaining soldiers charged him, only to be tripped by the chain. The giant smiled as the man fell. His massive fist followed the soldier's body to the ground, crushing bones and tearing through flesh.

The giant quickly got back up and watched another soldier decide to run for his life. He wound up the ax and rocketed the weapon after the fleeing man, striking the poor soul's back. More soldiers decided they no longer wanted to continue fighting and fled to random locations, but Chike thought otherwise and inexorably hunted them down.

He whipped the massive chain around a soldier's neck. With a slight pull of the chain, the man's face began to turn beet red as his circulation was cut off. Seconds later, Chike quickly yanked the chain, severing the head from the body.

I am great! I am a warrior! If I die, I will take him to hell with me! General Anthony thought.

"DIE!" Chike roared, his sight fixed upon the man who stood before him. "Rah!" the giant screamed, exerting all possible force in his swing. The general ducked in the nick of time, leaving another man in the giant's path. The ax slashed the man clear though from side to side, ripping him in half.

The general parried each strike with finesse, watching Chike carefully and mirroring his movement. Once more, he watched the ax swing by. This time it was much closer than the last. *I will not have another chance if he keeps this up. Thankfully, he is a little slower because he's used most of his energy already.* Watching the axe strike down like lightning and crater the earth below, General Anthony jumped back and slashed his sword at the giant's hand, creating a shower of sparks like fireworks as his weapon hit the chain.

Chike pulled the weapon back and thrust the edge of the ax at his foe. Instantaneously, the general brought up his shield, saving himself from imminent death. He assessed the situation. *Not just yet . . .* As the copper shield caved in from the sheer force, the giant continued to press with all his might against the little man.

If he continues like this, my shield will be my own hand. Losing ground, the general leaned all his weight into the shield, trying to slow down the giant's progression to no avail. He changed his tactics, striking at the hand once more, but this time through the small crevasse between the chains. The blade slid in, touching skin and the giant showed signs of pain. *Finally, I have a chance.*

Pulling away from the discomfort, Chike thrust the ax back into the shield. This time, General Anthony used both hands to brace for the attack. The rattling blow shook General Anthony, coursing through his body. Another strike came just as quickly, fatigue now becoming a factor.

The shield on his left arm felt like a burden more than protection as it caved in. The last strike from the giant was the last straw. The general lifted his shield one last time, and Chike's brute strength finally overpowered it. The shield completely caved in, and the bruises on the general's arm turned purplish-black and blue. Throwing away the shield, he felt the numbness left by multiple hits.

This animal shows no sign of slowing down. Fuck! Taking a few steps back, General Anthony tripped on a dead body and fell to the ground. *Fuck! Fuck, fuck, fuck, fuck!* Gasping for air, the general blinked a few times, attempting to refocus on the giant's location. Quickly, the ax came down to strike like a hammer to a coffin nail. The general rolled over, narrowly dodging the blow. Chike slashed the air just above his enemy, anticipating that he would regain his feet, but the general was lucky with every roll.

Ah, a sword. General Anthony rolled once more and grabbed the sword he'd spotted. The giant watched his foe's movement and this time was a step quicker, crushing the blade of the sword and making it impossible for the general to use. In a flash, Chike's foe lay on the ground, crying out in pain and missing a hand.

Chike stood over his old enemy with a cold, vengeful look. Anthony could not bear to look up or at the throbbing stump of his missing hand.

"Kill me now," General Anthony spat.

Chike waited for the general to look up at him.

"THIS . . . IS . . . MY . . . REVENGE!" Chike bellowed.

He threw down his ax for the last time, splitting the head of his last enemy. The feeling of satisfaction would only last for a moment. He reclaimed the ax from the ground. An empty feeling filled him thereafter when he walked away from the battlefield, tying up the ax and chain to his arm.

Through the town, the women and children ran, screamed, and hid in fear, but the giant did not pay any mind to them.

"One day you will understand… You are meant to do greater things in life. Greater things in life, greater things in life, greater things in life…" The voice of his mother echoed in the back of his mind.

This is my true calling.

CHAPTER 24
—PLANTING THE SEED

The instructor glanced at the last page of the book and then looked up to the class. With a ruler in hand, she began to walk through the aisles of students at their desks. She carefully observed each individual to see if they were paying attention.

"Only a hand full of soldiers survived that historic fight and documented the massacre. Does anyone know the importance of this moment in history?" she questioned. Walking down another aisle, she asked again, "Anyone?" A moment later, she continued waiting for any volunteers and scanned the room with her eyes.

"Abel," she called, stopping at his desk.

Anxiety made the young boy freeze. His mind could not function fast enough to answer, because it frightened him to be called upon. A chill as cold as a winter's bite gave him shivers and goosebumps although it was a mid-spring day. He simply drew a blank. Every student turned a watchful gaze to him, waiting for an answer.

Across the room, another student called out, "Be like Abel. Frozen, you will destroy everything."

Laughter erupted in the room and lightened the mood, but the chosen boy did not change. He kept to himself, trying to figure the answer to the lesson at hand. Illythia stared at her neighbor for the day and then, when he remained silent, returned to her studies.

"Class. Quiet down," the instructor ordered. The laughter came to an end as the teacher held the ruler firmly

"Power," Abel finally answered.

"What about power?" the teacher prompted him.

"The power to be great and the power he used to change the future."

"Good answer, but it is not what I am looking for. Does anyone else want to give it a try?"

"One person can change the course of the future," Rowland mumbled softly.

"Can you say that again, whoever spoke? Speak up! Speak up."

Rowland raised his voice slightly. "One person can change the course of the future."

"Very good, and do you know why, class?" The instructor paused. "One's own actions, choices, and ideas can change and shape the future."

On a parchment paper, Illythia began to jot down her thoughts. The classroom started to get restless as the day dragged on. Knowing that the school day was nearing its end, the class started to bubble over with chatter. At that moment, the faint shadow of a figure graced the side of the building through the window, and a few of the students caught a glimpse.

A knock sounded on the door, and the instructor left the aisle to answer it. With a surprised look, she whispered so that the students could not hear, "Father Jean? How can I help you?"

Father Jean was, as usual, decked out in his black cassock and cross necklace. He wore a welcoming smile on his lined face and patient brown eyes.

"I need to have a little talk with you, alone if possible," he responded.

"Certainly." She turned around to face the class and called out, "Class dismissed."

The chairs' feet screeched on the floor as the students got up. In singles and pairs, the children exited the classroom, greeting Father Jean on their way. Saying her farewells to the rest of her students, the instructor smiled as they left.

One of the last to leave, Illythia slipped a note on Rowland's desk when he was fixated upon the instructor and Father Jean. *I will give him some more years. This one will soon come seeking answers*, she thought, leaving the classroom.

Looking down at the parchment left like a gift in front of him, Rowland slipped it into one of his pockets like a love note. He gathered up all his belongings like any other day. Rowland was always the last one to leave. Unlike everyone else, his thirst for more knowledge could not be fulfilled during the normal hours of school; he wanted the satisfaction of knowing more. Slowly dragging his feet on the way out, he would sometimes think, *I wish I could stay here forever, just learning . . . I need to know more.*

"Have a good day, Rowland," said the instructor as he left.

With a half-smile, he replied, "Have a good day."

Father Jean gave Rowland a warm smile as the boy left the classroom and continued down the pathway. Then the priest closed the door behind him and walked with the teacher to her desk.

"What brings you here today?" she asked.

"I have some concerns that have been brought up to my attention," he replied.

"About?"

"Rowland."

"Rowland?" she was baffled.

"Yes . . . he is not like the other children. He is unique."

"Unique. Indeed." the teacher sat down. "If he had the choice, I think he would live here," she smiled.

"I think so . . . also, he does not seem to get along with any of the other children." Father Jean rubbed his chin with his fingers.

"He will get around to it. He is very eager to learn, very intelligent. I would not worry too much about it."

"And that is why I worry. Over the years I have watched over him, and he is still the same boy I met back when his parents were killed," his hands rested on his hips.

"Just keep him on the right path, Father. Rowland is bright and he has a bright future ahead of him," the instructor reassured him.

A small field of grass surrounded a circular fountain in the center of the courtyard, surrounded in turn by trees, and hidden from the buildings. In the shade, alone, Rowland sat beneath a tree, pouting. *I am not ready to go home.* The thought of returning to the residence always plagued him, yet there was nothing else to return to. *Why did you have to leave me? Mother . . . Father . . . I miss you.*

A light breeze sent a cold chill into the shade where Rowland sat, making him shiver. Watching the other kids laugh and play out in the sun on the sides of the courtyard or out in the field, Rowland still felt a void lingering within. Moving from sitting cross-legged to hugging his knees, he heard the paper rustle in his front pocket.

Curiosity overcame him. He quickly opened the piece of paper and read a few letters, "N. S." Farther down more words were added: "One day our paths will cross."

As he looked at the orphanage home, Rowland had a bitter taste in his mouth knowing that the bullies shared the same living quarters. *Why do I go through all this torture . . .?*

Time flew by as Rowland sat beneath the tree. He watched everyone pass by once or twice to the orphanage house or to the church. Nonetheless, it was all the same, and he watched the bully walk into the house with no care in the world. Always stalling for another moment, he tried to figure out what he wanted to do next.

The afternoon came to an end and dusk started to set in. Father Jean walked the courtyard one last time to see if there were any stragglers still out and about. Rowland got up and met him exiting the courtyard, and they entered the church together.

■　　■　　■　　■

Events seemed to follow the same routine as any other day. However, something felt off, a little different. The bullies walked right past Rowland as if he did not exist. *Today must be a good day,* he thought.

School flew by as usual, with no hiccups or disturbances during class. Before Rowland knew it, the school day had ended. The new student who sat next to him did not say a word. That did not bother him, though. He was used to the silence and awkwardness that surrounded him.

Again, Rowland was the last to leave the classroom, as was his preference. He enjoyed being the last to leave since it prevented any altercations with other students. The last voice of the day he would hear was always his instructor saying, "Have a good day, Rowland." *She is always nice to me.* Walking out the door, he gave her a nod of acknowledgment and continued along the path he always took to the courtyard.

Others were chattering in the middle of the courtyard. Rowland looked on from the safety of the shade trees, where he customarily spent his time. He enjoyed being the spectator, watching the other kids talk about anything and everything, never once looking at him, as if he were invisible to the world.

He often stared out into the sky, watching the clouds roll along through the cover of branches and leaves. It was a reminder of the days when he used to lie on the blanket during a family picnic and stare at the clouds with his parents. He yearned for the past; always wishing he could go back to those carefree days.

Walking silently along the tree lines, the new student, Illythia, crept by. For a moment she stopped and stared at the lonely boy lost in his thoughts. *I wonder if I would be in the same position as he if I were still a slave.*

"Hi," Illythia broke the silence, holding a book close to her chest.

Turning his head toward the voice, Rowland remained otherwise still. His eyes opened a little. "Uh . . . Ah. H-Hi."

"May I?" she gestured to the open spot beside him.

As a precaution, Rowland looked from side to side to make certain that she was really addressing him. "S-Sure."

"Why are you all by yourself?" she asked.

"N-N-No reason," he responded.

A moment of silence passed, both of them gazing into the sky above, before Illythia spoke again. "I was speaking with my father about the lesson we learned yesterday."

"Uh-hmm."

"The story about the giant."

"Yeah . . . I remember."

"Can you imagine if people like them ever existed?"

For a moment, Rowland thought about what to say. "Do you think people like him exist?"

He does. She chuckled. "It is told in stories . . . So it must be true."

"Yeah." His mind began to drift away.

"What would you do if you had the strength of the giant?"

"I don't know . . . Change my past, maybe."

"Hmm. I told my father about you and how smart you were. He gave me a sly smile and said that I'd taken a liking to you, but I told him otherwise. He went through some items he has been collecting for some time now. Then he blew the dust off of the cover of this book and wiped it clean, and said to make sure you read this." Illythia revealed the book to Rowland.

"It is blank . . . It doesn't have a title. What is the book called?" Rowland asked.

"The Four."

"The Four?"

"Yes. The story is about four legendary warriors throughout history. I think you might like this. Here, it now belongs to you," she handed Rowland the book.

Reaching to accept the gift, Rowland replied, "Th-Thank you."

Illythia gave Rowland a half-smile and then looked out to the courtyard. Realizing the time, she got up and said, "It was nice talking to you, and now I must go before my father is displeased with me."

"Okay," he replied, watching the traveling merchant's daughter walk away.

"It all begins here. The thirst for power will consume you." —Morgana

CHAPTER 25
—A SICKNESS

1674

"You will come back to me. I know you will."

Susanna sat near the window, her sad blue eyes and pale, wan face reflecting from the glass. Just as she did every day now, she stared out the window lifelessly, waiting for her special someone to come waltzing through the door yelling out, "Honey, I'm home."

Those days came to an end a month ago when it all changed. Though the days were nice and warm with not a cloud in the sky to hinder the sun, the Newmans' home was now as cold as winter.

Susanna coughed, covering her mouth with a handkerchief.

Joseph displayed a mix of his parents' features: blue eyes, square face, heart-shaped chin, and dimples when he smiled. He was slender and healthy, and his blond hair was cropped short. He sat on the wooden living room floor, dressed in his brown pants and white shirt, as usual, playing games with his imagination. Every so often, he would pause to look at his mother as she stared blankly out the window, but could not tell if she was focused on something or in another daydream.

Susanna had begun neglecting all the chores she would normally do around the house after the incident had happened. A new cold, empty nothingness left her feeling brittle and hollow, consuming her from within. Seconds turned into minutes and minutes turned to hours as she sat unmoving.

Nothing seemed to be accomplished until the night crept around the corner, and then Susanna would work in the kitchen. The simple act of deciding what to cook that night was a dreadful thought. She had once loved to cook, surprising her love with gourmet food that she would conjure from the simplest ingredients. That enjoyment was taken away from her now.

Joseph would wander around inside the house with little care unless he needed to be tended to. He had become accustomed to being ignored unless his mother was having a better day. Those came far and few between.

Visitors would come to the house every so often and knock on the door. Susanna's hacking cough could be heard from outside. Today, she opened the door and gave a faint smile to her brother-in-law as she nodded for Father William to enter. He closed the door with a faint click, and both of them headed to the living room.

"How is Joseph?" he asked.

"Still lively, even more than ever," she replied. A few coughs followed her response.

"Are you okay?" William asked, concerned. He sat down in a chair.

"Yes, I'm fine," Susanna sat next to William.

"Are you sure? You don't look well. Maybe you should come to the church so we can help you out," Father William suggested.

"Yes, I'm sure," Susanna tried to reassure him. Again came that hacking cough.

"Where is my little nephew?"

"Right there," she nodded in the other direction.

"Oh, I didn't see him hiding there."

"Yes, he is rather quiet now."

"Have you thought about coming and living at the church?" William tried again.

"And leave everything we have?" Susanna sounded appalled.

"No, I didn't mean it like that. I'm just suggesting that you get help every now and then, you know."

"Well, thank you for the offer."

Walking to the where the adults were having their discussion, Joseph hugged his mother's side and peeped out at William. He wore neither a smile nor a frown, only an expression of curiosity. He wanted to know what was going on.

"Well, hey there, buddy, how are you?" William asked cheerfully.

Joseph responded, with a shy smile, "Good." Trying to hide from his uncle's sight, Joseph hugged his mother a little tighter, concealing his face. Seconds later, someone knocked on the door. Their attention turned in that direction and Susanna proceeded to answer the door.

"Ah, yes," William remembered, getting up from his seat.

"Hmm?"

"I'll get the door for you."

"Okay . . ." Susanna paused near the door.

Father William went to Susanna's side and opened the door. Who might come knocking in the wee hours? Susanna thought it odd. A man dressed in a black cassock, like her brother-in-law, stood on the threshold. His features were concealed in the shadow.

"Father William, I brought you what you asked for," said the visiting priest.

"Thank you."

The man took his leave just as quickly as he'd appeared, vanishing back into the darkness outside. Father William immediately closed the door.

"These are for you," William handed the provisions to Susanna.

"Ah, thank you," she replied. "Care to join us for dinner? It is almost finished."

"Thank you for the offer," said William, "but I must be going."

"Okay." She almost sighed, and then was overtaken by a coughing fit instead.

Kneeling down, William rubbed Joseph's head, rumpling his hair. They exchanged a brief smile, and then the priest stood up.

"You take care of yourself, for your own and Joseph's sake, alright?" William said with concern.

Susanna nodded.

"I will come back tomorrow and check on you," William opened the door.

The warm presence that had filled the house left with William. The cold, dreary atmosphere crept back in, and Susanna welcomed it with open arms. Joseph resumed running around in the living room, playing imaginary games again.

Susanna went back to the kitchen. The worsening cough continued to plague her. She also felt dizzy and light-headed, hot and cold at once. Still, she continued to push and work to the night's end. The rest of the world, to her, was nothing but a blur.

CHAPTER 26
—A LOVE BIRD'S FATE

The repeated thudding on wood sounded in the distance, disturbing Joseph's sleep, yet no one answered it. Normally his mother would have answered the door. Extending his limbs from the comforts of his bed, Joseph drew in a deep breath and shook off his slumber. Pushing back the comforter from his body, he rubbed the sand from his eyes as quickly as his fatigue would allow.

Walking past his parents' bedroom, he heard no sound from within the room. He passed by obliviously, not thinking to check inside. A loud creak screeched forth when he stepped on a loose plank in the floor. This sound would usually have woken his mother, yet she did not stir.

As the boy made his way down the staircase, the squeaks continued with almost every step as he neared the door. Another round of loud knocking sounded.

Something was different. Joseph scanned the living room, but his mother was gone. She usually stared off through the window, waiting for her husband to return, as the sun seeped through and cast its rays across the floor.

Continuous knocks rapped forth once more, snapping him back to reality. Finally, the person outside unlocked the door and stepped inside. A smile lit up Joseph's face; it was Uncle William.

"Hey there, big guy. Where is your mother?" Father William inquired.

"I don't know." Joseph shrugged.

William entered, closing the door behind him, and began to look around. Joseph followed in his footsteps. They strode quickly through the living room and into the kitchen. No sign of Susanna there, either. Everything was in its place, spotless.

"Hmm," William pondered.

"Hmm?" Joseph wondered.

"Could your mother be in her room?"

"I didn't hear her at all upstairs, but I didn't check her room," Joseph replied.

"Well, let's check then. I'll race you up there!"

"Okay!"

"Ready . . . Set . . . GO!" Father William set the pace.

Joseph bolted like a cannonball in flight, leaving his uncle in the dust. He flew from the kitchen and past the dining room table, thinking only of winning this competition. The top of the staircase was his goal. Without a glance behind him, the child pounded rapidly up the stairs.

His uncle followed behind, walking casually up the stairs. He knew that moments like this, when he could give his nephew the pleasure of playing together, were few and far between. After his brother had passed away, he knew the boy's only chance for such play was when he came over. When he looked up, Joseph was already at the top of the stairs. *He is getting faster every time!*

"I win!" Joseph shouted from the top of the staircase.

Father William wore a wide grin, proud of his nephew. He ascended the stairs and tried to calm Joseph by putting a finger to his lips, hushing the young boy down. Silence came when Joseph understood what his uncle was conveying. No sound could be heard from the entrance of the master bedroom, but the door was left wide open. Then, a faint noise came from within. "Uh."

William rushed into the pitch-black room, where heavy drapes kept out the sunlight. He opened them slowly to let the light creep in and get a view of the room. Susanna's eyelids twitched in the light, as if they wanted to open, but could not.

Another light groan came from the woman on the bed. William came to the bedside and sat down. He noticed that the area around her was drenched with sweat, and he felt her forehead with his palm. Feeling the blaze of heat upon her skin, he realized that she had a raging fever. *Damn it . . . I should have brought some medicine with me.* Her skin was even paler than it had been the day before. William got up and hurried downstairs to grab a towel, and soaked it in cold water. He sped back into the room and placed the wet towel on her forehead in an attempt to reduce the fever.

I need to get to the church to get some medicine and ask for help to get Susanna out of here. I must go; I must hurry. Getting up from the comfort of the bed, William knelt down to Joseph. "Hey, big guy, stay here and I will be back as soon as I can."

Joseph nodded and allowed William to lift him up to sit next to his resting mother. Quick as the wind, William was gone after a few thumps of his feet down the stairs and the bang of the door closing hastily.

Left alone with his mother, Joseph waited patiently. Time seemed to be at a standstill. He did not play around as usual; instead, he was intent on helping in any way possible.

"Mama?" he called out.

At first, she did not hear his call. She tried to fight off the fever, her face twisted in pain and occasionally twitching. Her son's voice sounded like a distant echo in the wind as she tried to pinpoint the origin of the sound.

"Mama . . . Mama . . . Mama?" the cries sounded so far away.

Susanna finally achieved full consciousness and opened her eyes to see her son sitting by her side. Her warm smile consumed most of her energy. The fever made her ache, and her body stiffened as though her muscles were made of stone. Joseph smiled back with the biggest smile he could possibly present to her. In that very moment, they both felt the touch of heaven upon them.

"My dear Joseph . . ." Susanna spoke, her voice parched and dry.

"Mama," he replied.

Swallowing the little saliva in her mouth gave her the voice to speak. She reached out to caress the boy's cheeks. "I love you, Son," she smiled once again. "I am sorry for not being there when you needed me the most, but I am here now."

"I love you, mama," Joseph hugged his mother. Tears began to run down his face as though his eyes had a mind of their own. Emotions ran high, and at that very moment, Susanna joined in with tears of her own. "You are always there for me, Mother." Joseph stumbled on some of the words.

"I was not . . . I kept hope alive every day, thinking that Abraham would come back to us. I neglected everything else, even you."

"But . . . Papa is with us."

She did not understand at the time, and wondered what he meant. Susanna took Joseph's hand and caressed it. Her frail state continued to decline.

Behind Joseph, a transparent white figure hovered, his face dimpling with a smile. Abraham looked around the room and down upon his wife, reaching out his hand toward her.

"I want you to know, even though I may not be with you in life, I will always be with you in here," she moved Joseph's hand to his chest. "I am Abraham's love bird."

The door opened and closed downstairs, and footsteps thudded up the staircase, followed by William appearing in the bedroom doorway with a small pouch in hand. William set it on the foot of the bed and Susanna gave him a smile.

"You don't have to," she said, watching him unpack the medicine.

William gave Susanna a blank look of confusion.

"I want you to take care of my son for me. He is meant to do great things . . ."

"We will get you through this," William reassured her.

Her eyes slowly closed for the last time as she drew her final breath. Neither pain nor suffering remained, only an easy passing. At last, in peace, she joined the one she loved.

Pausing a moment to take it all in, William let Joseph spend those final moments with his mother in peace. As he returned all the medicine to the bag, he tried to remain unobtrusive, so as not to disturb the pair.

Father William left the bedroom and began to gather Joseph's belongings in the boy's room across the hall. One by one, he gathered Joseph's clothing and hung it across his arm, taking as much as he could carry.

He left Joseph in the other room and made his way down the stairs, out the door to the small single-horse wooden carriage with a small flatbed behind. After setting the clothes near the front, Father William returned to his brother's house and collected more of Joseph's belongings. The carriage soon filled up with things that Father William thought Joseph might keep along with some other cherished items.

Joseph watched a white glow from his mother's body rise and sit up. She looked around the room and smiled, taking Abraham's extended hand, then standing and embracing him. For a moment, time stood still, and then they walked together to the hallway. Before leaving, they looked back at Joseph and spoke: "One day, not this day, we will come back for you. We know you are going to do great things with your life. Never forget that we love you and will always be with you."

Joseph's parents then disappeared from his sight, and the warmth went with them. Left alone in the room, Joseph laid down to rest with his departed mother in bed, tired from the morning's trauma. Nothing else mattered besides rest.

The last few items Father William took were in the living room, including a small portrait of Abraham, Susanna, and Joseph together. He took a short break, thinking back with a sad smile, *Oh, brother, I miss you.* After taking all the photos back to the carriage, he returned upstairs to finally collect Joseph, who slept comfortably next to his mother.

He cradled Joseph in his arms and carried him from the room, leaving Susanna behind for the moment. William turned back to the hallway and descended the staircase for the last time. Joseph did not once move or squirm in his uncle's arms.

Having been placed in the backseat of the carriage, Joseph turned around to find a comfortable position and continued to sleep. Walking back to the doorstep, William stopped and gazed into the living room and the staircase one last time. *I have to bury my sister next to my brother.* He shook his head in disbelief. *I never thought that this day would come. I will be back.*

Though he knew it was the end of a family, it was the beginning for his nephew. Father William closed the door, and the flow of memories of his brother and sister-in-law played in his mind, leaving him with a smile.

"Hmm," Joseph groaned, stretching out on the bed.

Thinking that he was still in the bed next to his mother, he turned over to see if she was still there, but there was no sign of her on the other side. *Is this a dream?* He did not recognize the room; it was completely different from his parents' house; he knew that something was wrong. Finding himself in a new place, all he could do was wonder. On the countertop, across the room, a candle wick sputtered. He could smell the burning wax. A light white smoke floated in the air like a snake, and then the flame had no more wax to burn.

A small strip of light came through the curtains. In a trance, Joseph stared at the bar of light on the floor for a while. Then, the doorknob turned with a slight squeak, and, peeping through the door, his uncle asked, "Can I come in?"

Joseph nodded.

"I hope you like your arrangements. I tried to match it, the same way you had your room." Father William moved to the side of the bed and opened the curtains wide.

Joseph looked puzzled by his uncle's comment. He thought about getting up, but in the end, he stayed in bed, watching his uncle walk around the room. Either he was too tired to respond or too stunned to distinguish what was real and what was not. He hadn't had time to process what was happening around him. William left the room with the candle stub and returned quickly with a new one.

"Where is my mother?" Joseph broke his silence.

Father William took a moment to think before responding. "Your mother is in a better place now . . . She is with your father."

But I was just right next to her... Joseph quickly added it together, understanding his uncle's intentions and remembering what his mother had said. A feeling of sadness swooped down around him like thick fog; he wanted to mope and seclude himself from the world and the people around him. He knew better, though, as his parents had taught him well. Forcing himself out of bed, Joseph stood, a little shaky, eyes brimming with tears, and weak from having lain still so long.

Scanning the room, he felt as if he were still in his own home. Through the window, he watched a small group walking along the street. The young boy wondered where his house was, relative to his new location. However, he had no time to relax and consider it; instead, he followed his uncle.

The child's mind ran freely. Though he felt a little discouraged, Joseph was still the same, full of life. His imagination ran wild when his uncle gave him a tour of his new home. The sound of William's voice seemed muffled and distant, as though he were barely there.

Father William's next words caught Joseph's attention: "Right behind you, to the right, is the bell tower."

Joseph looked with a smile on his face, wanting to see the tower for himself, but his uncle continued his slow pace to the church. Passing the last window of the hallway, William stopped at the window. He pointed to a little shack outside. "That right there is the outhouse. Whenever you need to use it, you know where it is."

Before Joseph lay a grand wooden hall, bigger than what Joseph was used to seeing on a daily basis. There were three walkways, one on each side and one in the middle of the room. To the sides of the center walkway, long pews sat in rows almost to the back of the room. He looked through the windows briefly, then back to his uncle.

At the center table, a large cup sat in the middle next to two golden bowls. Father William indicated it: "This spot right here is where I first helped the priest in Mass, as an altar boy." Reminiscing on the past, he smiled, his eyes going distant with the memory, "Maybe one day you will do the same."

Taken by the new scenery, Joseph did not speak a word the rest of the day. He walked by his uncle's side and continued to listen to him. The day flew by for once, the first such day in a long time. He could not remember what he had for dinner, or what they'd done before. Before he knew it, Uncle William was leading him back to his sleeping quarters.

Joseph quickly slipped into his pajamas and made his way to the bed. Father William sat on the side of the bed as he turned back the sheet for Joseph to slip into.

"How old are you, big guy?"

"Almost seven."

"Oh my, you are growing up too quick."

Joseph frowned. "When will I get to see mother?"

"What do you mean, Joseph?"

"When can I see mama for the last time? I mean, before she is with Papa forever."

"Tomorrow," Father William answered.

"Okay."

"We are going to dress you up and you can say your farewell."

"Okay," Joseph frowned.

"Remember this. Even though you will say your farewells to them here and now, they will always be here," William pointed to Joseph's chest.

The boy nodded his head and then lay back on the pillow.

"Just remember that you can always visit them in your heart when you are feeling down. In a few days, you will be going to school to learn about things I cannot teach, and you will be helping out around the church."

Joseph let out a big yawn, letting his uncle know it was time for the boy to sleep. William tucked the sheets snugly around his nephew. Darkness set in for the young boy as his eyelids closed like a gate. His uncle disappeared into the shadows as he closed the door behind him.

Mama . . . Papa . . .

CHAPTER 27
—FIRST DAY OF SCHOOL

"Nathaniel! Wake up, time for your first day of school," Bruce yelled from the living room.

As Nathaniel let out a long, quiet yawn, his eyes filled with water. He stared up at the ceiling and then rolled over to the side of the bed. Nathaniel planted one foot on the floor, then the other. Leaving the bed sheets messy, he scrounged around the room for a clean shirt and pants to wear.

He looked underneath the bed and found a white shirt and brown pants, and quickly put them on. Passing the dresser and window and moving to the door, he found his boots. After stepping over a few toys that lay on the floor, he quickly slipped on his boots.

Nathaniel opened the bedroom door, beyond which the living quarters were just in sight. The fireplace in the living room smoldered as the last of its flame went up in smoke. Near the stone chimney, two rocking chairs sat in shadow across from each other. He walked by and brushed his boots on the bear skin rug.

He quickly made his way through the living room and was almost to the door when he heard a shout from behind.

"Do not be late!" Bruce warned him.

"Yes, father," Nathaniel responded obediently.

Nathaniel picked up a glass container half filled with water, which reflected shades of light like a prism, and placed it on a nearby table. His father,

Bruce, sat in the rocking chair next to the fireplace and took another gulp of the dark honey colored liquid from a glass bottle. There remained no scent of carbon in the air from the once burning firewood, which had now turned white on the outside while the inner portion still glowed red.

"Do you remember where to go?" Bruce asked gruffly.

"I remember," Nathaniel replied, rushing to the door.

"Okay, good," Bruce took another gulp.

Bruce stared into the cooling fireplace, fixated on nothing. His eyes revealed the pain that he endured, yet he hid it as best he could with the help of liquor. The cold days lingered on since his significant other left him without a single word.

Bruce was endlessly haunted by the deal he'd made with Morgana. He wasn't in the right state of mind to concentrate. His thoughts were adrift, always remaining in the past. His only friend was the glass bottle in his hand, helping him wash the pain away, one gulp at a time.

The door opened and closed quickly with Nathaniel's departure, before the glow of the light outside could make its presence known in the house. Now, Bruce's son was gone for the rest of the day. The night still commanded the sky, but was soon to be chased away by the sun.

A narrow path from the house to the main road was barely visible in the darkness. The grass hung over the edges to the man-made road, ready to sprout up with life once the light shone around the corner. The trees surrounded one another like penguins huddled together for warmth, with no whispers from the wind. The only sound to be heard against the looming dead silence was the shuffle of the boy's footsteps shifting sand and gravel from their place.

The brisk morning finally came to life, and rays of light began to spread from the horizon. With every step, Nathaniel made his way closer to town. Crossing over a wooden bridge, he looked over the side to view a tree that stood alone near the river and bridge. The unique scent of the river made him take a deep breath, wanting and waiting to take yet another. Stopping in the middle, he watched the flowing water, awestruck by its beauty.

Annette . . .

Did I hear someone say something? Nathaniel thought.

Beyond the grass plains and isolated farm houses, he continued north along the road. Soon, he saw the first signs of life. Farmers sat atop their carriages, carrying loads of crops into town. Nathaniel would soon become familiar with the city that lay before him. Several two-story houses came into view as the road forked into two directions.

Feeling like he was in wonderland, Nathaniel danced around as though tipsy. The atmosphere of the city gave him somewhat of a rush. Swerving back and forth, he dodged the oncoming traffic of people and carriages.

Clusters of people who saw the young boy did not pay any mind to him or try to avoid him. Nathaniel wanted to say hello, but was too timid to say anything. It was all new and different, outside of the comfort zone he'd grown accustomed to at home.

Nathaniel could hear people shouting obscenities from one side of the busy street, above the ambient noise of the city's hustle and bustle. Farmers, merchants, and traders were beginning to set up shop as was their usual morning routine. People congregated around the merchants to see what was new, and sought out the fresh produce the farmers had to offer. Some came to browse, just killing time, and others were running errands.

Some clusters of people were engaged in gossip as well. Some of these stared at Nathaniel as he passed, making him feel awkward. He had no business with them and pretended not to notice.

A man among the group of gossipers, spectacles perched upon his nose, spoke up: "Whose kid is that?"

"Which one?" another man, wearing a hat, replied.

"The child who just passed by us?" a mustached man questioned.

"Yeah, that one."

"Oh! That one is the drunk's child. Bruce is his name," the mustached man answered.

"What about the child's name?" the man in the hat inquired.

"Nathaniel, I believe."

"Oh, that's right. I feel sad for that boy," the bespectacled man chimed in.

"Why?"

"Did you not know?" The mustached man looked somewhat shocked.

"I heard that child's mother just up and left them one night," the man adjusted his glasses.

"But why?" the man removed his hat.

"Maybe she didn't want him. Or maybe Bruce beat her up. Could be that she got sucked into some witchcraft. Who knows?" the man brushed his whiskers with a finger.

Turning their heads and following the young boy's movement, the men watched Nathaniel make his way to the other side of the market and disappear into the crowd. They could only wonder what it felt like to be in his shoes.

"I pity that boy," said the glasses-wearer, as he pulled a handkerchief from his pocket to clean his eyewear.

The other two looked on in puzzlement at that comment. They tilted their heads to exchange a curious glance, and then focused back on their friend.

"Why would you pity him?" the man returned his hat to its place upon his head.

"Look at him . . . His father is the town drunk, and he has no mother. How much worse could it be for him?"

"Worse," the man with the mustache pointed toward Nathaniel, who continued his way to school. They soon realized the gossip between them was reflected in reality. People among the crowd darted awkward glances at the young boy and moved aside farther, avoiding proximity with the child and giving him more room to walk. Those who watched him slowly turned their heads.

Nathaniel, meanwhile, loved the new sights he came upon. He was a stranger to every different scene, and took the time to soak it all in. He listened to the lowing of cattle, the chatter between people in conversation, and watched the white smoke rising from small cook fires. He did not stop to browse around, though, knowing he had to be at his destination on time. The aroma of food cooking over the fires was tempting. His body wanted to follow his nose to the food; his empty stomach rumbled with hunger.

The city folk were attending to their daily responsibilities, running their errands while avoiding collision with others. The populace flowed like a mini highway of bodies. Nathaniel resisted the city's temptations and distractions by walking a little faster. He mainly tried to avoid bumping into others, and got the same impression from the people surrounding him. At this point, the boy was starting to feel lost, for he still could catch no sight of the school.

The memories of the past few days were still vivid. His father's voice echoed inside his mind as though Bruce stood right behind him. *"Look for the bell tower of the church, and you will be going in the right way."* Farther down the road, the crowd of adults slowly faded away, and other children in the same age group were moving in the same direction. Finally, the bell tower finally came into view.

On the school's doorstep stood an older woman, clothed in a modest brown and white dress, her feet covered in sturdy brown boots. Her tanned skin was weathered by time and sun, and her brown hair showed the frost of age. Keen hazel eyes regarded the students, whom she greeted with a slight smile as they entered.

A pair of girls in front of Nathaniel greeted the teacher with soft-spoken words, too low for him to hear. He watched them turn their heads in his direction, briefly glance at the new student, and giggled between themselves before entering the building. The teacher, for her part, felt an unnerving presence emanating from the young boy, yet she still smiled and gave him the heartiest welcome she could.

Still early in the morning, Nathaniel thought.

As he took a few steps into the big room, a buildup of nervousness engulfed the boy, maintaining a chokehold on him. He saw a large table in the middle of the room, with an apple and a ruler set on its corner. The small student desks were organized at a distance from the teacher's large one. The two young girls who'd entered before him occupied the front two desks, so to avoid them, he walked all the way to the back and sat at the corner desk.

Slowly, one by one, more children filled the classroom, eventually filling most of the seats. However, no one sat next to the new student, leaving a palpable barrier like an invisible wall.

Nathaniel watched with anxious eyes as the teacher entered the classroom. It appeared that all the students were present. However, after she'd taken one last peep through the window and had begun to close the door behind her, a voice spoke out: "Sorry I'm late."

The teacher left the door open, and a young boy around Nathaniel's age entered and then closed the door. The students cast appraising glances over the tardy child: blond hair, blue eyes, a square face; and dressed in normal student attire. He made his way to the teacher's desk.

"Joseph, did Father William have you do chores yet again this morning?" the teacher asked him.

"Yes, Mrs. Clark. He wanted to make sure everything was tidy, even before I am ready for the day."

"Well . . . Tell your uncle you need to learn," she replied, a sarcastic edge to her voice.

Joseph simply smiled, "You know I will."

"Take a seat. The class will begin."

"Yes, Ma'am."

Mrs. Clark watched Joseph as he walked to the back of the room and took a seat next to her new student.

"Today, we will be working in small groups. Look around to find a partner; we are about to begin," she rubbed her forehead, as though she'd forgotten something. "Oh. Class, please welcome our newest addition, Nathaniel Smith." She gestured to the back of the room, where he sat, trying to be inconspicuous.

One by one each student turned around to see the new face. The staring eyes made Nathaniel feel uncomfortable. Anxiety tightened his chest, as if his heart were going to explode. He wore an uneasy expression, although he tried to suppress it, along with the pain in his chest. *What is this pain?* he wondered.

Students started to gather into small groups. Nathaniel felt the alienating effects of being the new student in this new environment, and it began to take a toll. The sense of not being wanted cut deep, reminding him of the way he was neglected by a mother who'd left him.

The day had just begun, and Nathaniel already wanted it to end. He stared straight ahead, not looking to the side or listening to the chatter of the other students.

"Hey... Hey, Nathaniel," said the student at the next desk.

The voice was like white noise to him, as he was caught up in the web of his anxiety and fear. Joseph waited patiently for a response to see if the person next to him was even functioning.

Though it took a moment for Nathaniel to shake off his funk, he summoned a small burst of energy and turned to the side. Another blink, and Joseph could see he'd finally come around.

"Do you want to be my partner?" Joseph offered.

"Um . . . Yeah . . . Sure," Nathaniel broke his silence.

"Well, very pleased to meet you. I am Joseph Newman."

"Nathaniel Smith."

"Class! For today's exercise, you will get to know your partner a little more. Then at the end of class, as a group, you will come up to the front and tell us something interesting about your partner," Mrs. Clark announced. She returned to her desk and slipped into her chair. "Feel free to move around the room and get comfortable."

Some of the students got up from their seats and moved next to their partners. Others were comfortable where they were. A few scooted their chairs closer to one another.

Joseph said, "Let's go there." He indicated the center of the room.

They both got up, and Joseph led the way. Chatter and whispers began to fill the whole room, as the groups initiated conversation. The former void of silence was consumed by questions and curiosity.

"Is this your first time in town?" Joseph inquired.

"No, it's my second," Nathaniel answered.

He looks like someone I know . . . But whom? Joseph thought.

"So where do you live?" he asked.

"The farmlands south of town. What about you?"

"Very close."

"Very close?" Nathaniel looked puzzled.

"Yes, I live at the church with my uncle."

"Oh . . . Is there a bedroom in the church?"

"No," Joseph laughed. "There is an extension in the back, and we live there."

"Oh. Okay."

Out of the blue, Joseph asked, "Do you want to go with me to the river bend later today?"

Joseph seems really nice. Everyone else seems to feel a little different . . . What should I do? Should I say yes? No? He thought. Questions loomed on top of other ones, and none of them had obvious answers.

Moments later Nathaniel answered, "Yes, I'll go."

Time flew by as they spoke of various topics. From sunrise to a little past midday, their conversation continued without pause. They eventually erupted into a sudden burst of giggles before Mrs. Clark stopped them from having too much fun.

"Alright, class. Who would like to be the first to share what you have learned about your partner today? Do we have any volunteers?" she asked.

In the center of the room, Joseph raised his hand high for the teacher to see. Nathaniel looked at him in shock, not wanting to be first to the slaughter. As he stood, Joseph whispered something to Nathaniel: "The sooner we do this, the quicker it will be over. Trust me."

Taking the initiative, Joseph commanded the room with his presence and voice. "Hello, everyone, this is my partner for today, Nathaniel Smith, and I am Joseph Newman. There are a lot of things I did not know about him until today. I didn't know that his father built the house where they live now."

Taking a moment to let everything sink in, the class waited for Nathaniel to say something himself. Silence hung in the air as he tried to muster the courage to say something. The crowd's eyes upon him made him feel awkward. However, he finally forced the words out.

"What I have learned from Joseph is that he is really easy to get along with. He makes any situation very easy and makes you feel welcome," Nathaniel managed.

Joseph whispered, "See, that wasn't too bad."

Nathaniel nodded in response.

"Very good, you two. Who wants to go next?" Mrs. Clark called out.

Nathaniel and Joseph sat back down in the middle of the room as all the attention was directed to the next group at the back. They stood up, like the previous group, and gave their introductions the same way.

Nathaniel looked down and smiled, giving no attention to the other group's presentation. He realized that what Joseph had said was correct.

The stress of the day finally came to an end once all the introductions were done.

At the end of class, the desks were straightened back to their original positions. Everyone returned to the seats they'd started in. The instructor got up from her desk and walked down the middle aisle of the class.

"We are done for today. It was a pleasure to meet each and every one of you. Tomorrow will bring another day. Class dismissed."

The students left their desks and made their way to the door. Nathaniel waited a moment for the others to leave before making his own way to the exit. *I don't know where the river bank is,* he thought. *I will just follow Joseph if I can find him outside.*

Joseph was, in fact, standing outside next to the bell, awaiting his newfound friend. Shading his eyes with his hand, he greeted Nathaniel with a sunny smile. He felt like jumping for joy, but kept his composure as the other boy closed the distance.

"Ready to go?" Joseph was giddy with excitement.

"As ready as I'll ever be." Nathaniel returned the smile.

They walked away from the market, with its people buzzing around like bees, and made their way to the outskirts of town undetected. Freedom reigned as the babble of the busy town faded behind them.

Nature sang at its finest, and it felt refreshing. The river flowing serenaded their ears like a sweet melody, and the scent of the fresh air blown from the trees and the green grass surrounded them. An embankment slashed the wall through time along the river. Joseph pointed this out as the end of their journey.

The boys reached an uncharted road left by the cliff only for the ones who dared to come close and see. It gave them a view of the river where it met a larger body of water. Part of the view was blocked by towering trees. Nathaniel gasped in awe at the majestic sight. Joseph smiled, pleased to introduce this special location to his friend.

"This is amazing," Nathaniel breathed.

"Yeah, it is," Joseph responded.

Nathaniel moved from place to place in order to take in as much of the majestic view as possible. Joseph stood back, ready to pounce on the chance to amaze his friend with another feat.

"This is something," Nathaniel remarked.

"I have something else to show you."

"There's more?"

"Not exactly, but it's part of this place."

"Okay."

"Come, follow me."

Joseph led the way to the very edge of the river, and Nathaniel followed a few steps behind. All of a sudden, he was startled to see Joseph jump off the edge of the cliff without hesitation or even a look back. Frankly, it terrified him. He rushed up to see if his friend was alright, or had lost his mind.

Joseph shouted up, "Don't worry, I'm fine."

Nathaniel looked down over the ledge to a small shoreline of gravel and rocks. *This guy*, he thought. *He scared the living hell out of me.*

The rocks, pebbles, and sand at the shore more or less served as a beach. The water was clear enough to reveal the rocks that lay beneath the streaming water. The crystalline surface reflected the surrounding view.

Joseph pointed out to the water, "If you look close enough, you can a see fish swimming up and down the river."

Nathaniel gazed into the river to see for himself, but the speed of the rushing water was distracting. At first, he noticed only the rocks, but then was able to pick out some subtle movements back and forth beneath the surface. *Was he just imagining things?*

"Don't worry. It just takes time for you to spot them. It took me a while, too," Joseph explained.

"Do you know how to fish?" Nathaniel inquired.

"I thought you'd never ask." Joseph picked up a few rocks and stuffed them into his pocket. "Well . . . Do *you* know how to fish?"

"No," Nathaniel admitted.

"Well, I can show you. Let me get some poles, and we'll fish. Just give me a minute."

"Um . . . Sure."

Joseph climbed the ledge, where the rocks made a natural staircase. When he reached the level surface of the grass, he sprinted toward the tree line, blowing past Nathaniel.

Nathaniel stared after his friend, uncertain what he was up to. *He must have been here more than a few times,* he figured.

As he watched, Joseph bent down to gather something, and then returned with two wooden poles made of tree branches with string attached and a hook at the end of the string.

"There are some things I like to do here that I'd like to show you," Joseph offered.

"Okay," Nathaniel responded with a smile.

"Here," he extracted the rocks from his pocket and handed them to Nathaniel.

"What are these for?"

"You'll see soon enough," Joseph walked to the edge of the cliff.

Nathaniel followed shortly after, to see the method behind his friend's madness. Joseph separated one rock from the group and put it in his throwing hand. He then tossed the rock as far as he could into the water. The splash was somehow satisfying as Nathaniel watched the water ripple.

"You should try it. All the feelings you have, mad, sad, or happy, it takes them all away. It's very relaxing to me," said Joseph.

It does seem rather fun, Nathaniel thought. Imitating Joseph, he threw a rock, except that his throwing method was slightly different. Releasing the rock, and watching it fly and then splashdown, brought him a calming sensation.

"We can do more of this another time. Let me show you how to fish," Joseph offered. "It looks like you enjoyed that a little too much."

"Yeah!" Nathaniel answered, wanting to throw another rock, but also ready to learn something new.

Joseph bent down, grabbed a rock that looked like a spearhead, and then dug in the gravel. He continued to unearth more gravel from the ground to find what he was looking for.

"Ah, there it is!" He smiled.

Nathaniel hovered over the hole his friend had dug to see something squirming in the earth, something he'd never seen before. "What is that?" he asked.

"They're worms."

"Worms?"

"Yeah, food for the fish."

"Oh, okay."

"Here. Hold your pole," Joseph handed the second fishing pole to Nathaniel.

Bending back down, he grabbed a worm as it tried to squirm away from the tight grasp of his fingers. Pushing the worm's flesh into the pointed hook, Joseph said, "Make sure you put your worm on the hook, and everything else will do its work. Now you try."

Nathaniel walked over to the spot where Joseph had dug up the worm and tried for himself. Feeling the creature's slimy skin for the first time, he did not know how to react, whether to be disgusted or thrilled. He hooked the worm the same way that Joseph had demonstrated earlier and felt a sense of achievement. Satisfied with a job well done, Nathaniel smiled, the expression lighting up his face like a ray of sunshine.

"Good job," Joseph encouraged him.

"Thank you. Now what?" Nathaniel asked.

"We fish. Let's go," Joseph walked to the ledge.

Tossing the string and hook into the water, Joseph sat there and waited patiently, holding the fishing pole. Nathaniel watched, as always, and imitated the other boy as a little brother would copy the elder. Sitting right next to his friend, he felt that it couldn't get any better.

"Whenever you feel the need, you can always look up at the sky. It's always refreshing," Joseph suggested.

"Oh, yeah, it is."

I could never have asked for anything better, a new beginning, and a new friend to go with it. Life is good.

CHAPTER 28
—A LESSON WORTH KEEPING

There's a message
That follows a path
Where earth, sky
And water meets
Granted to all
The old withers
Inherited by the young
The flow of life
Into the blue
Gems of sapphire
Like a bird
Free like the wind
The sands and sapphire meet
An ocean of turquoise
Stream together
All as one, all as one

Grace hummed along with the sweet melody. The girl had inherited her mother's best features: blond hair, blue eyes, an oval face with a heart shaped chin, and lavender-tinted lips. Constance had once told her, "You have the look of an angel." Grace followed Shooting Star, just a few steps behind.

The pair made their way along a narrow path that most people wouldn't have noticed, designed by nature through time from animals. Grass, trees, and shrubs grew thick and green all around, more abundant than along the roads that people were accustomed to using. Yet, nature seemed to follow them: the birds in the tree branches above, the deer frolicking around in the distant bushes, and small furry animals dancing by their sides.

The light crystal-blue sky was scattered with clouds on a midsummer day. Birds chirped along, accompanying the melody that the two were singing. Occasionally, a ray of sunlight would peep through the heavy, thick branches and leaves that shaded them.

Grace paused her humming. "Nanny . . . Mama and Papa said that we are moving again."

Shooting Star continued to walk ahead, search for something. "Grace, if your parents choose to go, we will go with them. There is always a purpose for their decisions.

"But I don't want to go," Grace protested.

"Neither do I, but we must. I remember what your parents told me once, a long time ago. We were supposed to be in Salem, your father said. But we took a break from our travels and waited for you to grow up a little before continuing."

"Oh."

Walking quickly to keep pace with her nanny, Grace continued down the road, weaving her way between two trees that towered like skyscrapers. Shooting Star was just up ahead, bending down to look for something. Grace could see only her back.

"Come a little closer," Shooting Star beckoned.

Grace stood behind her nanny, waiting for further instructions. Shooting Star stood up with a flower in hand and tucked it over the girl's right ear.

"Beautiful," she commented.

Grace smiled brightly, yet something still troubled her. "Nanny, what is your real name?"

"Some of these things are not important," she responded.

"But they are to me. I have only known you as 'Nanny' since the day I was born. I want to know."

"Fair enough. It's Shooting Star."

Shooting Star. Shooting Star. Shooting Star. I have to remember this, Grace reminded herself. "Nanny, what are doing out here?"

"We are here to learn what is around us," Shooting Star responded.

"What is around us?"

"Yes, nature and the elements around us," the nanny turned to gesture at the landscape surrounding them.

Grace took the time to survey the surroundings and realized what she'd meant: *Nature and the elements around us.*

"Life is precious," Shooting Star began.

She turned to the side, where two small hares were playing in the bushes. The girl and her nanny watched them running back and forth, crashing around in the bushes, so easy to follow. Both of the hares popped in and out of the brush from time to time.

"See those two hares? If I hunted and killed one of them, a life would end, but the spirit of the animal would return to the earth. We have to make sure that we use everything that they gave us."

"Make use of everything?" Grace questioned.

"Yes. The fur you can use for clothing or blankets. The meat is for nourishment, and the bones, you can use for medicine or other things you can imagine."

"Oh," Grace started to piece it together.

"You see, we are all connected. You and I are connected in life. We are also are connected through another bond, in spirit. We are all intertwined with the land."

"What about the plants and animals?" Grace asked.

"They are all the same way, like us. They serve a different role, but in the end, we are all the same. No one is more important as the other; we are all equal," Shooting Star answered.

The cry of an eagle sent shivers down the young girl's spine, and she looked up to the sky. Wondering where the call had come from, Grace twirled in circles in an effort to pinpoint the cry again. Shooting Star could only smile as she enjoyed the view of Grace spinning around and around.

"What is that?" Grace asked.

"That is an eagle," Shooting Star responded as the eagle perched on her shoulder.

"Is that your pet?"

"No, dear. This is my guardian."

"Guardian?"

"Yes, a guardian. He's the one that led me to you before you were born, my very own protector."

"Does it have a name?"

The eagle swayed back and forth, rocking with Shooting Star's movements as she walked the path through the forest. Grace followed closely, trying to get a better view of the bird with every turn and bend of the road. He perched there stoutly, and from time to time, he would move his head from left to right as if scanning the area.

"His name is Soaring Eagle, after my late husband," Shooting Star answered.

"Soaring Eagle," Grace repeated, as her eyes grew bigger and brighter.

As the pair continued along the road, the maze of trees briefly gave way to a field of lush green grass, brightly lit by the sun. The movements of the young girl and her nanny were the only thing to stir the grass as it bowed below their feet momentarily and then reached for the sun again.

Oh, do I miss days like these, Shooting Star thought nostalgically.

Without any notice, Soaring Eagle took flight into the ocean of blue above.

"Without him, things would have been different," said Shooting Star.

"How so?" Grace asked.

"Maybe I would have never met your family, but that is another story to tell for another day. Well . . . It's starting to get dark, so we should head back."

"Okay," Grace agreed as they turned and walked back into the forest.

CHAPTER 29
—MY SALVATION

1677

The shuffling of dirt and gravel made a distinct sound early in the morning. The main door of the house was ajar, as though someone had forgotten to close it. The sun was not yet ready to shine its light over the land. A young boy stood in the distance, away from the door, patiently waiting. Suddenly, a gust of wind blew hard enough to open the door, making it bang into the wall. Inside the house, someone finally began to stir, and the boy could see a face looking out the window.

"Nathaniel! Time to go!" Bruce shouted.

"Uh," Nathaniel grunted from his room.

The small circle of light from a candle pressed forward against the darkness, moving from the bedroom to the living room. The very sight of his son and wife used to move mountains for Bruce with every breath he took, but that feeling was gone now. From the time his wife had left without notice, his world had changed. Though there was nothing he could do to change it, Bruce continued to sulk and live in the past. He hoped that the decision he'd made was the right one. The cold feeling of winter always surrounded him, even though the weather outside told a different tale.

He just didn't know anymore. The indecisive feeling vacillated from day to day, either to care and love, or to resent everything. Today was one of Bruce's better days. He watched Nathaniel make his way from his room to the door, illuminated by the candle.

Bruce briefly uttered from his place in the shadows, "Have a good day at school. I'll see you later tonight."

Nathaniel acknowledged with a nod, and then left through the open door. His footsteps padded away from the house, drifting away from Bruce along with the chatter of the two boys, eventually muffled completely by the sounds of nature. Bruce went back to his chair, as usual, with the gleam of light from the candle to guide him. He dropped heavily into the rocking chair to get a little rest before the break of dawn.

With so many things in mind and so much to do, Bruce could not decide what to do first, and his lack of motivation lingered. Something else strummed the chords of his brain like a guitar. A feeling of pain loomed, and suddenly he felt the weight of the world on his shoulders. It was the void that was once filled with love, which had been torn away by force.

Moments later, dawn broke and another morning began. Neither deep into thought nor doing anything productive, Bruce stayed in his rocking chair in a state of trance for the remainder of the morning until his stomach ached from hunger. Then, he decided to start his day. He stood up, stretched out the aches from sitting so long, and left the house.

Bruce swung the door shut and followed the gravel path. The sunlight clung to his back, like the shadow that imitated his movements in front. He gazed from side to side, taking in the view of grass and trees, and then stopped. Looking back at his home, he thought, *Damn . . . I have a lot of things to do around the house.*

Bruce stood still and thought for a good while about what to do, but first something else called for his attention. It ached, like a chest pain, enough for Bruce to grasp the area with both hands. The throbbing inside felt endless. One thing, and one thing only, he knew, could relieve him of this horrid pain.

As he walked towards town, he also journeyed down memory lane. The feelings were intermixed, both good and bad. They were hard to differentiate from one another; he really just wanted all his feelings to go away. He closed his eyes, only to be haunted by more memories of the past. When his eyes were open once more to see the light of day, his mind continued playing the same tricks on him. Not knowing if the illusions had been real, or if he wanted them to be, Bruce continued down the path to where it had all begun.

There was one memory that he definitely wanted to forget. In his mind, he approached the site where it had all happened, a wooden bridge just ahead. As he continued further, a chilly reminder sent shivers rippling down his spine like a shock.

Next to the bridge, just a little distance ahead, stood the lone tree where it had all happened. *Where all my nightmares haunt me*, he thought. Step by step, in his memory, Bruce approached the bridge. With every blink, in his mind's eye he could see the recurring images that had haunted him since the day the deal was made. When his eyelids closed to darkness, he was returned to the plague of his wrongdoing, watching Fayth suffer in pain, and again Bruce blinked his eyes.

When his eyes opened next, the sky came back into view as his eyelids rolled back. A heavy, thick cloud cover hung overhead, and rain that felt like needles fell from above.

He imagined Fayth lying there at the base of the tree trunk, with blood flowing from between her legs like a river of life draining away. A frantic younger version of himself stood there, paralyzed with the fear of not knowing what to do as time continued ticking by.

The vision of the cloaked man on the horse came back clear as day; in his memory, Bruce continued his steps toward the bridge. Nothing else mattered when he relived that moment. He recalled the mesmerizing feeling of the rain pouring down with no sign of stopping.

Upon the trotting horse, the rider continued along the bridge as the rain sizzled down upon the earth. The cloaked man turned toward the two helpless people beneath the tree, while Bruce, in his mind's eye, reached the top of the bridge and looked down upon the tree where Fayth and his past self were. This granted him some degree of separation. *Oh, thank goodness*, he thought, *just another daydream.*

"I need a drink . . . It's not too far now," he mumbled.

Within a matter of minutes, he reached the town, rushing through the streets and passing through the crowds. His eyes lit up like those of a child seeing fireworks for the first time when he saw the pub straight ahead. Focused on his objective, Bruce did not care to greet anyone or reply as they spoke. Everything else came a distant second to the task at hand.

As he opened the pub door, Bruce felt the relief wash over him. He felt at home gazing upon the familiar wood flooring, small round tables in the center room, and the bar near the far side wall. Just now, the bar looked like a ghost town. Bruce was ecstatic, not having to deal with any other soul. He looked toward the staircase that went along the side of the wall to vacant rooms above.

"Bruce, how are you?" the barkeep greeted him from over the counter.

"Good," he quickly answered.

"How can I help you?" the man asked.

"The usual . . . Can you add another one?"

"Sure thing, just give me a second," the barkeep walked over to the stockroom.

Coming out with a few glass bottles in hand and another tucked underneath his arm, the bartender came back to where Bruce stood. One by one, he placed the bottles on the countertop side by side, and then he knelt down to grab a cloth from underneath the bar. He quickly laid the bottles on their sides, upon the cloth, and began to wrap the cloth around the bottles.

"Leave one out for me, for the road," said Bruce.

"Okay," the bartender replied, tying the bottles securely in the cloth padding. He then handed the bundle over for Bruce to carry. "Thank you for helping me out patching up the place," he added.

"Don't worry about it," Bruce replied.

"Would you like some food? I'll take care of it."

"No, thank you. I have some housekeeping to do, and I still have some meat in the kitchen."

"Okay. Feel free to come back here anytime."

"Will do."

Hastily grabbing his purchases, Bruce bolted for the exit. The sun now dipped a little past noon. *Where did the time go?* The crowds were denser now, and the road ahead disappeared below the movements of men, women, and children alike.

The palpable anxiety of the people surrounding him felt overwhelming after a moment. Bruce cracked the first bottle open and took a big gulp. A rush of liquid ran down his throat, and soon enough he forgot all about the people and the stress that came with his anxiety. Putting the cork back in the bottle loosely, so he could take another sip later, he walked into the congestion of the crowd.

As the scene around Bruce became a blur, he breezed through the town remembering nothing but the goal of making it back to his own doorstep. In opening the door, he stumbled, weaving left and right, unable to walk in a straight line. The bottle was now nearly half empty. Bruce made it back to his chair.

He gulped what remained in the bottle as though he were parched, stuck in the desert, with the feeling of sand and dust in his throat. The last thing he could remember was the sight of the ceiling spinning in a circle; then his heavy eyelids rolled down to cover his eyes.

Not long after Bruce's return, the wooden floor squeaked with soft footfalls that did not disrupt the slumber of the drunken, tired man. As Nathaniel entered the house, he noted that the door was in the same position it had been when he had left. He looked around to see if anything had changed, but everything seemed the same. Approaching the living area, the boy saw an empty bottle beside his father's hand, as though he'd been reaching for it.

That's something new. Ah, there's something covered in cloth on the other side . . . I wonder what it is? Oh, well, forget about it. Nathaniel continued to his father's room. Bruce's room was just as empty as his son's, but much cleaner. A dresser stood by the side wall of the room and the bed was in the middle, illuminated by the light that shone through the window. In the closet, he knew, his mother's belongings still remained.

Nathaniel pulled the sheet from the bed, rolled it up in a ball close to his chest, and walked out to the living room. Loosening the bed sheet to slowly fall to the ground, he held onto the top of the sheet and carefully tossed it over and around his father, leaving his face untouched.

After briefly glancing at the fireplace, Nathaniel instinctively went back outside and around the house to the back. Just a few feet behind the house was a large knee-high tree stump that showed gouges from an ax blows. He made his way across the back wall of the house, where layers upon layers of wood were stacked.

Nathaniel selected a few logs from the very end, carried them back inside the house, and placed the wood into the fireplace. He went back outside and repeated the process until he felt he had the right amount of wood to start the fire. Lastly, he pulled some dry tinder from the remaining wood and set that on top of the rest.

Nathaniel collected the two pieces of flint that lay next to the fireplace and struck them together several times. After several attempts, a spark finally landed on the tinder and caught. He lightly blew on it to ignite the fire, which began to dance with life. Nathaniel turned around to see if his father would be woken by all the noise he was making, but Bruce remained in a heavy slumber.

Daylight came to an end and the night began its reign. Nathaniel got up from the fireplace and closed the door. He wandered into the kitchen, grabbed a couple of rabbits that his father had killed recently, and began to skin them. His stomach started to rumble in between skinning them and looking for a stick with which to skewer them.

The boy headed back to the fireplace and constructed a spit roast to slow-cook his dinner over the heat. Sitting front and center, he had time to enjoy the comfort of the heat as the night grew colder. The silence was his partner for the night; his father made no sound, silently asleep just a few feet away. The scent of roasting meat was alluring and made Nathaniel's mouth water. *Just a little longer*, he thought, *and the food will be done.*

The aroma of cooking meat had no effect on Bruce, who shifted from side to side every now and then in his sleep. When the meat finally finished to a golden brown, Nathaniel set one of the cooked rabbits aside for his father and kept the other for himself.

He did not mind the silence. Nathaniel blew on the meat to cool it a bit. His hunger was slowly satisfied with every bite of the chewy meat. Bite after bite, he ate and watched the fire rage on, burning through the remaining firewood. When it looked like the flames were beginning to recede, he would toss in a log or two to keep it maintained.

Nathaniel yawned with fatigue, realizing that it was almost time for bed. Leaving the bones by the fireplace, Nathaniel resolved to cleanup in the morning. He licked his fingers clean and savored the taste of the fat. Most importantly, it was time to rest. He made his way back to his room.

As Nathaniel drifted off to sleep, his father finally woke. Bruce opened his eyes to the surrounding darkness and realized that a blanket covered him. *For the first time in a long time, I did not have that horrid dream,* he thought. Something else was causing him more trouble than the dream, however. Sharp pains arose in his head, as if someone were stabbing it with a knife.

Bruce blinked, trying to adjust his vision to the darkness, with only the dim glow of the smoldering logs to shed any light. His blurry vision did not help with the throbbing pain. At the moment, though, his stomach rumbled with hunger, and that was all he really cared about. As his vision slowly adjusted to the dark, he noticed the roasted rabbit next to the fire, kept warm by its proximity to the heat. He leaned forward to pick up the skewered carcass, and took a moment to catch his breath with a deep sigh. Bruce's other arm swung freely near the floor, knocking into the empty bottle near his hand. Blood came rushing quickly to his face like a tidal wave.

The sudden rush made him lightheaded and disoriented. His head spun, sending the room into a spiral, but he tried to simply concentrate on eating his food. The first bite was the most fulfilling as his teeth broke through the flesh. It gave him a moment of heavenly bliss, as though he'd died and gone to heaven.

As Bruce leaned back in his chair, another type of hunger began to set in, and he looked for the cloth holding his purchase. He unwrapped the cloth like a Christmas present, uncovering the other bottle. Finishing the last few bites of food, he tossed all the bones from his and Nathaniel's meals into the fire.

Bruce opened the bottle with urgency. He gulped down the alcohol as though he were drinking water. It gave him a content, fulfilled feeling. He then stoppered the bottle and was ready for rest again.

The very last of the flame burned down hours later, with colors of orange, yellow, red, and touches of blue. It turned the wood black and white in the open fireplace, while shades of darkness engulfed the rest of the living room, and Bruce slept in the comfort of his chair. Within arm's reach, two empty glass bottles lay, barely touching, next to the rocking chair.

A simple sense of unease seemed to swirl through him, although unnoticeable to others. Every so often, his face would twitch convulsively. He still slept deeply from the intoxication of his new love.

Bruce looked up to the moonlit sky. A flash of light danced through the clouds with a monstrous sound, and suddenly a lightning bolt struck down. A few water droplets splashed on his forehead, and he closed his eyes. He knew what next was coming next. As he opened his eyes, the image of the tree appeared before him. *Not again . . . Why does this always have to repeat itself? Why me?*

The dream looked the same as always, and Bruce took a deep, slow breath. Another bolt of lightning flashed in the sky, a feature always present in these nightmares.

There in front of Bruce was his lovely wife, yet the lighting clashing with the darkness made it hard for him to see her face. The day that was supposed to be the best moment of his life had turned out to be the worst day possible.

Nathaniel, your birth will haunt me to the end of my days. Your beginning will be the death of me.

Another flash of lightning strobed in the clouds. The scent of the rain that day was different, almost toxic. Visibility was poor, and the pool of blood flowed like a river, only visible against the earth ground when the lightning illuminated it.

Why can I not remember my Fayth's face?

Another lightning bolt struck down with a vengeance, and Bruce looked up, attention drawn by the monstrous roar. A loud neigh sounded from the bridge, and Bruce turned to see a horse trotting across it. That man in the black cloak was unforgettable.

I guess some things never change, or do they?

The rain continued its downpour, a variation from the other nights. Usually, the rain would stop every time he saw the cloaked man approach. *Pain...* All he could feel was pain, from the tips of his fingers up over his shoulders. Heat rose from his palms, something sticky that he did not notice at first but later caught his attention. *Blood?* A dark red fluid covered his hands. Another flash of light illuminated the sky.

Bruce turned his gaze back to the tree. *Where is Fayth? She cannot just disappear like that! Where did she go?* He turned to the right and scanned the darkness, both near and far, but there was no sign of her. The silence was a killer, aside from the rain beating down on the earth. He continued his search of the surroundings and made sure that no stone was unturned. When he returned to the bridge, the cloaked man and his horse had stopped right where he remembered. *This dream is all wrong... Why, though?*

Where Bruce's wife had lain lifeless all those years ago underneath that tree, with death ready to carry her away, bottles stacked on top of bottles now filled that gaping, vacant hole. In the years after she'd left him, the countless bottles stacked up like a tower.

The horse neighed for attention, Bruce looked up, and there they all were.

Fayth stood right next to the horsemen with Nathaniel in her arms, and all of them stared at him.

I wonder why this has all changed.

The horseman took off his hood, revealing his face. His head was hairless, covered in scars, and his features were unusual: black eyes and nearly colorless eyebrows.

The man dismounted from his black horse, its red eyes making Bruce uneasy. The dirt and water shifted away from his feet, as though it did not wish to touch him. The sound of his feet striking the ground shook the earth with a deep, hollow thud, a unique sound that Bruce did not recognize.

Where is the young girl? Bruce wondered. He expected her to pop around the corner or appear from behind the man, but not this time. The cloaked man towered over Fayth and the baby, and swung his arm down like a whip. His hand clutched Fayth's neck, lifting her off the ground. She never cried out in pain or struggled, almost like a doll being raised up. She kept her gaze fixed on Bruce while holding Nathaniel close to her chest.

"You are weak," she declared.

"What?" Bruce blurted.

"You are weak," Fayth repeated.

"How am I weak?"

"You left me there to die."

"I didn't know what to do..." he pled.

"Now, you are doing the same to our son."

His eyebrows rose as he tried to swallow her harsh words. Baby Nathaniel turned his head to his father and opened his eyes for the first time to catch a glimpse. Bruce saw that the child's eyes were black, without even a small speck of white. He did not cry, just stared at his father like a statue. The cloaked man reached within his garment to reveal a knife.

"Toughen him up. I do not want him weak like you," Fayth said.

"What the hell are you trying to tell me?" Bruce shot back.

She ignored the question and continued, "I am dead to you. Soon, your son will be dead as well. Weak . . . Pathetic . . . What do you know? Nothing . . . Nothing at all."

Another voice echoed in the background, a familiar female voice. "You will come to me soon."

Bruce tried to distinguish where the voice was coming from. It seemed to issue from the cloaked man, but his lips never moved. Slight movement ruffled his cloak, as though someone else moved inside it.

"You will come to me soon," the girl's voice spoke once more.

Hands finally appeared from within the cloak, pushing it aside and a face appeared from the middle. *That's the girl! What?* He did not know what to do or say; instead, he stood like a statue, frozen with surprise.

"Goodbye," said Fayth.

Seconds later, the cloaked man stabbed Fayth from behind, and the point of the blade protruded through her chest. Her eyes closed with the shock, and, like a doll, her head bobbed lifelessly. Bruce couldn't do anything but stare, just as he had done in the past.

Then, the man turned his attention to Nathaniel, and Bruce screamed, "NOOOOOO!"

The knife pierced Nathaniel's chest, and it was all over. The cloaked man smirked, and lightning flashed again.

"NO!"

CHAPTER 30
—A DEBT PAID IN ADVANCE

Answers are in the past. Seek them and find the truth.

Vengeance will be mine. –Shadow–

A large fire, burning brightly inside a crater, lit the room. Four large pillars spaced around that crater were illuminated white and yellow by the flames. The walls inside the lair did not require any light, though the light from the fire sufficed for all necessities. On one end, a throne was visible in the dim light, and on the other side was the corridor that led to the room.

Entering through the colossal door and descending the bone steps, he entered the corridor like a shadow, carrying his cloak and wearing nothing but a loincloth and sandals. His black eyes showed no fear. The firelight revealed a network of scars covering his tan skin. A man of no words but instead, all action. Shadow walked past the pillars and stopped at the steps of the throne.

His Master sat upon his throne, a man made physically perfect by the gods. He wore a silk black robe with ancient words embroidered in red.

"Shadow, it is time," the Master spoke.

Two monstrous wolf dogs slept at the foot of the Master's throne. One of the beasts was white, and the other black, with pointed ears, thick fur, and fangs that showed even at rest.

"I took the liberty of having your gear brought here," the Master announced. "I altered your sword just a little; you will notice a difference in battle. Also, there is a certain house I want you to visit before you do your work.

The parchment with the information is attached to your shield." With a wave of the Master's hand, all of Shadow's attire appeared.

Shadow bowed, kneeling on one knee. He kept his head bowed, not once looking directly at his Master. Nodding his head to acknowledge the request, he stood, turned around and looked over his gear. He selected what he knew best, what had served him through thick and thin against many foes: his metal greaves, gauntlets, neck guard, right shoulder plate, sword and shield. After putting the shield over one shoulder and stowing the rest of the gear beneath his cloak, he was ready.

As he returned to the massive fire pit, another voice spoke inside his mind.

Leaving again? Morgana asked.

Yes, Shadow answered.

Ask our Master if I can accompany you. Would you do that for me, please?

Ha-ha . . . Sure. Let me ask him for you.

Did he tell you where you're going?

No details. I'll figure it out when the time comes. He just wants me to do what I do best.

Have fun, brother! Take me with you!

You know I will . . . Sure, if you can fit beneath my cloak. Shadow smirked, thinking it unlikely.

Let me try.

Um . . . No.

You're never any fun.

Maybe next time, sweet sister.

The Master waved his hand, and the air between Shadow and the fire pit began to shimmer and pulsate, defying the laws of time and space. Shadow stood there for a moment in silence, dwelling on a memory.

A monstrous and memorable rumble sounded; he remembered the din of thousands of men and women stomping their feet on the Flavian Amphitheatre ground. Shadow took a deep breath and exhaled slowly, thinking back to his days of gladiator battles as he closed his eyes. Almost like a ritual, he flexed his muscles tightly, building up adrenaline in his system. He then opened his eyes and walked into the teleportal. Limb after limb, all of his body disappeared.

Stepping through to the other side, he could feel the plush carpet tickling and caressing the side of his foot. As he planted his other foot on the ground, the ripple of air behind him vanished in silence. Shadow looked to the left, scanning up and down the room, and then turned full circle.

Candles lit the room from all corners and from the chandelier above. It was rather a plain room nonetheless, with a bed against the center wall, a dresser, and few ornaments to decorate the room.

He walked to the end of the room, where a section of the wall had been replaced with dark red curtains that hung to the floor. The wind was not a factor, only strong enough to ruffle the fabric. He pulled the curtains aside and stood for a moment, looking into the vast darkness ahead. As he took a few steps forward to the stone balcony, he vividly remembered the days past.

Hmm . . . The nights still feel as cold as I remember then. He gazed up to the stars, and it brought back memories of his gladiator days, when he always looked to the sky from behind his prison cell bars, a reminder of the freedom that he had to earn. Only his thoughts were of value as he kept wishing for the day of freedom to come. Yet, in that cage, he remembered that the stars burned brighter, and sometimes he would imagine reaching for them, inching closer and closer.

Now, without the bars holding him like a caged animal, the view seemed to change from what he remembered. The lust of wanting something already within reach had disappeared, and now the stars seemed to not shine as brightly as they had when he was enslaved. Tired and ready for rest, Shadow turned around and went straight to bed. *Tomorrow will bring a new day.*

Time breezed by as the sun shooed away the darkness, making its presence known. By that time, Shadow was up and about, ready to leave. He gathered his belongings and opened the door.

A child sped by the door, rushing down the hallway. Peeping out the door, Shadow looked left and right to make sure the coast was clear before he closed the door behind him and made his way to the staircase.

Downstairs, Shadow was greeted by the concierge behind the desk, "Good day to you, sir."

I don't remember ever paying for the room? Maybe the Master had someone do it earlier. He nodded in acknowledgment, making eye contact with the elder man.

Shadow's attention was more for the door, trying to gather as much information as possible about what he was supposed to do. He knew if he did not leave the premises quickly, the man would want something. The concierge stared at his guest, looking closely at all his scars. Shadow knew that if he lingered any longer, the man behind the counter would attempt to strike up a conversation with him. *Good thing I have no tongue. Heh.* Shadow smiled.

Shouts and screams sounded outside in the crowded street. Shadow rushed out to investigate the commotion, choosing to slip in unnoticed behind the crowd. The people were gathered along the side of the road.

Some soldiers were mounted on horses and others marched on foot. The crowd cheered and screamed for them as they passed by.

The crowd dispersed from the end as the last soldier disappeared from their sight. One by one, they began to go back to their everyday lives and normal routines. *Everything looks so familiar,* Shadow thought. Following the last soldier, he lingered close to the men at arms.

Just in front was a young girl who resembled his younger sister. Shadow caught a glimpse of her as she passed by. **What are you doing here?** He tried to communicate with her. She did not reply, however, and kept walking in the opposite direction. It made him recall a past memory.

80 A.D.

They sat on the second-floor balcony, watching the view below as the clashing steel and screams of fighters echoed outside. A cloth-covered canopy shaded the owner and guest as they watched. A small round table sat between the two, with fruits for refreshment and cups of red wine on each side. Two gorgeous young women, barely dressed in silk, stood by the men, fanning them for relief from the dry heat. Some of the fighters sparred with other men or with wooden mannequins, prepping themselves for the battle ahead.

"That young man there, is he your best fighter?" a senator asked, sitting up and watching the fighters carefully.

"Yes. He is the best fighter I have. He's also the best investment I have ever made," the slave owner replied.

"Ah."

"He has the will to live. No man or god can break him."

"Does he have a name?"

"You know his name; everyone does! It is The Shadow of Death," he exclaimed.

"No, no, no, no, no. His real name."

"I don't know."

"How many fights has he been in?"

"Many... He has made me a rich man."

"I'm pretty sure he has. Also, I hear you have a sibling of his?" the senator inquired.

"Now that I think of it, yes. Maybe she could answer your question." The slave owner waved off his servant girl to fetch The Shadow of Death's little sister.

"A sister?" The senator sounded somewhat astonished.

Moments later, the servant girl returned with the fighter's little sister. Appearing before them was a young girl, wearing a simple white cloth from shoulder to knee, with a rope tied into a noose around her waist. The senator inspected her from head to toe, carefully examining at dark brown hair, lightly tanned skin, rosy pink lips, light gray eyes, high cheekbones, and pointed chin. Indeed, she was lovely. With a courteous bow, she greeted her master and the senator.

"What is your brother's name?" the slave Master asked.

"The Shadow of Death," Illythia responded.

Both the senator and slave master smiled and shared a good laugh. When their laughter died down, the slave Master asked the question again, in a rather different way. "No, no, no, no, no. What is his *real* name?" he questioned.

She told them a white lie. "I don't remember anymore... We were very young when they took us. You would have to ask him."

"Alright. You heard the child," the slave owner remarked to the senator.

He waved off the girl to leave. She bowed and made her way back into the house to return to work in the infirmary. The senator couldn't take his eyes off of her. Until she disappeared from sight, he could only imagine and admire. Turning his attention back to the owner of the house, the senator smiled a different type of smile.

"Taken a liking to this girl, I can see," the slave master remarked, raising an eyebrow.

"I am quite taken," the senator replied.

"Feel free to go to the arena where they are training, or to his living quarters, wherever he may be now. You can ask my fighter for his name." The slave owner nodded toward his gladiator, changing the subject.

"What is her worth to you?" the senator asked.

"She is not for sale."

"Not for sale? All slaves have a price."

"Not this one, *especially* this one."

"Times change. I'm sure someone of your stature can make this happen. I will pay a substantial amount for her, that you may be assured," the senator stated arrogantly, getting up from his seat. "I will see this gladiator of yours, if one of your men will accompany me and lead the way."

Whistling down to the lower level, the slave owner caught the attention of one of the guards on duty. The man rushed up the stone side stairs and greeted them with a bow.

"Take the senator to meet The Shadow of Death," the Slave owner commanded.

"Yes, Sir."

Several more guards joined them and led the way down the stone steps and into the fighting pit, where all the gladiators were training. As they walked along the wall, the senator marveled at the spectacle. The guards surrounded the dignitary tightly for his protection. Far away, still relaxing on the balcony, the slave owner signaled for the men to lead the prized fighter into his cage.

The guards started a subtle shift, stopping the gladiator from his training and leading him back to his prison. They led The Shadow of Death to a clay prison farthest from the other gladiators, with bars that faced the arena. His cell was fairly comfortable, with a bed large enough to fit more than three people and other furniture to comfort him at night. By the time the senator made it to the holding cell, the fighter was sitting on a carved wooden seat near his bed.

"Gladiator . . . How many fights have you won?" The senator began.

The senator was not expecting his question to be met with silence. Though the gladiator did not answer, for the time being, he looked up from inside his prison cell to see who addressed him. *This man is of no importance to me*, he thought.

The Shadow of Death rose to his feet, pushing his chair closer to the bed, and slowly stalked his prey along the cage. Stopping in front of the man, face to face, the predator could feel the fear of the prey.

"Too many," The gladiator growled, responding at last.

"I have a question for you that no one seems to know the answer to."

"I am listening."

"What is your real name?"

"Why do you want to know?"

"Curiosity, of course."

"You already know my name. They chant it day in and day out. I have seen you watch some of my fights before," he pointed out.

"Hmm," the senator acknowledged.

"If you want to know my real name, you will have to fight me in the arena," the gladiator stated boldly.

"Why, may I ask?" The senator chuckled incredulously.

"I whisper it to my foes before they die. They will remember it right before their passing. That is my parting gift to them," The Shadow of Death responded.

Chills from those taunting words sent tingles all over the senator's body. All he could do was smile and nod before walking away from the fighter, knowing that he was not going to get the answer he wanted. Not being foolish enough to pit himself against the fierce gladiator, he returned back to the slave owner to bid him farewell.

"Did you get what you wanted from the gladiator?" The slave master questioned.

"I did not," the senator responded.

"He isn't one to talk a lot."

"Hmm. Well, think about my other offer while you are at it," the Senator prompted.

"I will take it into consideration," the slave master replied.

"Your gladiator has a sharp tongue. Maybe I will keep that as a trophy one day. Think about the offer; I know you will be pleased and I hope you will not disappoint me." The Senator left a large pouch of coins on the table next to the slave owner and then took his leave.

After the senator had left his property, the slave master cupped the pouch full of coins in his palm, and the bag jingled a sweet melody in his ears. As he repeatedly tossed it up in the air and caught it, he realized had a lot of things to consider, yet he did not want to think of the consequences that surrounded the predicament. He truly was stuck, knowing that both causes were not going to benefit him whatsoever.

Later that night, as a full moon peeked out from behind the rolling clouds, a visitor came to the Shadow of Death's prison cell. As on any other night, Cethin and Illythia slept close to each other, huddled close as they'd done as children. Some things never changed.

A sound tickled Cethin's ear. He lay there quietly, listening to the shuffling of sand and soft yet heavy breathing outside his cell. He knew that it was not a visitor from outside. He kept his eyes shut, pretending not to notice, and continued to listen.

"Wake up . . . wake up," the voice whispered.

Turning over, he faced the side of the metal bars and opened his eyes to see a black shade. Cethin got up from the comforts of his bed and drew closer to see who it was. The person clutched the bars as if it were a matter of life and death. *A woman?* The dim light of the moon exposed the woman's pale skin, though her face was covered by something black, like a mask. There was no wind, yet she trembled from the chill of the night.

"Please hear me out," she continued.

"I am listening," he whispered back.

"I overheard our Master and the man who met you earlier today."

"What of it?"

"The man wanted to buy your sister."

"Why?"

"I don't know. The moment that man laid eyes on her, he wanted her. That is all I heard. Also, he left a big pouch of coins with our Master," she answered. The girl then released the bars and left quietly, like a thief in the night, unnoticed.

"My master would not do such a thing," Cethin thought. He did not want to think about the conversation.

Looking at Illythia, he wondered what it would be like, living without her. Anger boiled within, he concealed his temper. *Those are only unconfirmed words,* he thought. *We shall see soon enough.* Cethin closed his eyes, and the night took care of the rest.

The morning came quickly. Cethin felt as though he'd only blinked for a second, yet the commotion of the everyday routine was going to begin again. Illythia came up beside the bed and gave him a big hug before the beginning of the work day, as always. They both appreciated every moment together and the promise that was given them to be permitted to stay together through the long years.

Cethin left his cell, turned the corner, and continued to the training grounds. There, the slave master and a few guards appeared before him. He was brought to a screeching halt and pointed back to his holding cell. The other gladiators continued their sparring and training, barely paying any mind to their surroundings or the other events taking place around them. Back in his chambers, Cethin was surrounded by several guards posted both inside and outside the cell, each and every one of them spread out.

The slave master went straight for the seat near the bed and sat down. His prized possession stood in the middle of the room. He watched his Master with suspicious eyes, uncertain what to expect. He downplayed the game, like a chess match, methodical; giving nothing away.

"Maybe you know why I am here, maybe not," the Master began.

"I have an idea," Cethin responded.

"Good . . . It will make things easier, then."

The Shadow of Death nodded and began to stretch his stiff muscles. The slave Master got up from his seat and made his way to his prized champion, pausing only a few feet away. Their conversation was conducted in whispers.

"You remember that man who paid you a visit yesterday?"

"Yes, I remember," Cethin answered.

"That man is very powerful. He offered me a lot of money for your sister."

"And?"

"I have not agreed to anything just yet, but he is a man who always gets what he desires, no matter the circumstances."

"When is this going to happen?"

"It will happen during your fight; then, you will be a free man." The slave master walked away.

"But our deal . . . !" Cethin's voice erupted with anger.

On his way out, the slave master stopped at the door. "I am sorry. There is nothing I can do about this."

Anger was Cethin's closest companion. Like a little devil on top of his shoulder, it goaded him so that he continually made the wrong decisions all day. Under the circumstances, he did not care about the possible consequences.

During his normal sparring routine, using a wooden shield and sword, he fought another gladiator chosen by the captain of the guard. There was no finesse today, and the battle showed all the purity of his rage. Cethin's thoughts were elsewhere, as the rage continued to consume him due to those wretched words exchanged in the slave cell.

Without strategy, his strikes were fierce, chopping from side to side, removing his opponent's shield. The crowd watched in awe as the shield flew across the arena. Before it had registered in his head, his opponent lay on the ground, battered and bruised from the numerous blows.

Cethin stared up and smiled dangerously at the guards surrounding him. Beyond the guards, on the second story balcony, the slave master sat, unhappily watching the sparring session. His serious expression and the tension between his eyes told the story alone. Having his investments injured before their main fight in the upcoming days did not bode well. Getting up from his comfortable seat, he nodded in disappointment and stormed away into the house.

The guards kicked the Shadow of Death behind the knees, forcing him to the ground. All the other gladiators stopped all their training to watch the conflict.

"Wipe that smile off your face or I will do it for you," the officer snarled.

Cethin was exuberant in his arrogance. Feeling almost like a god; untouchable, he continued to test his luck. Picking himself back up one foot at a time, Cethin rose back only to be felled again by another assaulting blow. *They think this is a game! Well, let us see who has the last laugh,* he thought.

"You cannot hurt me! What are you going to do to me? Huh? Nothing! I am the reason why you work here!" Cethin shouted.

"Hold your tongue, slave, or I will take it away from you," the officer threatened.

"Fuck off!" he spat, getting up from the ground.

The guards moved in, trying to restrain the gladiator, but he had other thoughts in mind and retaliated, punching one of the guards in the stomach. The guard fell to his knees, wind knocked out of him, and the rest of the guards swarmed the gladiator, restraining him. One guard on each side bound his arms, and one stood behind him to prevent him from getting back up.

"Do not test my patience," the officer snarled.

"You cannot do anything to me," the gladiator reminded them.

"Are you sure about that? I do not belong to you or him."

Nodding his head, the top ranking guard signaled the other guards to bring the whip. Pointing in the other direction, he directed the other guards to grab a small wooden table, waist high and the length of a small child.

The officer yelled out to the other guards, "Training is over! Take them back home."

One by one, the fighters left the training arena and returned to their cells. The officer circled around the troubled gladiator like a shark in a fish tank. The guard handed over the whip once the officer circled around.

"Still think you cannot be touched?" the officer questioned from behind the gladiator.

Seconds later, the whip cracked loudly upon Cethin's back, causing him to scream out a horrific cry of pain into the arena. The pain shivered up and down his spine as Cethin tried to free himself from the guards' grasp, but every attempt failed.

Through the pain, he still managed a short, cynical laugh. That did not sit well with his tormentor.

All the other gladiators silently watched the spectacle from their cells. They felt their comrade's shivers of pain as though they themselves were being tormented.

Another lash struck Cethin's back, and he grunted in pain a second time. Multiple lashes inflicted in the same area broke and reddened the flesh. The surrounding skin separated and peeled back; blood flowed like a red waterfall.

"Just you wait," Cethin taunted. "Just you wait."

"Wait for what?"

"I know who you are." He let out a few sharp breaths.

"Do you now?" the officer taunted back.

A brief gust of wind swirled in the arena, stirring up a small dust storm. Tension hung in the air. Arrogance still filled the gladiator, body and mind, a rage that consumed him from the inside, wanting, waiting to be free to destroy each and every foe. He knew that if he did something at this moment, it would mean his imminent disposal, but his tongue would not be stilled.

"Just you wait," he repeated. "When this is all over, I will come to your home, bind you and force you to watch me slaughter your children, rape your wife while she cries in agony, and you, you weak fuck, will not do anything to help. And when I am finished, you will watch her die in front of you. Then you will be the last to suffer."

"You will be the first to go to hell."

"I will take you with me."

Something clicked in the officer's mind, from either terror or fear of the gladiator's dreadful threats. He signaled another guard to replace him and continue the whipping.

"Give him ten more lashes before I return," he ordered, then departed to a room nearby.

The screams and cries of the gladiator echoed continuously, audible throughout the entire training facility and to the ears of all the prisoners. Until the last few lashes, Cethin ceased to cry out, for the numbness took over his body and, to him, the pain was beyond a state of mind.

Holding a forceps, the officer came storming back like a hurricane on the path of destruction. He sucker-punched the gladiator a few times on the side of the jaw. Cethin's head bobbed around as his mouth fell open with the pain.

Spitting out blood, he tried to gather himself back. However, he felt groggy, and his vision was now blurred.

The officer directed the guards to move the table in front of the gladiator. Forced to lean forward, the gladiator's chest lay on top of the table. With the forceps, the officer clamped Cethin's tongue and pulled ferociously.

"Today you will learn to hold your tongue," the officer spat as he unsheathed a knife from his side.

The slave master returned to the balcony and looked over to the training grounds, only to find his gladiators in their cells rather than training. It surprised him to see the guards in the middle of the arena with his prized champion.

A thud echoed in the silence as the knife struck the table, severing Cethin's tongue from his mouth.

"AH!" Cethin gasped, the only sound he could make.

The guards released the gladiator to watch him roll on the ground in pain. The sand of the arena covered his back, and blood flowing from the mouth soaked the ground. His slave master rushed down the flight of steps and down to the training grounds.

"What the fuck are you doing?" he demanded.

"The Senator sends his regards for his early payment," replied the officer, holding the forceps with the severed tongue.

The slave owner signaled to the other guards near the cell to open the door and let the other gladiators out to carry the injured fighter. The Shadow of Death opened his eyes to stare at the man who had inflicted all the damage. *I will forever remember your face. You will die at my feet. This I swear to you.* Then, darkness and pain overtook the fighter, and he slipped away, wavering in and out of unconsciousness, not feeling the other guards lifting him from the ground.

"Take him to the infirmary," the slave master commanded. *You cannot leave me just yet, you fool.*

The sound of an aftershock brought Shadow back from his daydream. He opened his eyes to see his sister's lookalike disappearing into the crowd. He turned to the direction of the sound. In the rush of innocent people fleeing from the clash of swords and shields, he saw his opportunity for fun.

Here I go!

CHAPTER 31
—THE BEGINNING OF CHANGES

SALEM, 1678

The bright sunlight seeped through the open curtains at the window. Grace's room was radiant with the bright colors of white and sky blue. Even the dresser was light wood, and the room was well organized. The toys were all stacked neatly together, along with the stuffed bears along the wall. The young girl's bed was set sideways away from the glare of direct sunlight, but the white sheets covering the girl still began to warm in the morning light.

The door opened with a soft squeak; the footsteps on the wooden floor were silent and swift. Shooting Star entered, her appearance still different from that of ordinary folk in the area. Her clothing was the traditional style for her tribe. Though she'd lived with her new family for quite some time, some things never changed. She continued to wear her tunic with a comet embroidered in beadwork, a necklace with a single eagle feather, deerskin leggings, and her comfortable leather moccasins. She made no sound as she glided quietly to the bed and looked upon the sleeping form of the girl she cared for.

The girl, soundly asleep, did not hear the door open. The sun lit up her pale skin and blond hair, like the finishing touches on a canvas.

Grace was at last rocked awake by her nanny's gentle touch. "Wake up, my sleepyhead," Shooting Star whispered in her ear.

"Umm," Grace mumbled groggily, turning over and facing the ceiling and blinking in the sunlight.

Shooting Star bestowed a gentle kiss on the girl's forehead.

"Umm," she grumbled again.

"Wake up, little one. Your mother and father are waiting for you in the dining room for breakfast."

With deep, calm breaths, the young girl stretched. Rubbing away the sand, Grace began to open her blue eyes and caught a glimpse of her nanny on the side of the bed.

Shooting Star gave a warm, welcoming smile for Grace, as always. The young girl remained motionless except for a yawn, not yet ready for the morning.

"Can I lie here a little longer?" Grace pleaded.

"Alright, just a little bit longer. Did you have a good time last night?" Shooting Star asked.

"It was okay." Grace sat upright, leaning on the headboard.

"Just about everyone showed up to the ball your mother and father hosted," Shooting Star exaggerated.

"No, Nanny, not everyone." Grace gave a sly smile.

"Well, you know what I mean. You know there were a few boys who couldn't stop staring at you. Did you enchant them with some sort of spell?" Shooting Star teased.

"No!" Grace replied, blushing furiously.

"Are you sure?"

"Well . . . I did have a good time."

"Good."

"It's just . . . There were a lot of people the same age as mother and father. There were only a few around my age."

"Well . . . that will change," Shooting Star replied. Grace gave her a puzzled look. "Your mother and father are sending you off to school."

"School? But I don't want to go," Grace pouted, her eyes fixed on the wall ahead before turning her attention to the open door, where light seeped through.

"I know you will enjoy it. Learn and expand your mind with knowledge and meet new people," Shooting Star encouraged.

"I have a perfect teacher here . . ."

"I can only teach you the things that I know, the knowledge that was passed down from generation to generation of my people. You will get to learn things that I cannot teach you. Now, let's welcome the morning with your parents." The nanny stood up from the side of the bed.

Grace pushed back the sheets and slipped out of bed, revealing her white nightgown with designs of flowers embodied along the midriff. She slowly followed her nanny out the door and into the hall. Candlelight reflected from the mirror, helping to illuminate the area. The sun had begun its journey in the east, but the west side of the house was still in shadow.

As the pair made their way down the hall, Grace thought the objects she passed by looked twice the size they should have been. The place was still new and unfamiliar, as though she were a tourist in her own house.

Just a few steps ahead, Shooting Star started down the staircase, where candles in sconces provided light, the flames protected by small glass jars. Pausing at the top of the stairs, Grace recalled her old home, where the staircase curved down to the middle of the foyer, and again she was the princess in the palace. She then grasped the handrail and planted her feet firmly on each step, descending carefully. Shooting Star waited patiently at the bottom, ready to guide the child to her parents.

Grace's reverie was quickly broken by the aroma of food from the nearby dining room. She hurried her little feet to catch up.

George sat at the end of the small, rectangular wooden table, its center draped with embroidered white linen. He welcomed Shooting Star and his daughter with a warm smile. George was sitting tall and looking dapper this morning in a white button-up shirt and black trousers.

"Good morning, Sunshine," he greeted them.

Today, Constance wore a black skirt and white blouse, so that she coordinated with her husband. From her place at the table beside him, Constance gave the same welcoming smile. The resemblance between mother and daughter was striking. Grace had the same light blond hair, and sparkling blue eyes set above high cheekbones in a heart-shaped face.

Grace responded with a sleepy smile as she approached her parents. George rose from his seat to greet his daughter with a big hug and a kiss on the cheek. Constance remained in her seat on the other side of the table and continued to smile. Two open seats remained across from Constance. All the plates had covers on top, hiding the food and keeping it warm. The silverware was already placed neatly on both sides of the plates.

At last, Shooting Star pulled the chair out for Grace to sit and pushed it back in once the child was in place. Another screech issued from the last chair scraping against the floor as the nanny took her seat.

Grace stared at the mountain of food: thick slabs of bacon, yellow and white scrambled eggs layered with diced potatoes, and sliced oranges on the side of the dish. She watched the steam rise from the freshly cooked meal. It was difficult to resist tucking in immediately.

"I am blessed," said George.

"For?" Shooting Star questioned.

"I am blessed to have a beautiful wife, a loving daughter, and the best care-taker I could ever ask for," he elaborated.

"Yes. We are all blessed," Constance agreed.

"Breakfast is served. Let's eat."

The family took up their silverware and began to satisfy their appetites. The food was delicious, and the sensation was practically euphoric. They ate in silence without a peep, simply relishing the meal. From time to time, they exchanged glances, acknowledging each other quietly. After a while, Constance set her utensils back on the table. She asked her daughter, "Are you ready for school?"

Grace politely put her silverware on top of her plate and looked up to her mother. Taking a moment to answer, she wanted to respond "No," but instead she replied, "Yes, mother." Her voice was somewhat strained, giving away her nervousness.

"We know it was sudden, sweetheart, but we want what is best for you," George explained.

Grace wanted to scream, "I want to stay here with my nanny!" However, she kept quiet and nodded.

"It's alright. You'll have a good time. I will always walk with you to and from school," Shooting Star reassured the girl.

"Promise?" Grace replied.

"Promise. Now, let us get you ready for school."

Grace's spirits improved considerably at that, and at last she smiled. Ready to leave her seat and hurry back to her room to change, she requested, "May I please be excused?"

"You may," George replied.

Grace looked at her mother, who nodded with a smile. Grace hurriedly pushed her chair back, and then gave each of her parents a kiss on the cheek before rushing back to her room.

The adults remained seated, still comfortable in their chairs, with their now-empty plates before them. For a moment, the only sound present was the loud thudding of their child stomping quickly up the stairs.

"Shooting Star, we wanted to ask you something," Constance began.

"Hmm?"

"When the school year is over for Grace, we would like you to come with us to England and visit our parents with us. We'll be visiting for about a year, and then return home. It will be a surprise for Grace to meet her grandparents, and we'd appreciate it if you would come with us."

"I will go . . ." Shooting Star paused for a moment. "But first, I would like to visit my own family before we leave."

"Certainly. We have a long time before we leave." George smiled. "Just let us know when you plan to go to visit your family, so we can take care of Grace while you're away."

"Of course," Shooting Star agreed.

"It'll be fun," Constance said encouragingly.

"I know I'll enjoy it as much as you will." Shooting Star smiled and leaned forward to clear the plates.

"Just leave the dishes. We'll take care of them," George offered.

"You do a lot for us, Shooting Star. It is the very least we can do you for you from time to time," Constance added.

Shooting Star nodded her head and sat back upright in her chair. At that moment, Grace came clomping back down the stairs, followed by the light clicking of her boots as she made her way to the dining room.

"My, oh my, does she look beautiful. It looks like someone's ready for school," George declared encouragingly.

Shooting Star turned to Grace. "Are you ready for school?"

Grace nodded and replied, "Yes, I am."

Shooting Star rose, pushing her chair and Grace's back up to the table. She turned and walked with Grace to the foyer.

"Have a good day at school!" George bade them as they left.

Grace looked back to give her parents one last smile before leaving. George and Constance's chatter receded into the distance as Shooting Star and Grace left the dining room. As the door closed, silence swept in and the sounds of nature took over.

Birds chirped a lovely melody from the trees nearby, others flew and danced in the air. Squirrels ran through the long grass, which rustled with their passage. Grace tracked the animals with her eyes as they passed.

With the sun shining before them they walked along the narrow road side by side, a line of grass separating them. As they walked, Shooting Star hummed a familiar melody. At first, Grace simply listened to the tune, resisting the temptation to join in, but in the end, she hummed along.

Soon, they reached a wooden bridge wide enough for a carriage to cross. Shooting Star ceased her tune and gazed at the town in the distance. The call of her guardian sounded from the heavens above, and she stopped at the foot of the bridge.

Soaring Eagle glided effortlessly down to perch on the highest point of the bridge. *Hm . . . Soaring Eagle usually comes to me first before going elsewhere,* she thought. *I wonder what is going on.*

Only houses lay before them, as far as the eye could see. Suddenly, like a rush of adrenaline, energy swept through Shooting Star's body as she detected a presence that she remembered from the first time she'd encountered her new family. The feeling seemed slightly different, though, covered by another layer of disguise. She couldn't pinpoint what it was, though. Her stomach churned with nausea, and an eerie aura seemed to tighten around her.

Shooting Star found herself unable to move forward any farther; her feet were like immovable stones clinging to the ground. She turned to Grace and said. "This is where I will meet you at each end of the day after school."

"Will you come with me?" Grace asked.

"I cannot. Maybe we will try another day." Shooting Star responded.

"Oh . . ."

"Don't worry, dear, there will be more opportunities."

"Alright," Grace pouted.

The nanny smiled. "Now remember to make new friends, and learn as much as you can." Shooting Star pointed in the direction of the school. "The school is right next to the church. If you ever get lost, that is the easiest way to remember. Now move along before you are late."

"Okay." Grace felt a little disappointed.

Shooting Star kissed Grace's forehead as a temporary farewell for the day. "Have a good day and don't cause any trouble, you hear?" she teased.

"How?" Grace questioned.

"Your beauty and charms, silly. The boys will flock to you."

Grace blushed. "Nanny!"

She smiled. "Now go have fun at school."

"I will. I love you."

"I love you too."

Grace took her leave, walking alone across the bridge. She glanced back to Shooting Star once before her focus went somewhere else. Trying to remember everything her nanny taught her, she navigated in the general direction she'd been told and kept her eyes on the church.

Shooting Star realized this was the first time in a very long time that the two of them had been apart. Her heart sank, knowing that the child she'd raised from an infant was growing up. Little by little, she knew that Grace would grow and change, and eventually, one day, they would part ways. Many more days like this would come in the future, and she knew it was inevitable.

Young children and adults alike began to flood the streets as they left their homes for school or work. Soon enough, Grace disappeared into the crowd such that Shooting Star could no longer keep track of her. The nanny stood there for a moment, telling herself everything would be just fine. However, she couldn't help feeling that something else was brewing. She knew she needed to seek answers.

Soaring Eagle took flight back into the clear blue sky, heading back into the forest. Shooting Star followed him off the road, through the lush, damp grass and into the forest where the trees stood tall and majestic. Her guardian would lead her to the answers she needed. She cast one last look over her shoulder at the town, *I know Grace will be fine*

■　■　■　■

Grace paused in the middle of the crowd, turned, and looked back to the bridge to check on Shooting Star one last time. The moving crowd did not stop for the young child, but, as with a rock poking above the rushing water, the people flowed around.

She wanted to retreat and go back to what she knew best, but Grace's heart was set on attempting this new adventure, so she turned back around to continue on her way. The school was not hard to find, just as her nanny had said, "right next to the church," and sure enough, there it was. Children flocked to the building from all over the town, as the bell rang forth its melody.

The crowd closer to the school thinned out as the adults went their own way; here, it consisted only of children. Grace noticed an older woman with tanned skin and graying brown hair, clad in a black dress and boots, standing near the school bell. The teacher smiled at every student who passed by.

Grace watched the other children flocking to the school. As though she were in a daze, everything seemed to move in slow motion. Even the sounds of children talking and laughing amongst each other, it all registered to her slowly. Finally, she broke her stasis and strode, step by step, to the school, returning her perceptions to normal. *Could be my imagination*, she thought, passing by the instructor and walking through the open door into the classroom.

She found a desk all the way in the back, away from the rest of the students. Taking a deep breath of relief, she pulled the chair out and took a seat. Knowing that the day was only beginning, she dreaded the slow passage of time. As other children her age came waltzing in through the door, Grace was already in a state of trance, not paying any attention to those around her, but only to the daydream ahead of her. Her chin rested on her hands, and she looked wistfully out the window, wondering what she could have done with her nanny if she'd stayed home, as in days past when she was younger.

The last few students entered the classroom, and right behind them, the teacher closed the door. She wasted no time in standing before the class, clearing her throat for everyone to hear. Like good little students, they all stopped what they were doing and looked up at their instructor.

"Ah, there she is." Mrs. Clark skimmed the room for her new student. "I would like to introduce to you our newest student. Please welcome Grace Arnold."

Grace quickly broke out of her morning daze to see all eyes upon her. With a half-smile, she gazed back upon those who regarded her. She noticed that two of her classmates on the side were not paying any attention to her, instead preoccupied with their conversation. Curiosity teased at her, but she could not do anything until she was no longer the object of attention.

She was too shy to introduce herself to the class. They simply resumed like any other day. The teacher took command and walked around the room, up and down the aisles, and circled around the outer desks.

"Class, today we are going to learn. . ." The voice of the instructor seemed to drift off as Grace's attention wandered.

Grace sat there silently gazing at nothing; her mind and soul were somewhere else. She was reminiscing about the past and how happy those times had been. She wished she could just go back. Though she knew that was never going to happen in reality, in her mind, at least, that was the perfect place to escape.

Time flew by until Grace snapped back into reality at the end of the school day. She looked over to the exit and saw the teacher opening the door. She watched her classmates as they stood up and walked out, singly or in groups. The two who'd ignored her during her introduction at the beginning of class were now the last to remain. Making her way to the door, she glanced at the two briefly as she passed them, and the chatter between the two stopped.

Finally, I get to see my nanny, Grace thought.

CHAPTER 32
—AFTER SCHOOL

The bright sunlight returned as the clouds shifted northeast, uncovering the bright orb. Some of the children stood by the gate and around the schoolyard waiting for their parents to come along, while others stayed to spend time with their companions. A few small groups of friends chattered amongst each other to decide what they wanted to do for the remainder of the day, either mischievous or productive.

Near the school bell the teacher had rung that morning, five young boys now stood, huddled in a circle. They were busy planning their next adventure.

"What are we doing today, boys?" asked the smallest boy as he adjusted his cap.

"We're going to make you play in the forest like last time, remember?" answered a boy clad in overalls, who stood across the circle from him.

"Ha, ha . . . Very funny, Franklin," the first boy responded.

"Yeah, maybe we should do that again, Christopher. You were lost in the woods for quite some time," added another boy, this one with his sleeves rolled up to his elbows.

"Yeah! I think I heard Christopher cry that time, Matthew," Justin chimed in, unbuttoning the collar of his shirt.

"Maybe we can mess around in the market," Christopher interjected in hopes of avoiding another unpleasant afternoon.

"I don't feel like doing that today," Justin retorted.

"Yeah," Matthew and Franklin echoed their agreement.

"I would rather see you swimming in the river than to go to the market today," Matthew commented.

"That's not a bad idea," Franklin answered.

"Yeah, it's a great idea," Justin repeated.

"Nuh-uh... No. No, no, no, no, no, no." Christopher repeated anxiously.

Laughter filled the circle but there were two who did not laugh. Christopher was terrified by the taunting, and the other was deep into meditation, staring at the ground. Franklin, who was closest to the boy in thought, nudged him with an elbow. Not budging, like an immovable rock, Timothy continued his blank stare, fixated on the ground.

"What do you think, Timothy?" Justin asked from the other side. A brief moment of silence hung in the air as there was no response from their friend. "What do you think?" he asked again.

"Yeah, yeah . . . Let's do it," Timothy finally answered. The response sounded automated, robotic.

For a second, Timothy looked up from the ground and to the door of the school, where he saw an angel. The new student was exiting the classroom, the sun kissing her skin, beautiful in his eyes.

The others were very curious to see what he was looking at, so they all followed his gaze. As Grace stood in the doorway, she scanned the scene. The boys' eyes went back to their friend. Smiles lit up their faces.

"Ooo! I think someone is in love!" Justin grinned.

"No, I am not!" Timothy answered defensively.

"In *love*!" The group chanted.

"Shut up!" he demanded.

"You should go and talk to her," Christopher suggested.

"Yeah!" Franklin agreed.

"What for?"

"Introduce yourself," Matthew replied reasonably.

"Yeah. She is new here, and you can be friends," Justin added emphatically.

"Ummm," Timothy hesitated.

"Go, go, do it." Christopher nudged him.

"Chicken!" Matthew exclaimed.

"Bwok! Bwok!" Franklin and Justin clucked mockingly.

"Fine!" Timothy stormed away from the group.

"Good luck!" the group of friends shouted after him.

Timothy paced himself, neither slow enough that his group of friends would antagonize him nor quickly enough to know what to say. He kept a positive mindset, knowing that he was taking the initiative. His heart pounded as though he was running a marathon, thudding so rapidly that he thought it felt like a heart attack. Butterfly flutters filled his stomach just looking at her. He had a feeling of uncertainty.

Timothy's nervous energy began to make him shake and tremble; he felt like a train wreck. He tried to gather himself by tensing up, balling his hand into a fist, and conjuring up thoughts of anything tranquil. He glanced back at his friends one last time.

The four boys in the circle waved back to him. A few grimaced with twisted smiles, believing they'd sent him to the slaughter. Justin and Matthew fed off the upcoming pains of horror, imagining a big disappointment. Franklin was the only one skeptical of the result, and Christopher was the only hopeful one, wishing for a positive outcome.

"What do you think is going to happen?" Franklin questioned.

"I think it will go well," Christopher answered.

"You guys are crazy. You remember how long it took Timothy to become our friend; he's hopeless," Justin retorted.

"This will be interesting. The only thing we can do now is watch," Matthew added.

"We will see . . . We will see," said Franklin noncommittally.

Timothy found comfort in his friends. Sweat formed in his balled up fists. Upon releasing them, his hands were cooled by the breeze of air. Still trying to think of something to say, Timothy was not prepared, and realized it when he looked up to see how close he was. *Shit!* Grace stood directly before him.

She took a step forward, snapping out of her afternoon slump only to find her eyes opening wide like a frightened deer, afraid to move. All she could think to say was, "Oh, I'm sorry."

"Oh... No, I'm so sorry, I must have startled you," Timothy replied.

Grace looked silently at the stranger. They both stood there for a moment and seconds passed by, both of them feeling awkward.

Not knowing how to pursue the situation, Timothy felt the nervousness creep up on him. *I cannot let this happen to me*, he thought.

"Hi. I a-a-am Timothy, and you are?" he asked. *Stupid me! She was introduced in class!*

Nanny . . . You were right. She gave him a sly smile. "Grace." *Just pretend to be nice and hope that he goes away.*

This is an improvement, he thought, and returned her smile.

"You look familiar. I think I have seen you somewhere," Grace continued.

"Yes, your parents invited us to your housewarming."

"Ah! Now I remember, my nanny pointed you and a few others out that night."

"Did you have a good time?" Timothy questioned.

"Yes, I certainly did," Grace replied with exaggerated enthusiasm.

"How long have you lived here?"

"A few months." Grace began to look around for a possible escape.

"I can show you around town sometime, if you would like," Timothy offered.

"Maybe another time..." *I don't really like this person. Ugh, I wish you were here, Nanny.*

"Are you looking for someone?" Timothy asked, noticing her wandering eyes.

"Yes, I am," Grace lied.

■   ■   ■   ■

As Joseph stepped out of the classroom, his eyes began adjusting to the bright sunlight from the shade of the interior. He looked ahead to see the new student talking to another classmate.

"Why did you stop?" Nathaniel stopped right behind him.

"You think we should help her out?" Joseph asked.

"Who?"

"Look in front of you."

"I am looking at your back . . ."

"Come around." Joseph tipped his head to indicate the direction. "Who is she?"

"Grace . . . Were you even paying attention in class?"

"No," Nathaniel admitted. "Why do you think she needs help?"

"I don't know, just a hunch."

"Do what you like. I'm not going to stop you."

"Okay."

Without hesitation, Joseph stepped forward, leaving Nathaniel behind.

Wanting to smack his head, Nathaniel thought, *Why did I say that? I knew he was going to do that anyway. Well, let's see how this one goes.* He stood and watched Joseph approach the new classmate.

Joseph spoke to her as though they were lifelong friends. "I am so sorry to keep you waiting, Grace."

"Oh, that's okay," Grace responded, playing along.

"You know Joseph?" Timothy asked.

"Yes, he's the one I was waiting for," Grace fibbed.

"Nathaniel and I were discussing some stuff and forgot about the time," Joseph added smoothly.

"Oh, that's fine," Grace replied. "Nanny can wait a little longer." She smiled.

Picking up on the hint, Joseph continued, "Well, we cannot have her waiting too long."

Walking next to Grace, Joseph presented his arm to her courteously. *I have always wanted to do this.* He smiled on the inside.

Well . . . He is going to get his butt kicked for this one. Look at Timothy. He is mad as hell. Yeah, Joseph is screwed. I am pretty sure of this. Nathaniel nodded in disappointment.

She smiled at Joseph's gentlemanly behavior. Sliding her arm through his, she waited for him to take the first step.

"Have a good day; we will see you tomorrow," Joseph called out.

Anger began to fill Timothy's mind, knowing that his window of opportunity would never return. Joseph had ruined his one chance. *Maybe I will get another opportunity, but probably not,* he thought. Though he kept a straight face and was about to respond, he got cut off again.

"Relax," Joseph interrupted in a soothing tone. "You're a little tense."

Something triggered for Timothy, right then and there. He seemed to respond to the suggestion in Joseph's voice, and took his advice. The tension in his face dissipated, as though he had forgotten why he was upset.

Joseph and Grace left, walking down the road and out of the school grounds. Seconds later, Nathaniel followed behind the two. He was able to catch a glimpse of Timothy and his crew as he cautiously passed them by. Watching Timothy's face return from calmness back to anger was strange, incomprehensible.

Timothy went back to his group of friends, who still stood near the school bell. They buzzed around him like bees in a hive, wanting to know all the juicy details of what had happened. Timothy's face said it all, though they wanted verbal confirmation.

"How did it go?" Christopher asked curiously.

"Yeah! How did it go?" Franklin parroted.

"I don't know." Timothy shrugged.

"You don't know?" Justin questioned incredulously.

"What do you mean, you don't know? You were there for a while," Matthew probed further.

"Yeah . . ." Timothy let out a big sigh.

"What did the two of you talk about?" Christopher asked.

"Well . . . We talked about the party that her parents threw, and the possibility of the two of us hanging out," he responded.

"Ooooo. Someone is in love!" Matthew teased.

"Shut up! Shut up!" Timothy snapped.

"Did she say anything else, like that she would hang out?" Matthew inquired.

"Maybe, that is all she said."

"You know what that means, right?" Justin said.

"No."

"That means she probably will not hang out with you," he stated bluntly.

"Well, whatever. Let's go to the river." Timothy tried to change the subject. *I will get you for this, Joseph.*

"Okay." The boys agreed.

Before they left, a lingering thought seemed to dawn upon the group of friends. Some of them wanted to ask the question, but were not sure if they should. Still, they sensed it amongst each other.

"Um . . . Why did she leave with Joseph?" Franklin decided to air the question.

"She was waiting for someone, must have been him," Timothy responded.

"Are you sure she was waiting for him? Or could it have been someone else?" Franklin asked.

"I don't know . . . Maybe you should follow her," Timothy suggested. *I am pretty sure she was waiting for him . . . If she was not, that was pretty a convincing act.*

"No, I'm okay," Franklin demurred.

"It sure doesn't look like that to me. Maybe Joseph is trying to take her away from you, Tim," Justin insisted.

"The priest boy?" Matthew questioned incredulously.

"Yeah!" Franklin replied.

"I'm sure Timothy's right," Christopher added.

"Maybe he is trying to take her for himself," Justin said, throwing more fuel on the fire.

The voices inside his head began to talk. *Do not trust Joseph! He is there to steal your girl! You will lose . . . You will lose it all.* Timothy didn't know what to believe anymore. His friends did not support him the way he'd hoped they would. Timothy felt like he was caught in a cyclone spinning faster and faster. Anger boiled inside, but he kept it hidden within.

Trying to be calm and collected, he made longer strides on the road, moving quickly to the edge of town. Soon enough Timothy's friends came following behind, one by one. Normally they would talk amongst each other, but today was different. Silence filled the air, not a peep from one or the other.

Tomorrow brings a new day. Let's hope things will change, Timothy told himself in an effort to control his racing mind.

■　　■　　■　　■

As they passed by the last few houses along the road and approached the end of the edge of town, Joseph continued to walk alongside Grace. Trailing a few steps behind, Nathaniel focused on the ground more than his surroundings. His only amusement consisted of kicking the dust into the air as he walked.

"Thank you for earlier," Grace said to Joseph.

"Hmm?" Joseph answered.

"You helped me get out of that situation with Timothy."

"Oh! No problem. He can be intimidating." He smiled.

"Yeah . . ." Grace looked down for a second.

"Where are we heading?"

"Just up ahead. My nanny is waiting for me there." She pointed.

At this point on the path, there were no more houses, and the smell of the city had been left behind, replaced by the natural scents of fresh water and trees. The welcoming sound of the rushing water just ahead soothed them, like a lullaby for a tired baby. Wild grass like an ocean of green covered the landscape on the other side of the river, and the trees stood tall in a line like the wall of a fortress.

"Why does your friend not say anything?" Grace asked.

"Oh, you mean Nathaniel? Maybe he just needs time to warm up to you, that's all," Joseph responded, unconcerned.

"Oh."

"Yeah, he's been like that since I met him. It took him a while to warm up to me, too."

"Okay." She nodded.

"Is that your nanny?" Joseph asked as they spotted Shooting Star.

"Yes. She has helped raise me since the day I was born," Grace answered.

"Ooooooooh," he replied.

Shooting Star's moccasins lightly slapped the wooden planks of the bridge as she approached. She wore a big, warm smile for Grace, happy and relieved to see the child she'd helped raise come back to her after the school day.

"How was your first day of school?" Shooting Star asked. *What is this feeling, though?*

"It was okay . . ." Grace answered, blasé.

"Just okay?"

"Well . . . yeah."

"I suppose that's good to hear, and who might be this fine young fellow be?" Shooting Star inquired regarding Grace's companion.

"This is Joseph."

"Oh?"

"He helped me out earlier."

"Nice to meet you," said Shooting Star.

"Nice to meet you too," Joseph responded courteously.

"And who is this fine young gentleman hiding in the back?" She asked with a smile.

"This is Nathaniel," Joseph spoke for him.

A shock jolted through her body, her heart began to race, and she felt paralyzed for a second. Shooting Star was suddenly overwhelmed by the foreboding of a threat from the past. It was a suffocating feeling, with sharp pains that seemed to squeeze her heart. *Is this the feeling from this morning? Can it come from this young child? How does he not know of this presence?*

Nathaniel took his eyes off the ground to gaze upon the woman before him. He stared in amazement, his eyes bulging slightly, as he'd never seen a Native before. Everyone he knew had pale skin.

Shooting Star caught a glimpse of something sinister joined to the child's features. The face of a hidden person, from within, like an onion peel, covered the child's face like a mask. The eyes of this shadowed face glowed a dark red. She blinked, and the shadowy overlay of a face disappeared. *I don't like this at all. Something is wrong with this child . . . This is not good. I need answers.*

"Well, it was nice meeting the both of you," Shooting Star continued with a kind smile.

"It was nice to meet you as well," Joseph answered.

Grace took a few more steps, inching closer to her nanny's side. They took their leave from her new friends. Briefly taking a moment to turn around, she waved goodbye to the two boys. The pair then focused only on the path ahead and their journey home.

"Joseph seems like a nice young child," Shooting Star mentioned.

"Mm-hmm."

"The other child . . . What is his name again?"

"Nathaniel."

"Yes, that's it. He's very quiet. Almost too quiet."

"Yes, Joseph said that's how he is."

Grace took a few minutes, then asked, "Nanny?"

"Yes, my dear."

"Can you come with me to school tomorrow?"

"I promised you I would every day."

"I mean, all the way to school."

"I will tomorrow."

"Promise?"

"I promise."

Shooting Star was troubled her every time she thought about Nathaniel. The vision of the shadowed face with its dark red eyes plagued her. She knew that there was something wrong, but needed confirmation. *I definitely need to seek the answers. We might be in danger . . . Again.*

CHAPTER 33
—THE AWAKENING

Shades of gray clouds swarmed across the sky. Travel was not safe, as the fog appeared to consume the land. One could see only a few yards ahead, yet a young child braved the clammy air and the low visibility. Joseph consistently watched the ground to make sure that he stayed on the right path to his destination.

Hidden by the surrounding trees, a large cabin stood among the woods. Joseph caught a glimpse of the few windows visible once he was closer. He stood before to the porch on the gravel road, as he always did, and noticed the door was still open. *Hmm*, Joseph thought, *that's odd*.

■　■　■　■

Within, Bruce was tormented by his thoughts. *WHY! Why, must I ask, why! Why do you haunt me? Every night, it does not stop. Why, I ask, why?*

The firelight flickered on one side of the room as the logs burned in the fireplace. The fire was beginning to subside, dimming and starting to smolder. Bruce sat in his rocking chair and took no action.

Darkness was his best friend. Bruce watched the fire fight for its life, his gaze fixed intently upon it. He watched the shadow consume the light, not wanting to think of the past or the present. The empty glass bottles continued to grow in number around him and spread through the room, silently keeping him company.

The smell of smoke from the burnt wood, combined with the touch of damp cool moisture from the open door, crept into the room, and the chill started to overtake the heat. It was feeling that he could remember from the memories of long ago; it always crept back to him, but he wanted no part of it.

Since his wife had left him, the bitter taste of resentment accompanied memories of her, and Bruce would relive the events repeatedly, like a daydream. *"Memories . . . Memories . . . I do not want these memories.* Reaching to the side, he fished around in the air for another bottle of liquor. *Nothing! Nothing! Where is my drink?!*

The door of Nathaniel's room creaked open. As he did every morning, Nathaniel moved silently, like a little mouse, trying to make no noise so that his father could sleep peacefully near the fire.

"Nathaniel, where did you put my drink?" Bruce snarled.

"Huh?" Nathaniel answered, puzzled.

"Boy . . . You heard me! Where is my drink?" he growled once more.

Looking into the dimly lighted den, Nathaniel saw only the darkened silhouette of his father in the rocking chair. However, he knew that his father's eyes were focused upon him, watching every subtle movement. He looked around, scanning the surroundings where his father sat surrounded by empty bottles. Finding an unopened bottle was like locating a needle in a haystack. However, he was in luck: one full bottle stood on the other side, where his father did not think to look.

"Right there by your side," Nathaniel pointed out.

Bruce swiped again, reaching again for the side where there was only empty space. "There is nothing here . . . Do not play stupid with me, boy!" His tone was agitated.

"The other side."

Bruce swiped his hand again, this time on the other side. As his fingers grazed the tip of the glass bottle, a sensation of ease spread through his body. He opened the bottle quickly and began to guzzle the alcohol as though it was water. Gulp after gulp, the pain of the past slowly diminished in his mind.

Thinking that he could leave now, Nathaniel continued to walk to the door. He hoped that was all his father wanted, just the drink and nothing else.

He took another step toward the door, and heard his father breathing heavily after the consumption of liquor.

"Where do you think you're going?" Bruce inquired, inching forward to his son.

"School," Nathaniel answered.

The alcohol kicked in a lot quicker than usual. The rush made Bruce light-headed, causing him to stagger. "Yooooouuu . . . are not . . . goingggg . . . toooooo . . . school today," he slurred.

"Joseph is waiting for me outside," Nathaniel stated in protest.

"Don't give me . . . that attitude, mister. I . . . am . . . your *father*! You do as I say!" Bruce commanded.

Defiance prevailed this morning for Nathaniel. He wanted none of his father's drunken theatrics. He continued the last few steps to the door, ignoring the warning. *Father is drunk. I shouldn't worry about it.* As he reached for the doorknob, he felt Bruce's large hand clamp down tightly on his wrist. It caused a great deal of pain.

Your son does not listen to you. What kind of father are you? The voice inside Bruce's head berated him.

He has no respect for you. Another voice.

I thought you would be a better father than this, Fayth's voice chimed in this time.

He shook his head to dispel the voices. "I *told* you! You . . . are not . . . *going* . . . to school . . . today!" Bruce slurred again. He pulled Nathaniel away from the door. "Your father knows best . . . Why do you not listen to me?"

"Father, you are hurting me!" Nathaniel cried out.

Discipline. The boy needs discipline. The voice in his head again.

Yes . . . Discipline the boy. The second voice.

Get rid of his friend outside.

Yes! You must!

I cannot do this to my son. Another drink should make these voices go away, Bruce thought. Slightly loosening his grip on Nathaniel, he leaned back to take another gulp of drink.

Seizing the opportunity as his father's grip loosened, Nathaniel yanked his arm away.

As Bruce pulled the bottle away from his lips and swallowed the liquor down, the voices continued to taunt him

Our son has no respect for you, said Fayth's voice.

No respect. Another voice.

Maybe you should teach him some respect. Yet another.

If I were there, things would be different, she exclaimed.

Bruce looked out the door to see Nathaniel's friend waiting patiently by the porch. They exchanged a glance.

"Is Nathaniel coming to school today?"

"No. He is not feeling good today," Bruce lied.

"Oh, okay. Thank you, Mr. Smith."

"Now hurry along, you don't want to be late for class."

"Yes, sir." Joseph watched Bruce close the door.

Small beads of sweat began to form on Bruce's face as it became suffused with a drunken red glow. Anger washed over him with the harsh words from his mind.

Nathaniel had taken another step forward, when Bruce raised his free hand to the sky.

If I were there, things would be different, Fayth's voice echoed once more.

"BUT YOU ARE NOT HERE!" he screamed aloud.

With a quick swoop, Bruce brought his hand down to strike the side of his son's jaw. The blow echoed in Nathaniel's head like a thunderclap and spun him in a circle. The pain throbbed throughout his lower face and his little hands clutched it in pain.

As Bruce inched closer and closer, his vision became clouded. Shades of black took over as his memory faded, the noise that surrounded him turned to silence, and the bottle in his hand fell to the floor.

"Father! Father!" Nathaniel cried.

Those words meant nothing to Bruce. He inched closer and closer to the boy and raised his hand yet again.

"No, Father, *no!*" Nathaniel screamed again, pleading for mercy.

Another slap came crashing into Nathaniel's other cheek. Another thunderous crack; another loud cry of pain. The boy could not keep his balance and fell to the floor.

Nathaniel could only think of the pain throbbing throughout his face. He wondered when this madness would stop. *This is not my father*, he thought. *I need to get through to him. Somehow, someway, I have to try.*

Bruce unbuckled his belt and sized it up for a moment, looking up and down. He snapped the leather, which sent shivers down Nathaniel's spine. The young boy sat on the ground, paralyzed in fear, terrified of what he knew was coming. He wanted to flee, but knew that he stood practically no chance, and was also stunned and drained from the pain he'd already endured.

The only thing he could do was watch in fear of the father who was no longer there to protect him, only to inflict pain and cause misery.

Bruce gave him a chilling blank stare, showing that his old self was no longer present. Nathaniel made one final attempt to stop the madness. "Please! Please, Father. No!" Misery enveloped him, the barrier that could not be penetrated. Not a single word registered to his father, a man possessed.

Sweat poured down the terrified child's skin. The strike was swift and fast, drawing blood. Bruce unleashed more blows with the precision and accuracy of a trained fighter.

The boy no longer cried out or wept, but only sat there in shock. He felt unable to move. Knowing that more pain was coming, he tried to lift his arms in defense, but they felt like anchors. Turning around to expose his back, the most he could do was try to crawl away. *Hopefully, this will be the end*, he thought desperately.

Anger fueled the fire burning deep inside Bruce as he watched Nathaniel retreat. The anger seeped through his skin and radiated from him like an aura. He did not like the sight of his son inching away; it enraged him further. Raising his hand yet again, Bruce struck another blow.

Nathaniel jolted in pain. "Aaaaaahhhhh!" he screamed. He now began to moan in agony. Saliva dripped from his lips like small raindrops to the floor.

Bruce continued to stalk his prey, moving and adjusting to find the right position for the next strike. Because the child did not scream when struck, he took offense and only wanted to cause more pain.

When he felt he was in the right position for another blow, he quickly unleashed another lightning-fast strike of the belt. His face lit up with sadistic pleasure from the pain he was dealing out.

"Please, Father! Please . . . Please . . . Please . . . Stop!" Nathaniel choked out with every hit.

Ripples of shock and pain racked the flesh of Nathaniel's back. He wanted to roll over and stop the onslaught, but was stopped by his father's foot holding him in place.

Bruce's aggravation escalated to another level as his fun was disrupted by Nathaniel's squirming and attempts to crawl away. The madness continued; he reached down and viciously ripped the remaining tatters of shirt off the boy's back.

Again the leather belt seared the child's skin. The pain felt completely different now without the slightest protection of cloth. Nathaniel's eyes bulged wide as his terror soared. Never in his life he had felt this much pain. A downpour of tears rushed from his reddening eyes, running down his cheeks to spatter the floor.

Another lash to his back, and the pain mounted ever higher. Now, Nathaniel was screaming, louder with each blow, until the young boy could no longer cry. The pain was so excruciating that all sensation numbed away as shock began to set in.

The pure amazement of his son's bloodied back gave Bruce pleasure. Through the pain, Nathaniel still showed signs of life and resilience. Attempting to crawl away from the madman's attack, he tried to inch away, moving one arm in front of the other.

Far from finishing, Bruce felt the slight movement of his son trying to move from under his restraining foot. He glared down at the helpless child and applied more pressure. Then, pushing Nathaniel to his side, he let loose with a fist to the boy's abdomen. Nathaniel gasped faintly for quite some time as he fought to catch a breath of air. Tears and saliva continued to run down his face.

Reaching down, Bruce grabbed the boy's arm and hauled him up to eye level. "Ah!" Nathaniel cried in pain. "Father . . ." he choked and sniffed.

"You think this is a game?" Bruce shouted in the boy's face, now wearing a twisted grin.

Lowering Nathaniel back down, he balled his hand into a fist and swung it forward. Then, he lifted him backup. The child bobbed back and forth like a pendulum. His punch did not matter where it landed, as long as it inflicted pain. Bruises were forming all over the boy's body.

Nathaniel's eyes were suffused with red. Tears ran down his cheeks like a river and fell to the ground, where they quickly disappeared in the dry summer heat. With every blink, his eyes felt like sandpaper. *Is this ever going to end?* He wondered. His breathing now came in erratic gasps. The boy looked up at his lunatic father, expecting a final judgment. The anger he saw in Bruce's face was a sign that the end was not in the near future.

Bruce's vision of darkness began to recede. Slowly, with every blink, he saw a body starting to take shape in front of him.

A voice echoed in the back of Nathaniel's mind. ***Releeeeeeeease meeeeee.*** He darted his eyes around the room to see if there was someone lurking in the darkness. *Am I going mad? Am I going crazy? Where is this voice coming from?*

Releaseeeeeeee meeeeee, the voice in his mind cried once more.

Bruce wanted to speak the words that he thought, but ended up choking, the words remaining unspoken in his throat. *Why cannot I speak? Why cannot I control myself?* He took a step forward, elevating his limp son like a teddy bear. Another step, and Nathaniel's body bounced back like a spring.

With no more room behind him, the young child's body had collided with the wall, knocking his head upon the hard surface. Nathaniel cringed in pain as the remnants of his energy fled. His head lolled from side to side like a broken toy, unconscious and dead to the world.

A quick change took place in the atmosphere, like the flicking of a switch. Bruce's rage morphed into something else, something almost demonic. The suffocating feeling inside him intensified. Nathaniel was now convulsing, slowly at first. The spasms intensified and slowly gained complete control of Nathaniel's small body.

"Heh, heh, heh, heh-heh-heh." A laugh rang out, in a voice Bruce did not recognize.

Nathaniel's convulsions came to an end. His head slowly lifted up, his eyes opened, and his gaze leveled with Bruce's eyes. The child's eyes were now black, and what gazed back at Bruce was no longer his son.

A low, snarling, demonic growl issued from under his breath, as the boy's nostrils flared out like a warning call. Without notice, whatever possessed Nathaniel struck like lightning, swiping like a ferocious wildcat, clawing at any available flesh. The young boy's fingertips grazed Bruce's chest, and at that moment Bruce's grip loosened.

Nathaniel crashed to the floor.

"If you harm this child like that ever again, *you are a dead man*," the alien voice threatened from Nathaniel's mouth.

Then, the atmosphere changed again, one last time. Bruce returned to his normal fatherly state. Horrified by his actions, he reached down to cradle his son. *What have I done?* Silence hung in the air. Bruce carried the battered child to his bedroom.

The coolness of the room was a welcome contrast from the sweaty heat of the den. It was soothing. Bruce could no longer feel the heat boiling inside him, or the sweat rolling down his face.

Setting Nathaniel on top of his bed, Bruce tucked the bed sheets over his son to let him rest and recover in peace. *This is the consequence of the things I have done. I screwed up. What have I just unleashed? Nathaniel . . . I am truly sorry.*

Outside, Joseph could not miss the commotion from within. *What did I just hear?* he thought, taking a few steps back. It did not sit well with him, but he was helpless to intervene. *Oh, my! Nathaniel*

. . . I hope you are okay. He took his leave and ran back to town.

CHAPTER 34
—JUST ANOTHER BAD DAY, PART 1

THREE WEEKS LATER

The sun rose on the horizon just as it did every day, lighting the sky a bright yellow and orange that suffused the heavens with the color of red like an ocean of blood. A few clouds brushed the sky in different shades of colors, lighting the land below in a glow.

Joseph walked along the road, his hands brushing the tips of the grass, swaying the grass back while he moved forward. In the distance, he could see Nathaniel's house. Pieces of wooden shingles were missing from the roof, and the left corner of the house near the ground showed signs of termite infestation. Some of the wood had holes and showed more signs of deterioration. Joseph saw the door left wide open once again.

Inside the house stood a small rectangular dining table with two wooden chairs on each side. Empty liquor bottles sat on top of the table, collecting dust, and behind the dining table was the kitchen counter and window covered with dust. Some light struggled through the grime all the same.

Joseph moved to the side to see farther inside the house. A couple of rocking chairs sat in front of the chimney. In between the two rocking chairs, a soft bear skin rug lay atop the wooden floor. The boy then caught a glimpse of a tall male figure in the back, which looked like a shadow in the darkness. He could also hear screaming from within the house.

"Where the fuck did you put my drink?" He recognized Bruce's voice.

"You had the whiskey bottle last. I don't know where you put it," Nathaniel answered, exasperated.

"Don't you lie to me, boy! Get your ass over here," Bruce demanded.

Suddenly, a loud slap echoed throughout the house. Joseph could hear it clearly from his place just outside the doorstep. Seconds later, a few whip cracks thundered from inside, accompanied by Nathaniel's cries of pain. Joseph tensed up and squeezed his eyes shut in sympathy.

Bruce peeped out the door and saw Joseph quietly standing there, listening to the whole ordeal. He told Nathaniel, "Hurry up and get ready for school; your friend is waiting for you." He gave his son eyes of disapproval and regret.

Nathaniel replied, "Yes, father." He walked into his room to grab a shirt.

Seconds later, he left the house, not once glancing back to his father, but walking out the door shirtless, the garment still in his hand. Joseph looked in horror at the bruises on his friend's back, along with the new marks from the belt. Nathaniel pulled his shirt on, concealing the wounds.

"Let's go," said Nathaniel flatly.

A dirt road paved the way for miles on end. The ground made a soft crunching sound under their feet as they walked alongside each other, separated by a strip of grass. The weeds on the edges of the road stood wild and untamed, as tall as their knees in certain areas. Trees shaded the surrounding ground from the morning sunlight.

Joseph's eyes closed for a second as he listened to the soft flow of water where the river sung in the distance. He turned to Nathaniel and asked, "Are you okay?"

"That was nothing. He can be worse," Nathaniel replied, offering no more on the topic. He stared straight ahead, as though in a daze.

Joseph looked intently at Nathaniel and commented, "I notice someone in class likes you."

Snapping out of his daze, he replied, "Hmmmm? What? Who?"

"Grace," Joseph answered.

"In your dreams. I haven't been to school in a while now."

"I've seen how she looks at you. In fact, she asked about you the other day. You should go and talk to her."

Nathaniel blurted, "I do not know . . . She is one of the nicer girls in town, and her family is well off. What does she want with me?"

"Well, if you don't talk to her, then I will talk to her for you," Joseph declared.

"Huh? Ah, fine . . . but not right now," Nathaniel grunted.

"But why?"

"You already know why."

"No, I don't."

"Do I have to show you?"

"Oh, that's right."

"I have bigger things to worry about right now. Eventually, I will though, Joseph."

"Alright."

"I think her nanny doesn't like me."

"Why do you say that?" Joseph questioned.

"Well . . . She looks at me weird."

"I haven't noticed."

"Well, you should pay attention when you have the chance."

"Okay."

Suddenly, Joseph stopped a few feet before the bridge they'd crossed daily for the last few years on their way to school together. Nathaniel stopped a few feet ahead, when he noticed Joseph was no longer moving. Something must have spooked him, like seeing a ghost; his face was contorted from fear.

"Is something wrong?"

Joseph watched the townspeople walking to and fro, buying, trading, and talking to one another in the town. Five young boys around his age had caught his attention. He watched them carefully as they walked around the market and finally disappeared from his vision. Swallowing hard, he responded, "N-nah, no, nothing's wrong."

"Let's get some breakfast," Nathaniel suggested.

"We're going to be late," Joseph responded.

"Your house is right there." Nathaniel pointed.

"Yeah, but my uncle is home. He'll kill me if we're late."

"Fine," Nathaniel conceded, disappointed.

He gazed past the white church, its bells ringing from the tower. Farther east, a river flowed, carving a ridge through the land.

"Are you sure you're okay?" Joseph changed the subject.

"That was nothing compared to some days. Often, he is worse than that," Nathaniel replied.

"What do you mean, worse than that?"

"You've seen the bruises."

"Uh-huh."

"I don't know . . . It's hard to explain."

"Well, try."

"Okay . . ." Nathaniel sighed. "Well, there are days when he's my father, and then there are days when he's someone else."

"Oh . . . Let's take the shortcut. It would be a whole lot faster than going through town," Joseph suggested.

"Sure."

They walked into the forest, where the edge of a trail revealed itself underneath the overgrown grass, a secret path that the two of them knew as a shortcut around town. The thick green grass swallowed their legs to the knees as they walked alongside the riverbed and past a few chestnut trees that grew beside the hidden trail.

Joseph asked, "What do you want to do after school?"

Nathaniel pondered for a moment before responding. "I don't know. What do you have in mind?"

"Fishing! We haven't done that in a while," Joseph replied with a smile, pleased with his great idea.

"Sure. If you cook what we catch, then I'm in."

"Deal," Joseph responded.

The boys came upon a narrow bridge made of rope and wood, which looked fairly new, as if it had been recently built. Nathaniel and Joseph crossed the bridge one by one, teetering left and right with each movement. Beyond the bridge, a small patch of wilderness hid the church.

To the left, in the school yard, Mrs. Clark rang the bell. The children passed through the yard, converging upon the small white schoolhouse from various directions.

Closing the door behind her as she did every school day, the instructor glided swiftly and softly to the front of the room, not making a sound as she crossed the floor. She surveyed the classroom and noticed several empty seats that were usually filled.

"My, oh, my. We are missing a lot of students today," Mrs. Clark stated, more to herself than to the assembled students. *Well, this is going to be an easy day, I suppose.*

■   ■   ■   ■

The day progressed, slightly overcast. Five young boys sat on a ledge, staring down into a breathtaking view of the river flowing into a larger body of water, which met the horizon such that it looked as though the lake reached for the sky.

"You think it was a good idea for us to skip school today?" Christopher sought reassurance from his friends as he gazed down at the flowing water.

"Who cares," said Justin thoughtlessly as he got up and moved to the nearest tree to lean upon it.

"We're only missing one day of class. It won't hurt us," Matthew added, moving back to lie on the soft, springy grass.

"Yeah, but . . ." Christopher paused for a moment.

"You can go back to school if you want, Chris. We've already missed the majority of it, though," Franklin chimed in, moving back as well to lie next to Matthew.

Tossing a fishing line into the river, Timothy felt at ease, with not a care in the world. "You can always walk back to school. Do what you want. No one is going to stop you."

"Yeah . . ." Christopher sighed. *I would rather spend time with my friends,* he thought.

"Relax a little," Matthew suggested.

"Yeah, relax. You think that Mrs. Clark will tell our parents, though?" Justin asked.

"You think she would?" Franklin reacted to Justin's comment.

"I don't think so," Timothy replied.

"But what if she does?" Matthew questioned, thinking better of it.

"Yeah . . . What if she does?" Justin echoed.

"No! No, no, no, no, *no*!" Christopher stood up, overtaken by anxiety. "We have to go to class!"

"What for?" Franklin yawned.

"If she tells my parents, I'm done for!"

"You should just come fishing with me, Chris. Don't worry about it. I'm sure these guys are just messing with you," Timothy commented reassuringly.

"Yeah," Justin said, grabbing the fishing pole next to his side. "Hey Chris, catch."

Turning around toward Justin, Christopher was unprepared. The pole smacked on the forehead, making him stagger back. They both watched the fishing pole fall to the ground.

A big smile spread across Justin's face, which he tried to conceal by covering his mouth with his hands. However, small chuckles escaped and soon turned to hearty laughter.

Matthew and Franklin heard the laughter and sat up from their comfortable place on the grass. They saw Christopher rubbing his forehead while Justin laughed hysterically. The contagious laughter spread amongst the others like wildfire and they joined in.

The laughter did not seem to die down anytime soon, Christopher grabbed the fishing pole from the ground and made his way back to Timothy. Not a word spoken to Timothy, Christopher sat next to him. He watched the young boy manage only a smirk but knew his friend was feeling a little down.

"What is wrong, Chris? This is not like you at all," Justin asked once he had control of himself again.

"Ah . . . Nothing. Nothing is wrong," Christopher replied.

"Are you sure?"

"Well . . . I have been thinking about what the guys were talking about earlier . . ."

"About school?"

"Yeah."

For a moment, Timothy chuckled at the thought. "You know that they were joking, right?"

"No . . ." Christopher looked down. "Well, come to think of it, my father didn't want me to go to school in the first place. He thought it was a waste of time and wanted me to work with him instead. My mother thought differently. She wanted me to get an education, you know."

"You shouldn't worry too much about it. It's only one day and, besides, I'll have your back if anything happens."

"Okay," Christopher answered with a little more confidence.

"Now, let's do some fishing and enjoy the rest of the day," said Timothy brightly.

Moments later, sitting at the edge of the cliff beside Christopher, Timothy enjoyed the silence. The call of nature was the only occasional disturbance. He caught a glimpse of his friend, who was now concentrating only on the task of catching a fish. Everything seemed to flow pleasantly. Timothy leaned back and began to doze off, drifting into a dream in which scenes from the morning visited him once more.

ONE WEEK AGO

On their way to school that morning, the boys had blended into the early flow of foot traffic up and down the street. As they'd walked down the middle of the path, they watched the people passing by, like the flow of the river. Oftentimes, they were lucky enough to see a carriage pass by.

"Timothy. Timothy," Justin called.

"Hmmph?"

"Let's go to the market and mess around," Justin suggested.

Timothy looked in the direction of the school. *I just want to see her*, he thought. "Well, I don't know . . . We're so close to school already."

"We're close to the market as well," Justin noted.

"You can do what you like. I'm thinking about going to class, though."

Christopher quietly approached his friends. The sound of his footsteps was drowned out by the noisy crowd. Timothy turned around, startled to see another friend standing right next to Justin. "Hey, Christopher. When'd you sneak up on us?"

"Not too long ago." He smiled.

Soon, the rest of the group arrived. Matthew came walking from the south and Franklin from the east.

"Well, well, well. What do we have here?" Matthew grinned.

"I can smell trouble from a mile away," Franklin said, closing in on his friends.

"Hey, guys."

Timothy led the way, not once looking back, and the rest of the group followed quickly. The center of town disappeared behind them, and he felt the distance grow. Only Christopher turned to look back.

As Timothy blinked, the sound of the townspeople faded away like a distant dream. It happened so quickly. His head was spinning faster and faster, looping in a circle, unable to see in the dark. When he opened his eyes, everything came to a halt.

"Hey, hey. Look who it is," Justin called from the left.

"Oh, yeah! It's your *girl*, Timothy." Matthew nudged his arm.

Timothy scanned the road from right to left. It was mainly empty, with a few kids around their age coming to school. Houses and small side roads filled the other side of the street, but they all seemed like a blur from his perspective.

Timothy had drifted off into his own little world for a moment. It took a while before he looked over. Sure enough, at the limit of his vision, he could see Grace coming up the road. *I always wondered why Grace's parents don't walk her to school. In fact, I seldom see them at all. She always comes with her nanny.*

The boys walked along the road, chatting and paying no mind to their surroundings. Timothy's attention, however, was riveted on Grace. He could hear his heartbeat in his ears. *Damn, I feel that rush every time I see her*, he thought. His palms were sweaty; his hands clenched tightly. He felt like a nervous wreck. *What if she looks at me? How do I look? I hope I'm not blushing.*

It seemed as though time itself slowed down as Timothy's eyes locked onto Grace and her nanny, walking up to the school. *Did she notice me? I hope she does! Oh my goodness, she is a beauty.*

"Timothy, walk with her to school," Franklin suggested.

"Hmmph?"

"You should go talk to her," Franklin added.

"Yeah, lovebird," Matthew teased.

One by one, they began to whistle in imitation of bird calls, each one trying to outdo the other, whistling louder than the person before. *Gosh*, Timothy thought, *they can be annoying at times!*

"Well, she is already with her nanny," Timothy noted.

"So?" Justin responded.

"Maybe he's a chicken." Matthew taunted.

"You were talking to her a lot, you know," said Christopher.

Something feels wrong... "Yeah . . . Not today."

"You'd better do something quick," said Franklin.

"Why?"

"Look." Justin pointed at Grace.

What now? *He'd better not be playing a trick on me. Well . . . Maybe, maybe not.* Remaining patient was the bane of Timothy's existence. Justin was making him anxious. He wanted to scream aloud, "Tell me what is going on!" However, he forced himself to remain calm and collected.

"In three . . . two . . . one . . . Here he comes," Justin counted down.

"There he is! Right on time," Matthew acknowledged.

"Who?"

"Priest boy Joseph," Franklin replied.

Joseph . . . Emotions boiled inside Timothy: anger, hate, rage, and something more. The thought of Joseph made his stomach churn. *Why does he have to try to go after the one person I like at school?* Timothy seethed internally. *This fucker is going to pay!* His anger was beginning to show.

"Ever since the town drunk's boy went missing in action a few weeks back . . ." Matthew explained.

"Who? Nathaniel?" Justin asked.

"Yeah. Since he hasn't been coming to school, Joseph has been really close to Grace," Matthew continued.

"What are you going to do, Timothy?" Christopher asked.

"One day, when Joseph is by himself, I will take care of him."

"Oh! I like that," Franklin egged him on.

"Yeah! I like it too!" Matthew added.

■　　■　　■　　■

Timothy blinked again and everything melted back into darkness. His friends' voices became distant and quickly faded away. Alone, he floated in the empty dreamscape, waiting.

Suddenly, he caught a glimpse of light in the distance, and heard a sound. What was that? He started to move toward the sound. Water, that's what he was hearing. The flow of the rushing river through the land was like a vein carrying the blood of life to a beating heart.

Is this another dream?

Timothy sat and opened his eyes to the clear blue sky above. A fishing rod was in his hand. Quickly turning to the side, he saw Christopher's familiar face. His friend sat beside him, focused intently on his fishing. Still, Timothy could tell that he had something else on his mind. Despite the attempt to keep his preoccupation from his friends, it was easy to read on his features.

Timothy turned his head to the other side, still getting his bearings, and saw Justin sitting near the tree trunk, partly concealed in the shade. Behind him was the forest. Justin seemed to be watching something among the trees and grass there.

He could hear something, or someone, rustling the grass and foliage. Timothy turned to see Matthew and Franklin rise from where they'd been relaxing, stand, and stretch, looking cynically upon the newcomers.

Timothy reeled in his fishing line from the river and tossed the pole to the side as the others walked closer to the group of friends. Christopher imitated his friend's action.

"Well, well, well, well. Look at what we have here," said Franklin.

"Yeah . . . A priest and the town drunk's boy!" Matthew snarled.

Nasty chuckles filled the air. Like vultures circling a fresh kill, Matthew, Franklin, Christopher, Justin and Timothy surrounded Nathaniel and Joseph.

"Nathaniel, you can go home now. We do not have any business with you."

Timothy motioned Franklin and Matthew over to have a word with them. They moved closer, closing the gap so no one else could see or hear what they were planning.

"Yes?" Matthew inquired.

"I want you two to take Nathaniel out of here."

"What if he doesn't want to come with us?" Franklin asked.

"Force him. He has no choice."

"But what if Nathaniel just comes right back?" Matthew suggested.

"Take care of it."

■　■　■　■

The darkness consumed Timothy once more; for the last time, he hoped. *Again? Why?*

His hands throbbed in pain.

He heard a familiar voice sobbing in agony. "Please stop."

■　■　■　■

He opened his eyes to a blinding light, as though the sun were directly in front of him. It consumed his vision momentarily, and he blinked once more, trying to focus. *Fuck . . .* Three solid figures were before him; two were the shapes of his friends, and another was down on his knees, arms out as though he were being crucified.

Did I wonder why the scenery did not change as it had the last few times? There was no time to think. From the groggy haze that clouded his vision, Timothy could finally see Justin and Christopher holding Joseph down, just as he had imagined in his dreams for quite some time.

"Timothy! Please, no! No!" Joseph begged.

Timothy wore the biggest smile, stretching practically from ear to ear. Joseph watched in dread as he took his time walking closer. Timothy thoroughly enjoyed the other boy's discomfort. Step by step, his anticipation rose and the adrenaline started to set in. *Thump, thump. Thump, thump.* His heart began to race, faster and faster.

Joseph's eyes widened with fear. "Please, Timothy, please, no," he begged again.

Timothy balled his hand into a fist, ignoring the pleas. He punched with all the force he could muster. The blow landed on the side of Joseph's ribcage. Christopher turned his head away, avoiding the brutal scene, but Justin, on the other hand, watched in fascination.

Joseph grunted in pain while Justin and Christopher held him in place. Timothy threw another punch, aiming lower this time, dead center on his victim's stomach.

Timothy watched his nemesis lose his breath and gasp for air. Tears began to form in the boy's eyes and fell to the ground when he blinked. *The sweet taste of victory!* For some reason, Timothy was not satisfied. He wanted more.

"Why? Why do you hate me so?" Joseph choked out between gasps.

"You know why," Justin answered.

"No, I don't! I swear, I don't!" Joseph replied, exasperation warring with pain on his features.

"Ever since your friend left you, you have been close to his girl," Christopher accused.

Joseph drew a blank. "What girl?"

"Don't act stupid."

Then it dawned on him. "Grace? We are just friends, nothing more," Joseph cried.

"Uh-huh. Sure. That's what they all say," Justin retorted.

"I swear! I swear it! We are just friends," Joseph screamed as he struggled to escape the clutches of his captors.

Timothy believed differently, though. *This lying piece of shit thinks I'm blind?* Just as he inched closer to throw another punch, something jerked him around. His hands jerked and shook uncontrollably up and down and side to side.

The loud noise of someone cheering and screaming claimed his attention. "Timothy! Timothy! You got a fish!"

The darkness swallowed him again for the last time. The pleasure of tormenting Joseph was stripped away from him. Joseph . . . Justin . . . Christopher . . . Meanwhile, the cries grew louder and louder. "Timothy! Timothy! Fish on!" *Why does this have to happen? I want my dream to come true. Why must I wake up now?*

Timothy's eyes opened to the view of his fishing pole jerking around in his hand, swinging wildly. He yawned, trying to bring himself back around and struggling to reel in the feisty fish on the end of his line. Christopher enjoyed the action, cheering him on.

As Timothy pulled the fish closer to the shore, Christopher yelled, "Looks like we have lunch!"

But Timothy could not stop thinking of his dream. *I wish it were all true.*

■　■　■　■

Meanwhile, the afternoon sunlight streamed through the classroom window, where Nathaniel sat at his desk in the back of the room, staring blankly into the sunbeam. Oblivious to his surroundings, he was lost in space and time. The students all sat silently at their desks, side by side, as Mrs. Clark kept watch from her place in the front of the room.

Then, at last, she spoke the longed-for words: "Class dismissed."

The seconds seemed to stretch before the first student's chair screeched back on the floor as the child moved to leave. The rest soon followed, streaming to the doors together like a school of fish.

Something felt different to Nathaniel as he watched all the students walk out the door one by one. He noticed that Joseph was not waiting for him as he always did. That threw him off. *We are always the last to leave class. Was I gone for that long? Strange . . . Something is not right.* After glancing around the empty room, he decided to get up and make his way past the line of desks to the open door.

Mrs. Clark dismissed Nathaniel cheerfully. "Have a wonderful day!"

Nathaniel watched her expression carefully. He could tell that she was making her best effort to smile and look happy for him. He sensed that something or someone was troubling her, but he gave no sign of noticing; he simply returned her smile.

"Thank you, Mrs. Clark. Have a good day," Nathaniel responded courteously.

It was another warm afternoon. Nathaniel paused just outside the door for a moment to gaze up into the cloudless blue sky. Then, a whistle in the distance broke his concentration. He looked around and caught sight of Joseph standing next to Grace. *I hate you, Joseph . . . literally*

"Nathaniel!" Joseph waved to him. "Let's go!"

Nathaniel wanted to cringe at the sight of Grace, but kept his composure. *Ugh . . . I have to talk to her one day, or Joseph will do it for me . . . I'm not ready.* He took his time, approaching them slowly. *This is not like Joseph,* he thought. *We always leave together.*

The crowds outside flooded the streets, causing Nathaniel to lose sight of his friends momentarily as he dodged and weaved between the other people. There was a good bit of noise as well from people chatting amongst each other and boots scraping the ground.

"Slowpoke!" Joseph teased as Nathaniel finally caught up with them.

He is always in a cheery mood, I will give him that. Nathaniel's left eyelid began to twitch. He rubbed it until the twitching stopped.

"Are you okay?" Joseph asked.

"Yeah, everything's fine," Nathaniel responded.

"Okay, let's go."

Following the flow of the crowd through the busy streets, they followed the wall of people northwards. Some of them left the crowd upon reaching their destination, thinning the herd. The three children continued their way to the edge of town, the school and church disappearing behind them in the distance.

Joseph and Grace would usually chat about anything and everything on their minds, and Nathaniel would silently listen to their conversations. Today, the atmosphere was different. The normally talkative pair kept to themselves, which struck Nathaniel as strange. The enjoyment of silence was very rare for their group. Soon enough, the rest of the travelers had left the road, and the last houses at the edge of town were past, leaving the group of three on their own. Only the green of vegetation covered the land.

Nature took hold, replacing the buzzing of human speech with the babble of the flowing river nearby and the melodious chirping of birds. Though hidden in the surrounding forest of green, the area was teeming with animal life.

As she did every day, Grace's nanny stood at the end of the bridge, waiting ever so patiently, welcoming the children with the smile that even Nathaniel had become accustomed to.

"How was your day at school today?" the nanny always asked when the children approached her.

"It went well, Nanny. It felt rather short today in class," Grace responded.

"How so?" the nanny questioned.

"I'm not really sure."

"This is around the same time I always come to pick you up."

"We were missing some classmates today," Joseph noted. "Maybe that's why it felt so short."

"Oh, okay."

Together, they continued further down the road and farther from the town. Small conversations took place from time to time, but silence dominated the majority of the walk. Coming to the crossroads where the roads split into two, Grace and her Nanny slowly separated themselves from the two boys and headed north. Nathaniel and Joseph paused for a moment, watching them leave.

"See you at school tomorrow," Joseph called.

As Grace and Shooting Star continued to walk, Grace turned around to wave back. "See you at school tomorrow."

"Have a good night!" he called back a little louder.

Together, the boys watched their friend fade away into the distance. For themselves, they had other plans in store. Along they continued down the other road, distancing themselves further from town and the crossroads. Joseph wanted to jump for joy as they got closer and closer to their normal hangout spot.

"I cannot wait! I cannot wait! We're going to have so much fun!" He sounded ecstatic.

"Yes, we are," Nathaniel agreed enthusiastically.

Layers upon layers of trees surrounded the two boys as they branched off the road and into the forest. The grass entangled their legs, as though it didn't want them to progress forward. Birds chirped loudly all around, and squirrels and other animals ran along the tree trunks and rustled the brushes below. The rushing river gradually grew louder as well.

"We are almost there!" Joseph called out in excitement.

"Wait . . . Do you hear that?" Nathaniel asked.

"Hear what?" Joseph sounded puzzled.

"There are people here."

Joseph took a moment and listened for anything out of place. "You must be hearing things," he replied, not detecting anything over the sounds of forest wildlife.

"I could have sworn I heard something," Nathaniel insisted.

Upon reaching the end of the tree line, they entered a plain, with a view of the large body of water ahead. Above them was the blue sky that the trees had hidden earlier in their travels. Grass covered the ground for as far as the eye could see. They continued to press forward, wrestling with the overgrown grass.

"Oh my, we have a couple of special guests here," a familiar voice spoke.

"Justin?" Joseph asked.

"And us," spoke another voice.

"Franklin, Matthew, Christopher, Timothy . . ." Joseph's voice turned hoarse, and he swallowed nervously.

Rising from the grass, Matthew and Franklin stood and stretched. Their smiles were cynical, making the newcomers apprehensive. Timothy and Christopher pulled their lines from the river and tossed the fishing poles to the side as they walked closer to the rest of the gang.

"Well, well, well. Look at what we have here," said Franklin nastily.

"Yeah . . . A priest and the town drunk's kid!" Matthew snarled.

"Y-you g-guys missed class to-today," Joseph stammered.

"Yeah! And what of it?" Justin retorted.

Chuckles and snide laughter filled the air. Like vultures circling a fresh kill, the boys slowly surrounded the other two.

"Nathaniel," Timothy said.

"Hmm?" Nathaniel responded. *Well, fuck . . . No wonder today didn't feel right.*

Timothy motioned Franklin and Matthew to come closer so he could have a word with them. On command, they moved closer, closing the gap so no one else could see or hear what they were planning.

"Yes, Timothy?" Matthew replied.

"I want you two to take Nathaniel out of here. My business is not with him," Timothy ordered.

"What if he doesn't want to come with us?" Franklin asked.

"Force him. He has no choice in this matter."

"But what if Nathaniel returns after we take him away?" Matthew suggested.

"Just take care of it." Timothy motioned. *Why does it feel like I have been through this before?*

With a cynical grin, Matthew took his leave. Franklin followed along, not far behind. Timothy watched them take a couple of steps. Everything that happened felt so surreal, with a strong sense of déjà-vu.

"Hey! Nathaniel, can I have a word with you?" Matthew approached.

"Um . . . Sure," he responded, not knowing what else to do.

"Come with us." Matthew led the way, away from the river.

Joseph felt an eerie chill creep up his spine. The cold sweat ran down every inch of his body even though the afternoon sun continued its blazing heat. All he could do was watch his best friend being escorted away by people he barely knew.

Nathaniel, Franklin, and Matthew disappeared along the tree line, and Joseph felt he had no choice but to look back. He knew that something else was brewing. He felt another presence, an evil one, crawling right around the corner.

Timothy's glare left Joseph feeling suffocated, distinctly worsening the tension. In response, he suddenly felt submissive, as though he would have obeyed almost any command. With tightness in his chest, he moved slowly forward to meet his doom.

Like statues in the sun, Justin, Timothy, and Christopher stood there motionless, waiting for Joseph. He felt like he was looking at three giant mountains as he approached, feeling less significant with every second that passed.

There he stood, alone, frightened and shaking on the inside, but he knew he had to stay strong somehow. A slight breeze swept across the land from west to east, making Joseph squint. *The winds of change.*

Timothy briefly looked over at Justin and Christopher, giving them both a nod to progress forward. Together, they marched to Joseph's side, leaving him no room. Words wanted to come out of Joseph's mouth, but they froze at the tip of his tongue.

He felt Christopher and Justin place their hands on his shoulders. Another nod from Timothy, and he was restrained by the two, unable to move either forward or back.

What is going on here? Joseph wanted to cry. The fear was overwhelming.

Timothy took a step forward, his feet thudding on the ground. Joseph imagined the earth beneath him splitting into two.

Hoarsely, Joseph forced out, "Timothy."

"This is my judgment. This is what you deserve," Timothy thought.

Joseph squirmed as much as he could within the restraint that Christopher and Justin applied. They felt the fight and applied more pressure to make sure that he was held down. It hurt. He felt like a prisoner waiting for his judgment. "Why are you doing this?" he begged.

"You already know why," Justin responded.

"Yeah!" Christopher chimed in unhelpfully.

Timothy moved forward wordlessly and punched Joseph in the gut. His victim flinched, falling to the side, losing all of his breath and gasping for air. Timothy smiled nastily, watching his enemy squirm.

Trembling in fear and not knowing what to do, Joseph wanted to scream, *"Nathaniel! Nathaniel! Please help!"* but he knew that his friend was already far away. *Why am I not as brave as you?*

"Why? Why?" He cried.

"YOU KNOW WHY!" Timothy threw another punch at his foe.

Joseph gasped for air. This blow was harder than the last. The excruciating pain was enough to bring tears to the boy's eyes.

"I don't! I don't! I swear, I don't know!" He screamed and choked for air.

"Well, maybe this will remind you!" Timothy punched him yet again.

Joseph struggled feebly, trying with all his might to escape the grasp of Justin and Christopher. *What in the world is he talking about?*

"I swear! I swear, I don't know what this is about!" Joseph continued to plead.

Timothy's blood boiled with anger. He was certain that Joseph was withholding the truth from him. *How could I make him talk?* His face reddened with anger. He paced around like a caged animal, trying to figure out what to say.

"You want her all for yourself! Is that right, Joseph?" he snarled.

Her? The throbbing pain made it hard for Joseph to think. Tears fell freely from his eyes. *Who is he talking about?*

"Why? Why do you hate me?" Joseph gasped weakly.

"You know why," Justin answered unhelpfully.

"No, I don't! I swear I don't!" Joseph argued.

"Ever since your friend left you, you have been close to his girl," said Christopher.

"Yeah, don't play stupid," Timothy added.

"G-Grace?" Joseph replied incredulously, stumbling over her name.

"BINGO!" Timothy answered angrily.

"W-We are just friends!"

"That's what they all say," Justin retorted.

"I swear! I swear! We are just friends," Joseph screamed, renewing his struggle to escape. *I am doomed if I don't get away.*

Timothy's response was to make a punching bag of Joseph, raining blow after blow upon the other boy. The cruel smile on his face revealed his enjoyment of Joseph's pain. Still, something was missing to make his satisfaction complete.

"Liar!" Timothy screamed.

"I swear!" Joseph gasped weakly.

"Tell the truth for once!"

"I am!"

This time, Timothy slapped Joseph's face, hard, reddening his opponent's cheek. Still, he was itching for something more, more than what he had in front of him. A thirst was growing inside.

"Let him go!" Timothy demanded of his accomplices.

"Timothy . . ." Justin replied.

"I said, let him go!"

They released their hold on the helpless boy, and Joseph collapsed to the ground. Like a frightened animal, he kept his eyes down. *It is not over*, he thought. *It is not over. Someone help me. What is he planning next?*

"Get up!" Timothy demanded. "Fight me!"

Joseph shook his head. "No,"

"You can take my girl, but you cannot fight?"

Again Joseph shook his head, too terrified to look up.

"Get up and fight me, you little fuck!" Timothy provoked his foe again. He took another step forward, paused for a second, and then unleashed a sharp kick into Joseph's ribs.

The force of the kick flipped Joseph over. He gasped shallowly, and through his blurring vision, he could just discern Timothy approaching again.

"*I wish this day were over. Please be over,*" Joseph wished futilely.

Chapter 35
—Just Another Bad Day, Part 2

The group of young boys walked along the path back to the main road. An uncomfortable silence that felt awkward for Nathaniel hung in the air. The tall trees that surrounded them were not stirred by wind, nor did the animals make a peep. Nathaniel noticed Franklin and Matthew's silence. The shuffling of dirt beneath their feet was the only sound.

I wonder why they brought me out here to talk to me, he thought. An eerie feeling of tightness constricted his chest, and it seemed that he was carrying weight of the world on his shoulders. He was certain something was about to go wrong.

"You wanted to talk?" Nathaniel questioned his companions.

"Yeah, we do," Matthew replied robotically.

The faint echo of a voice sounded in the distance. "Why? Why?"

Nathaniel paused for a moment. Was that Joseph? *Am I just hearing things?*

Franklin stopped abruptly behind him, nearly crashing into Nathaniel's back. "What is wrong with you? I almost ran you over."

"Nothing. Nothing's wrong. I'm sorry," he responded. *I could swear I heard Joseph's voice, though.*

Franklin moved around Nathaniel to catch up with his friend. Matthew looked back to see what was going on. After briefly contemplating whether to continue walking or wait for the other two, he halted.

"Matthew," Franklin addressed his friend softly.

"Yeah?"

"We might have to do something soon." He watched as Nathaniel, also, stopped and stood still.

"Soon?"

"Look. Nathaniel is suspicious."

"Yeah, so?"

"He might go back."

"Well, if he does, we will just have to take care of him, like Timothy said." Matthew nodded to the ground, where a thick tree branch lay. It was about the size of a baseball bat.

"Okay . . ." Franklin replied warily.

The two separated, Franklin returned to his original position, and Matthew inched closer to Nathaniel. Matthew knew that he'd have to stay on his toes and do some quick thinking. The time in which he could stall for time was quickly dwindling away.

Matthew decided to try some small talk. "How have you been, Nathaniel?"

"Fine."

"It's been a while, right? How long has it been since the last time we hung out?"

"Never," Nathaniel's answer was as brief as the last.

"How about your father?"

"Hmm. He's still the same." Nathaniel considered refusing to answer this last inquiry. *Why all these stupid questions all of a sudden? They don't care about me. It doesn't make sense.* He took a step back toward the river.

Franklin stood between Nathaniel and the path, blocking his way. "We're just worried about you, that's all."

"Yeah," Matthew added unconvincingly.

A voice, faint but clear, could be heard from the direction of the river. "Fight me!"

Nathaniel peered over Franklin's shoulder in the direction of the sound. Taking another step forward, Franklin stood his ground.

Am I really just hearing things? I should go back and check.

"I'm sure that Joseph and the others are fine," Matthew said.

"Yeah, I'm sure they are just talking," said Franklin.

However, another shout covered the distance, belying the boys' statements: "Get up and fight me!"

Upon hearing that, Nathaniel darted around Franklin with lightning speed, but Franklin reacted just as quickly and tackled Nathaniel to the ground. However, his grip on the other boy quickly began to slip.

"Do something!" Franklin yelled.

Rushing to the branch he'd spotted earlier, Matthew snatched it up as a makeshift weapon. Nathaniel kicked and squirmed until he'd broken free of Franklin's grasp. In a last-ditch attempt, Franklin reached out and tripped him back to the ground.

Nathaniel quickly scrambled back to his feet and tried to avoid his attackers while making his way back to the river.

However, Matthew came swiftly and silently from behind and swung the thick branch like a baseball bat into the base of Nathaniel's skull.

Upon impact, Nathaniel saw a tunnel of darkness open before him. His head jerked forward and he crashed to the ground, face first, like a felled tree. Matthew looked on with a blank stare.

Franklin quickly scrambled to his feet. "Why the hell did you do that?"

"Timothy said . . ." Matthew paused.

"Fuck what Timothy said! This is crazy!" Franklin shouted back.

A moment of stunned silence hung in the air. The whole scene had become surreal.

Franklin knelt down by Nathaniel. "Is he dead?"

"I don't know. Check!" Matthew snapped back.

"How?"

"Check to see if he's breathing, idiot!"

Franklin lowered himself closer to Nathaniel's still form to stare at his face. "I cannot tell."

"I am sure he's fine," said Matthew dismissively.

"Are you sure?" Franklin didn't think so.

"Yeah. Now let's go back to the others," Matthew barked.

Matthew joined Franklin and led him back to the river, carrying the branch like a souvenir. Franklin looked back at Nathaniel, hoping he wasn't really dead. What he saw wasn't so reassuring. A dark reddish-black fluid surrounded Nathaniel's forehead on the ground, and his chest did not visibly rise and fall.

"Fuck it. Let's go!" Franklin agreed. There was nothing he could do about it now.

■ ■ ■ ■

Joseph lay in the fetal position to protect as much as possible of his body from Timothy's relentless assault. As another kick landed on his side, he held back the scream that threatened to tear from his throat. He knew that making noise would only encourage Timothy to continue beating him. *I am truly alone in this struggle. Mother . . . Father . . . If you are here, please help me,* he prayed.

"Get up and fight!" Timothy tried again to provoke his victim.

Joseph shook his head once more.

Just then, Matthew and Franklin came around the bend and Timothy paused for a moment, affording Joseph a lucky break. Christopher and Justin silently welcomed the other two back.

"Where is Nathaniel?" Timothy questioned.

"I took care of him," said Matthew as he tossed the bloodied branch on the ground.

"Well now, at least someone did their job," Timothy praised his comrade.

"What about this one?" Franklin asked.

"He will not give me a fight," Timothy responded, frustrated.

"Well then, let's finish this," Matthew said decisively.

"I like that idea."

"Justin . . . Christopher . . . Are you going to join us?" Matthew pressured the other two.

Franklin decided on blackmail as a tactic. "Christopher, if you don't join us, I will tell your father you skipped class with us."

Like vultures circling a carcass, they slowly circled around the child lying on the ground. Joseph briefly peeked up at the five forms encircling him. *This is not good.* Closer and closer they came, and he could no longer see the light of the sun.

"Get him!" Timothy yelled.

Dust rose into the air as the boys unleashed relentless kicks upon Joseph. He was bounced around like a human soccer ball, slightly moving in a small circle. While Timothy and Matthew smiled with cruel intentions, the others joined in on their fun with unease.

Nathaniel lay on the ground, tasting his own blood that poured from the wound on his forehead. As he rolled over to his side, a small rock embedded in the ground was revealed as the cause of that wound. He gasped and coughed.

A voice called to Nathaniel from within: *Release Me.*

His body began to convulse, surging full of energy, and his eyes darkened to black. Nathaniel's hands stretched across the dirt and gravel and dug in when his hands balled into fists. Something within him relished the feel of the cold dirt and the refreshing taste of the air.

"Heh, heh, heh," Nathaniel chuckled in voice not his own.

Ugh, where am I?

Finally, he rose from the ground and stretched his limbs. *I will have to get used to this vessel. Oh, it feels so good to be alive once more.* For a moment, he surveyed his surroundings, watching the wind dance amongst the trees, making the branches and leaves follow suit, swaying from side to side. Then, something else piqued his interest.

Nathaniel sniffed the air and smelled something enticing. Trying to pinpoint the location, he took another whiff, moving his head from left to right. *I smell fear . . . I smell blood! Where? Where is it? I must seek it!* He noticed the road leading to the river. *Ah! There it is! I want to enjoy this.*

His hands returned to the ground, and Nathaniel pushed off with his legs, running like an animal. Dirt sprayed from the ground with each footfall. Trees flew by, left and right, quicker and quicker.

He followed the trail, weaving left and right as the turns came. His focus was on the scene unfolding ahead; tunnel vision blurred the immediate surroundings and painted them red in his sight. Seconds later, as he turned into the river bend, a vast opening of the horizon lay before him, where the sky took over and trees were few and far between.

Catching sight of Nathaniel, Justin shouted, "The hell! Guys, turn around! You did not take care of him!" The rest of the group turned, Franklin and Timothy landing a few last kicks on Joseph before shifting their attention.

Franklin and Justin burst into laughter at the sight of Nathaniel running like an animal on all fours. Following suit, the rest bellowed with laughter as well. Nathaniel stopped short, leaving a gap between himself and the group of boys. His body shook fiercely, as if by the hand of another.

"Has Nathaniel been like this before?" Christopher questioned.

"I don't know," Franklin responded.

"He is just like his father, a drunk," Matthew declared.

"Do we really care?" Justin retorted.

Timothy ordered Matthew, "Better take care of the job you didn't finish."

"Don't worry, I got it," Matthew answered. *I should have swung a little harder, after all.*

The shaking ended and Nathaniel collapsed to the ground like a doll being dropped. He appeared to be struggling from within as he screamed aloud. Finally, calmness overtook him, and he lay face down on the ground.

Release me before it is too late.

Okay, then go.

Matthew walked over to Nathaniel, who still lay on the ground. He had a decision to make. He looked down at his foe on the ground, and then glanced at the tree branch he'd dropped on the ground earlier. *Should I pick it up or not?*

He walked past the branch. "Not that again," Matthew muttered to himself.

Standing over Nathaniel, he paused for a second to examine his opponent and choose an angle of attack. Matthew took a step back and took the measure of his victim's body, then planted his left foot firmly on the ground and swung his free right leg quickly down like a club to its target.

However, Nathaniel's quick reaction thwarted the incoming blow, leaving Matthew's foot thudding uselessly into the ground.

"Heh, heh, heh, heh." The chuckle from Nathaniel was not his own.

What the hell is going on? He couldn't have seen that one coming. The fuck . . . This freak! Nimble like a cat, Matthew quickly jumped back to safety.

"Play?" Nathaniel's voice carried a sadistic tone.

"Oh, I'll show you some fun, alright!" Matthew pressed forward, enraged, closing the gap to Nathaniel once more. *This time, I am not holding back.*

Nathaniel balled his hand into a fist on the ground and collected some dirt. Regaining his feet, he threw the content into the charging Matthew's face like a smokescreen. The soil and pebbles hurt Matthew's eyes and blocked his vision, stopping him in his tracks. The rest of the debris scattered around him in a dusty cloud, bits of rock bouncing into the grass. Blinking furiously, Matthew rubbed his eyes repeatedly in an attempt to alleviate the pain and clear his vision.

Like an animal, with both hands and feet planted on the ground, Nathaniel stared down his prey. Through the lingering cloud of dust, Matthew pressed forward again.

Nathaniel lunged like a pouncing feline. Matthew, his eyes only partially cleared, merely caught a glimpse of something coming at him in the air.

Nathaniel's fist drove straight into Matthew's face, driving him back into darkness. With the force of the blow, his feet left the ground and he flew backward.

Nathaniel then leapt upon Matthew, slamming him to the ground with a loud thud. Nathaniel dropped his prey, watching the boy's eyes roll back, knocked out cold from the collision.

For the first time, the others felt actual terror at the sight of their friend being manhandled in such a gruesome way. They looked to each other in confusion and astonishment.

Timothy broke the trance and stirred the group to action. "What are you waiting for?" he screamed. "Get him!"

The three remaining combatants slowly moved to Nathaniel, conquering their fear to show that they were tough. Timothy took the hindmost position, guarding Joseph. Not knowing what to expect, the boys tread lightly, maintaining caution. They gazed into those black eyes and felt the chills run down their spines. They saw something they were uncertain of, something frightening.

Nathaniel returned back to his striking pose. Something felt different; he was a little lower to the ground. He eyed the four remaining boys warily. One by one, they slowly closed in and surrounded him. One of them still stood over their fallen friend. They kept an arm's length of distance, ready for the unexpected, having learned from experience.

Suddenly, Nathaniel ran toward one of the boys, like a wolf hunting sheep. Covering the ground with amazing speed, he lunged at his enemy.

Horrified, Justin watched the black-eyed demon child come at him. He felt petrified and stood like a statue. Though he wanted him to run away from this ill-fated place, his body would not cooperate. His eyes widened in fear of what was upon him.

Nathaniel extended his left arm as he lunged. His hand closed tightly around Justin's neck, lifting him a few inches off the ground like a weightless doll. He began to, choking the life away. Justin grabbed onto Nathaniel's hand, trying to pry it off.

He gasped for air, then tried to strike Nathaniel's forearm. Redness suffused his face as the struggle became dire. Trying any possibility to break free, Justin flailed his legs, kicking Nathaniel, but it was no use. His life slowly drained away, and the darkness began to consume him.

Seeing his friend in grave danger, Christopher decided to take action, running at Nathaniel without any real idea what he would do. *I have got to help out my friend.* He felt as though he had an advantage, the perfect position behind him, where he wanted to be. He moved nimbly and silently until he was within striking distance. Winding up for a punch, he came lunging in.

In a split second, Nathaniel's free hand rose up in the air. He swung his hand swiftly behind him, like a lightning strike, giving Christopher little if any time to react.

Christopher tried to change his trajectory and dodge the attack, his feet skidding on the gravel like a runaway train slamming on its brakes. Nathaniel's striking hand looked horrifyingly like a claw. Bending backward and sliding to the ground, Christopher thought he was in the clear. But then he felt a burning, stinging pain, one that was more intense than he could ever have imagined.

He looked down and noticed that a portion of his shirt had been torn away. Christopher's hands flew up to cover his shredded chest. Tears rolled down his cheeks, but the shock was too great to allow him to cry aloud.

Simple human . . . I don't even have to use any strength. Pathetic. Nathaniel's returned his attention to Justin. He shook the shreds of Christopher's clothing from his hand.

Balling his hand into a fist, he launched it like a missile to its target. As he struck, he released his grasp on Justin's throat so that the boy flew backward, half dazed and barely conscious. Justin slammed to the ground, his head bouncing as it struck.

Nathaniel did not stop, consumed with the hunger for more violence. He immediately chased after Justin, smiling devilishly, to sit on top of his chest.

There, he paused momentarily to take a deep breath and slightly reposition himself, preparing for his next move. Then, his fists came roaring down like two sledgehammers into Justin's chest. Convulsing in shock, Justin's body twitched and his head jerked erratically.

Before any further damage could be dealt, Franklin closed in. Looking down to the ground, he remembered that Matthew had tossed the tree branch not too far away. He hurriedly scanned the area. *Where is it? Where did Matthew throw it?* He hoped that he could find the equalizer quickly. As he took another step, Franklin's foot struck something. *Ah, there it is.* Bending over, he quickly grabbed the branch. *I will finish the job that Matthew could not do.*

Nathaniel continued his merciless onslaught, accelerating the pounding on Justin's chest. Then, he changed his tactic and started to swing at the boy's head. The defenseless Justin could only take the oncoming blows, his skin reddening and bruising.

Cocking back his fist for another strike, Nathaniel paused. *NO! STOP! WHAT ARE YOU DOING?* A voice rang from within.

His fist trembled in the air as though a rope held his wrist, tugging back. Trying to force another strike down, lower and lower the fist crept to a certain point before slowly rising back up in the same fashion. The darkness in his eyes slowly began to disappear.

Franklin took his last step before planting his feet firmly on the ground. Following through, he swung the branch with all his might, slicing the air with a whoosh. A hollow thud announced its collision with the back of Nathaniel's head.

"Yeah! There you go, Franklin!" Timothy cheered.

Blood rushed from the open wound in Nathaniel's head. As he toppled forward like a felled tree the redness in his eyes returned to black before he met the ground. Nathaniel planted his hands firmly next to Justin's head, and with an instinctive reaction, he kicked out like a donkey, giving Franklin a concussive blow to the chest.

Dropping the tree branch on the ground, Franklin slid a few steps back from the impact and grasped his chest, gasping for air.

He gradually buckled to the ground, his knees meeting the gravel. The tears in his eyes made it hard to see. As he blinked to restore his focus, his tears fell to the soil below. Once again, he looked around to find the branch that he'd dropped.

Franklin crawled forward, the pain throbbing sharply in his chest as though he'd been spiked. One hand in front of another, he moved, but the distance felt like miles. The rough bark of the branch was as welcome to him as a mother's warm touch.

Franklin could feel something watching over him. The eerie presence covered every inch of him, like the freezing air of a cold winter night. Goosebumps covered his body and a chill ran down his spine. He did not want to look at that demon again. Blinking once more, he gave in to the temptation to raise his head, even knowing his resistance was futile. His eyes opened wide at the sight of the figure that stood before him.

With a devilish grin and murderous intent plain in his eyes, Nathaniel belittled his foe with fear. With what little resistance Franklin could conjure, he swung the tree branch wildly at Nathaniel.

Nathaniel's unrelenting glower fell upon him, the demon boy not once blinking or shifting his black eyes away from the prize. His hand rose and intercepted the oncoming weapon with a loud smack like a whip cracking. His arm did not recoil in the slightest. The crack of the impact reverberated from his hand all the way to the shoulder. Having the crude weapon from yanked from his grasp left a burning sensation and splinters in Franklin's hands. Another spiking pain coursed through Franklin's body as he looked upon his shaky, now useless hands.

Nathaniel raised the branch above his head and then swung it down like the blade of a guillotine, striking the side of his opponent's neck. Franklin collapsed to the ground, his eyes rolling back into his skull.

For a moment, Nathaniel paused, his nostrils flaring as he caught a tantalizing scent. He turned and looked up from his prey. The lust still consumed him. *I . . . want . . . more . . .* The smell of fear made him smile.

The burning sensation in Christopher's chest dulled. Oblivious to his surroundings, his only concern was the pain and the likely repercussions of this conflict on his chest. *Papa . . . Papa . . . He is going to be mad at me . . . Mama . . . Mama . . . What should I do? Mama . . . Help. Help me, Mama! I want to go home!*

Nathaniel bolted over to Christopher. The thrill of combat excited him and renewed his desire. Licking his lips and closing in on the enemy, he reached out.

Reacting belatedly, Christopher snapped back to reality as Nathaniel's hand cupped the contour of his neck and slowly tightened its grip.

I cannot breathe. He felt weightless and not in control, and that bothered him. Being lifted off his knees and into the air, he clenched onto Nathaniel's wrist with both hands and held on for dear life. Releasing his clutches on Christopher, Nathaniel stood, stretching his limbs and rotating his head around in a circular motion, cracking the cartilage in his neck.

As Christopher fell back to the ground, his back took the brunt of the collision. His head struck next, bouncing like a ball with a sickening crack, and then the darkness finally set in. The last thing he saw before passing out was the black-eyed demon child's face, and the blue sky above.

Timothy trembled in fear. He was the last of the group still standing. He tried to avoid the confrontation by sneaking back along the road, back to town, being as discreet as possible. Not looking back, he hoped that Nathaniel would not notice him escaping.

Nathaniel looked over to where Joseph laid, battered and bruised, and noticed that one boy was missing. He sniffed the air and looked around. The crunching of gravel off in the distance made his ears pulsate with interest.

Timothy could feel an evil gaze boring into the back of his head. He picked up the pace. All he cared about now was escape and getting as far away as possible from Nathaniel.

Grabbing the branch off the ground one more time, Nathaniel focused on Timothy. He wound up and threw the branch like a boomerang at his quarry. It rotated as it flew, traveling faster than Timothy's feet could carry him. Nathaniel followed the branch he'd thrown like a dog chasing its toy.

The branch clipped one of Timothy's heels, causing him to trip and lose balance. His arms extended reflexively, bracing for impact. His hands met the gravel before the rest of his body slid to a halt. Fear pumped through him with each and every breath, knowing that Nathaniel was right behind. He barely noticed the abrasions on his hands. Instead, he was overcome by the panicked thudding in his chest. *Oh, no! Help me!*

Nathaniel heaved the last few steps and chuckled in delight. He watched Timothy turn around to wipe the dirt from his hands. Patches of blood stained his shirt.

"Please! Please! No!" Timothy pled desperately.

Nathaniel took another step, ignoring Timothy's plea. His murderous intent had returned; he thirsted for more blood.

"I—I didn't do anything to you!" Timothy cried as he backpedaled. "I didn't do anything!" He looked back occasionally as he still attempted to scuttle away to safety.

Evil laughter sprung from Nathaniel's mouth. Closer and closer he drew; the gap between the two diminished.

"Pl-please don't hurt me!" Timothy screamed, terrified.

In place of a response, Nathaniel kicked Timothy square in the chest, knocking him to lie on his back. Nathaniel towered over his new target. He closed his eyes for a moment and took a long, deep breath.

"I—I did not do a-an-anything to you," Timothy tried again.

Nathaniel opened his eyes and smiled devilishly.

"Please, please, please, do not do this. I swear . . . I will never fuck with you ever again," Timothy begged.

"It's already too late," Nathaniel responded.

Nathaniel sat down atop Timothy's stomach, raised his hand, and balled it into a fist, a sight that Timothy was now all too familiar with. As he clenched his eyes shut in terror, his life flashed before them. He knew what was coming; he could already imagine the damage dealt.

Nathaniel struck, and Timothy gasped for air.

"Pl—please stop!" Timothy cried.

Nathaniel ignored his pleas, raining down blow after blow. Tears rolled from Timothy's eyes, and warm fluid emptied from his bladder, soaking into his clothing and the gravel below.

"N—no," Timothy choked out.

Battered and bruised, Joseph still managed to sit up while Nathaniel's attention was focused elsewhere. He saw his friend receiving the same treatment he'd gone through, and Joseph knew he had to act quickly. *I have to stop Nathaniel. Somehow, someway, I must.* Exerting all the energy he had left, he stumbled up to stand on both feet. *Nathaniel, please stop! Please stop . . . Do not be like them.* "S—Stop," Joseph called hoarsely with what remained of his voice.

■　　■　　■　　■

Timothy's legs kicked wildly around as he squirmed futilely to escape.

Meanwhile, Joseph approached. With every step he took, his feet felt like anchors dragging on the ground. He wobbled along unsteadily, swaying like a pendulum from one side to the other.

Joseph could see Timothy's fight for dear life progressively slowing down. He no longer cried out. Nathaniel's rage only seemed to intensify as he unloaded punch after punch. Timothy's head bobbed left and right with every blow.

"STOP!" Joseph roared.

Nathaniel's frenzied movement came to a halt. Looking down at his hands, his body trembled as though he were cold. Joseph peered from the side to look into Nathaniel's face. Something he could not recognize lurked behind those eyes. Neither Nathaniel nor anyone else seemed present in the empty vessel before him.

Epilogue
—The First Encounter

"Ugh . . ." Nathaniel rubbed his eyes, clearing the rheum.

Nathaniel stretched out, and a quick chill slithered down his spine. He opened his eyes in hopes of seeing a light glimmering down from the sky above, but the pure darkness of the night loomed all around with no stars, clouds, or moon in the sky.

He blinked once more, hoping for the image to change, but it did not. *Where am I?* He waved his hands in front of his face, but nothing was visible in the blackness.

"Heh, heh, heh, heh." He could hear a voice laughing from far away.

Spooked by the unfamiliar voice, Nathaniel quickly stood up. *Where are my shoes?* He felt the cold ground beneath his wiggling toes, but he remembered putting on his shoes that day. *Where could they have gone?*

The unknown voice spoke again. "Come here."

Nathaniel turned around in the direction of the voice, or at least, what he thought was the right direction. The darkness didn't help one bit as he turned full circle, scanning for sound.

"Who's there?" Nathaniel questioned, puzzled.

"How could you have forgotten me?" The voice was now tinged with sadness.

"Who are you?"

"Come to me and you will understand."

"Umm . . ." What reason did he have to trust this person?

"Heh, heh, heh, heh." Laughter again.

Where am I? Nathaniel wondered.

TO BE CONTINUED . . .

SPECIAL THANKS

First and foremost, I'd like to give a big thank you to Chad. Without you, my dream wouldn't have been a reality. You helped me with many, many things that I can't thank you enough for. To Marvin and Ed, you guys are my best moral support, even when things were looking down for me. You guys always had a way to look at the brighter side and let the best of me come out. All three of you guys are my pillars.

Thank you, Luka, for being a thorn in my side. You've helped me in ways that I can't even imagine. You stuck with me even though I felt it was a lost cause. You're irreplaceable.

A big thank you to Miranda for taking me in at the last minute and working on the final touches to the journey. All the wonderful things we share with each other are amazing and I wouldn't trade that for anything. You get my humor and vice versa.

I can't forget about Christa from Into the Woods Tattoo and Art Gallery. Thank you for the wonderful art and willingness to deal with me. The amount of fixing and adjusting you had to do and take everything in stride; I don't know how you managed but you did it anyway.

For all those who read my samples and gave me feedback, I can't thank you guys enough for taking the time to read what I had. Thank you to my friends and family that supported me along the way. It's gratifying knowing I have a nice circle around me, and for that, thank you all.

Thank you